GERMANIA

BRENDAN McNALLY

SIMON & SCHUSTER
NEW YORK   LONDON   TORONTO   SYDNEY

SIMON & SCHUSTER
1230 Avenue of the Americas
New York, NY 10020

First Simon & Schuster hardcover edition September 2008

SIMON & SCHUSTER and colophon are registered trademarks of Simon &
Schuster, Inc.

For information about special discounts for bulk purchases,
please contact Simon & Schuster Special Sales at
1-800-456-6798 or business@simonandschuster.com.

Designed by Kate Moll

Manufactured in the United States of America

10 9 8 7 6 5 4 3 2 1

Library of Congress Cataloging-in-Publication Data

McNally, Brendan.
  Germania / Brendan McNally.
    p. cm.
1. Jews—Germany—Fiction. 2. Jewish entertainers—Germany—Fiction.
3. World War, 1939–1945—Germany—Flensburg—Fiction. 4. Speer, Albert,
1905–1981—Fiction. 5. Flensburg (Germany)—History—Fiction.
6. Germany—History—1945–1955—Fiction. I. Title.
  PS3613.C58575G47 2008-
  813'.6—dc22

                                                    2008003144

ISBN-13: 978-1-4165-5882-8
ISBN-10:   1-4165-5882-9

To my wife, Katerina,
for her faith, love, and support;
to my father, John Joseph McNally,
who died before I could finish it;
also to my daughter, Kathleen,
who joined us and made us a family

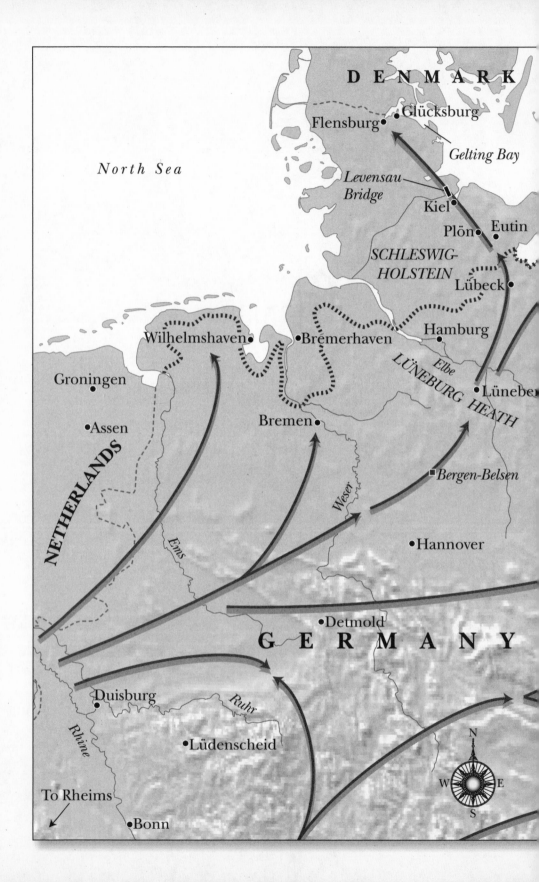

DENMARK

Flensburg
Glücksburg

Gelting Bay

North Sea

Levensau Bridge

Kiel

Plön
Eutin

SCHLESWIG-HOLSTEIN

Lübeck

Wilhelmshaven
Bremerhaven

Hamburg

Groningen

LÜNEBURG HEATH

Elbe

Lünebe

NETHERLANDS

Bremen

Assen

Weser

Ens

Bergen-Belsen

Hannover

•Detmold

GERMANY

Duisburg

Ruhr

•Lüdenscheid

Rhine

N

W   E

To Rheims

S

•Bonn

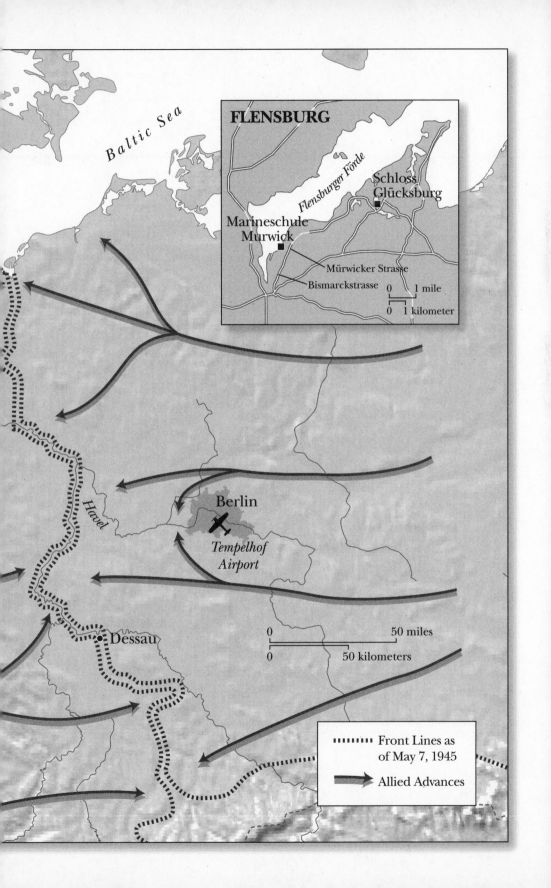

FLENSBURG

Baltic Sea

Flensburger Förde

Schloss
Glücksburg

Marineschule
Murwick

Mürwicker Strasse

Bismarckstrasse

0   1 mile

0   1 kilometer

Berlin

Tempelhof
Airport

Havel

Dessau

0   50 miles

0   50 kilometers

••••••• Front Lines as
         of May 7, 1945

Allied Advances

❨ PART I ❩

PROLOGUE

Gustav Loerber was a large man. His vast belly hung down from his chest like a barley sack, his jowls were fleshy saddlebags casually slung between his nose and ears, and his neck a shapeless, jiggling extension of his chin. Old Gustav was horrendously, obscenely fat. Yet nobody who looked at Gustav Loerber ever quite thought of him that way. It might have been the exquisite cut of his Italian silk suits, or his commanding smile, or his poised, impresario's way of carrying himself. It might have been something else. Gustav Loerber was, after all, a magician. But in either case, whoever looked at old Gustav thought only one thing: Magnificent!

Of course, it hadn't always been that way. Once, thirty years earlier, when Gustav Loerber was just another hungry young acrobat making his way in the world, he had been every bit as slim and wiry as his four sons were now. His sons; his celebrated sons; Manni, Franzi, Ziggy, and Sebastian; known to Berlin and the world as the Flying Magical Loerber Brothers. At any other time, Gustav Loerber would have told you they were his pride and joy, except at this moment three of them were screaming at him over his latest business decision.

He'd just come into their dressing room, waving the telegram sent by Adolf Hitler himself, inviting them all to perform at the upcoming Nazi Party gala celebrating his recent ascent to chancellor of Germany. Naturally Gustav agreed. But when he had gone to tell his sons, he found to his astonishment that they were anything but pleased.

"Father, how could you?" cried Manni Loerber. "We can't work for them!"

"But I thought you despised the Nazis, Father," shouted Franzi. "You've been saying it for years."

This was true. Gustav Loerber had never made much secret of his low opinion of the thugs and gutter politicians who made up the Nazi Party's ranks. But Hitler? Well, it turned out Hitler was a different story altogether. Old Gustav had secretly gone to a party rally or two, more for research than anything else, and seeing the Führer in action before those crowds, Gustav immediately recognized Hitler as a genius like himself: a fellow showman whose sense of spectacle and presentation nearly equaled his own. And now it turned out Hitler saw old Gustav the same way, and was inviting him and his sons to "add your magic to the New Germany."

"But Father, the man's evil," said Franzi.

"That's simply a matter of opinion," shot back Gustav.

"He's a psychopath," said Manni.

"Oh, come on! They always say that about visionaries. Boys, listen to me: we're on the ground floor of something really big."

"No!"

"We mustn't, Father."

Gustav fumed. That his own sons would do this to him. After all he'd done, couldn't they obey him just once? He should have known there would be trouble coming when Manni and Franzi started hanging around with those left-wing types.

"Father?" asked Ziggy, desperately waving his hand to be allowed to speak. The good thing about Ziggy was that he wasn't argumentative and didn't get into constant trouble like Manni and Franzi.

Gustav nodded. "Yes, son?"

"But Father," said Ziggy, "we're Jews, remember?"

Gustav Loerber shut his eyes and tried counting to ten. Why was the kid so bloody obtuse?

4

"Do you have to keep bringing that up?" Gustav groaned. "It was all such a long time ago and it never meant anything in the first place."

Eyes still closed, Gustav shook his head. What was with his sons? After all he'd done for them, this was how they rewarded him!

Devils though they may be, Franzi and Manni were unmistakably Gustav's sons. But Ziggy and Sebastian? The way they acted, they might as well have been someone else's. They really shouldn't be his. They were both far too odd.

Gustav wondered what Ziggy's problem was. To begin with, he seemed to possess no imagination whatsoever. He was a literalist who wanted everything fixed or controllable, something that Gustav found truly bewildering. Ziggy might not get into trouble like Manni and Franzi always did, but some of the things he did that he never got caught at did not sit well with Gustav.

Saturday mornings when normal people were still sleeping in, Ziggy would sneak off to watch a morning cartoon matinee where everybody else was under twelve. Or worse, other times he'd go to temple. Sebastian was also odd, but at least he was a genius.

His eyes still shut, Gustav Loerber picked his words carefully. "Adolf Hitler is going to do great things for Germany," he said. "All that talk about Jews is nothing more than a gimmick to keep the masses' attention. As magicians, we're supposed to recognize it when it's happening before our eyes."

"Um," said Sebastian, who as a rule never got involved in political discussion. Everyone turned to hear what he had to say.

Sebastian spoke quickly and decisively. "Their stuff is stupid, Father," he said. "It's stupid, it's ugly, it's corny, and it's pointless."

"And?" asked Gustav.

"And we can't get associated with that kind of schlock. It would ruin us." Sebastian fixed them all with an angry glare and immediately they were bombarded with mental images of chorus girls in swallowtail coats and swastika-laden top hats kick-stepping to a bouncy, uptempo "Horst-Wessel-Lied" while a red sea of Nazi Party flags shimmered behind them. It looked really ridiculous.

Manni and Franzi both rolled their eyes. "That's real nice, Sebastian, but there are bigger issues here than kitschiness," said Franzi.

"Maybe to you," he answered.

"Either way," said Ziggy.

"Yes," said Franzi, "either way, we're not doing it."

"We're unanimous," said Ziggy.

Gustav Loerber snorted and stamped his foot. "Well, I'm still the one making the decisions around here. You will do as I say or you can pack your bags and get out!"

"Fine with me," said Ziggy.

"Fine with me," said Manni.

"Fine with me," said Franzi.

"There's this avant-garde troupe in Wilhelmsdorf—" began Sebastian. But before he could say anything else, Gustav Loerber stormed out of the dressing room, slamming the door behind him.

Everyone returned to their mirrors, silently powdering their faces and applying eyeliner. Finally Manni broke the silence. "'Horst-Wessel' . . . uptempo?" he asked.

Then Franzi snickered, "Top hats with swastikas? I mean, really, Sebastian."

That immediately got Sebastian riled. "Hey! I was trying to make a point."

They all laughed.

As the others continued their mock-bickering, Ziggy kept staring at himself, as if the made-up face in the mirror were someone he'd never met. What was going on? The entire world seemed to be coming apart right in front of his eyes. The other day at the synagogue he'd heard people arguing about whether they should flee Germany for Holland or England or the Argentine. But Ziggy didn't want to leave Germany for somewhere foreign. He liked being a Jew, and he liked being a German.

He stared sadly at the souvenirs of Betty Boop, Mickey Mouse, and Bosko lined up along the bottom of his mirror. The others thought he was an idiot. But then all Ziggy had to do was offer to quit and they'd all start apologizing. Ziggy was, after all, the act's straight man and they needed him more than he needed them. Besides, neither of the other two could do improvisation work with Sebastian.

The door opened and the stage manager's assistant stuck his head in. "All right, Flying Magical Loerber Brothers, let's go!" The four got to their feet and followed him down the narrow backstage corridor, past the stagehands, chorus girls, and other performers who didn't have their own dressing rooms. But as they approached the stage-right wings, a group of stagehands blocked their path.

"Which one of you is Ziggy?" asked one, holding out a small square of paper.

"Right here," said Ziggy, stepping forward. He knew what they wanted.

"Settle a bet for us?"

Ziggy nodded for them to proceed. Rare was the night when this didn't happen. The stagehand cleared his throat.

"Tell me a number between fifteen and forty-nine."

Ziggy stared dully at the folded-up paper. "Twenty-two," he answered.

"Now a number between fifty and eighty."

"Sixty-three."

"A number between three hundred and seven hundred."

"Five hundred and seventy."

The stagehand unfolded the paper. On it was written *22-63-570.* He laughed and turned to his friend. "Pay up," he ordered. The other stagehand handed him a small wad of bills. He peeled off two and gave them to Ziggy before pocketing the rest. "Much obliged," he said.

"Not at all," Ziggy answered.

"So how'd you do it?"

Ziggy shrugged. "I'm magic," he said.

Entering the wings, the four brothers took their positions. By now the orchestra was already well into a bouncy medley of "Sweet Georgia Brown" and "Harlem Rhapsody," the Loerber Brothers' two signature tunes. Onstage the bright lights were going down as two spotlights played about the stage, as though looking for a prisoner who had just escaped. The music went on for a few more bars before the horns and strings dropped out and the drums took over with a frantic jungle rhythm, as if to say, *Tonight, folks, we're really going to have fun!* Then the stage manager shot them their cue, the lights went up, and Ziggy and his three brothers dashed out onstage. Seeing them, the audience burst into applause.

They formed a line in front of the audience. Behind them upstage, four very proper-looking couples—top hats, bonnets, and parasols—promenaded among black cutouts of park benches and trellises. The clarinets jumped in, sarcastic and leering, so the audience would know exactly what to think about what was going on. The four brothers began to sway back and forth, turning out their empty pockets one after the other and singing:

> *Spring is in the air,*
> *And pretty girls, they're everywhere.*
> *But, oh, how I wish it were wintertime still.*
> *Because when you're ragged and broke,*
> *You haven't a hope, and*
> *No girl wants you anywhere near her.*

Manni and Sebastian both stepped back while Ziggy and Franzi threw out their arms and continued:

Now, in Paris, they say, each dog gets its day,
And raggedy Jacques has his little Marie.
But here in old Berlin, ladies demand style from their men.
So you'd better dress smart, you'd better look right,
Or alone down the avenues you'll be walking tonight.

Ziggy remembered how Manni had once observed that after you've performed Gustav Loerber's different routines several thousand times, you realized they were all exactly the same: boy meets girl, boy loses girl; everything's fine and then something goes wrong, or everything is wrong and then something goes right. Two verses and then a chorus followed by a big dance number that has some tenuous connection to the story line.

Berlin girls have their standards
And don't you know it's a fact.
You'd better have money, nice clothes, and a hat.
Then they won't care if you're ugly, dull or fat.
Propriety, my friend, is the name of their game,
And spotless reputations girls must always maintain.

At that, the girls stepped away from their beaux and scurried together and in the sweetest harmony declared:

You've patches on your overcoat, holes in your shoes.
What would folks say if I were seen here with you?
Yes, Heinrich is tiny and ugly and dull, dull, dull.
I really don't care because his wallet is full.

And giving a tart turning-up of their noses, the four ladies scurried back to their beaux, who smiled back at the brothers with a blandness so overarching it bordered on arrogance.

The brothers wrung their hands in mock desperation. Then big grins came over their faces and suddenly they all

9

stepped forward with a wiggle of their eyebrows and began singing:

> *Well, if we can't go out, couldn't we just stay in?*
> *Be a pal, give me a try, I'll give you something special*
> *That Heinrich's money can't buy.*
> *So let's just sit on your couch and you're welcome to sup,*
> *A crop of fresh asparagus that's starting to pop up.*
> *It'll be our secret, we can shield it from society.*
> *No need to fret about the bounds of propriety.*

And then the dancing began. The girls flittered to them like a stream of butterflies, twirling first with Franzi, then working their way past Sebastian, then Ziggy and Manni, until the boys all had partners. Ziggy's was a blonde named Stella. Once, the previous fall, she'd come on to him, and Ziggy, eager to be rid of his virginity, went upstairs with her. But it had been a terrible mistake. Halfway into it, she broke off and began weeping about how the other girls had put her up to it and about a daughter that nobody knew about back in Munich. After that, whenever they'd perform together, she'd act like neither was anything more than an automaton. But this time, as they held each other and twirled to the music, her dark eyes flashed at him like she was thinking, *You're about to get yours!*

After that they switched partners and the girls worked their way back up and down the line, twirling and jumping and straddling the brothers: first Sebastian, then Manni, then Franzi, and back to Ziggy, back and forth, left and right, trading one for another and then another, and every fourth turn a different brother would hurl a different girl into the air, while on every seventh turn one of the brothers would jump up. All the brothers hated this routine, especially Sebastian, who abhorred any suggestion of lasciviousness. But the audiences could never get enough of it.

Around and around they swirled in a mad orgy of synchronized movement. Weave up left, weave down right, circle back left, swirl twice with the girl on his right, and then line up between Manni and Franzi and their girls, while upstage the abandoned beaux were being slowly blown backward like so many dry leaves until they disappeared behind some upstage curtains, all to the audience's howling approval.

They did their last frantic twirl, and the music stopped. The audience roared applause. The girls stepped back and the brothers stepped into the spotlights and bowed low to the cheering audience, holding it down for a count of three.

But as Ziggy straightened up, he saw that except for Sebastian and himself, the stage was empty. Manni, Franzi, and the girls had all left. Ziggy looked around, wondering what was going on. At that moment they were supposed to shift upstage to get into position for the next act, but instead it was just Sebastian grinning like the devil and the audience still cheering wildly. Was this what Stella had been trying to tell him: that he was being set up for another one of Sebastian's strange improvisations? Sebastian had a way of ensuring that Ziggy never saw them coming, while all of Berlin felt like they were in on it. Now he'd done it again and Ziggy was stuck having to do a very abstract impersonation with him. He looked at Sebastian still grinning at him.

Are you ready?

Ziggy nodded.

All right, then. Follow my lead. I'll let you know when to break.

Sebastian bounded upstage and did a flip, followed by another, which Ziggy immediately repeated. Sebastian began running clockwise in a wide circle; Ziggy waited until Sebastian was half a circle ahead, then followed behind him. Sebastian did another flip and then another, which Ziggy repeated. Then Sebastian turned and began running toward Ziggy with his hands out. It was the signal. Ziggy immediately dropped down on one knee and put his hands out. A second later, Sebastian dove at him. Ziggy caught his hands, and as Sebastian pulled the rest of his body into a ball, Ziggy leaped up, propelling Sebastian feet-first into the air, faster and farther than he knew it was possible to throw him.

Up Sebastian flew, his hands flapping earnestly from his hips like tiny wings, while snapping his legs open and shut. In an instant everyone saw an alligator being rewarded with the all-too-brief gift of flight. The audience let out a gasp. The gaping monster continued shooting upward, as if still fully believing that gravity would continue being negotiable. Up, up the alligator went, rejoicing in its newfound ability, but then, inevitably, its ascent slowed, stopped, its head tipped, and down it plunged, its jaws snapping, *Uh-oh! Uh-oh!* as it did.

The audience howled.

Sebastian landed and immediately resumed running circles and flipping, with Ziggy a half circle behind doing the same. Then Ziggy turned and this time Sebastian dropped down, Ziggy dove onto Sebastian, and a second later he was hurtling feet-first into the air. It seemed like he was shooting upward an impossibly long time.

Do something! Now!

Ziggy let his legs bend, grabbing his feet with his hands, and began wriggling his body like a caterpillar. He heard a roar erupt from the audience as they seemed to declare in a single voice: "A moth!" And even before he'd started coming down, there was thunderous applause.

An eternity later, Ziggy's feet hit the stage and he went back to running circles behind Sebastian. Once again, Sebastian changed direction and Ziggy dropped down, caught him, and tossed him up into the air. Sebastian shot upward, propelled by a force Ziggy knew he did not possess.

Once aloft, Sebastian performed another ballistic animal impersonation, legs bent, arms clenched, head bobbing, which the audience immediately saw as a hare. Then it was Ziggy's turn. This time, as he shot upward, he quickly bent his right knee and placed his left foot against his kneecap, while leaning his head against his left leg with his palms clamped against the sides of his head. Ziggy then flapped his elbows, which made the audience scream out in a single voice, "An elephant!" and applaud even louder than before.

It went on like this again and again, and each time all they had to do was move their arms one way, their legs another, and do something with their head or fingers, and each time the audience reacted with such profound amazement that Ziggy himself was amazed they'd completely lost sight of the fact that the brothers' time in the air was a flagrant violation of the laws of gravity and physics.

Flying above the stage, Ziggy noticed all sorts of things: that Stella was standing behind a scrim in the stage-left wing, watching them and laughing uncontrollably, like a child being tickled; that there were dozens of brownshirts sitting in the audience, they used to never come here, at least not in Nazi uniform; that Franzi and Manni had been watching them from the wings but were now both gone. One of the few ground rules of Sebastian's improvisations was that Manni and Franzi had to remain on hand in order to step in and force a conclusion, something that Sebastian, for all his genius, was absolutely clueless about. Where had they gone?

Ziggy landed and resumed running behind Sebastian. He looked ragged. Sebastian turned and ran toward him. Ziggy dropped, caught him, and tossed him into the air. He watched Sebastian spinning up toward the rafters, fluttering froglike with his arms and legs. As usual, the audience marveled at the genius of Sebastian's interpretation. Sebastian started his descent and Ziggy began running his circle. What was it going to be next? A gorilla? A pangolin? A giant sloth? Ziggy guessed it was up to him to make up an ending. He stopped, turned, and ran toward Sebastian, who was already down on one knee poised to catch him. But instead of going into his brother's hands, Ziggy dove several feet short, going into a somersault that brought his legs up onto Sebastian's shoulders. As Sebastian tumbled backward, he brought his own trunk up against Ziggy's backside, wrapping his legs around Ziggy's neck and chest just as Ziggy's feet reached the ground, followed by his knees and hands. Then it was Sebastian's feet, knees, and hands, then Ziggy's. Locked together, they rolled about the stage, backward and forward, as the audience roared its delight. At the center of the stage, they came apart and jumped to their feet and took their bows until the applause finally died away.

"Where'd they go? Where'd they go?" Sebastian kept screaming once they were offstage. Ziggy followed him to their dressing room. They were almost at their door when one of the wardrobe women stepped in their way. She looked worried. "Herr Ziggy, Herr Sebastian," she whispered. "Your brothers, they have disappeared. They must be found immediately." Ziggy wondered why she was concerned. It wasn't her responsibility in the slightest. She took a quick look over her shoulder and put her head closer to them. "Someone is waiting inside for them," she hissed. "The matter is most urgent!" Then she added, "It is a woman."

"What?" shouted Sebastian, not very politely. "You say they've got a woman waiting inside? Well, get rid of her right now! I don't have time for this. I need to rest!"

Ziggy looked at the wardrobe lady's expression and wondered whether Sebastian was even capable of being anything other than an utter penis all the time. But then, he did have a point. That last improvisation had wiped them out and they just needed to sit down quietly and not have to deal with some strange woman with an urgent problem. He watched Sebastian push the wardrobe woman away and step inside. Through the crack left by the partially closed door, Ziggy could see the gray and black shape of an older woman in a heavy coat getting up from one of the chairs. "I'm sorry, madam, but you're going to have to leave right now," he heard Sebastian say coldly. But then he paused. Ziggy went in to see for himself.

It was a heavyset middle-aged woman, her face bruised and bleeding, her gray sealskin coat roughed up and muddied like she'd been on the ground. She stared at them wild-eyed, slowly realizing they might not be who she'd come for.

"You're not . . . ?" she rasped.

The wardrobe woman spoke quickly in a low mutter. "Frau Lachmann, these are their brothers, Herr Zigmund and Herr Sebastian. We cannot find the boys. They are missing." The beaten-up woman stared back at her as if to ask, *What am I supposed to do with these two?*

Sebastian was still speechless. He stared at her with an open mouth like he'd never seen a woman beaten like a whore who wasn't a whore. Who was she? What had she done to make someone angry enough to do this to her? The wardrobe woman had addressed her as Frau Lachmann. Could she be married to Felix Lachmann, that surgeon who wrote those columns for one of the left-wing papers?

Ziggy put a hand on the wardrobe woman's arm. "Don't worry, we'll take care of her," he said and held open the door. "Keep looking for them!" He quickly closed the door behind her.

"What happened?" asked Ziggy. "Was it the brownshirts?"

The woman gave a nod as she slumped back down into the chair. "Please," she croaked. "I must speak with your brothers. Where are they?"

Sebastian turned to Ziggy. "What happened to her? Did she say Nazis did it? Why'd they want to do it to her?"

The woman looked into space. "They killed Felix," she said.

"The Nazis killed Dr. Lachmann?" Sebastian sounded almost like he thought it might be a joke. "Shouldn't we get the police?"

"Manni, get Manni," groaned the woman. "I have to tell them something."

"Frau Lachmann, we don't know where they are."

"Ziggy, why would the Nazis kill Dr. Lachmann?"

"*Sebastian!*"

"He's not Jewish or anything."

"Sebastian," shouted Ziggy, "do you have to be such an idiot? Besides, we're Jews, remember?"

Sebastian glared back at Ziggy.

"Sebastian, what do you think has been going on outside?"

"Father said it doesn't have anything to do with us."

"For God's sake, Sebastian, Father's an asshole!"

Frau Lachmann stood up from the chair and fixed Ziggy with the one eye of hers that seemed to focus. "I have to leave quickly," she said. "But you must tell your brothers this. Tell them the organization is finished and not to trust any of the others. Tell them they must get out! All of you! Get out! This thing is finished!"

Then the door opened and a different wardrobe lady stuck her head in. "Your father is coming and he's got two Nazis with him," she barked. She pointed at Frau Lachmann. "Get her in the closet! Now!"

Ziggy and Sebastian moved quickly. A second later, they had the bleeding woman and her sealskin stuffed inside the closet and were already at their tables, doing their eyebrows, when the door opened.

In all his years in show business Gustav Loerber had never quite tired of the way everyone turned whenever he passed through a backstage hallway. And it was even better with two extremely prominent Nazi gauleiters in tow. Big boys too, not that either of them had anything like Gustav's commanding girth or his panache. But still, they were the right sort, he decided: good-spirited and endlessly, endlessly worshipful. To them, Gustav Loerber was a god in whose presence they were blessed to be, and righteously eager to let some of his grand style rub off on them. And truth to tell, both could have used some. But then, even the greatest of epochs usually started off with some rough edges. And if it should be Gustav's job to polish them down a little, then he was just the man to do it.

As he came to the dressing room door, three of the wardrobe ladies bowed with delirious subservience. "Why, Maestro Loerber," they said, giggling. "And who are these lovely men you've brought us?"

Gustav smiled at them. "So good to see you again, ladies." Then, turning to his guests, he said, "Just a little visit, perhaps?"

He opened the door, and there were Ziggy and Sebastian. He started to demand they tell him where the others were, but the way his two sons jumped up and expressed immediate enchantment at the gauleiters' presence, it kind of slipped his mind.

"Why, Father, what a surprise," said Ziggy. He went for the fattest one's eyes. "Welcome," he said.

Gustav smiled. "Boys, I'd like you to meet some new friends," he said. "This is Gauleiter Gunderson and Gauleiter Boehm. Sirs, may I present my sons Ziggy and Sebastian Loerber."

Ziggy and Sebastian both snapped into bows, then snapped back up and extended their hands to the eager gauleiters.

"A pleasure, lads," said Boehm.

"So where are the others?" asked Gunderson. "Where are Manni and Franzi?"

Gustav looked at his two sons and wondered why the question hadn't occurred to him. "Where are they?" he asked.

Both brothers grinned.

"I'm afraid they've been kidnapped by some of the Tiller Girls, Father," Sebastian said quickly. "Isn't that right, Brother?"

Ziggy nodded.

Both gauleiters let out a laugh. "Hah! That's good," said Gunderson. "Perhaps we should organize an assault team to rescue them, what do you say to that, Maestro?"

Gustav grinned. Good idea, but first, business. "Boys," he said, "I've invited these gentlemen to meet you because they have a message for you from the Führer himself."

Sebastian and Ziggy each clapped a hand on their throats. "A message from the Führer?" they gasped.

"That's right," answered Boehm. "Though the Führer wanted it delivered to all four of you, I think we can do it right now, since it mainly concerns Herr Sebastian here."

"Me?" asked an impossibly delighted Sebastian.

"I just can't believe how much you two look alike," said Gunderson. "Gustav, how do you tell them apart?"

Gustav Loerber smiled graciously. "They even manage to fool me sometimes."

The two gauleiters laughed. The fact was they were themselves nearly identical; both fat and bald, with comb-overs and meek little mustaches cowering under their noses. Once, they both might have been fighters, but that had been a long time ago. Now all they wanted was to eat good food, drink French champagne, and have someone pretty play with their dicks.

They looked at the two smiling young men, attentive in their chairs. Gunderson nodded to Boehm. Boehm cleared his throat and began. "First of all, the Führer greets you and invites you four wonderful boys to add your magic to the National Socialist Revolution. He wants to assure you that you will have complete artistic freedom to create new variety pieces."

Then Gunderson spoke. "And the Führer would like to commission Sebastian to compose a special dance number for the show. He said you should feel free to make it as abstract as you'd like. The Führer has personally told me that he loves your avant-garde work the most. Do you think you can do that, Sebastian?"

Sebastian smiled. "Please tell the Führer I am honored."

Both gauleiters smiled. Good. The Führer would smile.

Boehm raised his finger. "The Führer was also wondering if any of you had ever thought about studying architecture."

Ziggy stepped in. "Well, now, isn't that amazing! We were just this minute talking about the subject and we both agreed that architecture is the noblest of all the professions. Isn't that right, Brother?"

"Absolutely." Sebastian gleamed.

Then Gunderson's gaze fell on the line of figurines at the bottom of Ziggy's mirror. His smile faded. He jabbed his finger at the tiny big-eyed flapper with the garter on her thigh. "What is this, then?"

"Betty Boop and Bosko, Herr Gauleiter, characters from American cartoon films."

"I know they are characters from American cartoons, young man. The real question is, what do they represent? In your youthful idealism, you are probably thinking Betty Boop merely represents a free-spirited flapper and Bosko a funny animal, and therefore equally innocuous."

"Aren't they?" asked Ziggy.

"Sadly, no," said the gauleiter. "In truth, Betty Boop and Bosko each represent a cleverly disguised attack on the purity of our Aryan youth and our Aryan culture. Why? I am sad to be the one to inform you of this, but you must understand that Betty Boop is, first and foremost, a Jewess. Yes! And Bosko, he is not a funny animal at all, but represents a little colored person! And so both represent degeneracy and disease. You must get rid of them both. Mickey Mouse can stay!"

He held out his large hand and waited as Ziggy handed over the unwholesome figurines. "I am very sorry," he said, looking contrite.

"Just never let it happen again," the gauleiter muttered, letting the matter drop.

The door opened and in came Franzi and Manni, both wearing overcoats and looking startled. Sebastian and Ziggy went into action making introductions, and soon everyone had agreed to help the Führer in any way they could, smiling and laughing and shaking hands.

Gustav Loerber gestured at his guests with an upraised thumb and forefinger. "A little drink, perhaps?"

The two gauleiters nodded and giddily exchanged glances as Gustav started over to the cupboard. Manni and Franzi shot Ziggy an alarmed look, like they already knew what was inside.

Gustav pulled open the cupboard door. Inside was Frau Lachmann, trembling, wild-eyed, her bloody mouth gaping in fear. He reached in past her and took out a bottle and a tray of small glasses. Then he closed the door.

As Gustav began pouring schnapps into the glasses, Franzi and Manni looked over at Sebastian and Ziggy. Suddenly they all grinned.

The three fat men held their glasses aloft. "Gentlemen," declared Gustav, "to our Führer and success!"

"Success and the Führer!" added Sebastian.

They were raising their glasses to their lips when the door opened again. A much younger, much thinner man in a storm trooper uniform came in. He looked worried.

"Herr Gauleiters, we are in an emergency situation," he said.

"Well, what is it?" demanded Gunderson.

"Two of our men have been found dead in the alley across the street. Their throats were cut. We need to get you both out of here at once."

Neither gauleiter liked that. "Out of here? Why?"

"In case whoever did it is in the building."

"But it happened in the street. Why are you assuming the killers would have come in here?" asked Gunderson.

"We have no way of knowing," the man answered. "But the police need to do a check."

"Check?" Boehm snorted.

Gunderson didn't like the idea either. "You don't intend to halt the show, do you?"

The man looked at them a long moment before answering, "No, of course not, Gauleiter."

"Good," snorted Gunderson and signaled for him to leave. He turned to Boehm. "We should let these young men get ready. Let's go back to our box."

"Good idea," said Boehm. The gauleiters were all smiles. "Thank you very much for letting us in. We'll talk again soon," they said.

"Yes, sir, looking forward to it," said Sebastian.

"Heil Hitler!"

"Heil Hitler, sir!" shouted Manni, Ziggy, Sebastian, and Franzi. "Auf Wiedersehen!"

They waited with frozen smiles until the gauleiters were gone. Manni and Franzi both broke into hysterical laughter.

"So where were you?"

Franzi and Manni looked at each other. Manni grinned and said, "Doing the Lord's work!" Everyone laughed and a moment later they were all back at their mirrors, frantically reapplying makeup and eyeliner. The stage manager's assistant stuck his head back in. "Franzi, Manni, Ziggy, Sebastian, let's go!"

The four looked up, put down their brushes and combs, pushed their chairs back, and stood. Franzi, who was nearest the clothing rack, began handing out billowy-sleeved, sorbet-colored shirts. Ziggy's was orchid, Manni's papaya, Sebastian's lime-green, and his own passionfruit. They left the dressing room, walked over to the stage-right wing, and took their positions. Onstage a springboard and trapezes had been set up for them. The Hawaiian Hallucination was their big acrobatic number.

"One minute," said the stage manager's assistant. The four brothers nodded back. The lights went down onstage and the orchestra started playing "Call of the Enchanted Islands." "Bring the lights up," said the stage manager, and a moment later shot them their cue. The four Magical Loerber Brothers ran back out onstage, the audience burst into thunderous applause, and they went into their second routine.

First they tossed Manni up high into the air, and as he was coming down, Sebastian jumped to the far side of the springboard. Manni came down onto the other end, propelling Sebastian high into the air to the first trapeze. Then Ziggy boosted Franzi up onto his shoulders, Franzi jumped down onto the springboard, launching Manni upward, where he was caught by Sebastian, who swung him around and around before flinging him off to the other trapeze. Manni spun around several times on the second trapeze before coming down onto the springboard, sending Ziggy upward. Then Sebastian and Ziggy flew around and around before Sebastian flew off from the second trapeze, leaving Franzi to catch Ziggy.

It worked like an assembly line: every somersault, every spin calculated precisely, so that downward was causing upward, momentum feeding momentum, and the velocity and force always increasing. In this exactitude, each brother found his own mind and body melding with the others' until they were four separate parts of a single whole.

As he flew from one trapeze to the next, the thought of Frau Lachmann languishing in the closet briefly flashed through Ziggy's mind. Coming down, he told himself he needed to do something about it. But by the time he hit the springboard and began flying back upward, he had already forgotten about it.

(1)

Maybe it was because he would soon turn forty that Albert Speer repeatedly found himself dwelling on the course his life had taken. Maybe it was knowing that none of the miracles that were supposed to turn the war around were ever going to happen. Maybe it was because with the end looming, it now seemed possible to look beyond and speculate how things might go once the war was over.

Or maybe it was because the other day, someone visiting from the Foreign Ministry had showed him a captured Allied intelligence report that named him, Albert Speer—Hitler's architect, protégé, and minister for armaments and war production—as the likely head of a post-Hitler government. *Speer*, it said, *is an able technocrat who, despite his extreme closeness to Hitler, remains relatively untouched by Nazi ideology.*

Naturally, Speer's first reaction had been one of alarm. "Has von Ribbentrop seen this?" he asked. The last thing he needed was for the foreign minister to have something on him that he could take to Hitler. Things between Speer and the Führer were already bad enough. But the man allowed the tiniest smirk to appear on his otherwise impassive face, like a waiter might when sharing dirt with a favorite customer. "Well, *I* certainly haven't shown it to him," he said. "And I can't imagine who would. No, no, this information is strictly for you, Herr Reichsminister, a little gift from your friends at the Foreign Ministry."

... Untouched by Nazi ideology ... able technocrat ... The words came back to him that afternoon during a bombing raid while he and his office staff huddled in their overcoats and helmets deep inside the ministry shelter, and suddenly what the report had said no longer seemed so ridiculous. Why not? Speer thought. They're going to have to pick somebody.

Eventually the all-clear sounded and Speer and the others trooped back upstairs to their offices. By now everyone had lost track of how many times the Armaments Ministry had been hit. Their memory didn't go much further beyond the fragmentation bomb that had killed ten people from the strategic materials section the week before. All the other bombs and all the other people killed or injured had already congealed into a monochromatic, undifferentiated mosaic.

Back in his office, Speer hung up his helmet but kept his overcoat on. The paper on the front windows had been blown out in the bombing and all that remained were a few jagged triangular strips fluttering along the edges like race pennants. It had been at least a year since anyone had replaced a window. Usually the electricity didn't work and since the roof was mostly holes now, everything smelled damp and musty. Speer lit a cigarette and stared out the window. It was early March and the skies over Berlin were perpetually gray. He wondered if by the time the actual spring came the war might already be over. A number of the women in the office had already come up and asked if, with his connections, he could get them suicide pills. He promised he would look into it, but he still hadn't started asking around.

The intercom on his desk buzzed. Speer went over and pressed down the switch. "Yes?"

A female voice crackled on the other end. "Colonel von Poser is here to see you."

"Send him in," said Speer. A few seconds later the office door opened and in strode a short, frowning, white-haired soldier easily twenty years his senior. Colonel von Poser was Speer's military liaison to the Army General Staff and one of the few men he trusted completely. Von Poser was of the old school. He hated Nazis and dilettantes and he hated discussing things in rooms he assumed were bugged. "Speer," he grunted, "it has happened."

Speer knew it could only mean one thing: that the Americans were now across the Rhine, Germany's last barrier in the west. He got up from his desk and followed von Poser to the wall map. "Where?" he asked in a low voice.

Von Poser put his finger on a town called Remagen. "Apparently efforts to blow up the railroad bridge had not been as successful as originally claimed," he muttered.

"Any chance they'll be thrown back?"

Von Poser shook his head. "We don't have anything to throw them back with. But you see what lies next." His finger made a circle around the area just east of Remagen. It was the Ruhr, Germany's industrial heart, the biggest concentration of mines, steel mills, chemical plants, and manufacturing anywhere in the world. "You know what's going to happen next, don't you?"

Speer nodded. Hitler would now have all the excuse he needed to unleash a spate of scorched-earth orders, just as he had done when the Russians had moved into East Prussia a few months earlier. All the factories, all the mines, the rail yards, electrical plants, telephone exchanges, everything, would get blown up, smashed, and destroyed, leaving behind a mangled, smoldering wasteland.

Blowing up the Ruhr's factories was not going to keep the enemy from winning the war. Nothing could at this point. All it would accomplish was to ensure that the Germans who survived would spend the rest of their lives in the Dark Ages. This was Hitler's new vision for Germany.

"So are you still willing to go ahead with our plan?" asked von Poser.

Speer nodded.

Von Poser gave a grim smile. "You know what your friend will do if he finds out?"

Speer shrugged. He knew.

"All right," said von Poser. "I'll get the auto ready. We leave when it gets dark."

After that Speer had meetings that went on through the afternoon. When everyone had finally gone, Speer went back to his quarters and packed all his things into two pigskin traveling bags. In his valise he stuffed some reports and letterhead stationery, along with a thick sheaf of stay-of-demolition orders, which his ministry had no authority to possess, let alone hand out, along with an inkpad and an assortment of rubber stamps from different governmental authorities. Then he gathered all the canned food from his personal larder and bundled it into a pillowcase from his bed.

With still an hour to kill, Speer lit a cigarette and went over to the couch and sat down.

You know what your friend will do if he finds out? Speer had always hated that they referred to Hitler that way. Hitler wasn't his friend. Speer may have been Hitler's friend, perhaps even his only friend. But that wasn't the same thing, was it? Besides, Speer knew what Hitler would do when he found out.

Reasonably speaking, all they could hope for now was to keep enough of Germany's industrial base together so that some sort of civilized life could continue after it was all over. He'd carefully broached the matter with Hitler during the winter, but Hitler dismissed it. "There is no need to preserve anything for the survivors, Speer," he told him. "They will have proven themselves unworthy."

Speer went over to the window and stared out. By now the bombing had taken out most of the city's landmarks, leaving him without his usual points of reference. Locating Alexanderplatz had always been a matter of simply finding the old Town Hall's clock tower and then going a little bit left. But now the tower was gone. So were the Karstadt department store, the Columbus building on Potsdamer Platz, the twin steeples of Saint Nicholas Church. He tried to remember what they looked like, but they were already excised from his memory.

Instead what blazed unforgettably in his mind was the skyline of a city that had only existed on paper and tabletop scale models. He saw the dome, stretched out before him, larger than a sunrise, with its dozens of gigantic columns and a massive bronze eagle perched ominously atop its cupola.

And he heard Hitler's voice reciting the numbers to onlookers: *Sixteen times the size of Saint Peter's in Rome!* And he saw the rest of the imaginary city, the broad avenues, the monuments, the palaces and plazas, the gigantic ministry buildings, cinemas, concert halls, hotels, and storefronts, miles and miles of it. The two of them had spent years dreaming it up; a city greater than Rome, a light among nations, a capital fit to rule the world for a thousand years: *Germania!*

Speer had actually believed in it back when Germany's future still loomed bright, enough so that he went ahead with demolition orders for whole neighborhoods in order to make way for it. Berlin's destruction hadn't started with the first British bombing raids, but with the bulldozing he had himself engineered.

Once the war had started the whole thing should have been shelved, but it only stoked Hitler's enthusiasm. And when the enemy bombing did come, Hitler acted gleeful. *They're only doing our work for us, Speer,* he'd say. And Speer accepted it without question. Even after things went bad in Russia, Hitler had insisted it be kept on as a top priority, summoning Speer to the studio in the middle of the night so they could discuss the changes that still occurred to him on a daily basis. They'd spend endless hours bent down at eye level to the miniature streets and buildings, peering under archways, discussing each gallery and staircase.

Even now, with the enemy at their door, Hitler wouldn't let it go. In his mind, Germania was still every bit as real as the miracle weapons, inevitable victory, and all the other shabby fantasies that he insisted everyone believe in. And it was all Speer's fault for wanting a thousand years of glory.

Going to pick up his bags, he paused for a moment to look at himself in the mirror. Was this the face of a future world leader? Except for some rings under his eyes and a receding hairline, there was still far too much boyishness in it. He was neither handsome nor ugly, his face was round, his chin soft. It was only the face of a technocrat. No, that's not completely true, he told himself. His eyes had it. Dark, brooding, even without a night's sleep, they had a sharpness to them, inquisitiveness too, and sardonic humor. The face of a man who could put things into perspective.

Speer went downstairs to the garage where Colonel von Poser was waiting beside a supercharged, six-wheeled Mercedes. They drove out after nightfall, heading west.

{ 2 }

At first a war is a cause, a crusade. But ultimately it becomes nothing more than an intersection of x and y axes; a cost-benefit analysis, a calculus of conditions and circumstances. In this particular war, the lines had been crossed long ago and there was no longer any benefit, just cost. It wasn't a question of belief or will, only numbers. And the numbers had said only one thing: the war was lost.

While the Western Allies kept to the western bank of the Rhine, Germans hoped it might somehow stay that way, as it had been two thousand years earlier when the Rhine had marked the Roman Empire's northernmost border. They wondered what it might take to ultimately convince the British and Americans to stay put. The French could keep Strasbourg and the Alsace, the Russians the eastern bank of the Vistula. As far as fallback positions went, it almost bordered on the agreeable. Not that the Führer would have seen it that way. But then again, the Führer wouldn't be around forever.

But now of course the Rhine was breached and the Americans were racing the Russians to Berlin. Now it was a question of trying to limit the destruction so that there might be something left for the future. It should be something everyone could agree to.

He and von Poser had gone in thinking it would be easy, since by now Speer was on a personal basis with nearly every factory director in the Ruhr. Despite his youth, they all looked to him as a guiding light, someone who understood their needs and concerns, who respected their expertise and knew what could and could not be done. And he was someone they could speak frankly to about the suicidal course the war had taken. They'd all been acutely aware of what Hitler had done to the industrial areas in the east and were adamant the same thing not happen to their beloved Ruhr. Some had even dropped broad hints about their willingness to go against the regime should Speer elect to break with Hitler and lead a revolt. But now that Speer had come to do just that, they were suddenly overcome with reticence.

Had I said that, Herr Reichsminister? You must be mistaken.

Don't say these things, Herr Reichsminister. It's treason.

Perhaps we should stop the conversation right here, Herr Reichsminister.

Herr Reichsminister, what you are suggesting is quite impossible.

Herr Reichsminister, you must not ask this thing!

Herr Reichsminister, I've always had the utmost respect for you, but if you do not leave at once, it will be my duty to inform the local party militia of your subversion.

Now please, you must leave, immediately.

Get out.

Leave now!

Go!

Not that it was surprising that everyone was suddenly so scared. With everything in complete disarray and communication with Berlin hopelessly tangled, the local Nazi party chiefs, the gauleiters, now held absolute power. Their "flying squads" seemed to be everywhere, examining travel documents, searching vehicles, questioning people about what they were doing away from the front lines, and then acting as judge, jury, and executioner against anyone whose enthusiasm for the war they found wanting. Their victims were either taken away for torturous interrogations or simply strung up from the nearest lamppost, where they remained for weeks as a reminder for everyone else.

By the end of the first day Speer was ready to throw in the towel and head back, and he would have except that von Poser's steely determination showed no hint of flagging. So they went on, day after day, visiting chemical plants, steel mills, coal mines, electrical generating stations, ammunition works. Most of the distance driving they did at night, the sky teeming with enemy aircraft during the day. Sometimes they traveled with military convoys, but more often alone. The roads were kept dark and with their headlights masked down to tiny illuminated squares, they had to proceed slowly, as the roads were full of bomb craters and debris.

It was anyone's guess where the roads would take them, since everything had been rerouted and changed. The front's actual location was kept secret and more than once they ended up at the front lines with less than half a kilometer between themselves and the nearest enemy tank. Even more confusing was the fact that nothing looked familiar anymore. In his years as armaments minister, Speer had visited every factory town there countless times and knew the region like the back of his hand. But with half the buildings flattened and the sprawling industrial plants transformed into forests of twisted metal girders, frames, and broken pipes, Speer and von Poser often found themselves disoriented. But underneath the wreckage, Speer knew that a surprising amount was repairable. Factories were often up and running again in a matter of days, machine tool works sometimes within hours. Of course, if the militiamen really tried, they could purposely render everything completely unfixable. And that was Speer's biggest worry.

They drove around, visiting the factories that came their way. They'd talk to whoever was around, sound them out, listen to their excuses, nod sympathetically, and then move on to the next location, hoping they'd get lucky. They'd knock off late in the afternoon, sleep a little, then drive through the night. Usually toward dawn they'd find a command post where there were cots, or they'd simply pull over and rest for a few hours. Sometimes they ate from their stock of canned food, but mostly they tried to eat whatever was being spooned out for the troops.

Then one night they were driving between Lüdenscheid and Dessau on a particularly badly bombed stretch of autobahn. Speer sat beside von Poser in the front seat, an air defense map spread on his lap, while the radio alternated between piano concertos and a lifeless voice reading out positions of enemy aircraft: *"Fighters reported in Grid E-6 heading westward, enemy fighters in Grid F-12 bearing east. Enemy fighters in Grid D-9 heading east, enemy bombers in Grid C-7, C-8, and C-10, high overhead heading west."*

Then suddenly they heard the metallic scream of aircraft engines as machine-gun fire ripped up the ground in front of them. Von Poser slammed on the brakes and before they knew it, the car was plummeting down the embankment. They pushed open the doors and jumped out onto the ground. A twin-engine Heinkel roared over them, with a smaller American fighter tight on its tail, firing away. The Heinkel's starboard engine was aflame. Then its wing crumpled and it turned over, plunging into the darkness. A second later they heard the dull explosion and saw the flash of fire in a distant field.

They tried getting their car out of the ditch, but the mud was too thick and the back wheels only spun uselessly. They stood around in the darkness unsure of what to do next. In another hour it would be light enough for the American Mustangs and Thunderbolts to return and begin strafing anything that wasn't already blown up.

Then they became aware of the easy clopping of horses' hoofs. They peered into the mist to see what it was. The clopping came closer until suddenly he was in front of them: a tall thin figure in a long coat and floppy-brimmed hat, leading a team of four large sputtering farm horses. "Hey, there," he called out. "I see you had an accident. Let's see if my boys here can't get you out." His name was Jakob and he was a farmer, tending his cows in a nearby field when he heard the noise. So he went back to the barn and hitched up his team. It used to be that there were hardly ever any accidents on this stretch of the autobahn, he told them. But now it seemed like barely a night went by without someone smashing up.

It didn't take five minutes to pull the car back up the embankment and onto the road. Jakob worked his horses with a good-natured firmness that struck Speer as the utter embodiment of German peasant virtue. Speer imagined Germania and the pilgrimages that all the Jakobs of the Greater German Reich would make at least once in their lives so they could see the city and stand inside the Great Hall. Supposedly this war had been for them. Now all it would do was chew them up in its maw.

"Jakob, what will you do when the Americans come?"

Jakob gave a big smile. "It'll never happen," he said. "The Führer has those secret weapons of his. And once the Americans have gotten themselves too far in to escape, boom!" Jakob clapped his hands together joyfully. "He'll fire those secret weapons and then their goose will be cooked!" Jakob smiled guilelessly at them. Von Poser looked away uncomfortably.

"Where did you hear about this?" asked Speer.

"Oh, you know, around," said Jakob. "Everybody agrees about that."

"They do?"

"Of course," he said. "The Führer knows what to do. People just need to have faith, that's all."

Speer felt sick. They'd really done a good job indoctrinating people. "Jakob, listen to me," said Speer. "All that stuff they're telling you, it's all a lie. There are no secret weapons."

Jakob stared at them uncomprehendingly. "But I've heard them say it," he insisted. "Over and over . . . on the radio . . . that they're almost ready." Then he laughed nervously. "You're joking with me, aren't you? I know, this is all a test. You're testing my faith, to see if I'm worthy."

Von Poser stepped in. "Speer, we need to get going."

But Speer waved him off. "No, we're not testing you, Jakob. We're trying to help you, just like you've helped us. When the

33

Americans come, find a place to hide with your cows and let it all just pass you by. That nonsense they're telling you will only get you killed. Please, Jakob, hide. Save yourself."

He watched Jakob shifting back and forth on his feet as he stared down at the ground. But then he looked up and his eyes were blazing with anger.

"Traitors!" he spat the word out. "You betray our Führer. You betray Germany! And to think I helped you out. Look at you! You're betraying your uniforms, your country, your people. You're worse than Jews! And you," he said, pointing his finger at von Poser. "Look at you, an army officer, of all people. You should be ashamed of yourself!

"I'm getting my gun," he shouted. "And if you are still here when I get back, so help me, I'll kill you both!" Giving a shake of his reins, he put his horses into a brisk trot and left them.

"Speer, are you insane?" shouted von Poser. "You're going to get us hanged."

Speer felt like an idiot. "I'm sorry, Colonel. I just couldn't stand thinking about somebody like that getting killed."

"Well, don't ever do it again! Things are dangerous enough as it is. I don't need you screwing it up with some weak-hearted do-gooding. Get in the car. Let's get out of here."

For the next half hour, von Poser drove as quickly as he could. Speer made several attempts to apologize, but was rebuffed. He sank into an uncomfortable silence.

An hour later, outside Dessau, they came to a roadblock where grim-faced party militiamen came at them with machine guns and yanked them both out of the car.

"How dare you?" roared Speer, feeling their hands at his shoulder. "Do you know who I am?"

That got him a hard punch in the jaw. "Shut up!" the militiaman grunted, knocking him to the ground. Speer rolled on the pavement, hands, elbows, and shoulder stinging. He tried to push up onto his knees, only to feel a boot heel coming down hard against his side.

"Stop!" wailed Speer. "You're making a mistake. I'm minister for war production . . ." He waited for the militiaman to step back, but he didn't. Speer felt the man's boot stomp down on his shoulder.

"You think we don't know what you've been doing?" he heard the man hiss. The boot came down again, this time hard into Speer's ribs. Speer stopped moving. He put up his hands, got onto his knees, and looked up at the two men standing over him, their machine guns pointing down at him. Von Poser was also on his knees. He looked angry and tired.

The militiamen stepped back and let Speer and von Poser get to their feet. They kept their hands up while the men went through their pockets. Then one of the militiamen pulled Speer's arms back behind him while the other snapped a heavy pair of iron handcuffs onto his wrists. They did the same to von Poser. Then the two were shoved into the back of a police van, which took them to a fortresslike police building. After being led down a series of narrow gray steel-paneled corridors, they were thrown into an empty cell, where their handcuffs were finally removed. Then the doors slammed shut and once again it was just the two of them.

Hours passed. Neither of them said anything. Von Poser's furious expression told Speer not to bother offering any more apologies. So this is how it ends, he thought miserably. The best thing they could hope for now was a chance to shoot themselves before getting strung up. They might give von Poser back his pistol with one round, but not Speer. Would he get the Führer or would he be passed directly into the hands of Heinrich Himmler, the Reichsführer SS? They'd never been friends. Speer knew Himmler resented him for his closeness to the Führer. It wasn't enough that Himmler held all the power, that he was the Führer's *faithful*

Heinrich. He wanted the Führer to share his dreams with him the same way he did with Speer, to share his dreams of salmon skies and buildings, of civic spaces and a city that would be a thousand years of glory, a light upon nations. Germania, Himmler wanted that too. What a laugh, thought Speer. And how he will smile when I am brought before him. Unless they shot Speer right off, this would definitely happen.

But will I have the Führer first? Will I get to listen to him rage on about the betrayal? How I, Speer, the man Hitler trusted enough to share his dreams with, have betrayed him and befouled the purity of our joint vision? *If I've loved just one person in my life, it was you, Speer,* he'd say. *After all I did for you, you did this to me. Oh, Speer, how could you, how could you?*

Colonel von Poser's fate would be much more immediate. For him it would mainly be a question of selecting a suitably prominent lamppost to string him from. Speer could see in von Poser's face the anger at having just thrown away his life and honor gallivanting about with some civilian dilettante like Speer. Like a fool.

More time passed. Gradually they became aware of laughter coming out from the other side of one of the steel doors. Then the door opened and a group of men came out and stared at them through the bars like they were impounded animals.

There were five of them, all in party uniforms. The local gauleiter's boys, fat as though life had been good to them. All except one, a younger man, about thirty, taut and lit up like he was having a hell of a good time.

He blew smoke from his cigarette as he grinned at Speer. He took his cigarette out and turned to the others and remarked, "Yes, I'd definitely say these are some fish you've got." Immediately the four fat men laughed like it was absolutely the funniest comment anyone had ever made. "Yes, we've definitely won the prize here today, gentlemen." He smiled at Speer and von Poser as though he were looking forward to eating them. But once they'd left, Speer found himself thinking only that the young man's face seemed really, really familiar.

He saw von Poser looking at him.

"I'm sorry, Colonel," mumbled Speer.

Colonel von Poser looked away.

The laughter continued in sporadic bursts. Speer kept listening for other sounds, someone yelling, screaming, arguing. But all he heard was the laughing, loud and growing more hysterical, like whatever it was had them busting their guts. Then suddenly it stopped and everything went quiet. Von Poser looked at Speer. This was it! They heard a lock turning on the steel door. Then it opened and out stepped the young man, only this time he wasn't smiling or trying to look menacing. He quickly handed them their identification books and gestured to them to follow him. "Quickly," he said.

They followed him down the corridor to another steel door. He took out a key on a long chain, put it in the lock, turned it, and popped the door open. Dull gray daylight burst in. The young man stuck his head out but then pulled it back in and shut the door.

"Back," he told them.

They went back up, past their cell, all the way to a place with three steel doors. Choosing the one on the left, he put his hand on the handle and looked at Speer and von Poser. "Just walk through quickly," he told them in a quiet voice. "Don't look around, don't stop. Okay? Let's go."

He pushed the door open and led them briskly down another corridor through a small comfortable office with two desks at one side and a low table surrounded by stuffed club chairs on the other, where the other four men with automatics were sitting slumped over and leaning back, their mouths gaping open, the rest of their faces shot off. There was blood and flesh everywhere. Speer did his best not to look.

The young man opened the far door and ushered them

through, locking it behind them. They went up another corridor, much wider and lined with shelves and file cabinets. Halfway down, two men were going through an overhead cabinet. The young man turned back and fixed his eyes on Speer and von Poser. "All right," he whispered. "One, two, three . . ."

They followed him past the two men, who barely acknowledged them when they walked past. The next room was full of people at desks and typewriters and people carrying papers. Some people looked up, but nobody said anything. Twice people looked like they were going to say something, but somehow the young man's nod quieted them and made them forget they had been about to ask something pointed. Speer watched as the young man nodded to different people and he guessed he had been somebody back when he was younger. Somebody whose face had been in photo magazines, always smiling, clean, bright-eyed, youthful Aryan laughter.

Who was he?

He took them through a lobby, past desks and rows of chairs and rifles and party militiamen in brown coats with holster harnesses and black ammunition bandoliers strapped across their shoulders. He waved to a couple of burly men in feldgrau coats and constable's hats. "Next time I'll bring you some photographs," he said as though he knew it would probably never happen. They nodded back like they didn't really believe it either but looked forward to it just the same.

Outside, they went over to where Speer's Mercedes had been left. The young man opened the back door and let them get in. Then he shut the back door, opened the front, and put himself behind the wheel. The engine started up, he shoved it into gear, and drove out.

They motored past milling groups of militiamen who ignored them, then went out a gate where no one stopped them for papers. A few minutes later, they'd gone past streets full of bombed-out buildings and then found themselves out of town and speeding up an empty road. Speer and von Poser sat back and exchanged looks of astonishment.

They drove past fields and pastures where cows were busy grazing, oblivious to everything but the grass.

Then the young man turned back to address them.

"All right, so here's the deal," he said. "I'm going to be your driver from now on.

"You're trying to keep the Nazis from blowing everything up." He said this like it was something everyone already knew. "Well, you're going about it the wrong way."

"Apparently," grunted von Poser.

"I can get you what you want," the young man said. "I'll have them eating out of your hands."

"How are you going to do that?" asked Speer.

"I'm magic," the young man said. "No one ever refuses me."

They looked at him, dumbfounded.

"Why?" asked von Poser.

"I need to get around," the young man explained. "Business to take care of."

"Who are you?" asked Speer.

"Never mind who I am," the young man snapped and returned to his driving.

Nobody said anything after that. Speer and von Poser settled into their bewildered silences. Speer stared out at the passing countryside. In the late afternoon sun, the winter fields no longer looked so bleak. He thought he saw hints of green beginning to emerge.

As he drove, the young man began whistling something Speer remembered orchestras playing back when he was still a young man with lots of dreams, but no job. A lyrical and melancholy number that expressed how everyone seemed to feel back then. Then he remembered it was called "Harlem Rhapsody."

He remembered seeing the words in white lettering inside a black circle on a magazine page. And a crooked headline snaking across it, asking, *Which One Is Your Favorite?*

And suddenly the names came to him like waves: Ziggy, Franzi, Sebastian, and suddenly Speer knew exactly which one he was.

"Yes?" asked the young man.

"You're Manni of the Flying Magical Loerber Brothers."

The young man dazzled them with his smile. Then he turned back to keep his eyes on the road.

(3)

That first day they visited ten different factories and at each of them, whoever was running it, the owner, the general director, the workers' committee, or in one case an elderly one-armed ex-infantry general, all immediately agreed to join Speer's campaign. It was as if everyone's fear had suddenly evaporated. The day after that, they visited two mines, a railroad roundhouse, an electrical generation station, and the Bayer Pharmaceutical Works, which was now host to an artillery battery. There too, everyone agreed not to obey the scorched-earth orders when they came in. "Let 'em come here and try to tell us what to do," shouted a bunch of electrical workers waving machine pistols in defiance. "We'll show those Nazi pigs what for!" And even the artillery battery commander, under strict orders not to move an inch, readily agreed to relocate his guns to a less sensitive spot. "They don't have to know anything," he told Speer. "None of it makes any difference anyway. Let's keep the chemical works intact."

And in each case, Speer and von Poser hadn't done anything any different than what they'd done in previous visits. The only difference was that at some point, Manni would step in and say something completely unremarkable like, "I can understand your misgivings on this, but if you'd just let me explain something to you . . ." And then he'd say something that, on the face of it, wasn't that different from what Speer had tried himself. But this time it worked. Whatever they asked for, they got.

He seemed to know exactly what each person would respond

to. He was able to convince Field Marshal Model, a diehard Nazi, that the Führer's across-the-board destruction orders required a radical reinterpretation to spare sixteen factories that manufactured components for the new miracle U-boats. And once Model conceded the logic in that, Manni got him to add a neighboring steel mill, a power plant, a machine-tool works, and a couple bridges to the exemption order. With another, he'd reminisce about the old days with his brothers and what a grand character old Gustav was. Others he would get to talk about the world they wanted for their unborn grandchildren. In three days, they'd visited twenty-two different sites and were successful at each one. And no matter where they went, they never encountered a problem from the Nazi militias.

Still, it was hard to enjoy any of it. The uneasiness was too ever-present, and Manni Loerber's manner with them was brusque. Everything about him said to Speer, *Do exactly as I tell you and don't try to get away.* And so they didn't.

One time he came out leading a frightened-looking man by the elbow. The man had on a raincoat that fit him so poorly Speer guessed they'd stolen it on their way out. Manni opened the rear door and let the man get in beside Speer. "He's a friend of mine. I told him we'd give him a ride," he said. Then he got behind the wheel, put the car into gear, and they were off again. For the next two hours the man remained rigid, wild-eyed, and trembling, like he thought he was still sitting under the interrogator's lamp. Eventually Manni asked Speer to find him something to eat. Speer went into his bag and pulled out a tin of mixed vegetables. He went to work opening it, then pulled back the lid and handed it to the man, who stared at it warily before taking it in his hands and gulping down its contents in a few seconds. Once he finished, he looked around ravenously, then sank back in embarrassed silence. Finally, just as it was getting dark, they drove into a forest and let him out near a logging road. Without saying goodbye or waving, the man hurried up the path and disappeared into the trees.

And each time, Speer and von Poser found themselves waiting for Manni in the car and mostly avoiding each other's gaze so they wouldn't have to ask each other what the hell they were doing.

Speer tried to remember what he could about the Flying Magical Loerber Brothers. Like everyone else, he'd seen them perform many times, and certainly he'd enjoyed their act. It was impossible not to. Still, Speer had been largely bewildered by all the Loerber Brothers mania that had gone on for so many years back before the war. He remembered all the photo and variety magazine covers. Some trademark picture of their four identical clean-cut and smiling faces arranged like a crescent moon. *Which one is your favorite?* it always asked. And people had their favorites and would tell you, which to Speer didn't make any sense, since they were all indistinguishable from one another. It was like having a favorite corner of a square building.

But everyone else apparently could distinguish between them and they'd dote endlessly over the supposed minutiae of their lives that the fan magazines would concoct. *Franzi's Secret Crush! Twenty Things You Don't Know About Manni!*

What Speer did recall was that one of them had disappeared; it was news for just an instant and then, suddenly, public memory of him vanished. Suddenly there had only been three Flying Magical Loerber Brothers. Sebastian. He was the one who had disappeared and no one had ever talked about again. Speer remembered it played up big in the afternoon papers and how everyone had bought several to compare stories. But by the morning, Sebastian Loerber had ceased to exist. And he'd been the brightest one of them. That was what people had said. It had been back in the early days, when the power scramble was far from settled, and the SA still had more power than the SS and even Göring and Hess were running their own police forces. They never found out who arrested Sebastian, but the finger-pointing must have been murderous that day. In the end whoever was in charge must have decided it would be easier to make Sebastian Loerber cease to exist than get to the bottom of it. So for a while there were three of them and then after that Gustav Loerber died and there was that big, big state funeral that the Führer and everyone else attended. It had been on the newsreels how only one of the brothers was able to attend because the other two were in uniform and away.

So, *were* they all magic? Had Sebastian Loerber been killed or had he just unraveled in some metaphysical spasm? What about the others? Ziggy and Franzi? What were they doing now? Perhaps some variation on Manni's wandering assassin?

Magic? What was it?

Speer didn't exactly consider himself an atheist; he'd just always considered believing in a god to be mostly beneath him. That held true even now, although now he could say he believed in magic. Unalterable numbers and logic all could be bypassed. It only took Manni Loerber opening his mouth and asking. And every time, everyone agreed to whatever he asked for. Food? Ammunition? Diesel? Join the uprising? Sure. Anything else?

What had happened to their fear, to their survival instinct? What had happened to their need to protect at all costs their families from the gauleiters' flying squads? Time and again, people would smile and agree to misplace a sheaf of destruction orders, or to shove a half ton of explosives into a sump hole, or to carelessly drop a grenade into a room full of fellow militiamen. It had to be magic. There was no other explanation.

(4)

Even in the best circumstances, magic doesn't work forever. For two weeks things went without a hitch. Then one day they visited the local offices of a deputy gauleiter, a short, fat, red-faced man, who they'd hoped would block an order to blow up a nearby series of canal locks.

At first everything seemed to go well. "Whatever can I do for Herr Reichsminister?" he asked solicitously. Speer started with his usual bit about heavy industry being the lifeblood of the German nation, and then about "ultimate victory" and how the Ruhr's infrastructure would be vital once the Americans got thrown back by the Führer's secret weapons, which, Speer let the deputy know, were now only days from completion.

But try as he might to come off humble and unpretentious, Speer could tell that the deputy really only saw things in terms of weak and strong; of someone mighty and sophisticated like Speer begging favors from a relative nobody like himself. There was something of the inequity of it that he couldn't accept. The whole time Speer talked, he kept staring at Speer's tailored gray suit; crumpled as it was, it still somehow made his own sumptuous party uniform look like a servant's.

Speer thought that perhaps he should just stand up and thank the man without coming to the point of his visit. Make an excuse, say he'd be back later. But he hesitated and before he knew it, Manni had taken over. "What we need from you is to sign these declarations to prevent the unnecessary destruction of the canal locks." The man nodded. "It's for the future," Manni added. The man nodded again. He took his pen and flipped open the lid of a rather ornate eagle-on-a-swastika inkwell, dipped the pen into it, and then started contentedly scratching his signature onto the first of several documents.

But then he stopped. He blinked and shook his head like a horse trying to jolt off a fly. It was like Jakob all over again: a detonation that couldn't be controlled. His eyes flared at Speer.

"You! You! You betray the Führer! Of all people, you, Herr Reichsminister! You are the Führer's *friend* and you do this to him?" He stood up from his chair. "I'm going to have you killed!" he declared. Again and again he tried to pull his pistol out from its holster, but for some reason his hand wasn't able to find it. He opened his mouth to shout out something, but then suddenly his eyes went blank, his jaw dropped, and he slumped back into his chair with a heavy plop.

"Quick," barked Manni, grabbing the sheaf of papers off the desk. "We've got to get out now!" They ran down the corridor, causing the secretaries and typists and party functionaries to look up from their desks.

Once outside, Manni tossed von Poser the keys. "Colonel, you're driving," he shouted. "Drive fast!"

He got in the back beside Speer, pulling out several automatic pistols from under the seat, while looking out the back window. Just as Von Poser fired up the engine, the deputy gauleiter stumbled out of the building entrance, pistol in his upraised hand as he screamed at them like a rabid dog.

He shot at them as he ran down the steps, striking the car, shattering its rear window.

Von Poser began easing the huge car out into the street, only to slam his foot on the brake when he saw a truck barreling toward them. More shots rang out, but this time none of them hit the car. Speer saw the deputy running out into the street, right into the path of the oncoming truck. It ran straight over him and kept on past Speer's Mercedes. Von Poser waited until it had gone past, then pulled out, heading in the opposite direction. The last thing Speer saw as they drove away was the crowd of people running up to the deputy's body.

Then he looked over at Manni and saw he was slumped against the door, a pistol fallen from his hand. "He's been shot," he gasped.

"Stay calm, Speer," barked von Poser. "Try to see where he's been hit."

Speer bent over the young man to check his face and chest for wounds, but other than some glass cuts he didn't see anything. "I don't see any wound," he said, his voice quavering with panic. "But he looks like he's dead."

"Is he breathing?" asked von Poser.

Speer put his ear to Manni's chest. He could hear breathing, but it was shallow, like he was in shock. His face was ashen. Speer pulled open his eyes, but they were not reacting. "He's breathing, but he's out," he told von Poser.

"Just keep an eye on him."

Von Poser kept driving as fast as he could, swerving occasionally to avoid the potholes and debris. Speer pulled out a blanket and draped it over the young man. He tried to feel his pulse, but he couldn't tell whether it was there.

A few minutes later they came to a checkpoint. The militiamen looked at the bullet holes and the shattered windows without interest. Von Poser let them examine his papers.

"Where are you going?" one of them asked.

"We're trying to find Field Marshal Kesselring's headquarters," answered von Poser. "Any idea?"

"How would we know?" one of the militiamen answered. "Everything keeps moving around. The field marshal probably doesn't even know." He pointed at Manni, still lying unconscious in the backseat. "What's with him?"

"He had too much to drink. His wife just died," Speer answered.

The militiaman gave a wave of his hand. "You can go," he told them.

They drove through the night, changing direction frequently and sticking to back roads where there were fewer checkpoints. Manni Loerber remained unconscious the whole time. Every hour or so, Speer checked on him. His pulse had returned and his breathing seemed almost normal, but nothing would rouse him. The roads were mostly empty now. There wasn't fuel for convoys to move around much anymore. But in contrast to the stillness on the ground, the sky was full of constant buzzing. The Allied fighters were everywhere, roaring low overhead without a moment's warning. Sometime before dawn they found an abandoned farmhouse on a hillside overlooking Detmold. Von Poser helped Speer carry Manni inside. They put him in the large bed and covered him with a blanket. Then they ate something, opened their bedrolls, and went to sleep.

After weeks of never more than an hour or two of sleep at night, Speer fell into a deep uninterrupted slumber. If at any point he dreamed, he wasn't aware of it. It was late morning when he finally awoke. For more than an hour he remained under his blanket, vaguely aware of snatches of conversation going on between two voices. Finally getting up, he found von Poser and Manni in the other room sharing a cigarette at the hearth, where a small fire was burning.

Manni looked over. "Hello," he said in a small voice.

"How are you feeling?" asked Speer.

"Terrible," he answered sourly, but still managed a grin. "I was just telling the colonel that I think I've pulled my last trick for a long time."

"That's all right," answered Speer. "I think we're finished with it."

Von Poser held up a battered-looking coffeepot. "It's fresh, compliments of Herr Manni."

"You have coffee?" asked Speer. As far as he knew, it had been a nonexistent commodity for more than a year.

Von Poser handed him a steaming cup. "Here's to new beginnings," he said.

For a long moment, Speer luxuriated in the coffee's deep aroma, then took a sip. "So what do we do now?" he asked.

They spent the afternoon milling about the farmhouse, not doing anything in particular. The few conversations they had were sparse and inconsequential. The young man himself spent most of the time in silence, but it seemed to have none of the brittle edginess that had marked his previous regime. He seemed relieved that whatever he'd been doing was now over. He was relaxed, shared his cigarettes and coffee, and though he didn't join in much of the conversation, his presence didn't deter it either. Once when Speer was in the other room half dozing on the bed, he heard the other two briefly laugh at something.

They took turns sitting by the fire or standing at the windows or doorway, staring outside as American Mustangs and Thunderbolts roared low overhead in continuous waves, hunting for things to kill. They seemed to operate with almost reptilian brains, striking at shiny things that moved. The Mercedes stood in the middle of the field, with only a thin layer of netting over it, and though its profile was still unmistakable, it didn't seem to register with them.

Speer wondered where the front was. Von Poser's map was by now several days out of date, and it was likely that in that time the situation had changed radically. What was certain was that they were inside a shrinking fishbowl.

In the late afternoon they made more coffee, sliced some bread, and opened their last remaining cans, which they passed around, spooning beets and potatoes and chunks of fish onto their plates.

They ate with the reserved familiarity of three strangers of the same class sharing a table in a dining car. When they were finished, von Poser took out a cigarette from his silver case, lit it, and, after taking a puff, passed it to Manni.

"Did they ever find out what happened to your brother?" he asked.

Manni Loerber looked back at von Poser in languorous silence. "No, they never did."

"No explanation one way or the other?"

Manni shook his head.

"My daughter wept for many days. He was her favorite."

Manni let a slight smile cross his lips. "Who was her second favorite?"

"I believe it was Franzi," said von Poser.

For several minutes Manni fell into deep, meditative silence. Then he stood up from his chair.

"That's it," he declared brightly. "Herr Reichsminister, come with me, please." He headed for the door.

"What are you doing?" asked Speer.

"Herr Reichsminister," said Manni, "it's time you learned to juggle. I'm going to teach you. At times like this, a man needs to know how to juggle. That's the problem with the world. Nobody in charge of anything can juggle. It's a scandal. I'm getting my balls out of the car now!"

"Don't go outside, you'll get killed!" said von Poser.

"Watch me." Manni laughed as he strode outside.

Speer looked from the doorway while Manni went out to the car. Immediately an American fighter roared low overhead. More screamed past while he rummaged around the trunk, pulling a number of gaily colored balls out of one of his bags. Heaping them in his arms, he began walking back.

Then he stopped. "What are you waiting for, Herr Reichsminister? Come on out."

"Are you crazy?" answered Speer. "It's not safe out there."

Manni looked around, like he was trying to see what danger Speer could be referring to. Down the hill, Detmold was on fire. Fighters and twin-engine bombers swooped down low over the city's factories, dropping bombs as they did, which exploded with an evil burst.

"I know, but the ceiling inside the farmhouse is too low," Manni answered. "It'll never work in there. Come on out. You'll be fine."

"We'll get killed. Come inside right now!"

Another fighter swept low over the field, but Manni didn't flinch. "Forget them," he said. "They're not interested in us. Come on out!"

"No," said Speer and turned to go inside.

"Herr Reichsminister, this moment will never happen again. Aren't you interested in knowing how magic works? Well, this is how it starts. Right here.

"Herr Reichsminister, just turn around."

Speer didn't know why he didn't just go inside and hide himself in the farthest corner of the farmhouse. He really should have, but instead he turned around. A ball flew at him and he caught it, but barely.

"Now toss it back to me," urged Manni.

Speer tossed it back. But Manni had already tossed another ball at him. He caught it.

"Quickly toss it back," said Manni. "Don't stop. As soon as you have it, shoot it back the exact same trajectory that you caught it. Don't think! It's easier that way."

Speer did as Manni instructed. He caught the ball and tossed it right back. A second later another ball came, and then another and another.

Manni took a step backward and Speer took one forward to catch the ball that was coming toward him. Manni took another step backward. Speer took another step forward. Manni added another ball, then another. "That's it! Keep it up!"

51

The balls were coming faster now, one after the other in quick succession. But even so, Speer was surprised at how much time he had to catch them and shoot them back.

He was aware of the airplanes flying just over their heads, of bursts of machine gun fire and explosions that had none of thunder's innocence. But Speer knew that as long as he could fix his attention on the balls, on catching them and throwing them back, he would be immune. He wasn't the Reichsminister for war production standing in an empty field, he was a tree, a brick wall, a part of a machine; a cog, a cam follower, a take-up spool, a reciprocating gear. Another one, another one, another one. More enemy planes screamed over their heads. More balls kept flying toward him.

"How many balls are we doing now?"

"Can't you count?"

"No," answered Speer with a laugh. "How many?"

"Five."

Five. Five balls. Speer wondered what his wife would think. Juggling five balls in the middle of an air raid.

"Are you afraid?"

"Of what?" Speer shouted back.

Catch it, throw it back, catch it, throw it back. There was a perfect logic to it, focused on the moment, on the *now*. Nothing else mattered but the moment, the motion. The spaces between the moments became vast, even though he knew they couldn't be more than a second apart. Enough time for flawless reaction. Enough time for an eternity of thought.

And somewhere in this wilderness of space was the room to alter outcomes. Here, somewhere, magic lay. And here, with Manni, Speer sensed he was walking along the very edge of it.

{ 5 }

Back on the road again, driving through the night. Fat raindrops spattered against the windshield as the pneumatic wipers made their faltering sweeps against the glass. They had the radio turned up high, blaring Bruckner along with enemy fighter coordinates. Speer was in the front seat, staring ahead into the garbled gray horizon, past the flashes of artillery and arcing streams of tracer rounds, and wondering what was going to happen to them.

They were driving toward Duisburg. They'd heard there was a refueling depot where supposedly they could fill their tanks with unlimited diesel. By now their crusade had deteriorated into an aimless shuffling about the ever-shrinking confines of what was now being called the Ruhr Pocket. Most of the region's factories were already in enemy hands. The rest were still in the hands of the gauleiters and militias, who seemed content to let the Americans bomb and shell them all to bits.

"Night fighters in Grid C-1, Mosquitoes in Grid B-9, squadron of bombers flying east-southeast Grid B-14," the voice on the radio announced, before returning to a piano étude.

Speer glanced over at Manni Loerber sitting behind the wheel, cigarette dangling from his mouth, staring dully out at the darkness. Now that his personal retribution campaign seemed to be over, he didn't appear to have any more idea what to do next than Speer and von Poser did. All Speer knew was he didn't want to go back to Berlin.

Odd guy, thought Speer. He remained largely remote toward

them. The only difference was that now when they were holed up somewhere he would break out the bag with the rubber balls and for the next hour he and Speer would juggle. And whenever they did, he would start asking Speer questions about his friendship with the Führer. And for all Speer's normally deeply engrained reticence on the matter, he would end up spilling his guts, time after time.

"Medium bombers in Grid C-8 and C-24 heading west."

Once he told Manni about the time Hitler had ordered the melting down of all the Luftwaffe's bombers and the building of nothing but fighter planes. Another time he told about the endless hours he'd had to spend sitting through American musical films, back to back. Other times he'd tell him about Göring, or the rivalry between Goebbels and Bormann, the Führer's secretary. He even told Manni about Germania.

"When we weren't spending the night watching musicals, we'd be staring down miniature plaster streetfronts and revising shopping arcades and inner courtyards. Or we'd imagine how the Great Dome would look in the light of a setting sun." Manni had smiled like he thought all of it was just too funny and weird.

"Night fighters in Grid D-16 heading north," said the radio announcer. *"Mustangs in Grid D-4 heading east. Mustangs in Grid A-6, A-7, and A-9, circling."*

That afternoon their conversation took an unexpected turn. After jumping from one topic to another, Manni brought up Himmler, the Reichsführer SS.

"What do you want to know about him?" asked Speer with a grin. When Manni didn't answer, Speer decided to goad him with one particular morsel. "Did I ever tell you how he tried to kill me last fall?"

Catch it, toss it back. Catch it, toss it back.

"No, I don't believe you did, Herr Reichsminister. What happened?"

"I'd fallen sick during the summer and had gone into the hospital. Well, the Reichsführer saw his opportunity and got a certificate issued to have me transferred to a special SS clinic run by Dr. Gebhardt."

Manni smiled as though he thought it was very droll. "And what happened?"

Catch it, toss it back. Catch it, toss it back.

"Gebhardt started administering poison to me in small doses."

"So what happened? Why didn't you die?"

"I escaped."

"You escaped!" Manni looked impressed. "Very wartime!"

"Yes, very," answered Speer, elated by Manni's response.

"As long as we're on the subject of the Reichsführer SS . . . ," said Manni.

"Yes?" asked Speer. Catch it, toss it back.

"If I may be so bold?"

"Yes?"

"What do you think he's going to do?"

Speer did his best to act surprised. "Do? How do you mean?" Catch it, toss it back. Catch it, toss it back.

"Somebody is going to have to succeed the Führer," said Manni.

Speer remembered the captured intelligence report that the Foreign Ministry man had shown him. Had that only been three weeks ago? It felt like years.

Speer allowed himself a tiny laugh. "Herr Manni, if you're suggesting the Reichsführer might succeed the Führer, then it's clear you still don't understand the first thing about either of them." Catch the ball, toss it back.

Manni looked flustered. "But the Führer cannot possibly last much longer. Somebody is going to have to succeed him."

"So why would it be Himmler?"

"How could it be anyone else? It has to be Himmler."

"Why?"

"Because Himmler is the one with the power."

"Herr Manni, the only reason he has the power is because his loyalty to Hitler is so absolute, he isn't capable of thinking on his own."

"You're suggesting Himmler would never betray the Führer?"

"Never."

"So he would never, ever seek a separate peace deal with the West?"

"Never," said Speer.

"That's not what we've heard," said Manni. "Apparently he's been sending his masseur up to Stockholm to meet with Eisenhower's people."

"His masseur?"

"So you don't think it's possible?"

"Look, anything's possible," said Speer. "Maybe Himmler will try. Who's to say?" Catch the ball. "It would actually suggest leadership, wouldn't it?"

"So, yes?" asked Manni.

"No," answered Speer.

"No? But he's got the power."

"But he hasn't got the balls."

Toss it back. Catch.

Morning found them on the outskirts of Lüdenscheid. After driving most of the night, they'd taken shelter inside a half-wrecked building that a Volkssturm battalion was using as its command post. Partially demolished buildings like this one had become valuable since they were less likely to be directly targeted for additional pounding. Speer stood at its entrance, huddled in his overcoat, staring out at the drizzle and the gray bleakness and wondering if this was the day he'd finally be caught.

In the yard below, some soldiers had a fire going, using wood pulled from the wreckage. A large cooking pot dangled from an iron tripod above the flames. Nearby stood the volkssturmers, gray and rheumy-eyed, shivering in their heavy coats. They were old men, retired bakers and clerks and librarians. Men who'd fought their own wars long ago and, having survived them, didn't see the point in dying now.

Breakfast was a thin, tasteless gruel, a cup of black, bitter ersatz coffee, and a cigarette shared between the three of them. Von Poser, choleric and bleary from not enough sleep; Manni, looking fixed and irreducible, like a soldier before his hundredth battle. Von Poser opened his map and briefed them on what he'd learned about the current military situation. They discussed it for a few minutes and then, baggage and bedrolls in hand, walked to where the Mercedes was hidden, rolled up the camouflage netting, and took their places inside. Manni started up the engine and they were off.

They headed toward Frankfurt and ended up that morning in the remains of a steel plant. Even now some of the armaments factories were still making weapons, and occasionally Speer was called upon to make phone calls to locate needed nitrogen or saltpeter or convince someone to give up his horded tungsten or chromium in order to make antitank shells. Here instead, all they found was a group from the local party militia, who had acquired a demijohn of Czech rum and were too busy drinking it to care about destroying anything. The steelworkers had already taken apart the rolling mills and they showed Speer where the parts were being stored. Speer congratulated them on their inventiveness and listened to their plans for convincing the Americans to come in and take over. Then someone recognized Manni and right away they all got excited and crowded around him, clamoring for stories about the old days, about old Gustav and Sebastian before he disappeared.

After that, they drove to a town outside Nauheim, where, according to their maps, Field Marshal Model was supposed to have moved his headquarters. But when they got there, it had already been shifted eastward. An infantry colonel told them nobody had any precise idea where the Americans were at this point. He noted that there was also an SS Panzer brigade in the area, supposedly, but no one had any idea where they were either.

They spent another hour driving through a pine forest. At first waves of enemy fighters flew low overhead, but then everything got so quiet it almost made them think the war might suddenly be very far away. Coming out, they entered a small town. Driving up the main thoroughfare toward the center, they craned their heads looking for a sign of life. No windows were broken, no roofs shattered. Everything seemed in good order, except that there were no people anywhere. "It looks like our troops have already withdrawn," observed von Poser.

They continued motoring slowly toward the center. Then they began to see them. Hanging from the lampposts, there must have been dozens: soldiers, civilians, old men, women, their faces in commedia-dell'arte grins, skin the color of concrete. Placards around their necks proclaimed: I WAS A COWARD AND A WRETCH. I DESERTED MY PEOPLE. I WAS A TRAITOR TO MY VOLK. I WAS A COWARD. I WAS A WISENHEIMER, I WAS A WORTHLESS WHORE. The birds had already been at them.

In the town square, a solitary soldier stood by a dry fountain, calmly smoking a pipe, two Panzerfaust rockets resting at his side. At von Poser's direction, Manni stopped the car, and all three men got out and walked across the square toward him. He seemed to regard their approach with little interest.

"Hello, soldier," said Speer.

The man said nothing.

"Where is everybody?"

He jerked his head around to indicate all the executed. "They're all here."

"Who did this?" demanded von Poser.

"Koehl, the party chief," answered the soldier. "He declared the town a fortress, demanded everyone fight to the death. Nobody wanted to."

"So where is Koehl?"

"He left." The man was grinning like he'd wholeheartedly endorsed Koehl's decision at the time.

"Then what are you doing here?"

"My orders are to wait for the Americans," he said, pointing down the street with his chin. For the first time Speer was aware of the nearby rumbling of tanks.

"So what are you going to do when they get here?"

The soldier smiled. "Oh, they're here."

The rumbling grew louder. The soldier tapped the ashes out of his pipe and put it away in his side pocket. Then, without saying anything, he picked up the two Panzerfausts and walked to the edge of the square, taking up a position behind the corner of a building. Up in the distance a large tank with a white star had turned the corner and come into view.

"Come on, let's get out of here," said von Poser.

But Manni had an idea. "You know, we can just let them take us," he suggested. "Five minutes from now it'll all be a different story. Come on. What do you say?

"For Christ's sake," Manni continued. "All that stands between us and the safety of the American lines is that shovelhead? Let's go!"

Von Poser looked at him angrily. "You can do anything you want," he hissed. "But this is not what we came here for. We are not deserters. Let's go, Speer."

Speer turned to leave. He looked at Manni. Manni shook his head. "It's been fun, Speer."

Speer nodded.

"Keep practicing."

"I will," Speer said and started hurrying to get back to the car before the tank made it to the square. Von Poser looked relieved when he saw Speer was alone. "Well, so much for that," he grunted as he turned the car around. Speer didn't say anything.

"Speer! We could juggle our way to freedom."

"Goodbye, Loerber."

They found the rest of the German army a few miles to the east. An expectant mood had come over the soldiers, like they believed their war was nearly over and in just a few more days they'd be home free. "Would you mind moving your car somewhere else, Herr Reichsminister?" one of them asked. "We don't want their artillery spotters unnecessarily zeroing in on us." A couple soldiers laughed. Then a wild pig came out of the woods, bleeding from a stray bullet, squealing wildly as the soldiers chased it around. Not bothering to ask directions, Speer and von Poser drove east. They ate supper with a factory director he'd known from the old days. Afterward the director produced a bottle of cherry liqueur and they finished it off watching the sun set over a horizon of bombed-out factories. They got going soon after that, driving through the night and reaching Nuremberg just as dawn was breaking.

The drive itself was uneventful, except for the last five kilometers where the autobahn was lined with the burning wreckage of army convoys that had been shot up an hour earlier. In the faint early light, the ghostly silhouettes resembled the skeletal carcasses of extinct ancient beasts, though the stench of the burning ammunition, rubber, and men kept any of it from seeming remotely like a fantasy. And they'd all been his animals, his machines. In a few more days they'd all be just as extinct.

That was when von Poser turned to Speer. "Do you know how many times I took my daughter to see them? We must have seen them twenty times. We did it for years. The Flying Magical Loerber Brothers. I wonder what the others are doing. Ziggy, Franzi, and the other one. Sebastian."

"I wonder. And Manni."

Enemy daytime fighters appeared with the dawn, flying low, attacking any vehicle that hadn't already found cover. But by then he and von Poser had already put the netting over the car. They found the army headquarters hidden among the half-bombed factories just inside the city. Field Marshal Model was expected at noon. With nothing else to do for the next five hours, they got themselves directed to a darkened corner where dozens of cots had been laid out for officers and quickly went to sleep.

An hour later someone was tapping his side impatiently. "Reichsminister Speer?" It was a stern-looking captain with a pocket torch.

"What is it?"

"I'm to escort you to the airfield," he said. "There's a plane waiting to take you back to Berlin. Führer's orders."

(6)

The Führer glared furiously at Speer. For the first time since they'd known each other, there was neither a greeting nor a handshake. He waited for the adjutants to leave before speaking.

"So, Speer," he began icily.

"Mein Führer?" asked Speer, knowing he didn't sound even remotely innocent.

Hitler looked terrible. His eyes rheumier than before, drooping eyelids, bags, gray oatmeal skin. He looked much older than his fifty-five years. That bomb last summer had taken a lot out of him. Hitler kept his palsied left hand clenched behind him so it wouldn't shake uncontrollably. His green uniform jacket had stains and Speer noticed bread crumbs sticking to one of the cuffs.

"Bormann has given me a report on your recent activities. He says you're telling people the war is lost and that they shouldn't carry out my orders." He paused and waited for Speer to say something. But Speer said nothing. "Well?"

"Mein Führer, I can't lie to you," Speer said finally.

But Hitler would have none of it. "Are you aware what the punishment is for that?"

Standing stiffly at attention, looking straight into Hitler's eyes, Speer said, "I am aware of the penalties for disobedience, mein Führer. And you may, if you wish, apply them as the law demands without any regard to our personal relationship."

Hitler slammed his good fist against the desk. "How could you do this, Speer?" he shouted. "How could you? You! Of all people!"

He paced back and forth in front of his desk, not looking at Speer. "Sit down!" he ordered.

"Mein Führer, I prefer to stand."

"Sit down."

Speer lowered himself into the chair.

"After all I've done for you, and you repay me like this. You were nothing, Speer. Do you remember? An unemployed graduate without a pot to piss in.

"Do you know what I do to people who betray me? What makes you think you're any different?"

Speer looked up at him. "The answer is yes, mein Führer, I know what happens to people who go against you. And I am no different."

Hitler didn't like that one bit. His head started twitching. He pulled his bad hand out to claw at the air. Everything was behind him now. His years of victory, of moving from strength to strength, were all gone. His charm, his wit, his animal vitality had deserted him. All that was left was this quivering shell. But even now his determination and will, the two things that defined him, were undiminished. He sat down at the desk and studied its surface for a long time. What comes next? Speer wondered. Will he declare me apostate? Throw me to the lions, the SS? Is Himmler going to jeer at me? *So, Speer, we were never good enough for you, were we? But now we'll just see how much better you really are.* It might have been better to have been shot by the gauleiter's deputy that time. For the first time he remembered his wife and children and how he'd loved being called Uncle Hitler by them. He hoped they wouldn't be included.

Hitler looked up from the table. Suddenly he looked forgiving. "Speer, you think I don't know things look bad? I've been a soldier for thirty years and I've seen more bad times than you'll ever know." The angry tone was gone. He sounded like someone offering encouragement to a wayward friend. "But I'll tell you something else: Bad times never last. Things turn around, sometimes very quickly. But the only way you can be there to take advantage of them is to have faith. Faith, Speer! Faith in yourself, faith in your volk, faith in your leader, faith in me!"

Faith, thought Speer. Faith doesn't matter when you're out of fuel, out of bullets, and out of everybody but seventy-year-old volkssturmers.

"Mein Führer, what I saw in the Ruhr—"

Hitler quickly waved him to silence. "None of that matters, Speer. What matters is inside you. Don't you see?" Hitler stood up from his desk, leaning forward so that he was close to Speer, his face a kindly grimace. "Now tell me, Speer, tell me you have faith."

"I'd be lying, mein Führer," answered Speer, making no attempt to sound contrite.

"Then tell me you have hope. Don't you at least hope everything will work out?" He looked imploringly at Speer. *Say yes.* His eyes looked so sad, as if every other tragedy, every other turn of fortune he could bear—but not this. *How could you do this to me? After all our dreams? Your hoping means more to me than anything, Speer. Hope. How could you not hope for a turnaround? Please, say yes.*

Speer saw the eyes, the trembling frame. He thought of how vigorous he'd been once, how full of life and joy. And now he was a sad old man asking for a tiny favor from his only friend; a favor only a completely unfeeling bastard could say no to.

"I'm sorry, mein Führer," said Speer. "But the facts do not lie." He wanted to add, *The war is lost,* but somehow he couldn't bring himself.

Hitler's face darkened and once again he grew cold. "I'm giving you twenty-four hours to think about what I've just said to you," he said brusquely. "I want you here tomorrow telling me you have faith in victory."

Back in his office at the ministry, Speer tried to write down what he wanted to tell Hitler. He thought about all the things he'd seen in the Ruhr that he wanted to describe to him. If he could have seen the elderly volkssturmers or the disorganized, fragmentary divisions, if he could have seen people like Jakob who still had faith in him, who still believed in victory, maybe then Hitler would be able to see the utter travesty in what he was asking. But the words wouldn't come and he knew Hitler wouldn't listen anyway. It was impossible to write it down, just as it was impossible to tell him to his face. What was he going to do? Speer didn't know. All he knew was that he was dead tired. He went back to his quarters and went to bed.

He woke up a few hours later with a dry mouth and a cold sweat and rather than try to go back to sleep, he put on his robe and went back to his office to work on his response. Faith? Hope? Do I say yes or no? If I say no, I'll at least get to maintain my integrity. Of course, at this point his integrity had to be about the most useless thing there was. But on the other hand, his reward for discarding it was hardly worth having.

Speer wrote a few sentences, then crumpled the paper and stared out into the darkness. The electricity was out again. The empty window frames either hadn't been repapered or what they'd put in had already been blown out. Perhaps the papering crews had all been mobilized and sent off to the front. Faith? Hope? Come on! There was nothing left.

After three weeks in the Ruhr, he was back here like the whole thing had never happened. He'd staged his own revolt against Hitler and now Hitler was going to take even that away from him by forgiving him. But Speer had changed. He was a different person now and Hitler's power over him wasn't what it had been. He'd learned to see things differently. He now saw things from the perspective of a juggler.

Juggling, perhaps that was what Speer should do. He hadn't juggled in two days. He didn't want to lose his edge. He wished he had some balls lying around. Of course, they don't have to be balls, they don't even have to be round or the same size or weight. Just remember the feel and the weight. What did he have? He lit another candle and went looking for objects. There was a small Bakelite ashtray, a pocket flask, a leather eyeglass case. What else? He rummaged through his desk drawer and found a small steel box. Why not?

He stood up and started juggling the ashtray and the eyeglass case. Once he had them going well, he snatched the steel box off the desk and threw it up to join the other objects in the air. Then the flask.

Keep it up, keep it going, one thing at a time. He kept it going and going and going and for the first time since his return from the Ruhr his head felt clear, his heart lighter. What will I tell Hitler? Flask, ashtray. Tell him all I have left is my integrity and my ability to juggle, not that there is any difference between the two. Leather case, steel box, flask.

Tell him he's dropped too many balls. The single ball he keeps throwing up into the air does not constitute juggling. That he should get off the stage. Ashtray, case, steel box. Here comes the flask, and now the ashtray and now the case.

And maybe if he'd bother to read *Mein Kampf* again he might remember what he himself had said about leaders who can no longer lead. Flask, ashtray. And he's asking me to reaffirm my faith in a man who's dropped all the balls and is just pretending they are all in the air when they're actually rolling around on the ground. I don't think so, mein Führer.

And what would Hitler tell me? *All I've got left is you, Speer. The others don't matter. Lapdogs are a dime a dozen. I need a man who will tell me the truth. All I require is this one lie.* Flask, ashtray, eyeglass case. *One lie, Speer. After all I've done for you, I'm not asking much, one little lie. Tell me you have faith.*

Here comes the steel box—and up it goes again! Flask, ashtray, case.

Faith? Hope? Obey? No, said the disobedient angel, I will not obey. My integrity is reduced to this act of rebellion and if you take it away from me all I have left is this . . .

Steel box, flask, ashtray, eyeglass case.

Only then Speer became aware of the presence of somebody else in the room. There was somebody standing in the shadows by the doorway. He must have slipped in. Somebody from his staff, perhaps; one of the secretaries, a deputy, a section chief. But he wasn't going to let his eyes off the flying objects. He didn't want to stop yet. He still had a few things to think through.

"Could you come back in ten minutes, please?" Speer called out. "I'm busy with something right now."

But the visitor did not stir, though Speer noticed he had reached up with his hand to touch his forehead. Speer kept on juggling and hoped the intruder would take the hint and leave. Finally the figure stepped out of the shadow and into the dim candlelight. It was Himmler.

In an instant Speer's focus evaporated and the objects crashed onto the floor.

"Reichsführer," he said embarrassedly. "What a surprise."

With the candlelight dancing upon the thick lenses of his glasses, Himmler's eyes were all but invisible to Speer. But then it was easy to guess what they looked like, because his eyes were always the same: cold, expressionless cobra's eyes.

"So, Speer," he began matter-of-factly, "I hear you have become quite the folk hero in the Ruhr. Going around charming the populace, getting them to disobey the Führer's directives, talking about tomorrow instead of today." But to Speer's surprise, Himmler's manner wasn't threatening. If anything he seemed nervous, as though he were looking for someone to confide in. Speer wondered what had happened while he was gone.

"Is there something I can help you with, Reichsführer?" he asked politely.

Himmler stared at Speer for a long time before finally saying, "These are exceptional times, are they not, Herr Reichsminister?"

"Yes, Reichsführer, very exceptional," answered Speer. Catch it, toss it back.

"These are dark times also, wouldn't you say?"

"Yes, Reichsführer, very dark times."

"But then, isn't it true that it is always darkest right before the dawn?"

"Yes, I've heard that said," allowed Speer.

"They also say that when you get to the bottom of a valley, there is nowhere to go but up."

"Yes, they also say that." Speer tossed it back. He wished Himmler would come to the point. Absentmindedly Speer picked up some pencils from the desk and began flipping them into the air, then catching them and flipping them back again. "Is there something you wanted to ask about, Reichsführer?" he asked. "Something about darkness?"

He caught them and then tossed them up from his shoulder, then stuck his other hand behind his back and caught them as they came down.

"Yes! Would you stop doing that!" snapped Himmler.

Speer put the pencils down. "Pardon me, Reichsführer, but I'm very nervous right now. What were you saying?"

"I was, ah, saying how some people are saying . . ."

"Yes?"

"That it may be time for a change."

"People, Reichsführer? What people?"

Himmler hesitated again before continuing. "People who are, ah, concerned with the way things are going right now with the war. People who believe we might be missing out on unprecedented opportunities with the Western Allies."

Speer suddenly realized what Himmler was trying to say. Was it even possible?

"Reichsführer, are you talking about a peace deal with the West?"

Himmler stared openmouthed at Speer.

"I'm talking about opportunities for Germany's future."

"Opportunities, Reichsführer?"

Himmler looked at Speer. "When you talk to the Führer again would you do something for me?" Speer nodded for him to go ahead. "Try to sound him out on his stepping aside for a brief period to allow for a realignment."

"I promise I'll get back to you on it," said Speer.

"Good luck, Speer." With that, Himmler left quickly.

Speer went to his desk and tried writing out his thoughts again, but his concentration was gone. He ended up pushing the paper and pencil aside and went back to reading the industry reports he'd been looking at before going to the Ruhr. Hours later, when the call came for him to report back to the Führerbunker, Speer still had no idea what he was going to tell Hitler.

He entered the bunker through the Chancellery garage, walking down a labyrinth of narrow, half-lit corridors and stairways, past heavy, pressure-tight airlock doors, until he reached the depths of the Führer's subterranean lair.

Hitler was waiting for him alone in one of the conference rooms. "Well?" he asked bluntly.

"Mein Führer," began Speer. He could see the desperation in Hitler's eyes. Everything was hanging on his next sentence. He thought about Jakob and the people hanging from the lampposts. I WAS A WISENHEIMER. I WAS A WORTHLESS WHORE. I have to be true to the facts. Hope will not stop enemy tanks. These are exceptional times, wouldn't you say?

"Well?"

"Mein Führer, I stand unreservedly behind you." Catch the ball, toss it back.

Tears came to Hitler's eyes. He smiled. "Then all is well," he said.

Hitler had some building plans he'd been wanting to show Speer, plans for a cathedral for his hometown of Linz. "It's just my way of giving back, Speer."

They spent thirty-five minutes going over the drawings, Speer fawning with him over cupolas and spires. Finally Hitler got restless and let Speer go.

As he climbed up the final flight of steps leading to the Chancellery garden, the late afternoon sunlight greeted Speer like an all-forgiving friend. So maybe he'd bungled it. Manni would have done it differently, no doubt. But it was enough that he was alive. It would be all over soon anyway. Himmler could do anything he wanted. So could Manni.

(7)

During the flight back from Stockholm, Schellenberg went over and over what he was going to tell Himmler. *The discussions with Count Bernadotte went very satisfactorily, Reichsführer,* he figured he'd start off saying. *He assures me General Eisenhower is receptive to our proposal. The Anglo-Americans are eager to join in an alliance against the Russians.*

Not that Bernadotte had actually said anything of the sort, but Schellenberg, the thirty-year-old head of Foreign Intelligence, needed to motivate Himmler into moving against Hitler and if fudging a few minor points was what it took, well, then so be it.

The count said he'd been told by Eisenhower himself that they now consider the Russians a much bigger worry than ourselves. They are absolutely convinced the Russians will turn on them.

Bernadotte hadn't said that either. What he'd said was that there was growing nervousness in Allied circles about what would happen with the Russians once Germany was defeated. Schellenberg was smart enough to know what that meant without having to be told.

Eisenhower is ready to make a deal, Reichsführer, he merely requires us to make the first move. Until then, his hands are tied. Of course, what Count Bernadotte had actually said was, "This is all very nice, General Schellenberg, but until I get some concrete declaration from the Reichsführer that he is taking over the reins of government from Hitler, nothing I say to Eisenhower will make any difference. There must be immediate action. Force Hitler to

71

step down, arrest him, kill him. How you do it is not his concern. Just get it done."

That was what Schellenberg really needed to tell Himmler, and perhaps in a perfect world he would. But he knew from experience how terribly skittish his boss was when it came to things like this. Anything requiring definitive action sent him into one of his massive panic attacks. His stomach would go into spasms and next thing he'd be screaming for Kersten, his Finnish masseur, to come in and take the pain away. Schellenberg didn't want that to happen this time because Kersten wouldn't be there. He was supposed to fly back with Schellenberg from Stockholm, but at the last minute he'd made up some excuse and stayed behind. That put Schellenberg in a doubly sensitive situation, since he'd have to force Himmler into making a difficult decision without having Kersten on hand to rescue him.

With a Finnish passport that allowed him to come and go seamlessly, Felix Kersten was the Reichsführer's secret envoy to Allied intelligence. Schellenberg had flown up with him the day before to see Count Folke Bernadotte, head of the Swedish Red Cross and a member of the Royal Family, who was their intermediary to Eisenhower to explore ways of making a deal to end the war.

Schellenberg and Bernadotte had both agreed that the single best choice for a new head of state would have been, hands down, Field Marshal Rommel, the gallant head of the Afrika Korps, who was admired by both the British and Americans and no doubt might have cut a very favorable deal, except of course that Rommel was dead. So Schellenberg proposed his own boss, Reichsführer SS Heinrich Himmler. Initially Bernadotte had reservations, worrying that Himmler's position as head of the SS would put off the Anglo-Americans. Then there was the issue of Jews and the death camps. But Schellenberg kept pushing the idea until the count finally relented and said, yes, Eisenhower would probably deal with Himmler as long as he could deliver.

So here they were, and all that remained to be done was to get Himmler to cross over. The problem was, for all his icy efficiency in carrying out Hitler's orders, when it came to thinking for himself Himmler was a hopeless waffler.

What could Schellenberg tell him that would make him act? *It is the eleventh hour, Reichsführer. It is late, but not too late. The sooner we do something, the more we can bring to the table. But it must be now. Time will not improve our position. You must move against the Führer immediately!*

The other possibility would be to appeal to the Reichsführer's obsession with the mystical. *This is our supreme hour of destiny, Reichsführer. We are at the threshold of a moment which might not come again for a thousand years.* And even though Schellenberg himself took a dim view of the Reichsführer's karma-laden ravings, in this case it wasn't an exaggeration. If Himmler moved boldly, the rift between Germany and the West could be healed in a matter of days. The fact was, even at this late stage, Germany had an awful lot to bring to the table. There were still more than a hundred army divisions, thousands of aircraft and tanks, and a populace dedicated to throwing back the Soviet horde. Eisenhower should be able to see virtue somewhere in that.

And of course there were other things they had to sweeten the deal with, things that, as head of counterintelligence, only Schellenberg knew about. There was, for instance, Source Moonpool, their secret network inside Red Army intelligence. Not only were they learning about the Soviets' intentions, their plans, and their capabilities, but more importantly, about their intelligence efforts against Germany and the Western Allies as well.

In fact, only the day before, Major Steiner, his man running Moonpool, had come to him with information about something he was calling the Cambridge Spy Ring, a group of deep-penetration agents whom the Soviets had recruited from Cambridge University during the thirties and who had since wormed their way to the top tiers of British intelligence. Steiner was confident that by the end of the month they would have their names. When Schellenberg thought about what that information might be worth, he got very excited.

Steiner was perfect, except for one thing. He was a homosexual and had found a boyfriend there at SS Headquarters among the Reichsführer's staff astrologers, and the transcript from a recent random bugging gave Schellenberg reason to believe their pillow talk might be getting too detailed. Once he had finished reporting to Himmler, his next order of business would be to see that little issue taken care of.

They started their descent into Berlin. He could hear the hydraulic whine of the aircraft's landing gear coming down and locking into place. He looked out the window and recognized Tempelhof Airport's long curving terminal buildings. Minutes later they had landed and were taxiing down the tarmac.

Reichsführer SS Heinrich Himmler received Schellenberg the way he usually did, standing with his back to him, staring intently out his office window. Himmler liked to meditate. Sometimes he remained there the entire time while one of his subordinates delivered his report. Schellenberg supposed this was a ploy to intimidate, but he had grown to actually prefer it to the icy spotlight of Himmler's blank, emotionless stare.

"Well?"

"The meeting with Count Bernadotte went quite well, Reichs-führer," began Schellenberg. "He believes some great opportunities will present themselves once we get things moving."

"What specifically did he say?"

Schellenberg brought up the things he had rehearsed: how amenable Eisenhower was to the idea of joining forces against the Bolsheviks and how it would launch a new era of European peace and order.

Himmler liked that. "Go on."

"Count Bernadotte agreed that with Rommel dead, you are the

single best candidate for a new German leader. Apparently Eisenhower also agrees."

"That I'm the best candidate? Did he say why?"

"Well, yes, he did, Reichsführer. Like Rommel, you're a military leader, largely nonpolitical. The fact that the SS is not connected to the Nazi Party is a big plus. He also pointed out that while you are not a Christian, you do believe in a god. Belief in God is very important to the Americans, you see."

Once Schellenberg started, he couldn't stop. He said that Bernadotte had told him how impressed Eisenhower was with the way Himmler had run Germany's unified police system before the war and that he believed they should model Europe's future internal security organization after it.

Himmler turned from the window and looked directly at Schellenberg, a look of utter amazement on his face. "Eisenhower said that?"

"Indeed he did, Reichsführer."

"What else did he say? Tell me everything!"

Schellenberg felt a twinge of guilt for having spun so far from the truth, but he knew the survival of Europe's soul rested on keeping up Himmler's enthusiasm. Besides, as chief of counterintelligence, he was in a position to make educated guesses about such things.

"Reichsführer, Eisenhower is concerned that Europe will fracture into many different competing jurisdictions. The French communists are already posing a problem. It will have to be dealt with by someone unafraid of using a firm hand. Someone not bound by existing alliances, who can mete out justice with fairness and impartiality. He's already finding that very difficult. The British are unable to grasp things. They tend to be too heavy-handed. And of course the French are even worse."

"How are the French worse?"

Schellenberg rolled his eyes and tried to come up with the

most appropriate explanation. "Come on, Reichsführer. You know how the French are. They completely lack nuance."

Himmler leaped up in excitement. "Yes! The French are like that, aren't they? Did he say anything about growing discord among the Allies?"

"Yes, Reichsführer, that is one of his biggest concerns."

"I was right! I was right!" exclaimed Himmler. "Well, you should tell Count Bernadotte to tell Eisenhower that he should—"

"Reichsführer," said Schellenberg. "We're in a unique position to cut a deal with Eisenhower. He needs to know just how thoroughly infiltrated British intelligence is right now. And with Source Moonpool, we can tell him that and a lot more. You need to sit down with Eisenhower and come to an understanding, general to general, world leader to world leader. I think you'll be quite surprised by what we might walk away with."

Himmler smiled. He liked that idea.

"But," said Schellenberg.

"Yes?" said Himmler.

"You have to make the first move."

"Yes," said Himmler.

Without his uniform, Reichsführer SS Heinrich Himmler would not look like a leader, world or otherwise. He was a pudgy, balding little man, with weak, watery eyes, who stared out at the world through thick-lensed pince-nez glasses. Without the uniform, he might be a barber or a clerk or a bathroom attendant. The eyes behind the glasses usually betrayed no emotion. But this time they glittered as he smiled at Schellenberg.

"Yes, I should," he said excitedly. "I'll tell him . . ." His voice momentarily trailed off. "Schellenberg, let me ask you this. When I go to Eisenhower and present myself to him, should I bow or should I offer to shake hands?"

Normally Schellenberg was wary of letting Himmler veer off the topic, but this was a good sign. It meant the Reichsführer was thinking about running things after Hitler was gotten rid of.

"Reichsführer," he began solemnly, "I would say the best thing to do would be bow. Why? Because it shows your gallantry and your readiness to approach him as a supplicant. Offering to shake hands right off could create the impression of being too forward. But when you bow, he will feel compelled to put his hand on your shoulder and be gracious."

Himmler was suddenly a whirl of activity, speaking quickly as he paced back and forth. "You're right, you're absolutely right. That's what I'll do. I'll come up to him and I'll bow."

Schellenberg smiled.

"Now I just need to see about getting the Führer's permission," he said, almost as an afterthought.

Schellenberg stood dumbfounded. . . . *Getting the Führer's permission?* Could he possibly have heard it wrong? The understanding had been that if Hitler didn't agree to step down, he should be shot. Permission? He stared up at Himmler, who stared back, his watery eyes imperceptible as ever behind the pebble lenses of his glasses.

"There is also the matter of my uniform. Should I wear the green one or the black? I think black would be ideal," he ventured.

Schellenberg tried to keep from exploding. "Reichsführer, you need to tell me, are we still on the same page on this?"

Himmler dabbed at his mouth with his forefinger. "Whatever do you mean?" he asked absently.

"None of this can happen until you confront the Führer and make him step aside. We've already discussed this."

Himmler twitched.

"Now, are you going to do it or not?"

A bigger twitch this time.

"Count Bernadotte is going out on a limb telling Eisenhower you are ready to take over the government. That was the whole point of my flying up to Stockholm. That was what we agreed on, wasn't it?"

Himmler's stomach jerked.

"They both expect immediate action from us, Reichsführer. And I'd say they are also definitely starting to lose their patience."

Another twitch. Himmler's mouth gaped.

Schellenberg pushed it further. "Reichsführer, the situation is critical. The Russians are going to chew us up and spit us out. They're going to rape and kill everyone they find. Is this what you want to happen?"

Himmler was all frantic motion now, waving his arms like he was battling an onslaught of flies. "General Schellenberg, you know it's not as simple as that. You really must understand my situation here. I owe everything to the Führer. Everything! And while yes, I might agree in principle, I just can't come to him and say, *Get out of the way, it's now my turn.* It's just not, it's just not, it's unthinkable—I've sworn an oath of allegiance, a sacred oath, and I, for one, take that sort of thing very seriously!"

"Reichsführer—" interjected Schellenberg. But Himmler waved him to silence.

"You must understand the karmic implications of what you are suggesting. It would be much better for everyone if the Führer elected to step down, that would minimize the celestial trauma. I think we should give it a few more days and see if something might alter the forces in our favor. Karmically speaking, it would be the thing to shoot for. And my astrologer assures me there are some major events on the horizon, so who knows?"

Schellenberg cursed himself. The whole trip had been a waste. All of his efforts over the last two years had been a waste.

"We need to be patient, Schellenberg, and not rush anything. It's the cosmic thing to do." Beads of sweat were forming on Himmler's forehead and his left eyebrow was fluttering.

Schellenberg began shouting. "Reichsführer, do you understand the situation we're in as a nation? We are facing racial extermination. And unless you move immediately, now, today, we will all be destroyed. You must find the strength inside yourself to do what must be done."

"But you don't understand," shot back Himmler in a high-pitched voice. "I owe him everything. I swore an oath to him." Suddenly Himmler clutched at his stomach and began shrieking in pain. "It's starting again, Schellenberg! The pain, it's tearing me up!" he screamed. "Aaahhhh, I can't take this! It's killing me, it's killing me. Call Kersten. Get him in here at once."

"Reichsführer," said Schellenberg calmly. "Kersten is still in Stockholm."

"Aaaaaaaahhhhhh!" Himmler shrieked as he collapsed onto the couch. "Do something, Schellenberg! Do something! I can't take it."

Schellenberg went to the door. In the outer office, Himmler's adjutants, aides, and secretaries all waited in hushed terror. "Shouldn't we send for Kersten?" suggested one of the women.

"Kersten isn't coming back," said Schellenberg. "Is there anyone else we can call?"

Everyone looked at each other helplessly. There wasn't a doctor Himmler would let touch him. There was only Kersten. Nobody could take the pain away like Kersten. Nobody could listen to him and give him advice like Kersten. In the next room Himmler screamed like he was being gutted.

"There has to be somebody," said Schellenberg.

One of the adjutants shifted nervously. "Ummm, there's Sublieutenant Loerber from the Astrology Branch. He's supposed to be pretty good."

Himmler shrieked louder.

"Then get this Loerber up here on the double!" ordered Schellenberg.

When they brought the young man in five minutes later, Schellenberg immediately recognized him: Sublieutenant Loerber was Franzi of the Flying Magical Loerber Brothers! Franzi, a crummy sublieutenant, while Schellenberg was a three-star general. Schellenberg remembered when he was eleven or twelve, gazing at the endless photographs and newsreel shots of the four brothers, performing their singing and dancing. Even though they were several years younger than him, their self-assurance and polish made them seem so much older that he secretly dreamed of being one of them. He looked at Franzi's face and wondered what had gone wrong. There were the same pale blue eyes, only the light had gone from them.

Then he remembered that Loerber was also the name of Steiner's boyfriend.

When the call came, Franzi Loerber had already officially gone off duty and was sitting by himself in the staff and junior officers' canteen having a cigarette while working out the final calculations on a large batch of horoscopes he'd been assigned to cast for senior members of the planning staff. It was crap work, very tiresome. Calculate algorithms based on the variations factored from the shifting positions of fifteen ascendant and twelve descendant groups of stars over twelve nine-day intervals starting a month before conception. It was all complete nonsense, something he'd invented on the spur of the moment a long time ago, but for some reason people swore by it. And far be it from Franzi to tell anybody what they should believe in.

All in all, horoscopes were fairly formulaic stuff. The calculations took forever, but the actual writing never took more than five minutes. You just had to make sure it offered so much opportunity, so much warning, and lots of ambiguity. Just write something down, and boom, you're done and you move on to the next one.

He went on number-crunching for another hour until the tediousness finally got to him. Putting the horoscopes aside, he took out his handwritten Moscow Center coding chart and began composing a long-overdue report.

47361 73908 66214 38947 03418 87451, he wrote. It was his way of saying everything was under control and that some promising leads were coming up. *15376 21294 97124 33965*, he added, more as an afterthought. Everyone believed the end would come soon.

Franzi looked up to see the cute captain from internal security eyeing him from the next table. Under normal circumstances he might have seen if he could take it somewhere, but since the captain was a spy-hunter and Franzi happened at that moment to be writing a coded letter to Moscow, he looked away instead. He thought about mentioning him in the report. Moscow seemed to like hearing who in SS Headquarters was queer. He tried to remember what the captain's name was. Hessler, Hindemann? *96101 49327 85634.*

He hated what he was doing. Ziggy was a U-boat captain, Manni an assassin. They got to live lives of adventure and excitement. And all Franzi had done this entire war was calculate horoscopes and report his fellow SS queers to Moscow and London. Franzi looked at the clock. There was a dead drop hidden in one of the lavatories on the second floor. If he posted the message in the next twenty minutes, he could have Moscow off his back for at least two weeks, maybe longer if things went downhill fast enough. He stared at the paper for a long time. When he looked up, the cute captain was staring at him again. What did he want? Sex? Betrayal? Both? Why not? The captain smiled. Franzi smiled back. He crumpled the paper into a ball, then tossed it into a wastebasket along the wall. Franzi rolled his eyes. The captain gave him a sympathetic smirk as though he knew what that was like.

He was done serving Moscow, Franzi decided. The war was all but over and now he had to start taking care of himself. Manni was already gone. He'd left for the Ruhr a month earlier and by this point he was probably safely behind Allied lines. Now Franzi needed to do the same. But how?

It had been a big mistake agreeing to spy for the Russians in the first place, but then at the time he hadn't felt like he had any right to be picky. If he'd only waited for two more weeks, he could have gone to work for the British. It turned out their friend Nigel Westerby was a British operative and had already signed up Manni. Though Franzi readily agreed to share his information with them, he remembered seeing the disappointment on Westerby's face.

The Russians had first come to him after they found out Gustav had wangled him a cushy research post with the Ahnenerbe, the SS-run racial heritage and occult studies institute. Franzi hadn't liked the idea of spending the war working with a bunch of charlatans and mystic crackpots, but the Russians insisted it would be an excellent career choice and a great way to fight the Nazis from the inside. It turned out he'd been right on his first guess: it was worse than being a librarian. For someone who'd spent his entire life in the celebrity spotlight, it was a living death. He remembered how, at first, everyone there was excited to have one of the Magical Loerber Brothers on the staff. People came up to him all the time to ask questions and reminisce, but it wasn't long before the utter midlevel facelessness of his new job wiped the shine right off him. And once that happened, everyone stopped thinking of him as anyone special.

He noticed two staff majors waving frantically at him from the canteen doorway. "Loerber, come here!" one of them hissed. They waited until Franzi was up close and whispered, "You're a masseur, aren't you?"

Franzi nodded warily. "I've done some," he said. "Not professionally."

"Get your things," one of them whispered. "You're needed immediately at the Reichsführer's offices."

Franzi picked up his papers and followed them upstairs to the fifth floor. He was brought past the guards and the identity checkpoint without anyone even taking his name down or checking his papers. Once inside, he was led through a warren of corridors and outer offices where an array of majors, colonels, generals, and secretaries all stood attentively, waiting for his arrival. Outside the Reichsführer's office, a young general stood before the door. Franzi recognized him at once. It was Schellenberg, head of SS intelligence—head of all German intelligence, foreign and domestic—and Franzi's boyfriend's boss.

"The Reichsführer needs your help," Schellenberg said. "Do the best massage you can. And not a word of this to anybody, do you understand?"

Franzi nodded.

But Schellenberg wasn't satisfied. "I mean nobody. Not your office mates or your fellow astrologers, and certainly not your boyfriend. Clear?"

Franzi nodded.

"Good," said Schellenberg. "Now go in."

"But Herr General, isn't Professor Kersten the only one . . . ?"

"Kersten is gone," answered Schellenberg, holding open the door and then following him inside.

There, writhing helplessly on the couch, flanked by two adjutants, was the Reichsführer, his naked body bulging and throbbing as if being eaten up from the inside. At the sight of Franzi, Himmler reached out and groaned, "Please, please! Do something! Please! This pain is killing me!"

Franzi looked at Himmler, then over at Schellenberg. What do they want me to do? I've never done anything like this. He'd heard about the Reichsführer's attacks, and knew that the only person on earth capable of helping him was Kersten.

Franzi pointed at the two adjutants. "You," he said to one of them, "hold down his legs at the knees." He gestured to the other. "You, hold him down by the shoulders. Take his upper arms."

As they did, Franzi bent down over Himmler's upper torso and ran his hands lightly up and down the chest and stomach. The abdominal muscles were churning so violently he could hardly tell their proper orientation. It felt like cats fighting inside a cloth sack. How am I supposed to fix this? he wondered.

"Pleeeease," moaned Himmler.

Not knowing what else to do, Franzi plunged his hand deep into the Reichsführer's abdomen. Himmler immediately let out a long breath. "Ohhhhhhhh," he said. "I can't belieeeeve thaaaat!"

Kneading the man's puffy flesh, Franzi felt the pulsations underneath: constricted, irregular, everything wildly, bizarrely unbalanced, as if holding together purely out of spite.

Slowly the abdominal muscles loosened. Himmler's groaning began turning to grunts of animal pleasure. "Keep going," he told Franzi. "Don't stop. Everyone else, leave now."

Obediently the two adjutants left. But Schellenberg remained where he was, nodding at Franzi not to mind his presence. Franzi noticed the thick spectacles lying on the desk and realized that without them, the Reichsführer probably couldn't see anything. Franzi finished with the abdomen and began working the chest, the shoulders, and the arms. He kneaded the muscles, methodically working his fingers deep into them, following the strands up to their ends, then moving to the next. All of them felt expended, moribund; as if, having been rid of their pent-up tension, they were now unwilling to recover any of their former elasticity. Himmler's body was a mess, shapeless and puffy, no tone, color like paste. Hadn't he ever taken any exercise? What kind of food did he eat? A man in his position could eat anything he wanted. But this was the body of someone who kept himself going on cheap sweets and canteen food. He couldn't understand how anybody could do that to themselves.

"You're very good," said Himmler, after Franzi had worked on him for fifteen minutes.

"Thank you, Reichsführer," Franzi answered.

"No, I mean it," insisted Himmler. "You're very good. You might even be better than Kersten. I haven't felt this relaxed in a long time. I want you on my staff full-time. What is your name?"

"Loerber, Reichsführer. Lieutenant Loerber. I'm with Ahnenerbe."

Himmler seemed surprised and delighted at his answer. "Loerber? As in the Flying Magical Loerber Brothers?"

"Yes, sir. I am Franzi."

Himmler let out a laugh. "And now, all these years later, you're here exactly when I need you. It must be karma."

"Yes," said Franzi, "I believe it must be."

For a while after that, Himmler didn't say anything more. Franzi turned him over and began working on his back. The minutes ticked by.

"Schellenberg keeps pressuring me," said Himmler suddenly. "He's making such demands of me. And he won't let it go."

"Oh?" asked Franzi. He looked over at Schellenberg, whose expression was somewhere between bemused and irritated.

"I'm certain that's why this keeps happening to me," Himmler went on. "He keeps bringing up things that are so unpleasant, just thinking about them makes me feel terrible. What do you think, Professor?"

"It's hard to say," answered Franzi. He looked up again at Schellenberg. The young general suddenly looked preternaturally still and alert, like a leopard deciding whether or not to pounce. . . . *You're in completely uncharted territory here, young man,* his wide eyes seemed to be telling Franzi. *You're walking on the very edge of the razor. How you handle this next minute will determine whether you see the sun rise tomorrow.*

"Let me ask you something," Himmler went on. "Do you know anything about destiny?"

Franzi cleared his throat. "Destiny is a funny thing, Reichsführer. Everyone has a destiny, but very few are men of destiny."

"I don't understand," said Himmler. "Explain."

"Well, look at me, Reichsführer. I know I am just an ordinary man. I may possess vision, and be able to interpret the stars, but ultimately I'll just live my life and die and then be forgotten. But you, sir, are clearly a man of destiny. You are destined to profoundly change things."

"How can you know that?" asked Himmler.

"Ah, Reichsführer, it's the difference between being able to see and having vision. I see things in the universe, but I know that it's not about me."

"But then who is it about?"

"It's about you, Reichsführer. The time has come to fulfill your destiny. Right now the universe requires that you step up and do what is necessary." He stole a glance over at Schellenberg, who looked like he was impressed. That was all Franzi needed.

He remembered that every time he'd been up on a tightrope, there'd be a moment when the worrying part of his brain simply shut itself off and he'd start having fun. There was nothing he and Manni liked better than spinning stories out and dragging people through the swamp. The razor's edge was no longer a frightening place.

"Reichsführer, do you know what happens to men of destiny who doubt themselves and fail to seize their cosmic moment?"

"No, what does happen to them?"

"No one knows, Reichsführer. It's as if they disappear from the face of the earth."

Himmler looked at him in stunned silence. For a long time he didn't say anything. Finally he spoke. "Let me ask you something else. I have a friend with whom I need to talk about something serious, but he's making it very difficult. He only talks about what he wants to talk about. And if you try bringing up something that is important to you, he'll just stare at you and then change the subject."

"I've had friends just like that," said Franzi.

"He drives me crazy, how he does it," continued Himmler. "I've known him for a long time and he's one of those people who is the greatest person in the world when everything is going well, but when things aren't, he won't face up to the facts. Either that or he starts making up excuses. Maybe the problem is I'm not good at confronting people if they won't at least acknowledge the problem so we can have a starting point for meaningful discussions. I've seen other people try to confront him, but he takes everything so personally. Honestly, I don't know what to do."

"We all let people into our lives who drain our energy away from us," said Franzi, "energy that we need for reaching our full potential as cosmic life-forms. And that is a dangerous thing, Reichsführer, because there is only so much energy."

"I never thought of it that way," said Himmler. "Time and energy, they're really the most valuable things we have."

"You're absolutely right, Reichsführer. And do you know why?"

"No, why?"

"Cosmically speaking, time and energy are both different manifestations of the same thing."

"That's absolutely incredible," said Himmler.

Franzi didn't say anything for a while, letting the silence speak for him. Then he added, "But you know, Reichsführer, they're our friends. You can't really change them and you can't abandon them every time they disappoint you."

Suddenly Franzi sensed he'd misstepped. He quickly corrected himself. "But sometimes putting up with it is not worth it. And then you have to confront them and let what happens happen. You tell them to straighten up and fly right and if they don't like it they can stuff it!"

The effect of his words on Himmler was explosive. He sat up and slammed his fist against his palm. "By golly, you're right!" he declared. "I'm going to have a straight talk with the Führer and I'm going to lay down the law with him, and goddammit, friendship or not, if he doesn't agree to end the war immediately, I'll shoot him myself."

Franzi froze. Warily he looked over at Schellenberg and, to his utter shock, saw that he was smiling like he'd just won the grand prize.

(9)

"You know, Loerber, I think you and I are going to make a great team," said Schellenberg as he and Franzi walked down the fifth-floor corridor. Only a week had passed since he'd joined Himmler's staff and this was the third time he and Schellenberg had lunched together, sitting off in a corner of the senior SS staff dining room. After seven years lost in the Ahnenerbe's perpetual mystic twilight, the shine was back on Franzi Loerber. And it felt good.

"Thank you, Herr General," said Franzi. "I am honored to be working for you."

"Just bear in mind one thing," cautioned Schellenberg. "Right now you and I have only one goal."

Franzi nodded. They'd been over it a dozen times already. Eisenhower had made it clear there would be no peace with the West until Himmler seized power from the faltering Führer. And Franzi, owing to his calming and persuasive abilities, would now act as Schellenberg's spear point in that effort.

The task was proving to be a challenging one to say the least. Though he had succeeded several times in getting the Reichs-führer fired up, to the point where he'd storm off to the Füh-rerbunker to "show Hitler what's what," each time something conveniently went wrong and his determination fizzled out just short of the breech. Even so, Franzi had brought him far closer to action than Schellenberg ever had, and Schellenberg remained convinced it was now just a question of seizing every opportunity to get Himmler to move.

"Another thing to keep in mind, Loerber. Since you're now part of the team, I might as well let you in on this little secret. Count Bernadotte is going to be coming down here very soon and he'll be bringing with him senior representatives of the World Jewish Congress to meet with the Reichsführer. They say they'd be willing to settle things with us because they recognize that what happened to the Jews was not really the SS's fault."

"That's good news, Herr General."

"Indeed it is, Loerber."

Franzi didn't see how this was possible. After all that had happened in the camps, after so many millions brutally murdered, how could anyone believe an offer like that could be anything but a ploy? Maybe this whole thing with Eisenhower was also a ploy. Why wouldn't it be? The American wasn't under any obligation to play fair with someone like Himmler.

There was muffled rumbling in the distance. The Soviet artillery was finally within earshot. They turned the corner and continued down the corridor back toward the intelligence staff offices. Several colonels and majors sprang to attention as they passed. They offered salutes that Schellenberg and Franzi returned without comment. Schellenberg was all right, Franzi thought; very collegial and incredibly bright, especially compared to some of the thugs who'd risen high in the SS ranks. He probably didn't even hate Jews. That's what made it so difficult to reconcile the crazy things he said with the grim reality around them. There had to be things nobody else knew about: secret deals, behind-the-scenes relationships that allowed Schellenberg to retain his blue-sky optimism. Franzi reminded himself that the man he was talking to was the most informed person in Germany. He would know it if the Western Allies believed the Russians would turn on them once the victory against Germany was complete.

Schellenberg continued, "I don't have to explain how important an agreement like this will be to the future of Europe. It is imperative Hitler be already out of power when they arrive, so that the Reichsführer can have a free hand to make deals on behalf of Germany. Use any method you can think of to motivate him. We cannot let this thing fall through!"

Franzi found his opportunity that very afternoon during a massage. Himmler required them several times a day in order to relieve stress even when his stomach wasn't actually bothering him. And it usually wasn't long before he began talking to Franzi about things.

"Do you know anything about dreams, Professor Loerber?"

"A little," answered Franzi. "Why?"

"Well, could you tell me what the relationship is between dreams and reality? Does reality cause dreams or do dreams cause reality?"

"That's an extremely good question, Reichsführer," said Franzi. "What kind of dreams are you talking about?"

"Well, I've been having some really strange ones lately," said Himmler. "I can't help but wonder where they are coming from."

"Really?" asked Franzi. "Tell me about your dreams, Reichsführer."

"Well," said Himmler, "I don't know how to say this, but lately all I've been seeing is people's faces staring at me."

"Really? What kind of people?"

"Criminals," answered Himmler.

Franzi didn't understand.

"You know, criminals," repeated Himmler. "Bad people who had to die. The kind of people whose faces I wouldn't look at when they were alive. But now when I'm asleep they're all I see, and I keep trying to wake up but I can't, and everywhere I turn they are there, staring at me from across the barbed wire. Then they start walking through it and come right up to me. Do you have any idea what it could mean?"

"Criminals, you say?" asked Franzi.

"Jews!" Himmler snapped. "I see Jews everywhere, everywhere!"

In his desperation he started to weep. "What can it mean?" he asked.

Himmler's obtuseness was astounding, thought Franzi. Why shouldn't Jews be in his dreams? He'd only killed millions of them.

"Please, Professor Loerber, tell me what it means."

"It's simple, Reichsführer," Franzi began. "The universe is in flux. When that happens, disruptions in the cosmic fabric become rampant. The gyres of destiny need to be put back in balance."

"Gyres of destiny?" breathed Himmler with reverence. "But how could a bunch of dead Jews have anything to do with that?"

"I'm coming to that, Reichsführer," said Franzi confidently. "Unless the harmonic balances are restored, spirits will continue to populate dimensions where they aren't wanted. You see, in a sense, the cosmic fabric is like any other kind of cloth. When it frays, people and things from other dimensions find places where they can pop through. The souls of dead Jews especially, since, as you know, they really have no rightful place in Valhalla, are gathering at the portals where they'll stream back into the dimension they had so recently departed.

"What the world needs right now is a man of supreme destiny, someone who has the courage and vision to put the balances back, restore harmony, and drive the restless dead back to where they belong."

"Oh?" said Himmler. "You mean me, don't you? But how am I supposed to do that?"

"Reichsführer, men become gods when they transcend the limitations of their mortality," said Franzi. "That's why it's so important to seize this moment and fulfill your destiny, Reichsführer. It's not just about you. It's about the whole universe and the balance and the order that will prevail!"

"It almost sounds like you're talking about a battle between the gods of old and the gods of new."

Franzi nodded. "Absolutely. I'll tell you this, Reichsführer: If it ever comes down to a battle of gods, we are sure to win, for we have many gods and they are all strong, while the enemy has but one, and theirs is a god of mercy and weakness."

"That's true. Ours are stronger," reflected Himmler.

"Yes, but at the same time, our gods have been through incredible trauma. They need to rest in order to regain their polarity. A cosmic showdown is not what anyone needs right now. What we need is healing, peace. And you can start restoring balance to the universe by making peace with the Jews. This is extremely important, so that the cosmic fabric will have time to repair itself. And you definitely need to stop thinking of Jews as criminals."

"I do?"

"Yes, Reichsführer. Start thinking of them as people, with hopes and dreams and fears that are not so different from anyone else's. Think of them as unfortunate victims of a terrible injustice, one that you are now willing to remedy."

"I can do that," said Himmler with surprising ease.

"Reichsführer, you need to tell them that even though you were responsible for inflicting suffering on them, you're not really to blame. Mistakes were made and you were misled, terribly misled. Do you think you can do that, Reichsführer?"

"I never wanted to hurt them, really I didn't. But they have to understand that I was honor-bound to obey the orders that were given to me. I'd sworn a solemn oath of allegiance to the Führer. Do you think they will accept that?"

"They might if you come to them with a sincere and open heart."

"I can do that," said Himmler.

"If I remember, Reichsführer, the ancient Jewish mystics had a saying: If you make peace with the living, then the dead will follow."

"They said that?"

"Indeed they did, Reichsführer."

"That's amazing."

Franzi looked at Himmler, who seemed to be glowing with the knowledge of the role destiny had written for him. He's taken the bait, thought Franzi. Now all that stands between him and godhood is a dying man living deep underground.

Himmler motioned for Franzi to hand him his shirt. "Really, this has gone on long enough," he said. He reached for the phone. "Call the Führerbunker. Tell them I'm coming over now."

Returning the receiver to its cradle, Himmler looked up at Franzi. "Well, Loerber," he said with an amused sneer, "I certainly hope that when Bernadotte brings his Jews down here, they're going to be a little more personable than those dead people."

"What do you mean?"

"I mean they keep saying really nasty things to me."

"They say things to you?" Franzi tried not to sound alarmed.

"Yes, didn't I tell you? Night after night, they keep saying to me, over and over, *The Blood of Israel will have its vengeance!*" Himmler buttoned up his uniform blouse. "I'll be back in an hour or two. Maybe we'll even have a little celebration tonight."

Schellenberg looked irritated. "He specifically said, 'the Blood of Israel'?"

"Yes, Herr General."

"Damn! We were trying to keep him from finding out about them."

"Who are they?" asked Franzi, pretending he didn't know.

"A Jewish terror group," explained Schellenberg. "Apparently there's a phrase in the Talmud that says, 'The Blood of Israel will have its vengeance.' We've known about them for years, but aside from the occasional mass killing, they haven't been much of a problem for us. Then a couple of months ago hundreds of SS men started complaining of having nightmares where dead Jews standing behind barbed wire threatened them with vengeance. Some were so rattled by it they killed themselves. We studied the reports and found all the dreams were identical.

"Our scientists were at a complete loss about this phenomenon. One of our Jungian psychologists suggested that their experience in the concentration camps may have been so overwhelming that it spurred an identical, uniform response."

"That's crazy," said Franzi.

Schellenberg nodded. "The Jungian didn't believe it either, but it was the best explanation he could come up with for that sort of mass phenomenon. The other explanation would be mass-projected dreams."

Franzi's objections came fast and furious. "Sir, it's impossible. It's completely crazy."

"And why is that, Lieutenant?"

Franzi rapped his fingers against the sides of his forehead. "Sir, magic doesn't work like that. Not at all!"

Schellenberg stared icily at Franzi.

"Mass-projecting dreams is impossible, General."

Schellenberg didn't say anything.

"Sir, it's as much a load of rubbish as the Philosopher's Stone and the Fountain of Youth. Magic doesn't work that way."

"But wasn't one of your brothers known to do it? Sebastian, I believe?"

"That was a trick. We were entertainers."

"Well, how did the trick work?"

"It wasn't my trick, sir. It was Sebastian's."

Schellenberg wasn't getting it. Franzi clutched his temples with his hands and tried to find a logical way of getting his point across. "Herr General, do you want to know what magic is? Ninety percent of it is distraction. The rest is manipulation. Period. The Flying Magical Loerber Brothers were entertainers. If people thought we were magical, it meant we were doing our job. We were paid to distract and entertain people. Sebastian's projecting dreams was just a trick. Besides, he's dead and this is a Jewish terror organization you're talking about. How could it possibly have anything to do with him?"

"Well, your family were Jews, weren't they?" Schellenberg said it casually, and seeing Franzi's nervous reaction, he smiled. "Yes, I know, Loerber. The first investigation I ever did was when your brother disappeared. I know a lot of things about you and your family. I know about you and Major Steiner. As long as you don't get caught, I don't really care what you do. I just need to know one thing from you: Who are you working for?"

Franzi's answer was immediate. "I'm working for you, Herr General."

"Good," said Schellenberg.

"Herr General, if someone is suggesting that Sebastian is alive and mass-projecting nightmares, then I'd say they're grasping at straws and you shouldn't believe them. Some advice, sir?"

"Please."

"Don't go around wondering whether or not magic exists or whether I'm the real thing or a phony, sir. The only question right now is results. I'm working for you, Herr General, and I'm here to bring results. Everything else is bullshit."

Eventually Himmler returned, acting as if nothing had happened. When they pressed him he explained that the Russians had apparently been pushed back from Küstrin and after seeing the elation on Hitler's face, he couldn't bring himself to confront him. Next time, certainly.

Later, alone in his quarters, Franzi wondered how much longer he could keep snowing Schellenberg like this. So their men were being hit by bad dreams. Could that mean Sebastian was alive? Franzi had always suspected his disappearance might be a trick and this certainly seemed like Sebastian's handiwork. In his day Sebastian had projected so many naked girls into his mind it had caused Franzi to wonder whether he might actually prefer them over boys. But the Blood of Israel? What the hell was that? It didn't seem anything like Sebastian.

Leaving the light off, Franzi pushed aside the blackout curtains and stared out at the night sky. So Schellenberg knew he was a Jew and that he was queer. Searchlights swept the cloud cover for signs of enemy aircraft. Tonight, it seemed, there was nothing. It wouldn't be long before the Russians were here. He still hadn't heard anything about the SS having a plan for evacuating Berlin, though he assumed there had to be one. Schellenberg, he told himself, was either fiendishly clever, someone who put Machiavelli to shame, or simply the biggest putz ever to call himself a spymaster.

(10)

It was April 20, Hitler's birthday. The day was declared a national feast day and in an effort to make it just like all the earlier ones, the last stocks of flour and sugar and sweets were opened up and distributed to the public. For several hours there was electricity and water again flowed from the pipes. People broke from whatever they were doing and took baths, baked cakes, and then went outside to watch the parade and cheer.

As in years past, there was a party at the Chancellery. But instead of the usual long line of limousines pulling up with smiling ambassadors, envoys, and high government officials, today the guests arrived in a handful of shared staff cars.

Speer came as he always did, driven in his ministry Porsche, which he had parked in one of the underground garages. He made his way through the wrecked halls, climbing over collapsed beams and shattered walls to the bunker's entrance. The Chancellery, *his* Chancellery, was falling apart. For five years it had stood up to the Allied air bombardment, but three days of pounding by Soviet artillery had reduced it to ruins.

Passing through the airlock's steel doors and going down the steps, it seemed he'd returned to a world of order. Here the concrete corridors were still clean-scrubbed and the lights all worked. But as he got down to the main level, he began noticing the uncollected dirty glasses, plates, and silverware gathering in the corners and beneath end tables. After weeks of serving endless parties, the housekeeping staff had clearly lost their enthusiasm for the job.

In the corridor outside the conference room, a crowd of aides and adjutants milled around, while liveried waiters swirled among them with silver trays of canapés and drinks. Everyone tried to act festive, though it was obvious that what was really on their minds was getting out of Berlin. The Führer had announced he would be flying out to the Obersalzberg to conduct the war from there. But so far he hadn't told anyone when he'd be leaving. The Russians were now rumored to be in the outer suburbs, and while it was anyone's guess when their encirclement of Berlin might be completed, until the Führer officially gave word for them to decamp the city, they were all stuck there.

Inside the large room the situation conference was already under way. General Keitel was giving the briefing. Even now, in the midst of the catastrophe, he managed to find morsels of optimism. Whenever the Soviets had elected to withdraw from a sector, Keitel seized upon it as the portent of an upcoming reversal. In each instance, Hitler reacted with glee, rubbing his hands and ordering Keitel to elaborate on how they would exploit it. There seemed so many possible paths to victory, it left scant opportunity to examine those other places where German forces were fleeing in disarray. It went on for another hour. Speer listened to Keitel and Jodl predict how the alliance between the Jewish Bolsheviks and the West was on the verge of disintegrating. Göring talked about the new jet fighter squadrons that were becoming operational that very day. Dönitz chimed in with news that the first of the new miracle U-boats had finished their testing and were beginning their first war patrols. Hitler loudly praised Dönitz for his indomitable fighting spirit.

Throughout, Hitler ignored Speer. Somehow he had fallen out of favor again, though he had no idea why. He supposed Bormann must have told him something.

Once the briefing had wrapped up, Hitler surprised everyone by leading them topside to the Chancellery garden, where a large group of twelve- and thirteen-year-old boys stood in ranks, waiting to be decorated for heroism in combat. It was criminal, Speer thought grimly, as he watched Hitler going from boy to boy, exchanging a few words with each, praising their courage and pinning Iron Crosses on their tiny chests. He doesn't believe in victory any more than I do, yet he happily sends children to their deaths.

The sight of Hitler plainly shocked the boys. He wasn't at all what they'd expected. The hero they'd been taught to revere since the day they were born was this decrepit old man? Those who'd fanatically believed in victory now knew they'd lost. Hitler immediately sensed their unease. His initial good humor and heartiness turned brittle and soon he was handing out the Iron Crosses without a word. Once he'd finished, the Hitler Youth were dismissed and he led the partygoers back to the bunker entrance. But at the threshold he stopped, turned to face everyone, and announced that he was staying in Berlin. Whoever wanted to leave was free to do so, he declared with an angry wave of his hand. Warily, they followed Hitler back down into the bunker for cake.

The rest of the party was a shabby, uncomfortable affair. Relieved as they were to have been given permission to leave Berlin, as long as they were down there in the bunker with him, they were still his captives. Precious minutes were ticking by and he was plainly in no hurry to let them go.

All this time, Speer had been unable to exchange even a few words with him. At one point he had approached Hitler as he was being beset by Ley and von Ribbentrop, carrying on with their customary drunken blandishments, which Hitler looked plainly tired of. Speer approached respectfully, positioning himself a few feet away like a waiter. But rather than avail himself of Speer's ready presence to get rid of the other two, Hitler shot Speer a dirty look and enmeshed himself even deeper with them. Speer waited awkwardly for several minutes before finally withdrawing.

Then Hitler called up Himmler and, hand on his shoulder, began to talk nostalgically about their early days of struggle on the streets of Munich, where day after day they'd fight it out with the Reds. Hitler lavished praise on his *treue Heinrich,* who had always stood by him, no matter how tough the going got. For some reason Himmler responded with only an embarrassed smile.

"Reichsführer," urged Hitler, "tell everyone what it was like back then."

Himmler awkwardly shifted on his feet. "Ah, yes, those days," he said with the greatest effort. "If I, ah, live to be a hundred, I'll never forget." Himmler paused. "But that is not to say, of course, that the best is still not to come." Everyone felt compelled to make agreeable noises to that.

Just then one of the Reichsführer's adjutants came in and handed him a message. Himmler looked at it and grunted, "Five minutes." The major gave Himmler a hard, nonnegotiable glare and withdrew to the corridor. Himmler stuffed the message in his pocket and continued speaking. "Yes, very soon the tide of this battle will turn and the Russians will be fleeing back across the Oder. All the karmic balances will be restored and our millennia of uninterrupted peace can resume." He was now getting into his stride. He began talking about the bright future of the German race, how, freed of negative racial pollutants, their full potentiality would blossom forth unhindered unto the very stars. Everyone was startled at the unabashed magnificence of his pronouncements. Speer noticed the SS major standing at the entrance, glaring significantly at Himmler. The major silently mouthed the word, *Now!*

Suddenly Himmler stood up and announced that he had to be going. The other guests looked at each other in shock. No one had ever done that to Hitler before. Not his closest, most favored underlings, not his most choleric, combative generals. People waited until Hitler dismissed them. That was the rule.

"Urgent business, I am afraid," mumbled Himmler by way of explanation. "The war."

Hitler was fuming. But Himmler paid him no heed. He

repeated his birthday greetings and his hope to see him again soon, and then turned on his heel and was gone.

"I guess he had to see to the new millennium," Göring muttered to Speer. Speer thought of the conversation he'd had with Himmler in his office. So apparently he was capable of independent action. He wondered what news had spurred this urgent move.

For another hour the party went on, more dispiritedly than before. Then, without Speer hearing it, permission to leave was given and all at once everyone was in a hurry to get out. They formed a line to bid the Führer farewell.

Colonel von Poser was in the doorway, waving at Speer to come over. The Russians had started a new attack in the northeast, von Poser explained. Berlin would be cut off in a matter of hours. They had to leave now. Speer looked back at Hitler, who was making his way down a line of generals and party bigwigs, shaking their hands, clapping each one's shoulder as he praised their dedication and loyalty. "I need to say goodbye to the Führer," he told von Poser.

The colonel shook his head. "There isn't time. We need to leave now." He followed von Poser up the stairs to the exit. "By the way, we've got company," von Poser told him.

"Who?"

"You'll see."

When they got to the garage, Speer noticed someone sitting beside the driver. As they approached the car, the driver got out and opened the rear door for them. Cautiously, Speer stuck his head in to see who it was. The man turned and Speer was face to face with Manni.

(11)

Someday in the future, when the history books were being written, this would be the moment they'd point to as the new beginning. This was when men of reason and vision came together, put an end to the most senseless and bloody conflict in human history, and forged a new era of peace and prosperity. And he, General Walter Schellenberg, would be forever remembered as the arbiter of that peace.

Schellenberg stood at the entrance of Ziethen Castle watching the Reichsführer's motorcade drive up. Inside the castle Count Bernadotte was waiting along with the Jewish representative. They'd flown down from Stockholm on what turned out to be the last commercial flight into Berlin, landing at Tempelhof just as the Soviet ring around the city began to close in. Luckily Schellenberg had gotten them picked up and whisked out not an hour before it did.

The long line of cars stopped. The driver jumped out and opened the door and the Reichsführer stepped out, followed by a host of aides, adjutants, batsmen, and the thirty-six heavily armed SS troopers who made up his personal security detail. He strutted up the driveway, his boots kicking up bits of the thick gravel. Seeing Schellenberg, he fixed him with his usual empty gaze, and then let a thin smile form briefly on his lips. *It is done,* it seemed to say. Before Schellenberg could greet him with the customary salute, he put his hand out for Schellenberg to shake. Side by side, they walked up the castle corridors toward the salon where their guests were waiting. He was back to his old self, observed Schellenberg. The nervous skittishness was gone, replaced by authoritativeness and control.

Schellenberg hadn't spoken much to the Jewish representative yet, but he seemed like a reasonable sort, with his eyes fixed more on the future than the past.

He was sitting in the parlor on a couch by himself, a little man, gray, finite, and dapper in his London suit and red and purple French tie. He stood up when they entered the room. Schellenberg made the introductions. "Reichsführer, I would like to introduce you to Herr Norbert Masur of the World Jewish Congress. He has flown down from Stockholm to be with us today."

"So good of you to come, Herr Masur," said Himmler with surprising affability. He quickly extended his hand for Masur to shake. "I trust you had a pleasant flight down?"

Masur nodded and assured him there had been no problems at all.

"Good, good," said Himmler heartily. "I can't tell you how happy I am to have you here. There is much we have to talk about."

Masur nodded again. Yes, there was, he said, his eyes quietly riveted on the Reichsführer.

Schellenberg had coffee brought in and they sat down to talk.

"I have asked you to come here," began Himmler, "because I believe the time has come to put an end to this terrible period between your people and my people."

Masur nodded, urging Himmler to go on.

Himmler adopted a solemn, sincere look. "You must understand I didn't have anything personally to do with all the terrible, unfortunate things that happened to your people. I am a soldier, Herr Masur. Do you understand what that means? It is my duty, my sacred duty, to obey orders, and that is what I did. No one asked me to agree with them. You must understand that it was never my intention to harm anyone or cause them pain. I always sought to solve the, ah, Jewish Problem by peaceful, humane means, by expulsion, emigration, and resettlement. But we were prevented from doing that by two things, Herr Masur. We were prevented by the extreme resistance of the outside world as well as by opposition from the Nazi Party."

On this point Schellenberg had expected Masur to raise some objections, but he appeared detached, smiling his mandarin smile and nodding in all the right places, but saying almost nothing. Perhaps the man was shy. In any case, he was listening.

"I never hated Jews, Herr Masur. I must tell you that growing up in Bavaria, many of my best friends were Jews. I thought they were all very nice people. And I don't want what happened to be a stain on our future relationship. We need to think about the future, Herr Masur, and I don't mind telling you that the future Europe which our peoples will share is going to be a most wonderful place." Finally Himmler finished and invited Masur's reply.

Masur clasped his fingers together as he spoke to them in a startlingly forceful voice. "What you say is very interesting, Herr Himmler. But my reason for coming here today is simple. Whatever has gone on in the past cannot be changed. What I would like from you today are assurances that no more Jews will be killed. Let me repeat that: not one more. I would also like your guarantee that the remaining Jewish prisoners will remain in the camps and that under no circumstances will they be evacuated away from the approaching Allied armies. I would also ask that you provide me with a list of all the camps where Jews are being kept. If you can do these things for us, perhaps we will have a basis for future discussions."

Himmler broke into a relieved smile. "I am happy to report, sir, that I have already given such orders. And just to show my goodwill, I would also like to propose releasing a large group of Jewesses from Ravensbrück." Himmler's smile became conspiratorial. "The Führer has already given me permission to free Polish women. It would be a very simple matter to have these

Jewesses reclassified as Polish. I could do that for you if you'd like."

Masur nodded and said yes, he would like that.

"So what do you say, Herr Masur?" asked Himmler jubilantly. "Are we burying the hatchet?"

The three shook hands. Masur remained polite, but ever so distant.

They left him there and went into an adjoining room to see Count Bernadotte.

"I am happy to inform you that you may now go to Eisenhower and tell him I am taking over command of the Reich and would very much like to start peace talks at the general's earliest convenience," Himmler said. "How soon do you think you could get something started?"

Count Bernadotte told him he'd get on it right away, except that with Berlin and Tempelhof already cut off, the only way they could get back to Sweden was by driving at least into Denmark before he could arrange for a neutral aircraft to pick them up. They decided Schellenberg would drive them in his car.

"Gentlemen," Himmler declared, "I think it's fair to say this marks the beginning of a whole new era."

(Part II)

❲ 12 ❳

Along the shores of Eutin Lakes, in the vast refugee encampments that had sprung up there, Speer's Ministry for War Production started to reconstitute itself. People from the different departments and sections began finding each other. Then they'd brought their tents and trailers together and started inventorying the files and equipment that made it out.

The drive out of Berlin had been a nightmare. Naturally, the order to evacuate came late. Ten thousand private vehicles that had been kept hidden and fully fueled for several years suddenly reappeared and converged on the one open road heading north. Everyone who could get exit papers—party fat cats, ministry bureaucrats, wealthy businessmen, and military officers, along with their families and prized possessions—were all trying to pull rank and cut each other off. And just as suddenly, swarms of enemy aircraft came out of the clouds, strafing them with machine gun fire and dropping bombs. And then there were the checkpoints, where stern-faced militiamen would examine their documents and send them back whenever they felt like it. It was hell. Getting to Schleswig-Holstein usually took only four or five hours, but with the traffic jams and blown-up bridges, it had taken three days. But somehow in spite of it all, Speer and the others had managed to get out.

Surveying the scenery around him, Speer wondered whether things might actually start getting better now or whether this was merely the last moment before everything slid into complete chaos. People were walking around with the vague sense that if they looked hard enough they'd find there was someone running it all, that sooner or later a bunch of trucks would show up and dig some regulation latrines or a field kitchen and someone would blow a whistle and gather everyone together to make announcements. But instead, there were only the militias and military police, whose involvement with them ended once they stopped moving from place to place.

Speer had spent the afternoon meeting with his deputies over what their priorities should be for reestablishing contact with different factories and power plants once the fighting was over. Some argued that since they were unlikely to get any guidance from above, they should take over the functions of the different industry and transport ministries to reduce any overlap. In the end, no decisions were made and they simply agreed to wait and see how things turned out.

Walking away from the lakeshore, Speer endeavored to find some solitude. He began heading across the fields toward a nearby wood. The encampment seemed to go on forever, everyone with their plot carefully staked out, guarding it as much from their neighbors as from strangers. Women tended fires, men fiddled with automobile engines and camp stoves. Everyone acted peaceful, but the tension was palpable. Not knowing what would come next weighed on everybody. People couldn't decide whether to eat all their food at once or ration it out and risk having it stolen. Having gotten this far, nobody had any petrol left and they worried that should there be an order to move, they'd have to ditch their cars. You could no longer tell who anyone was. On the trip up, all the Nazi Party officials wore their uniforms so that no one would dare bother them. But now they'd put them away so that aside from their ample bellies, they'd look no different from anyone else.

Eventually he did get past the endless campground and found

his way into open fields where there were no people about. Springtime had come to northern Germany. The grasses in the fields
were already getting long, and a host of violets, daffodils, and
primroses entwined themselves among the stone walls and hedges
separating the fields. Speer was glad to be finally by himself.
Having so many of his underlings there from the ministry, looking
to him for direction, made Speer uneasy. He didn't have contact
with anyone from the administration of the Northern Zone. He
knew that Admiral Dönitz was running it and he should report to
him and see what he could do.

The most troubling thing about this camp was having Manni
back. Strange as the whole Ruhr adventure had been, once Manni
had gone, Speer quickly compartmentalized it so that he no longer dwelt on Manni being a spy or Speer unwisely confiding in
him. But here in Eutin, hovering among his staff, his presence
was jarring. But even so, Speer still found himself slipping back
into the old routines. The other day Manni had come by with his
juggling balls. Speer could have offered some excuse, told Manni
he was busy, that he didn't feel like it, but instead he nodded. It
started with the usual patter, then Manni had bluntly asked him,
"Any news from your friend?" Speer had shaken his head and
Manni hadn't bothered asking him anything else.

"My friend," Speer said aloud to the trees and the grasses. He
thought about the birthday party and how in the end he'd walked
out without even talking to him. He should have tried harder
instead of just standing there, cloaked in his aloofness, waiting
for Hitler to make the first move. But now he was here and Hitler was in his bunker, surrounded by those horrible people. I was
Hitler's friend, probably his only friend, but when the time came,
I walked out on him.

Speer suddenly realized he was crying.

He came upon a road that cut across the field, and rather than
continue on to the woods, he took it. After walking a few minutes he saw small airplanes taking off and landing farther ahead

and realized there had to be an airfield somewhere nearby. He picked up his pace. A Volkswagen Kübel drove up to him and stopped. Two military policemen with submachine guns stepped out and asked him what he was doing there. Speer showed them his papers and they offered him a ride to the airfield. Most of the aircraft that were landing had just flown out of Berlin, they told him.

They left him off outside the operations hut. Speer went in and asked to speak to whoever was in charge. A weary-looking Luftwaffe colonel came forward. "Yes, Herr Reichsminister?" he asked.

"Can you fly me into Berlin?"

{ 13 }

Mostly they sat in chairs set up along the corridor facing the line of windows that looked down into the courtyard, the higher ranks at the far end, Franzi and the other junior officers down closer to the doors leading to the stairway. The Reichsführer had taken the large corner office with double doors while the three smaller offices were used by what was left of the command and operations staffs. Near the entrance, across from the lavatories, a hot plate was set up where they'd boil water for coffee and tea. If they wanted to smoke they could step outside to the top-floor landing, but beyond that, they couldn't leave.

This, they were told, was to be their new headquarters. After a week of moving from place to place, the SS had taken over the large gray building of the regional police presidium in the north German city of Lübeck. The small courtyard was crammed with half-tracks and open-roofed Volkswagens while dozens of heavily armed Waffen-SS troopers milled around. For the most part, discipline was being maintained, but even so, cracks were starting to appear. For the first time everyone had stopped pretending that victory was inevitable. The war was lost and they all knew it. Their one shred of hope lay in the Reichsführer's completing his deal with Eisenhower, and from what Franzi could tell, things were progressing nicely.

Each day a fresh stream of supplicants came in to confer with Himmler and assure him of their support. There were party officials, gauleiters, generals, ministers, deputy ministers, all eager to ingratiate themselves.

Out on the landing, there was endless, uninhibited speculation. They'd moved a wireless there to listen to the news reports coming out of Berlin, which weren't actually good for much since about all they ever said was that the Führer was continuing to lead the defenses of the city and that fresh relief spearheads were expected to arrive at any time. Franzi told himself that sooner or later *the Führer continues to personally lead the defense of Fortress Berlin* was going to get replaced by something more ambiguous, yet more telling. *The Führer has gone out to join the fighting. The Führer has left the bunker.* But then Radio Berlin stopped broadcasting, so they tried the Hamburg station, which turned out not to have any news, though the music was nice. Hearing two colonels complaining, Franzi took the bold step of suggesting they try Radio Atlantik.

At first the two stared at each other, wide-eyed, wondering whether they should. Radio Atlantik was an enemy propaganda station and listening to it was verboten. Finally one of them said, "Can you find it?" Franzi started twisting the dial and ten seconds later had it tuned in.

"Turn it up!" urged one of the colonels. Immediately they heard a young man's friendly voice reading reports of air strikes and armored thrusts and about British and American bombers now being used to drop food into parts of Holland where the civilian population was on the verge of starvation. Apparently, without a cease-fire being declared, the German military authority there had agreed not to hinder the relief effort. Now, that was real news. Was it part of the deal with Eisenhower?

Berlin was now almost completely overrun with Russian troops in the center of the city, they said, with only a few scattered pockets remaining in German hands. Meanwhile, in San Francisco, a large conference was being held for something called the United Nations.

They had been listening to it for a while when a voice behind them said sharply, "What are you doing?" They looked up and saw a Sicherheitsdienst major staring hard at them. Neither of the colonels acted like they cared what some pipsqueak major thought about anything. "What do you think?" one said, cigarette dangling from his mouth.

"That's Radio Atlantik, isn't it? You know that's strictly forbidden," said the major.

"Oh, stuff it," said one of the colonels.

"You're listening to Radio Atlantik, the voice of Free Germany," announced a young woman with a pronounced Swabian twang. There were three notes played on a chime, their call sign, and then the young woman said, *"And now for some happy music, here's Cab Calloway's 'Jumpin' Jive'!"*

The major nearly exploded. "How dare you? And right here outside the Reichsführer's offices!" His face shook with anger and disgust. "You're all under arrest," he said. "So help me, I'll have you all hanged." Then he turned to a captain having a cigarette alone in a corner. "Don't let any of them leave," he barked and turned to go downstairs.

In a searing instant of alertness, Franzi pitched himself into the major's mind just enough so that when he started down the stairs, he misjudged the second step by an inch, and the third turned to butter beneath his feet. He went flying head over heels, hitting the middle landing with a loud thud and a crack. He was dead, his neck broken.

The three stared down at him dumbfounded. Franzi reached over and turned the radio off. Word of the accident ran through the corridor, but no one bothered getting up to see. A few minutes later the body was taken away and the radio was back on. Franzi staggered back inside the office and slumped into the first empty chair he could find. He stared at the wall calendar for a long time, before the words and numbers began to make any sense to him. Today was April 30, Walpurgisnacht, the last night for resident witches to get out of town. Franzi wished there were some way he could use the occasion to justify doing the same.

He was no longer needed there. It had been more than a week since he had given Himmler a massage. Himmler's panic attacks had ended once Bernadotte went to Eisenhower. Having thus broken with the past, the Reichsführer was a changed man. Himmler the icy interpreter of orders had become Himmler the personable, Himmler the decisive and calm, Himmler the man of destiny. When Franzi got called in now it was simply as an advisor.

Not that Himmler had stopped dithering entirely, but his dithering was now focused on less pressing matters. He couldn't decide what form his new government should take. One day he'd want a two-chamber parliamentary system, the next he'd talk about reviving the old Nordic "Volksthing." Then he'd dither over who to include in his cabinet. But one thing he never wavered on: whatever its form, there would not be a place in it for Albert Speer. Once he announced to Franzi and the others, "Gentlemen, I do not anticipate having any need in my administration for a Reichsminister for mechanical drawing. Nor do I expect to rebuild Berlin as some twentieth-century version of *Rome*! And I'm sure Eisenhower will concur."

There was also no dithering when Himmler talked about running Eisenhower's security apparatus; their common vision of a new Europe would combine the universality of Charlemagne and the mystical grandeur of the early German monarch Henry the Fowler; the Soviets would quickly collapse under their combined power; the future of Europe was great now that Hitler was out of the way.

It was all very encouraging, except for one nagging little detail. Hitler wasn't dead yet. He was still in his bunker sending out radio messages hourly and ordering nonexistent armies about. Another nagging detail was that even though the peace discussions seemed to be at an advanced phase, Eisenhower still had yet to call off his armies. The speculation out on the landing was that he was waiting until the Russians finished off Hitler before moving ahead with the cease-fire. That made sense, everyone agreed. If Schellenberg's boundless optimism was any indicator, then the Himmler-Eisenhower alliance was a done deal.

Schellenberg was the hardest to keep track of. He'd disappear for a day or two, then drop by unannounced, meet with Himmler for an hour, and then leave again. Once he brought Steiner with him, who had been reassigned to a remote communications station outside Flensburg. In the few minutes they were together Steiner managed to inform Franzi not only that he missed him terribly, but that according to Source Moonpool, Moscow Center had determined that its agent in SS Headquarters had been two-timing them by sending exactly the same intelligence to London. "A double agent, Franzi, right here among us! I don't know what I should do about it." Franzi had just enough time to tell him not to do anything before Schellenberg whisked him away.

Most of the time, though, Franzi remained in his chair and, having nothing to do, wondered about things he'd previously been too busy to dwell on. He thought about the endless streams of refugees he'd seen clogging the roads all over northern Germany, millions of them, with nowhere to rest; no camps, no tents, no hospitals or sanitary facilities. And these were Berliners, people who used to come dressed up in nice clothes to see them perform. They weren't supposed to be hungry and wretched and dirty, pushing baby carriages full of their belongings.

He thought about Berlin and all the places that had been his world, bombed out and overrun. Until now he'd assumed it was only a temporary condition and that once the war ended, everything would return to its original state. He thought about his brothers, whom he'd also assumed would reunite once it was all over. But that had perhaps been as much an illusion as everything else.

❨ 14 ❩

Franzi had been asleep on a bunk in the basement cell block that had been converted to a dormitory for the junior officers when one of the Reichsführer's adjutants came down and ordered him to get dressed. "He wants to see you now," he said.

Franzi sat up. "Any idea what's up?" he asked. The adjutant shook his head. Franzi got dressed and followed him upstairs. When they reached the fifth-floor landing, the usual crowd was gathered around the wireless. "Any news?" he asked.

One of the colonels looked up. "The fighting has stopped in Italy. Some kind of truce," he said.

"I guess it won't be long now," Franzi said. The others all nodded back.

Himmler looked calm when Franzi entered his office. "Have a seat, Loerber," he said, pointing to one of the stuffed chairs. "I'll be with you in a second." He gestured to the adjutant to leave.

As Franzi sat down, Himmler quickly put his signature on a batch of papers and put them all into his OUT tray. He got up from his desk and walked over and took the chair opposite Franzi.

"As you probably know, Loerber, I'm putting together a government. We should become operational in another day or two, once things are over in Berlin. The question right now is, of course, who can I count on? Who is with me and who might be backing another faction?"

"Another faction, Reichsführer?" asked Franzi. "Is there another?"

"Yes, Göring," said Himmler. "My sources in the south tell me he is still hoping to exercise his old official designation as successor to take over. He has apparently been telling people that he is uniquely suited to reach a peace agreement with Eisenhower."

"Is there any indication that he has actually contacted Eisenhower?" asked Franzi.

"No, there isn't. But to be honest, that isn't my major area of concern right now. What I want to ask you about is Grand Admiral Dönitz."

"Grand Admiral Dönitz?" Franzi was confused. Dönitz might have been the head of the navy, but as far as political power was concerned, he was nobody.

Himmler noted Franzi's bewilderment and smiled. "He was just here a few minutes ago. You didn't see him?"

"I'm sorry, Reichsführer, but I was asleep. I was up till four."

"Oh, too bad," said Himmler. "I wanted to know how you read him. There is something about the man's karma that I can't completely grasp. Do you know anything about him? Isn't your brother Zigmund one of his favorite U-boat captains? Has he said anything about him?"

At the mention of Ziggy, Franzi felt cold sweat. Ziggy was the only other person who knew he and Manni were enemy agents. "I'm sorry, Reichsführer," he said. "But my brother and I haven't spoken in years."

Himmler fixed him with his blankest stare, like he couldn't get Franzi's measure. "I'm very sorry to hear that, Loerber," he said. "But you might be interested in knowing your brother has just been appointed to a very sensitive post on the grand admiral's staff." Himmler paused. "A strange choice, I thought, in view of some of his past activities."

"Activities, Reichsführer?"

"Well, you do know that on more than one occasion he has made statements critical of the Führer?"

That's nothing, thought Franzi. On more than one occasion he attended services at a Berlin synagogue. He's critical of the Führer and all Nazis in general, but he's a loyal U-boat officer and when we asked him to help us spy against the government, he refused.

Franzi adopted a sorrowful look. "Yes, Reichsführer, that's why we had a falling out. I couldn't tolerate hearing any more of it. I know I should have reported him, but he's my brother. Forgive me, Reichsführer."

Himmler gave an indulgent smile. "That's all right, Loerber. His loyalty doesn't interest me. My reason for bringing it up is simply that I'm trying to understand Dönitz. I asked him if he would support me. Everybody else is falling all over themselves to join my government. But you know what he told me? He said, 'Reichsführer, I will support unconditionally any legitimate successor.' Now, what's that supposed to mean?"

What it meant seemed obvious enough to Franzi, but instead he answered politely, "I don't know, Reichsführer."

"Doesn't he see what's going on? The Führer is determined to drag the whole world down with him. He doesn't *want* a successor."

"Did you tell Dönitz that?"

"How could I? And you know what else he said?"

"What, Reichsführer?"

"I was trying to give him a hint of our negotiations with Eisenhower. You'd think he'd be grateful that someone is actually doing something. But instead he was absolutely hostile. I can only interpret that as proof that he is backing Göring as a potential negotiator with Eisenhower. What do you think?"

Franzi thought of Göring, the fat, drug-addicted failure in his splendiferous uniforms, and laughed. "Honestly, Reichsführer? At this point I cannot imagine anyone taking Göring seriously."

"But what other possibility is there, if not Göring? He couldn't be backing Speer. Speer doesn't have any power. For God's sake, all he is, is the Führer's draftsman!" Then suddenly Himmler lit up. "I have an idea. What if I show you a photograph of Dönitz and you probe it for me, tell me what vibrations you're getting from it? I bet that'll work!"

"Probe?" asked Franzi with a sinking feeling. Where did Himmler get these ideas from?

Himmler got up, went over to the credenza, and pulled out a framed photograph portfolio from one of the drawers. He handed it to Franzi. "Go ahead, probe it. Tell me what you get."

Franzi took the photograph in his hands and stared at it. An intense-looking, dried-up little man in a navy uniform. These guys all look exactly the same, he thought. He could be a ferry-boat captain.

Himmler leaned forward. "Well? What do you see?"

Franzi tried to think of something meaningful to say. The man in the picture didn't look especially warlike or crafty or even as though he liked the sound of his own voice. He looked like one of those men who believed, first and foremost, in following orders; perhaps he was also more than a little sardonic.

"You've got him all wrong, Reichsführer," said Franzi. "This man doesn't know or care about politics. He's a soldier, he follows orders, he believes in complete obedience to whoever is in charge. I don't see him plotting against you with Göring or anyone else."

"But what about the war? What is his position on how to end it?"

"His mind is on his submarines, Reichsführer. He thinks about that and nothing else. The rest of the war is someone else's business."

"Actually, I think you're on to something," reflected Himmler. "There are those new miracle U-boats of his. They're supposed to be ready to launch."

Suddenly Franzi saw himself inside a submarine, but different from the ones he'd seen in magazines. It wasn't so cramped.

The equipment was modern, automated. He could feel the speed of it cutting through the water. And suddenly he saw his brother standing at its helm, looking through a periscope, calling out orders to his men. And then, just as suddenly, the submarine was gone and his brother was standing in the wreckage of a city, rifle in hand, helmet on his head, humming to himself, *Who's afraid of the Big Bad Wolf, Big Bad Wolf, Big Bad Wolf?*

Franzi opened his eyes and looked down at the face his fingers were touching. He looked up at Himmler. Himmler looked pleased. "You're a very bright young man, Loerber. Maybe you should go back to sleep now."

Franzi stepped outside the office into the corridor. The adjutant was waiting in a chair. He got up. "I trust that whatever the Reichsführer has discussed with you will remain private, Loerber."

"Naturally," answered Franzi and went to look for something to eat.

❨ 15 ❩

HAMBURG

Ziggy Loerber's assumption had always been that he'd die at sea. He was a U-boatman, after all, and that was how U-boatmen invariably died. By now the war had gone on for nearly six years and except for Cremer and Lüth and a small handful of others, everyone he'd ever known or served with had already found their watery graves. They died from enemy depth charges, from bombs and cannon fire. They bled to death, drowned, or asphyxiated from battery acid fumes or too much carbon dioxide when the air inside their submarines became unbreathable. They died when their boats sank or when they dived too deep and the water pressure crushed their iron hulls like eggshells.

Recently he'd embraced the idea of dying alongside his shipmates in one massive, glorious, final battle. He'd been given command of U-2514, one of the new "miracle" U-boats that promised to be everything the old boats were not. Underwater they were extremely fast and yet so quiet that they could run circles around the British and American warships without sonar picking them up. Once they were unleashed, their commanders would sow terror throughout the North Atlantic, torpedoing every destroyer, cruiser, frigate, and flattop they could find. Of course, they'd be killed in the process, but just to show those British and American bastards what for just one last time, it would, to their minds, be worth it.

But it didn't work out that way. Instead, a week after it had been launched, his boat was blown up in an air raid at the ship-yard while waiting for its special binary fuel to arrive. Suddenly, and without benefit of his dying at sea, Ziggy's career as a sea captain and U-boat sailor was over. Instead, he and his crew were issued helmets and rifles, put into a naval infantry brigade, and sent to defend Hamburg against the British.

For the last two weeks they'd been footsloggers in the vast no-man's-land of the outer suburbs, lurking among ruined buildings and burned-out vehicles, waiting for British tanks, trucks, and armored vehicles to pass through and then attacking them with grenades and Panzerfaust rockets.

This morning they had situated themselves in a wide field of bombed-out factories near what had been the marshaling yards for the city's western train station. Tanks frequently passed through, exploring, but once they ventured just a short distance up any of the side streets, they were lost in a jagged wilderness of wrecked buildings, chunks of walls, and collapsed floors, any of which were perfect for staging an ambush.

It was nothing like going after enemy ships, Ziggy told himself. A U-boat was like a wolf, pursuing its prey over long distances. Now Ziggy was more like a crocodile, waiting for its prey to come along. As a wolf, Ziggy Loerber had been fantas-tic, but as a crocodile, he was not so good. Ambushes required patience and timing and even under the best circumstances they easily backfired. In the last two weeks, he'd lost more than half of his men.

Even so, it occurred to Ziggy that with a little luck he might be captured by the Tommies, and then who knew? In a couple of months, weeks, or even days, if he didn't die of starvation or cholera, they would let him out and send him back to his loved ones. Except, of course, that Ziggy didn't have any loved ones, un-less you counted his family, which he didn't. All Korvettenkapitän Zigmund Loerber had was the navy, and it frightened him to think of what his life would be like without it.

It was a foregone conclusion that the defense of Hamburg wouldn't be successful. They had none of the men, weapons, ammunition, vehicles, or petrol to push the British army back. They could only hope to fend them off for another day or two. There was a massive seaborne evacuation under way in the eastern Baltic and each day dozens of freighters, warships, and fishing boats arrived with refugees and soldiers escaping from the last German outposts in Latvia and Russia. It was imperative that the navy keep Hamburg's port open for them to put in.

So they hung on with whatever weapons and vehicles they could get their hands on. That morning they had managed to commandeer some three-wheeled bread trucks and, with a couple crates of Panzerfausts in hand, drove out to the western suburbs. Their war chariots were noisy, underpowered vehicles with engines too small even for most motorcycles. Still, each could carry three people: a driver and two others kneeling on the back bed, machine guns at the ready. Everyone else followed on foot, rifles slung over their shoulders, keeping a wary lookout, as much for townspeople eager to stop the fighting as the British themselves.

As Ziggy sat with his back against a shattered wall, he closed his eyes and let his ears search out through the loose fabric of battlefield noise for the sound of approaching armor. He could hear a metallic clattering in the distance and as he listened closer, he began to make out the rumble and squealing grind of caterpillar treads against broken concrete.

He looked up from the wall to see the high rounded turret of a British Sherman emerging from behind the remains of a factory. He got his binoculars out to get a better look. It was a single tank, painted a brownish green with sandbags piled everywhere along the front below the turret, giving it the appearance of a moving pillbox.

The tank veered slightly to the left, giving him a full view of its side. There was an image painted on the hull. Ziggy tightened the focus on his binoculars. It was a nearly naked girl, busty, with big eyes, short bobbed hair, and a garter prominently gracing her thigh. He almost had to laugh. Betty Boop!

For a moment, he was a teenager again, watching American cartoons and serial movies at the Titania Palace or the Cinema Universum. Mickey Mouse, Oswald the Lucky Rabbit, Bosko, and Betty Boop; how he'd loved them all. To his brothers, his unabashed love of cartoon characters was all the proof they needed that he was brain-damaged.

As the tank lumbered forward, Betty Boop seemed to bounce giddily to a rumba rhythm. The tank continued coming closer, and to calm himself Ziggy started humming, *Who's afraid of the Big Bad Wolf? Big Bad Wolf? Big Bad Wolf?* He tried to remember whether he'd thought about cartoons at all during his years aboard U-boats. It sure didn't seem like it. But now that they were back, it seemed like they'd never been gone. What he'd give for the chance to talk with someone about cartoons. Who knows? Ziggy thought hopefully, staring at the tank. If anyone gets out alive, maybe he'd get to.

Betty, Betty, Betty. The real love of his life; in the last twelve years, she hadn't aged a bit. Except now she was adorning a British Sherman and Ziggy wasn't in a position to play favorites.

He gripped the rocket's launching tube, holding it like a lance, and stared a hole into his target. That's it, closer, come closer, a little bit more, a little bit more. He watched it climb over a mound of rubble, pitching its prow upward and, for a brief second, exposing its soft, lightly armored underbelly. Ziggy stood up, pointed the rocket, pulled the trigger, and in a hot burst of propellant smoke watched it slam into the flat plate just below the driver's hatch. There was a rumble, the tank shuddered, and bright plumes of red flame erupted from its different openings. Nobody climbed out. For nearly a minute he stared at Betty Boop burning. Then, turning away, Ziggy signaled his men to move to fresh positions.

Half an hour later, they were hidden along the remnant of a wall when they heard a familiar rumbling coming from the east. They looked up and to their surprise saw a lone German tank lurching its way across the moonscape. Something about its movements seemed stalwart almost to the point of being comical, like some self-important businessman trundling through an African jungle with his satchel and umbrella, determined not to let anything stay him from his appointed mission. It had been days since Ziggy had seen any German tanks moving around and he wondered what this single tank's presence could possibly mean.

But almost as soon as he thought it, the air filled with a ragged tearing noise that descended down from the sky. Artillery! "Everyone take cover!" Ziggy yelled. The men dropped to the ground just as the shells began exploding. It went on for nearly a minute and then stopped. Ziggy looked up and saw nothing but a dense cloud of dust that hung in the air. The tank was gone, not leaving behind even a smoking, burning carcass. Suddenly Ziggy imagined old Gustav, gloved hand to his top hat and giving a gracious bow, *Thank you, thank you, and now for my next magic trick . . .*

"Herr Captain," one of the men shouted. "Look! Someone's coming!"

The dust had slowly begun to settle and from it emerged a group of figures with rifles and helmets, tiredly picking their way through the rubble. Germans, in a pastiche of different uniforms whose only common feature seemed to be the yellow-gray dirt that covered them. Naval infantry, just like themselves.

"It's Captain Cremer!" one of the petty officers shouted. Immediately everyone sprang to life and began shouting out greetings. Korvettenkapitän Peter Cremer had been Ziggy's friend and shipmate from early on in the war when they'd both served under Wolfgang Lüth, the U-boat ace, who was as famous for his philosophy of taking care of his crew and keeping their morale sky-high as he was for sinking vast amounts of enemy ships.

Ziggy pulled his last cigarette from his blouse pocket and held it up for Cremer to see. While their men chatted, they walked off by themselves.

"Korvettenkapitän Loerber," said Cremer, giving a mock salute. "I'm shocked to see you here. Whatever happened to that miracle boat of yours?"

"Sunk. Yours?"

"No fuel," said Cremer, grinning with disgust. "Only a temporary setback, they assure me. You still believe in ultimate victory, don't you?"

"Of course," said Ziggy. "You?"

"It goes without saying, Herr Korvettenkapitän."

"Naturally."

"Naturally."

"And if I may ask, how is your crew handling this new assignment of theirs?"

"I'm running them exactly the same, Herr Korvettenkapitän," answered Cremer. "I don't think they even realize they're off the U-boat yet."

"That's right," said Ziggy. "That's exactly how I'm doing it too. Running them the way Lüth taught us. Constant drilling. I was thinking of calling a practice dive. You?"

"We're staging a poetry contest," said Cremer. "Each of them has to come up with a verse and then we're going to print it up in the ship's daily paper. Just like Lüth taught us."

"Just like Lüth taught us," agreed Ziggy. "Every day a Sunday."

"Every day a Sunday," repeated Cremer. It had been a key element in Lüth's famous philosophy of maintaining crew morale. "Lüth would be proud of us."

"Damn proud," said Ziggy. "But seriously, Peter?"

"Seriously?" asked Cremer.

"Yes," said Ziggy. "What now?"

The smile faded from Cremer's face. He looked weary. "I think we've reached the end of the line, Zigmund."

They went back to their men and pooled what rations they had and ate lunch together. Then they returned to where they'd hidden the bread trucks, loaded up their unused Panzerfausts, and headed west to where a line of British tanks had been reported. They took up a position in what looked like an ideal ambush point between two rows of half-leveled buildings and waited for the tanks to come.

They were visible in the distance, dozens of them, as though waiting for the word to move forward. Finally they started advancing, but at a glacial speed. For nearly an hour, Ziggy stared at them, growing nervous. The men were getting restless too. This was the largest force they'd come up against and it was taking too long.

Finally the first tanks came into range. Ziggy gave the order to take firing positions. "Pick your targets and wait for my order," he told them, speaking with a calmness he did not feel.

To Ziggy's surprise, the tanks began loudly gunning their engines, even though they were moving no faster than before. Why were they doing that? Then Ziggy saw one of his men jerk back and slump to the ground. A second later another fell, then another.

Snipers! He looked around frantically at building tops and shot-out windows, looking for the shooter, but the loud rumbling of the engines made it impossible to tell where the shots were being fired from.

Then the tanks began firing. Ziggy heard the groan of a shell coming at him and flattened into the brickwork as it exploded against a nearby wall. Rocket still in hand, he tried scrambling away. The tank fired again and once more Ziggy flattened, hearing the shell sizzling overhead before exploding against a building, showering him with a stinging hail of brick and masonry fragments.

Rising from his fetal crouch, he pulled himself up beside a hole in the wall and peered through to where he thought he'd seen a momentary glint. He noticed it again. It had to be someone with binoculars on top of a building. Then he saw them, two British soldiers with high-powered rifles.

He grabbed a Panzerfaust. He knew if he fired it at them

directly, it would either explode uselessly against the wall or fly completely over their heads, which would give them all the warning they'd need to move to another position. He had to lay it right on top of them. But how? Panzerfausts were meant to be fired point-blank, not along a trajectory. But then, in his nightclub days, Ziggy had been an expert at lobbing Indian clubs overhand and hitting targets dead-on.

He stared at the spot where the snipers were, pointed the rocket directly into the air, and fired.

The rocket arced upward and then came hurtling down right onto the rooftop. It exploded and he knew he'd gotten them.

One of the tanks exploded, then another. A machine gun opened up in a long, sustained burst. Ziggy got to his feet and started running toward another piece of wall as a stream of bullets raked the ground behind him. Then a tank fired, another loud groan, followed by an explosion cut short in midburst, and suddenly everything went black.

When the lights came up again, Ziggy saw another tank coming at him. He leveled his Panzerfaust at it and fired. But this time when the tank exploded, it broke into a dozen smaller tanks, which instantly grew to full size. He fired his rocket again and again, and each time he hit one it became many tanks, until there were too many to count. Ziggy turned and began running, but try as he might, his legs wouldn't take him anywhere. Suddenly a kid-gloved hand reached out and pulled him into a building. He found himself back inside the Blue Star sitting at a table across from his brother Sebastian. Next to him sat Betty Boop. "There's a young lady I'd like to introduce you to," Sebastian said, pointing at her. "She simply loves your work."

Betty Boop offered Ziggy her hand to shake. "That was some fancy shooting, cowboy," she said.

Sebastian raised a whiskey bottle. "Like some Johnnie? I can get them to bring a clean glass," he said, examining the one in his hand. "This one's got rubble in it."

There was an explosion, and then another. "When will it all end?" Ziggy asked.

"It's already ended," answered Sebastian. "You need to think about the future."

Tears were welling in Betty's big eyes. "A nice Jewish boy like you, a Nazi? How could you?"

"I'm not a Nazi," answered Ziggy. "And I'm not a nice Jewish boy. I'm Ziggy of the Flying Magical Loerber Brothers."

"No, you're not," said Betty. "You're not magical anymore. What have you done that's magic?"

"Pick a number between seventy-two and one hundred thirty-five," said Ziggy, but then he couldn't think up the number.

Sebastian frowned at Ziggy. "I can't believe you would betray your own people like this. Beware the Blood of Israel! The Blood of Israel will have its vengeance!"

Ziggy tried to tell his brother to piss off, but instead he heard himself saying, "If I should forsake thee, O Jerusalem . . . ," while Betty Boop slapped his face.

"Ziggy, wake up! Come on. You've got to come to now!" Ziggy opened his eyes and saw Cremer slapping him awake.

"What? Where am I?" Ziggy asked.

Cremer was looking straight into his eyes. "You were shouting in Hebrew again, Ziggy. If I hadn't slapped you, the men would have heard you."

They were in an aid station. Everywhere around them there were wounded and dead: soldiers, civilians, volkssturmers, kids in bloodied Hitler Youth uniforms with missing limbs and bandaged heads.

Cremer was smiling. "We've been ordered out of here, Ziggy. The whole bunch of us. We're moving out immediately to Plön. The grand admiral's orders," he said. "We're going to be his security battalion."

⦃ 16 ⦄

After eating something in the basement canteen, Franzi had gone back upstairs to the command corridor and found an empty chair. Nothing was going on and the others were restive and in foul moods. How much longer was it going to take for Hitler to die? Of course, for all they knew, Hitler was already dead and it was just being kept secret. This whole thing had gotten ridiculous. He wondered how the negotiations with Eisenhower were progressing and had tried pressing Himmler a couple times on the matter, but the most the Reichsführer would do was give a vague but optimistic look and mutter something about "good indications." Perhaps it was true. Schellenberg hadn't been seen in days and no one would say anything of his whereabouts. Franzi took that to mean that Schellenberg was probably now talking directly to Eisenhower, either in France or in Stockholm, and the reason nobody was saying anything about it was that they didn't want the Russians finding out.

And Franzi knew for a fact that the Russians were eager to find out what was going on here in SS Headquarters. Only the day before, he'd managed to peek out one of the windows looking out onto the street and immediately saw painted on a nearby building two parallel lines with a circle on the top left corner, the Moscow Center *all is forgiven, make contact* symbol.

"Here comes something," whispered the major sitting next to him. The colonel in charge of the signals staff was coming down the corridor with a radiogram in hand. He only brought in messages that came directly from the Führerbunker, an event that had become increasingly rare. He knocked on the door, went in, and then left a few seconds later, carefully avoiding eye contact with anyone. "I bet the Führer is dead," whispered the major. A minute later the door opened and one of the adjutants stepped out, walking quickly to the operations staff room, only to return immediately with three generals and a colonel in tow. Looking grave, they went into Himmler's suite, closed the door, and for the next two hours there was nothing. Then a junior signals officer came in with another radiogram.

Eventually the door opened and an adjutant popped his head out and began looking up and down the corridor, surveying the faces of all the colonels, majors, and captains sitting there, until finally he spotted Franzi and frantically motioned for him to come inside.

Franzi followed him through the padded door to the inner office. It was a far different scene from his earlier visit. Himmler was on the couch, his spectacles lying on the table, his shirt unbuttoned, and his undershirt pulled up above his chest, revealing his pasty white stomach, which was already starting to spasm obscenely.

"Oh, Professor Loerber," he groaned. "Something terrible has happened."

Franzi looked around at the others, who seemed frozen in a kind of alert helplessness, and wondered if the supreme moment had arrived. "Is the Führer . . . dead?" he asked.

Painfully, Himmler shook his head. "No, worse!" he answered. "He's found out about my negotiations with Eisenhower and now he's removed me from all my posts! I'm no longer Reichsführer SS. I'm not even in the party anymore." He wiped his forehead with a handkerchief. "Oh, God, I feel just terrible. I should never have listened to Schellenberg!" Himmler buried his head in his hands and began to weep.

Franzi looked at the generals, the adjutants, and aides-decamp. With their eyes, they all seemed to implore him, *Do something.*

Showtime!

"Reichsführer," Franzi began, "when you and everyone else in this room swore their oath of loyalty to Adolf Hitler, it was to a man who was the living embodiment of Germany. Well, he is no longer that man. What is happening in Berlin right now is merely the natural course of things, which each of us must embrace. Nothing lasts forever, change is constant. The old is always replaced by the new. The wheels of destiny are in perpetual motion. You can throw yourself in front of them, but you can't stop them. Regrettably, the Führer let himself believe otherwise. Had he possessed the grace to accept his destiny, things might not have become such a terrible mess. You did the right thing, Reichsführer, and in a few hours all this unpleasantness with the Führer will be over and you'll be free to lead Europe into a bright new day."

"But he has given my post to Gauleiter Hanke," moaned Himmler. "I've been demoted. This has never happened to me in my life! And now Grand Admiral Dönitz is coming to arrest me!"

For a moment Franzi felt thrown off. Then one of the adjutants handed him a piece of paper. It was a radiogram from Naval Headquarters, Plön, tersely informing Himmler that, on the instruction of the Führer, Dönitz was on his way there.

"He just met with me this morning. Why else would he be coming back here?"

Franzi gave a shrill laugh. "You've got to be kidding, Reichsführer! That little pipsqueak? He's more scared of you than you are of him. He's coming back here only because he's been ordered to. All you have to do is tell him that it's all enemy propaganda. You think he won't accept it? Of course he will! He doesn't need to get into a fight with you. He's got enough problems as it is. And the Führer no longer has the power to enforce anything. You need to let the grand admiral know who's boss and let the rest take care of itself.

"Honestly, Reichsführer, looking around me here, I don't see anybody leaving you to serve Gauleiter Hanke. Correct me if I'm wrong, gentlemen." Franzi looked at the shocked faces of the generals and colonels, giving them his very best drip-dry Gustav Loerber smile, and noted with great satisfaction how positively they all responded.

He turned back to Himmler. "Now, whether the Führer knows it or not, he's already dead. Reichsführer, you need to calm down and accept that your moment of destiny has come and it's right now. Not tomorrow, not in an hour. Now!"

Franzi faced the others and in his most commanding voice declared, "Gentlemen, I present to you our new Führer, Heinrich Himmler!" Turning back to Himmler, he snapped his right arm into a stiff salute and shouted, "Heil Himmler!"

There was stunned silence in the room as the others looked to Himmler to offer some qualification, to chastise the strange young man for his brashness. So what if he was a prophet? He was still only a junior officer. It wasn't his place.

But Himmler only smiled.

"Heil Himmler!" shouted Franzi again. "Heil Himmler!"

They joined him on the third chant. "Heil Himmler!"

Himmler stood up from the couch. His shirt seemed to have buttoned itself and his thick-lensed spectacles were back on his nose. When he spoke, he was as calm and confident as Franzi had ever seen him.

"Gentlemen, we have a new millennium opening before us. The cosmos requires that we seize this moment. We all have our jobs to do. Let's get to work."

Grand Admiral Dönitz arrived soon after that, and was gone five minutes later, apparently satisfied with whatever explanation Himmler had offered him. That seemed to take care of that, everyone said and began settling into a celebratory evening, toasting the new Führer of the German Reich and the man destined to lead Europe.

{ 17 }

During the flight back from Berlin, Speer sat by himself in the back of the airplane. The only time he spoke with the pilot was when they finally put down at an airstrip east of Eutin and the pilot muttered something like, "There you are," to which Speer might have answered, "Thank you." Now he was safely back, but somehow he felt even worse than before.

Why had he assumed Hitler would be glad to see him? That his appearance might even have brought tears of joy to his eyes, the same way he had that time a month earlier when he'd told Hitler, "I am with you." It had always been the small kindnesses that Hitler had appreciated the most from Speer. But this time he'd had Speer wait in an anteroom for eight hours. Then when he was finally brought inside to see him, they ended up having a disjointed conversation. Hitler remained cold and stiff. When the time finally came to say goodbye, Hitler said only, "So you're leaving now? Good. Auf Wiedersehen."

Speer didn't register climbing up the stairs, going through the airlocks, or which exit he came out of. Then he was back on the surface, where it was nighttime and the bunker guards flagged down a passing armored half-track that took him back to his plane.

By now the fighting was close by. The vehicle's hull was continuously struck by enemy bullets. But the half-track continued on its rounds with the same slow deliberation as if what they were going through was merely a very bad rainstorm. Speer sat in the back with a group of dirty, unemotional Waffen-SS troopers. They let him off on the East-West Axis, the city's main boulevard, which had been turned into an airstrip.

The pilot was plainly relieved to see Speer. He flicked away his cigarette and opened the back hatch and trundled Speer into the compartment behind the cockpit, where he nestled atop some mailbags. Then he got into his seat, started up the engine, and a minute later they were flying over the Brandenburg Gate and Speer was staring emptily at the inferno swirling below. If he'd actually thought anything, he couldn't remember it now. He felt too numb to remember much of anything.

They hedge-hopped the whole way north, avoiding the enemy fighters that now incontestably ruled the sky. When they finally put down it was just after daybreak and they were at a small strip crowded with derelict aircraft. He watched the pilot pull out his personal gear and then walk away from the aircraft with finality, as though he'd already forgotten he'd ever been a pilot. He wasn't going to check in at the operations hut, he was just going to keep walking.

Speer walked through the mass of abandoned aircraft, wondering deliriously if they possessed the self-awareness to accept their fates. These magnificently crafted fighting machines were the fruit of his work in managing the war industries. In a sense he'd overseen every rivet, rib, and spar that went into them. He'd allocated the chromium content in their engines, seen to it that the synthetic rubber in their gaskets had no more than .005 percent adulterants.

The Americans had tried to keep these planes from being built. Part of their bombing strategy was to cripple the key industrial activity upon which all others were dependent: ball bearing production. But no matter how hard the factories were hit, Speer and his people had gotten them back up and running, often within a matter of days. In the end it wasn't ball bearings but lack of fuel and trained pilots that finally defeated their efforts. Part of him tried to roust awake the feeling of pride in his accomplishment, but seeing all these dead aircraft made him only feel desolate.

Then he saw a familiar figure standing beside a Kübel waving at him. It was Manni Loerber. Speer knew he should heed the alarm bells going off in his head, but he needed someone, anyone, to take over, to lead him and do the thinking for him.

"How was it?" Manni asked.

Speer said nothing. Manni opened the door to let him in.

They drove for a while through the countryside. Speer tried looking ahead, but he kept nodding off. "You look like you could use some coffee," said Manni.

Speer opened his eyes. "You still have coffee?"

Manni reached behind his seat and pulled out a battered-looking metal thermos. He handed it to Speer. "Help yourself."

As he drank, Speer waited for Manni to ask about the bunker, but the questions never came. They stopped at a militia checkpoint. Manni held out a pass, but the militiamen waved them through without even a cursory examination. A few minutes later they reached a small naval base, an unimpressive collection of one- and two-story brick and wood-frame buildings and corrugated metal huts standing under a tall canopy of camouflage netting. Naval infantry in helmets milled around, rifles in hand, while an antiaircraft crew stood inside a ring of sandbags.

Manni stopped at the front gate. Speer looked around with sudden confusion. He'd assumed Manni had been driving him back to Eutin Lakes.

"Where are we?" he asked.

"Plön. Naval Headquarters," said Manni. "You need to talk to the grand admiral."

"Dönitz?" Speer remembered the last conversation he'd had with Dönitz and cringed. He'd gone to see the admiral a few days before going to the Ruhr and tried sounding him out on the question of ending the war. But unlike everyone else, Dönitz turned ice-cold and angry and told Speer that he was completely out of line. He let Speer know that even though he went around in something that looked very much like a military uniform, he didn't know the first thing about what it meant to be a soldier. Speer left feeling like a thief, worried that Dönitz might report him.

"I know you two had a bad falling out, but a lot has happened since then and I'm sure he'll be glad to see you," said Manni. "Offer your services, anything you can do. The man's got his hands full and, outside the navy, there aren't too many people he can trust."

Once inside the gate, Speer was taken to the command center and led up to Dönitz's offices. The officer at the front desk ushered him inside and explained that Dönitz had gone to see Himmler but that they were expecting him back shortly. Speer went into a vestibule in the inner office, where he sank into a chair and fell asleep. The next thing he knew, he was looking up and Dönitz was standing over him, saying, "Hello Speer, what a surprise. It's good to see you."

Speer got up, relieved that Dönitz was not frowning at him. "Hello, Grand Admiral, it's good to see you too," he said. "I've come to see if there is anything I can do for you."

Dönitz gave a grim smile. "That's very kind of you, Speer. If you'd like, we could start off by having dinner."

They ate in a small dining room adjacent to Dönitz's offices. Dönitz looked terrible. He explained that he'd been to Himmler's headquarters in Lübeck twice that day. Each time the drive was harrowing and the sight of all the refugees shocked him. "I'm not used to dealing with civilian problems, Speer," he confessed. "Not even in the best of circumstances. But this?" He gave a hopeless look.

He explained that for the last two weeks his only concern had been getting the new "miracle" U-boats ready for action. One was already on its first patrol and twenty more were starting their preliminary "shakedown" cruises.

Speer was amazed. "I didn't know they were actually ready," he said.

Dönitz gave a tired smile. "I could have a hundred ready next week if I could only get my hands on enough fuel. But you know something, none of it is going to happen.

"Today I got to Lübeck and I saw all those people on the road. I'm telling you, Speer, I've seen the reports, I've read the numbers, but I never realized what it means when hundreds of thousands of people are out there, without food or anything. Until today I really hadn't thought about them."

The door opened and a naval officer came in and handed Dönitz a telegram. As he turned to leave, Dönitz stopped him. "Wait a minute, Captain," he said. "Speer, do you know my adjutant, Lüdde-Neurath?"

Speer got up from his chair to shake his hand. After Lüdde-Neurath left, Dönitz waved the telegram at Speer. "See here, just what I was telling you. The grand offensive I've lived for is about to begin and all that it promises to accomplish is meaningless compared to all the misery here, which I can't do anything about."

He put the telegram aside and stirred his soup, then irritably put the spoon down. "This morning, Himmler summoned me to his headquarters in Lübeck. I went, even though as head of the Northern Zone I'm technically his superior. I thought, no point getting into a pissing match when there are massive issues at stake. And you know what he wanted to talk to me about? Karma, the spheres, the shifting from one epoch to another like it's the bloody Twilight of the Gods. And then he starts hinting that he's got negotiations going with Eisenhower and wants to know if I'll support him when he becomes the Führer.

"I must be an idiot, Speer. I didn't get what he was saying. Even then I didn't question his loyalty. But then I get back here and there's a message from the Führer saying that Himmler has committed treason and I am to move against him immediately. So I turn around and go back to see him and suddenly he denies everything, like that first meeting never happened. He just lies straight to my face. And what can I do? Arrest him? Call him a liar?" Dönitz laughed bitterly.

Speer nudged the conversation back to the new submarines. Dönitz told him they had gotten a large quantity of the special Ingolin fuel two days before and all that remained was finding a way of moving it to Norway where most of the boats were waiting. Speer listened to him explore the different possibilities: flying glass casks of it at night in large transport aircraft or putting them aboard fast patrol boats. The problem, of course, was that if anything happened to them in transit, they would explode.

Speer listened attentively and then tried to make some helpful suggestions. Of all Hitler's men, Dönitz was the only one he had felt any affinity with. They'd always gotten along well, because like Speer, Dönitz was an expert who put numbers and facts above talk. And in a way, one could even say he was an artist—except his canvas was the ocean and instead of paintbrushes and paints he used submarines.

Lüdde-Neurath came in again with another folder, which Dönitz read and scribbled a reply on before handing it back without any comment to either of them.

They finished dinner and started back to Dönitz's office, but Lüdde-Neurath intercepted them in the hall. He had another telegram, this one from the bunker. Speer watched Dönitz read the message and saw his face become still.

"What is it?" asked Speer.

Dönitz handed him the telegram. It said:

GRAND ADMIRAL DÖNITZ,

IN PLACE OF THE FORMER REICH-MARSHAL GÖRING, THE FÜHRER AP-POINTS YOU, HERR GRAND ADMIRAL, AS HIS SUCCESSOR. WRITTEN AUTHO-RIZATION ON THE WAY. IMMEDIATELY TAKE ALL STEPS REQUIRED BY THE PRESENT SITUATION.

BORMANN.

Speer reread it to make sure he hadn't missed the meaning. It didn't say anything about whether Hitler was dead or alive. He looked at Dönitz. "I suppose I should congratulate you."

"Please don't," said Dönitz.

"What are you going to do?"

Dönitz thought for a long time. Then he said, "I think what we need to do first is move against Himmler."

Nobody would tell Franzi why they were suddenly going to Plön in the middle of the night. All he knew was that they were traveling in a large column of Kübels, armored vehicles, and staff cars, everyone armed to the teeth. He sat in the backseat of Himmler's Mercedes, wedged between Himmler and Macher, the new head of security, sleepily wondering if this could be the beginning of a civil war, between the Himmler-led "peace faction" and the Hitler loyalists, led by Dönitz.

Himmler, for his part, seemed calm and determined, for once not prattling on about Eisenhower or the spheres of destiny. Instead he stared out of the window, deep in his own thoughts.

Finally Himmler tapped the back of the driver's seat. "How much longer?" he asked.

"About another hour, Reichsführer," said the driver.

Himmler stretched out and nestled his head between the seat and the cushion lining the door.

"In that case, don't wake me until we get there."

"Jawohl."

Franzi leaned forward, resting his forehead against the front seat. Macher drummed his fingers on the door. He didn't seem to be nervous at all; neither was Grothmann, sitting beside the driver. Both came from the Das Reich division and, being longtime veterans of the Russian Front, didn't appear the least bit worried about getting into a battle with anybody, especially members of the navy, if that was indeed why they were going there. Franzi

knew better than to ask them. He might be the Reichsführer's astrologer, but in their eyes he was just some glorified rear-echelon
malingerer who didn't know which end of a pistol the bullet came
out of.

Franzi was scared. He shut his eyes and wondered what was
going to happen. Then it occurred to him that if what Himmler had said about Ziggy's promotion was true, Ziggy might be
involved. What if they ended up shooting at each other? What
if during all the confusion Franzi had a chance to sneak away?
Maybe he could get Ziggy to help him. If things got really crazy,
would Ziggy quit being such a stick and pitch in with some magic
to help diffuse the situation?

For a Loerber, Ziggy had been spectacularly obtuse and imma-
ture. Perhaps if he hadn't had his head so full of cartoon characters he might have figured out that Franzi and Manni had actually
gone undercover when they joined the SS and Nazi Party. Later,
when they asked Ziggy to spy for them, he had acknowledged
that what they were doing was noble and right, but he couldn't
handle the "level of complexities" involved in both serving and
betraying his beloved navy.

Franzi could not imagine what might have made Ziggy like
this. For someone trained from birth to understand and ma-
nipulate the natural fluidity of reality, Ziggy insisted on living in a
world where things were precisely what they appeared to be, as if
such a world could exist.

Ziggy loathed the Nazis because they had dared suggest that,
being a Jew, he could not be a German, and he loved being both.
He joined the navy because it was considered the least Nazi of all
the armed services. Of course, he'd had to pretend he wasn't a Jew.
But, he told Franzi, he'd considered it preferable to the constant
duplicity and lying he'd have faced as a spy.

Franzi wondered what he was like now. Their last meeting had
not gone so well. They'd called each other a lot of names and in
the end each loudly wished the other would drop dead.

Himmler stirred in his seat. His breathing seemed almost mechanical, as if being controlled by an outside force. Franzi turned to look at him. His eyes were wide open, but unseeing, as if in a trance.

"Blood!" Himmler whispered.

"Reichsführer?" asked Franzi.

"Blood! The Blood of Israel will have its vengeance!"

"Reichsführer, are you all right?"

"The Blood of Israel will have its vengeance," repeated Himmler. "The Blood of Israel! The Blood of Israel! The Blood of Israel!"

"You want to tell me what the hell is going on?" demanded Macher.

"His mind's been invaded," answered Franzi. He tried shaking Himmler, but Himmler just kept shouting, "The Blood of Israel will have its vengeance! The Blood of Israel will have its vengeance!"

"Reichsführer, snap out of it!" shouted Franzi. But Himmler kept going on and on. Blood. Vengeance. Israel.

"Colonel Macher, I think we need to stop the car now!" said the driver.

"Keep driving!" shouted Macher. "You, Loerber, get him out of it, now!"

Franzi grabbed Himmler by the arm, shaking it. Then he started slapping his face, but Himmler continued to shout, "The Blood of Israel will have its vengeance! The Blood of Israel will have its vengeance!"

The driver was beginning to lose it, and Grothmann looked rattled. "We need to do something," he hissed.

Franzi bent down and pulled his medical kit from under the seat and began rooting through it. He found a bottle of smelling salts and stuck it under Himmler's nose, but it didn't even change the rhythm of his breath. Vengeance. Israel. Blood.

Franzi reached back into his bag and pulled out a crystal the size of a pinecone and held it against Himmler's forehead.

"Reichsführer, wake up! Please wake up!" Nothing. Franzi was beginning to feel desperate.

"The Blood of Israel will have its vengeance! The Blood of Israel will have its vengeance!"

"Somebody do something!" yelled the driver, now on the verge of panic.

Franzi dropped the crystal, pushed Himmler hard against the back of the seat, and shouted at the top of his lungs, "Sebastian, stop it right now! You're going to get me killed!"

Himmler stopped. Suddenly everything was quiet.

"How the hell did you do that?" asked Macher.

"I don't know, Colonel," answered Franzi.

Himmler yawned and stretched.

"You called out to your dead brother, didn't you?" said Macher. "What does he have to do with this?"

Franzi stared hard at him. "Colonel Macher," he began. "Rather than insult your intelligence with an idiot discussion about spooks and magic, let's just say there's stuff out there you don't know anything about. Now, I know you think what I do is bullshit, and, well, you're mostly right. But Colonel, the biggest mistake people make about magic is believing they can open a door halfway. If the Reichsführer had been more like yourself and just left it all alone, none of this would be happening."

Before Macher could say anything, Himmler interrupted them. "I just had the strangest dream!"

"How so, Reichsführer?" asked Franzi warily.

"I can't remember," said Himmler. "But I'd really like to go for a walk right now. Driver, stop the car. Loerber, you will accompany me."

"Yes, Reichsführer," answered Franzi.

"We'll continue this discussion later," said Macher. He rolled down the window and stuck his head out. "Five-minute break," he shouted.

Outside, the night air was cold and Franzi sucked it in like it was liquor. He and Himmler started down the road, past the troopers who stared down at them from the back of the trucks, until they were away from the headlights. Then Himmler stopped and pointed up into the sky. "Professor Loerber, tell me what the stars say."

Franzi looked up at all the low clouds drifting across the starlit sky and for the thousandth time wondered what it was about stars that made people believe they give a rat's ass about anything. He'd been gazing at them for years and they'd never given so much as a hint. But he needed to tell Himmler something, so he said, "The change is happening now, Reichsführer. The whole grand cosmic order is shifting. A thousand years will pass and it will be nothing compared to what is happening tonight. And you, Reichsführer, are at the very center of it."

Himmler gasped. "What else do they say about me?"

"It is a moment of great danger," Franzi went on. "But it is a moment of even greater opportunity."

"So what should I do?"

"You need to go with the flow," Franzi droned. "Stay the course, during all the instability, so that you will be the one left standing when the chaos has stopped."

"Ahh," said Himmler. "But go on."

The words were now coming to Franzi independent of any strategy. "The first shall be last and the last shall be first," he said.

"You mean the Jews, don't you?"

"The last shall be first and the first shall be last."

"Yes, it has to be the Jews," said Himmler, sounding relieved. "It's a good thing I buried the hatchet with them. It was the smartest thing I ever did. What else?"

"Beware!" whispered Franzi. "Beware!"

"Beware what?" asked Himmler.

"Beware the man."

"Which man?"

Franzi had no idea which man. "The man who serves with both hands!" he said, pointing to one of the far stars of Orion.

"Are you talking about Eisenhower?"

Franzi pointed to the sky again. Himmler looked up. A flash in the sky appeared: a comet or a meteorite, blazing from the west to the east, then burning out and disappearing.

"My God!" exclaimed Himmler. "That was incredible. I didn't realize you had such a powerful gift of prophesy!"

"You must warn Eisenhower," Franzi said.

"Warn him about what?"

"The man who serves with both hands."

"You're talking about the traitor, aren't you?"

Franzi felt a chill.

"It's got to be those Cambridge spies Schellenberg was telling me about," Himmler said excitedly. "Philby. He serves London and Moscow. That's serving with both hands, isn't it? I'll have Schellenberg tell Eisenhower about Philby and the others. You're right, it's more than a bargaining chip. It's our good-faith measure. Professor Loerber, you are a genius."

Then suddenly Himmler was in a big hurry to get moving again. "Come on, let's not keep the grand admiral up all night waiting for us."

(19)

It was midnight when they finally drove into the Plön naval base. In the darkness all that stirred was a single petty officer, who pointed a flashlight to where they should park. The men got out of their vehicles, weapons at the ready, and assembled into a tight cordon, with Himmler, Macher, Grothmann, and Franzi in its center. "Keep your eyes open," Macher told them. "Anybody sees anything, sing out. If any of these navy clowns try anything funny, we'll let them have it. Let's move."

The petty officer pointed them to a small cluster of buildings at the end of a walkway flanked on either side by groves of trees. They started down the path, moving slowly and deliberately. "There're men behind those trees," reported one of the troopers in a loud whisper. Franzi peered into the shadows between the moonlit tree trunks and tried to make out the shapes of men hiding among them, but could see nothing. "More behind that row of trash cans," said another. Macher nodded but kept the group moving closer to the buildings.

"Pathetic," muttered Grothmann. "If this is their idea of an ambush, they've got another thing coming." Someone else chuckled quietly. Franzi could hear guns being cocked and safeties clicked off. "This is going to be more fun than killing Russians," someone cracked.

Halfway there, Macher gave the order to halt. "Everyone pick a target." Then he shouted into the darkness, "Whichever one of you is in charge, I suggest you come out right now."

A naval officer in a long leather coat emerged from behind a tree as casually as if he had his desk there. Even in the dark they could make out the Iron Cross around his neck. "Good evening, gentlemen," he said pleasantly enough. "I am Korvettenkapitän Cremer, head of the Dönitz Guard Battalion. You are here to see the grand admiral?"

"What the hell were you doing back there?" demanded Macher.

"Just a routine security precaution," answered Cremer.

"You tell your men to come out right now," said Macher.

Without turning, Cremer raised his right hand and called out, "First squad, come forward. Everyone else, stay where you are." A dozen sailors stepped out from the trees with rifles pointed and advanced across the grass toward them. When they had come forward about twenty feet, Cremer put up his hand again and they halted.

"Tell your men to lower their weapons," said Macher.

"You're on our base, so you should lower yours first," countered Cremer.

"Forget it," said Macher.

"Have it your way," said Cremer.

A minute passed and nobody moved. The SS troopers maintained their steely determination as they faced off against Cremer and his sailors, who didn't waver. Himmler seemed distracted, as if none of it particularly concerned him. Franzi wondered how much longer it would be before someone started shooting. Then a light came on outside the operations hut. The door opened and a naval officer stepped out. "If you'll come this way, Reichsführer, the grand admiral is waiting for you," he called out. Without a word, Himmler walked the rest of the way by himself. The naval officer held open the door and followed him inside.

After that, both sides relaxed a little. They partially lowered their weapons and settled in to wait. Cremer walked around them, looking at their weapons and into their faces. When he came to Franzi, he stopped and stared at him with a puzzled look. "Loerber?" he whispered, as though he thought it was altogether amazing.

"Is there a problem?" growled Macher.

"I'm not sure," answered Cremer. Then he turned and waved toward the bushes. "Captain, come here," he called out.

A figure stepped out of the darkness. A naval officer in the same long leather coat, also with the glint of an Iron Cross at his throat. It was Ziggy!

He began walking across the lawn toward them.

"You stop right there!" said Macher.

Ziggy ignored him.

"I'm not going to say it again," said Macher. "Captain Cremer, keep your man back."

The naval guard raised their weapons again. The SS raised theirs.

Cremer kept signaling Ziggy to come forward. Ziggy was now close enough that even in the darkness Franzi could tell that he recognized him.

"Franzi?"

"Ziggy?"

"Colonel, do you mind?" said Cremer. "These guys are brothers. They haven't seen each other for a long time."

"Both of you, step away! Now!" said Macher.

Ziggy stopped, giving Cremer a worried look.

"Colonel Macher, you want to start something, go ahead, but I guarantee you, we'll finish it. Second squad, lock and load."

"Troopers, wait for my word," said Macher.

Franzi looked at Ziggy. Ziggy smiled.

What is he thinking? wondered Franzi. It was like the old days, standing in the wings just before going onstage, none of them talking, primed to act as a single unit. The orchestra would strike up "Harlem Rhapsody," and they'd wait five bars and then run out onstage.

"Harlem Rhapsody." Suddenly the memory was on him, so

incredibly vivid he could almost hear its lilting sadness; the song, he imagined, of a black man on a street corner, gazing up to the window of the woman his heart cries for as packed streetcars clatter by. They all loved that song. He could hear it now, crisp and sweet.

Wait a minute, he *was* hearing it! Someone was whistling "Harlem Rhapsody" from one of the other buildings! Ziggy heard it too. They both looked over to see where it was coming from and saw a figure leaning casually against the railing in front of the entrance, cigarette in hand, looking away up into the sky as the blue notes curled up like smoke from his lips.

Manni.

Everyone stood in spellbound silence, Cremer, Macher, Ziggy, everyone, as the melody drifted to them through the cold night air.

Then the light came back on and the door flew open as Himmler bolted out alone. He made his way as quickly as he could toward them. Two of the troopers stepped aside to let him into the cordon. Even in the darkness he looked livid.

"Reichsführer, is everything all right?" asked Macher.

"Let's just get the hell out of here," snapped Himmler.

Franzi looked back at the building and saw that Manni was gone.

❨ 20 ❩

From his desk, Grand Admiral Dönitz listened with relief to the sound of Himmler's motorcade fading into the distance. With any luck, he wouldn't have to deal with him again.

He'd come in like he'd owned the place, haughtily demanding to know why he'd been summoned. Dönitz handed him the telegram and watched him turn white. "I suppose congratulations are in order, mein Führer," Himmler had said. Without blinking, Dönitz told him not to call him that. After that Himmler got solicitous, asking to be made the "second man of the state." Dönitz shook his head and, when Himmler asked why, explained that he intended to form a government of a "less overtly political nature."

"But I'm not overtly political," objected Himmler. "Eisenhower said it himself!"

Dönitz decided to let it pass. "Reichsführer, the subject is not open for discussion. Do you have any more questions?"

Unfortunately, Himmler did. He asked him about what he planned to do about the war. Dönitz told him he hadn't decided anything, but until he did, the war would continue and everyone would obey the orders given them. He stared coldly at Himmler while making this last point. The conversation went on a while longer, but ultimately, when Himmler saw Dönitz was not going to give him anything, he got up abruptly and left.

Alone finally, Dönitz let his eyes close for a moment. It had been nearly six hours since the telegram had arrived from the Führerbunker naming him Hitler's successor, and only now, with

Himmler out of the way, was the weight of this new job beginning to sink in. Head of state, Reichspräsident, Führer, heil Dönitz! The last thought made him shudder.

He went back to his pile of reports and for two hours his attention remained focused only on paperwork. After thirty-five years in the navy, it had become second nature and now it provided him with a sense of reassurance that things were not as utterly chaotic as they appeared. Armies, even on their last legs, continued to generate reports, requests, tallies, statistics, strategic assessments. They kept streaming in and Dönitz continued reading them. But somewhere around four-thirty he looked up, rubbed his eyes, and realized nothing he was reading addressed the real heart of the matter; that the war was lost and as head of state, the only choice left to him was deciding how large the funeral pyre should be.

He picked up a report from Admiral Kummetz, the man in charge of the Baltic evacuation. Twenty more ships had come into different German ports with refugees and soldiers. Estimated numbers, thirty-five thousand men, women, and children. Tomorrow they hoped to get out fifty thousand. Every freighter, barge, and fishing boat they could get their hands on was now going to and from the Latvian ports of Lepaya and Ventspils, where upwards of a million Germans were still holding off the Russians. He knew as well as anyone what the Russians would do to them when they got them. He had to continue the evacuation. He couldn't give up on them.

He needed to put together a government. But how was he supposed to do that? He didn't know the first thing about government or diplomacy. He wondered if what Himmler had said about the Americans and British considering an alliance with Germany against the Russians could be true. It seemed crazy. But then, didn't he have all those spies and that whiz-kid Schellenberg with all his foreign contacts?

Besides, forming a new government was still only a means to an end. So what end was he seeking? What was left? A surrender?

A few hours ago, the idea had still been completely unthinkable. But now it seemed to be the only thing that made any sense. The irony was that the Führer had given the job to him because he knew he would never surrender.

So what should I do? Am I supposed to continue following the path of someone who has abdicated his responsibility and leadership? If Hitler wanted the war to continue, he should have stuck to his job. Where was he anyway? Was he dead? Or had he gone out to the streets to join the fighting? What difference does it make? he asked himself.

He remembered driving back from Lübeck that day telling himself that Himmler would be the next Führer—and the thought of serving under a liar like that seemed more than he could take. He found himself wishing he'd had the guts to arrest Himmler on the spot. Himmler's men would have gunned him down immediately, but at least he could have died honorably and remained true to all those young men he'd sent to their deaths.

Or, instead of returning to Plön, he should have gone to the nearest airstrip, commandeered a plane, and flown up to Oslo and gotten aboard one of the Type XXI boats to go out into the North Atlantic to raise hell. The first enemy warship they'd find, they'd sink. Then they'd find another and sink it too and then the one after that and the one after that, until they'd finally get sunk themselves. He had the right to do that. He was a soldier, and a soldier's last bullet is always for himself. But it seemed Hitler had taken that privilege from him so he could go out fighting on the streets of Berlin. So why had he done it? It wasn't right. Damn it, it wasn't fair! It wasn't. It was selfish!

So what do I do? What is the interest of the state? The interest of the state is survival. And at all costs, Germany must survive! Surrender, then? That's not why I was appointed by the Führer. But then, he's not Führer anymore. I am. I'm the Führer. Don't say that! Don't use that word. I'm head of state. I'm in charge.

Dönitz got up from his chair and opened the door to the outer office. Lüdde-Neurath was staring at the war log. "Sir?" he asked, looking up.

"Captain, I need to ask you a question and I want a completely honest answer," said Dönitz. "Do you ever get into conversations where during the course of them people say to each other or to you, 'This war has to end'? Do you ever get into these conversations?"

For one very long, uncomfortable moment, Lüdde-Neurath stared back hard at him as though he wasn't sure whether it was a trick question or something else. Then he answered, "Sure, all the time."

"All the time?"

"Sir, what do you think people talk about?"

Dönitz nodded and went back into his office. He finished off his coffee, set the cup back down, and rubbed his eyes. Then he switched off the desk lamp and in the darkness swiveled his chair around toward the window. As his eyes grew accustomed to the darkness, he saw first light was beginning to gather in the eastern sky. In another hour, the first Allied air attacks would commence. They would hardly discriminate between refugees and military traffic.

Today was May first, May Day. A funny time to start.

Later that morning, Dönitz convened his first government meeting. He announced to his staff that he was now the head of state and would be seeking an immediate cessation of hostilities with the West while continuing military operations to support the evacuation of the Baltic.

But it was May Day, the Day of Revolt. And in Hamburg, the surviving residents declared a socialist revolution. In keeping with a century-old tradition, they hung red flags from lampposts, buildings, windows, anywhere they could. Of course, the only red flags anybody could find had big circles with swastikas at their centers. But once those were cut out and discarded, everyone agreed they served their historic function quite sufficiently. Kaufmann, the Hamburg gauleiter, sent Dönitz an ultimatum: if he did not allow them to declare Hamburg an open city, they would turn against the city's defenders in order to avoid further British attacks. Dönitz was furious, but there was nothing he could do. He radioed a request to the British for a truce.

By now his government was seven hours old. It consisted of himself, Speer, and two advisors. Speer pointed out that they needed someone to handle diplomatic affairs. They spent the better part of the morning searching for someone to fill the combined post of chancellor and foreign minister. Within hours, candidates began to show up. The first was von Ribbentrop, Hitler's old foreign minister. As usual, he was drunk. He loudly demanded Dönitz restore him to his post, citing his close friendship with the current British Prime Minister, "Mr. *Vincent* Churchill." He was promptly ejected from the premises. Himmler arrived next with Count Schwerin von Krosigk, the old finance minister and a onetime Rhodes scholar, upon whose coattails Himmler hoped to ride back into power. Dönitz ejected Himmler and kept von Krosigk, if for no other reason than to prevent the Reichsführer from forming a shadow government.

They held another government meeting. Von Krosigk conceded that at this point their diplomatic options were few. He too had heard the rumor about Schellenberg's negotiations with Eisenhower, but after having spent the morning with the Reichsführer, he had no reason to believe it had any basis in fact. "One thing is certain, Grand Admiral," he said to Dönitz. "We've only got one card we can play: the Russian card. If we can convince them that without our help they too will be swallowed up by the Red Tide, we might have something."

Then someone pointed out that the question of whether Hitler was alive or not still remained and not knowing might hamper any negotiations. That glaring fact had slipped their minds. Not long after that, a final telegram came from the bunker informing Dönitz that Hitler had died the previous day, several hours, in fact, before Dönitz received word of his appointment. The Führerbunker and all of Berlin went silent. That night, Dönitz went on the radio and announced Hitler was dead.

The next morning, Dönitz summoned Admiral von Friedeburg, his longtime deputy and new head of the navy. "I want you to go to Field Marshal Montgomery and negotiate an end to the fighting," he told him. "Try to get him to agree to a partial surrender in the Northern Zone, but above all persuade him to give safe conduct to civilian refugees and to retreating military personnel. I know we are in no position to bargain. We are beaten. Nevertheless, you must do this for the sake of our people. You must get him to agree."

Watching von Friedeburg leave, Dönitz felt a momentary surge

of hope. Von Friedeburg was the best man he had: tough, coura-
geous, forthright, and professional. His presence made Dönitz
feel, at least in that instant, that his government might rise above
all the prevailing depravity and opportunism and make something
of it that was decent and good.

Von Friedeburg drove with a small delegation of army and
navy officers to Lüneburg Heath, where Field Marshal Montgomery's Twenty-first Army Group had its advance headquarters.
Dönitz waited for some word, but by midnight there was still
nothing. The next day, von Friedeburg radioed via the British asking Dönitz to meet him at the Levensau Bridge. Something was
wrong.

(22)

It had been four days since Ziggy and Cremer had come aboard as heads of Dönitz's security detail and other than the standoff with Himmler's men, they hadn't done much in that time besides salute and present arms a couple dozen times. When the order came for Ziggy to take a detachment of men to accompany the grand admiral to Levensau Bridge, he assumed it had to do with Admiral von Friedeburg's negotiations with the British. Levensau Bridge was only a mile or two east of the British front lines and in the last day all the fighting seemed to have come to a halt.

Though the bridge still stood, it had been too heavily bombed for vehicles to cross over. They parked on the road leading up to it and waited. For the first time in days, the bridge was empty. Presumably everyone on the other side who'd wanted to flee the British had already done so, and anyone who wanted to go west thought better of doing it there.

On the opposite bank a navy staff car was driving up. Then it stopped and Admiral von Friedeburg got out and began clambering across the bridge toward them.

For several minutes, Dönitz stood with his aides, silently watching von Friedeburg's progress through his field glasses. Then he abruptly took them away from his eyes. "Wait here," he said and started quickly up the bridge to meet him.

Ziggy put his field glasses to his eyes and looked over at von Friedeburg approaching. Something was very wrong, he thought. His footsteps seemed jerky and his face was frozen into a Greek mask of horror. He watched the two men stop and face each other. They began exchanging words back and forth. Dönitz remained stiff and arched, while von Friedeburg stood slumped. Then von Friedeburg put his hand over his eyes and Ziggy realized with a shock that he was weeping.

Dönitz started barking something at him, but von Friedeburg kept crying and shaking his head as though he were saying, *No, I tried but it didn't work. Hans, get ahold of yourself,* Dönitz seemed to be saying. *Remember what you are!* But von Friedeburg only kept pleading. *Please don't make me go back. Please, I can't take it. I can't!*

Ziggy kept his eyes on the two figures, clearly defined against the grayness of the river and sky. Their gestures seemed to describe what they were saying so completely it made Ziggy wonder if, without even knowing it, he was telepathically reading conversations again.

Whatever the case, there was no question about Dönitz's answer. *You have your orders and you will carry them out!* Then Dönitz softened his stance slightly and said something reassuring. Von Friedeburg set his mouth into a hard grimace and stood rigidly at attention as the rain pelted his face. Dönitz finished speaking, then turned and began angrily marching back. Von Friedeburg stood motionless for a few seconds and then started walking back to his side of the river.

Ziggy lowered his glasses. He wished he hadn't witnessed any of it. The way von Friedeburg was acting seemed less like head of the navy than some freshly minted ensign being dressed down after panicking during his first depth charge attack. What had happened to him?

Twenty yards from the bottom of the bridge, Dönitz stopped and gestured for his adjutant. The adjutant ran up, but before he even got there, Dönitz snapped out a couple words and the adjutant turned again and ran back to the others.

"Korvettenkapitän Loerber," he barked. "Report to the grand admiral on the double!"

"Jawohl," shouted Ziggy and ran to see what the old man wanted.

Dönitz looked at him cold and hard as iron. "Something has come up," he said. "I need you to go back with Admiral von Friedeburg to help him negotiate with the British." Then, softening his voice, he added, "You're a U-boat captain. You'll know how to handle it."

"Yes, sir," said Ziggy, completely bewildered.

Dönitz went on, "The admiral is having problems. He has a very difficult job ahead of him. You must help him, be his friend, but if things get out of hand you are to remind him of his duties, as a German naval officer and as a man."

Ziggy looked at Dönitz and saw how his eyes blazed with cold anger. "You speak pretty good English, as I recall," he continued. "That might be helpful. Loerber, you need to make sure he's able to function. The navy's honor is at stake. Do you think you can do that?"

"I'll do my best, Grand Admiral."

"No! That won't do, Loerber. The admiral just did his best and it wasn't enough. Whatever it takes, Loerber, you must see to it that he carries out his task. On this I am giving you full leeway. Do you understand?"

"Yes, Grand Admiral."

"It shouldn't take more than a couple of hours. Now get moving."

Ziggy saluted and started across the bridge. He hadn't been walking a minute when the grand admiral's words started sinking in. *Be his friend? Remind him of his duty? Full leeway?* If it hadn't been Dönitz telling him this, Ziggy would have thought it a joke.

The rain clouds that hung over them, low and heavy, cloaked everything in gray gloom, making the riverbank look more like it did on a forlorn late fall day rather than the middle of springtime. So the war was ending, he thought. Hitler was dead, Dönitz was head of state, and von Friedeburg was apparently in the middle of negotiating a cease-fire with the British. Peace was finally descending on Europe. Germany was finished. We'd wanted war and gotten it. He tried to imagine what peace would be like, but couldn't.

Ziggy walked across at a brisk pace. As he approached the admiral's Mercedes, the driver got out and came to attention.

"Come on, let's get going," said Ziggy, not bothering to salute back.

"Sir?" asked the driver. "Perhaps you might prefer to ride in the front."

Ignoring his suggestion, Ziggy opened the rear door and leaned inside. Admiral von Friedeburg sat empty-eyed in the back. "Herr Admiral?" asked Ziggy.

Von Friedeburg did not look at him.

"The grand admiral has asked me to accompany you, sir."

Von Friedeburg glanced at Ziggy just long enough to let him know he understood.

"I'll be sitting in the front if you need me, sir."

Von Friedeburg gave a slight nod like he thought it was a good idea. Ziggy shut the rear door and took the seat next to the driver.

Two minutes down the road, a pair of British army motorcyclists picked them up and, with their sirens blaring, escorted them past miles of parked tanks and milling British soldiers to a large encampment out on the Lüneberg Heath, where a British flag snapped arrogantly from a hastily erected flagpole. A hand-lettered white sign proclaimed TAC HQ 21ST ARMY GROUP. Hearing them approach, soldiers in mud-colored uniforms streamed out of the tents to get a look at them. The car stopped outside a tent where a group of unpleasant-looking sergeants stood waiting to receive them, rifles in hand. One of them opened the car's door and they got out. Inside the tent the rest of the German delegation was waiting. Ziggy immediately recognized Admiral Wagner. The others were a Wehrmacht general and a major who carried a leather satchel, which Ziggy assumed belonged to the general. They all seemed embarrassed by von Friedeburg's reappearance. As von Friedeburg stood silently with Wagner, the general took Ziggy aside and murmured to him, "We'd hoped the grand admiral would send a replacement. Did he not get my note?"

Ziggy looked directly into the general's eyes. "Well, I guess he didn't, Herr General," he said.

The general obviously didn't like Ziggy's answer, but before he could say anything, a heavyset British officer appeared in the entrance. "Admiral von Friedeburg, General Kinzel, if you're ready, the field marshal would like to proceed."

Von Friedeburg nodded emptily. The British officer gestured for everyone to get in line and then led them outside to another, larger tent crammed with officers and men with newsreel cameras. They were brought up to a large table where a short, prissy, domineering man dressed in a field jacket and beret stood glaring at them in irritation, as though he'd already had quite enough of them, thank you.

"Gentlemen, shall we begin?" he asked them in a shrill, accusing voice.

A soldier came up and set down four large documents in a row on the table. Next to them were pens set into tiny round jars of ink. The prissy little man, who Ziggy had surmised was Field Marshal Montgomery, gestured to von Friedeburg to come forward. As he did, glaring lights came on and a battery of newsreel cameras began loudly whirring. Von Friedeburg took a pen and bent over to the first paper, scratching his name onto it. Then, returning the pen to its well, he moved to the next document, where another pen was waiting. He put his name to that second copy and proceeded to the third and then the fourth. As he did, Montgomery signaled General Kinzel to come forward and sign, then Admiral Wagner. One after another they worked their way down the line, signing their names to the copies. When they were done, they stood in a group while Montgomery and two of his officers did the same.

Once they'd finished, Montgomery brusquely signaled for them to be taken away. As they stood outside in the rain, Ziggy approached von Friedeburg. "Admiral, what about the negotiations? Wasn't I supposed to help you with them?"

For the first time, Von Friedeburg looked directly at Ziggy. "Negotiations?" he exploded. "There aren't any negotiations, you fool! This is an unconditional surrender!"

(23)

As they walked back to their tent, Ziggy was aghast. Unconditional surrender? They had just given away the whole thing! Northern Germany, Holland, Denmark, Norway, and not the slightest concession.

Inside the tent, General Kinzel offered them cigarettes from his silver case and passed around his lighter.

"So what now?" asked Admiral Wagner.

Von Friedeburg said nothing. Kinzel cracked a poor joke. The major, who said his name was Friedel, brushed the ash off his cigarette by tapping it against the tent pole. Ziggy wondered whether they'd all be sent home or taken prisoner. He supposed by everyone's silence that they were thinking the same thing. All except for von Friedeburg, who didn't appear to be thinking at all.

Then the tent flap opened and a group of British officers stepped in. One of them started reading from a clipboard.

"General Kinzel, you shall remain here as a liaison with the German command. Major Friedel, you are to proceed to Field Marshal Busch's command with our orders to establish communications with Twenty-first Army Group. Admiral Wagner, you shall return to Grand Admiral Dönitz's headquarters with our instructions to him." He finished reading and nodded for a subordinate to hand each of them a buff folder containing their instructions. "You shall proceed at once," he added, in case they hadn't gotten the point.

All the while, von Friedeburg sat staring emptily at his

cigarette, as if none of it concerned him. He didn't seem to notice or care that his name had not been mentioned. Suddenly Ziggy understood why Dönitz had been so angry with him. If he couldn't stand his ground, he could at least adopt a haughty demeanor. He could throw them off by being an enigma. But he couldn't even do that. He looked negligible, like an unmysterious sphinx.

Ziggy looked at the British and then at the others, each with their folders. "What about Admiral von Friedeburg and myself?" he asked sharply.

The officer with the clipboard glared at von Friedeburg. "General Eisenhower wants you at Supreme Headquarters in Rheims to sign a more comprehensive surrender. You're flying out immediately."

They were put into a worn-out Humber and driven to the Lüneberg aerodrome, along with a dozen members of Montgomery's staff who were sent to escort them. But by the time they'd reached the airfield, the drizzle had turned into a downpour and they were informed everything had been grounded. They were taken into a hangar, where chairs had been set up for them: twelve for the British contingent, and a few feet away, two for the Germans. There was a large hole in the reenforced concrete roof through which rain poured into a Messerschmitt fighter, whose after-section had been crushed by a massive chunk of fallen concrete. The little airplane stood on its front wheels, wings still bravely stretched out, but with its nose pointing helplessly upward. They faced the wrecked airplane in meditative silence. It seemed to Ziggy like it was in pain.

Under the propeller, its wide, ovular air intake gaped in outraged protest, like the screaming horse in Picasso's *Guernica.* In the cold glare of emergency lights, the rain falling through the hole glittered like snowflakes. It battered the forlorn wreckage, pelting the glass windshield, rolling down the wings in heavy rivulets, and dripping from the propeller blades.

The British officers exchanged bits of conversation with each other, but it had been so long since Ziggy had used his English, their talk sounded more like birds' chirping than anything else. He couldn't tell what the admiral's state was. He made Ziggy feel restless. They'd been together since early afternoon, and except for screaming at him that one time, von Friedeburg had barely acknowledged his presence. Now they were apparently destined to be together for another couple of days and he had a feeling it was going to be the most thankless duty he'd ever pulled.

Ziggy wondered what would happen now that the war was ending. Had the Allies found out about all those camps the SS were running? There'd be hell to pay once they did. Everyone was already scrambling to disassociate themselves with them. It gave him a certain grim satisfaction.

Ziggy noticed a heavyset British officer wandering around the hangar, rifling through tool cabinets and drawers. He didn't seem to be part of the delegation; there certainly hadn't been a chair set up for him. The seated officers kept looking at him and exchanging terse noises among themselves, until finally the general in the group murmured something to his adjutant, the adjutant said something to the aide, and the aide got up and went over to the man as he went through a tray of screwdrivers. There was a brief, inaudible exchange of words and a moment later the aide sheepishly returned to the adjutant and muttered something. The adjutant turned to the general and ran his forefinger down the side of his nose. The general nodded and the whole matter was dropped. The man continued going through the drawers, handling the tools and acting like he was the only one there. Except Ziggy knew the man was watching him.

It went on like this for a while before the man at the tool rack looked back at the aide, gesturing with a thrust of his chin toward Ziggy. The aide got up and walked over to Ziggy. "Major Westerby would like a word with you," he said.

Ziggy stood up. "I'd better go see what he wants," he said to von Friedeburg, who didn't react.

Seeing Ziggy approach, the man dug into an inside pocket of his duffel coat and pulled out a packet of cigarettes.

"You're Major Westerby?" asked Ziggy.

The man nodded. "How is your admiral?" he asked in perfect Berlin German. "Do you think he'll be fit enough to perform his function?"

"He'll do what he has to," Ziggy replied.

Westerby nodded approvingly, then offered him a cigarette. Ziggy hesitated. It would be nice to know how he was expected to conduct himself in the situation. Could the bounds of icy correctness be stretched to include smoking a cigarette over business? He stole a look over at von Friedeburg, who seemed oblivious. The British officers, on the other hand, stared at them intently.

"Let's go around the corner," Westerby suggested. He led Ziggy to a spot along the side of the hangar where they were protected from the rain by the overhanging roof. Ziggy let him light his cigarette.

"I saw you perform many times at the Blue Star," said Westerby. "Your brother Franzi was a friend of mine. In fact, both your brothers are friends of mine."

Ziggy looked again at his face, trying to recognize him. He wasn't sure. Between the four of them, there had been constant traffic backstage of friends and acquaintances.

"Look, Major," said Ziggy, "if you don't mind, I'd rather not make this a social occasion."

Westerby ignored him. "The reason I'm asking," he said, "is we're trying to learn Franzi's whereabouts."

"How would I know where he is?" asked Ziggy. "I'm in the navy, not the SS."

"My understanding is you saw him a few days ago when the Reichsführer came to Naval Headquarters in Plön. He's apparently become part of Himmler's inner circle."

Ziggy didn't say anything. How could Westerby know that?

Westerby continued, "As I understand it, part of your falling out with your brothers came when they joined the SS and Nazi Party. I'm wondering if you're still as big an anti-Nazi as you were before the war."

"Major, if you don't mind, I'll just smoke this by myself."

"What if I told you that neither of them are what you think?"

"Major Westerby, if you're trying to drop broad hints that they're both Allied spies, then I already know."

"Well, if you know that, then perhaps you can tell me who Franzi's been working for."

"Well, the British, of course."

Westerby explained that Franzi was actually a double agent of sorts. He'd started out working for Moscow, but just around the time he'd begun having second thoughts about them, Manni—who by then was working for Westerby—convinced him to share the information he was sending eastward, assuming that no one in Moscow would ever be the wiser. Only it didn't work out that way.

Ziggy tried to listen, feeling his mind clouding over with the sheer assault of information. Cambridge, Moonpool, Schellenberg, and then the Russians. All he knew was that it sounded exactly like the kind of thing Manni and Franzi would find irresistible. Sowing chaos, playing different sides against each other, and with the help of their magical abilities, repeatedly escaping by a hair's breadth. Though supposedly there was a moral angle to it, he doubted they cared to think in those terms.

"Not that Franzi was pro-Bolshevik, mind you. Not at all. Like yourself, he was antifascist. They just got to him before we could," said Westerby.

"But why are you telling me this?" asked Ziggy.

Westerby looked at him searchingly. "Because Franzi is in great danger, and not just from the SS, whom he's trying to flee, but also from the Russians, who want to kill him to keep things he knows from getting out. And I don't mind telling you, Captain Loerber, that once it starts, none of you will be safe. We need to get him away from Himmler. My organization is thoroughly infiltrated by the Russians. There isn't anyone there I can trust. Manni and I will do what we can, but we need your help to get him out."

Ziggy was incredulous. "My help? How do you expect me to help you?"

Westerby was adamant. "Captain Loerber, you've got the guard battalion. That's more than we have. You can ask Cremer for help. He's your friend. You'll be at an advantage. Dönitz will be setting up his government in Flensburg. I'm sure Himmler will not be far away. It shouldn't be that difficult to locate him."

"How do you expect me to locate him?" asked Ziggy.

Westerby looked exasperated. "For heaven's sake, man, you're magic, aren't you?"

For a long moment the two stared at each other. Ziggy couldn't decide if Westerby was pulling his leg or completely nuts. He looked into the hangar and there was the injured fighter plane, its gaping mouth bellowing from the depths of its pain. *The Blood of Israel will have its vengeance!*

Ziggy looked down at the packet of cigarettes in Westerby's hand and snatched them. "I have to go back now, Major," he said quickly. "Thank you for the cigarettes."

He went back to sit with von Friedeburg. After another hour of waiting in silence, they were taken to an empty mess tent where two metal trays of food had been set for them. After that they were led to a small tent where there were two cots set up, each with a thin blanket. They were told they should be ready to leave at short notice, once the rain had lifted.

In the dim light of a kerosene lamp they prepared to go to sleep. Ziggy was about to blow out the lamp, but seeing von Friedeburg staring at him, he stopped.

"I've never treated anyone like this," von Friedeburg said. "Thirty years I've been in the navy, but I've never treated my fellow man with such disrespect. Why are they doing this to us? I don't understand why they're treating us this way."

Ziggy looked at him. Was this what had been on his mind the whole time? How could he be so stupid as to not know why they were being so nasty?

"Honestly, sir?" asked Ziggy.

"Yes!"

"Well, sir," said Ziggy. "I gather they've been finding out what we've done in the name of civilization."

"Civilization? What are you talking about, Captain?" asked von Friedeburg, a touch of indignation in his voice.

"Come on, you know, Admiral, what we did to the Jews."

"The Jews?" von Friedeburg asked, as if he'd never heard the word before. "Captain, may I remind you that we are military officers and we do not involve ourselves in issues of politics?"

"The British probably don't consider mass murder a legitimate form of politics, Herr Admiral," said Ziggy, feeling the anger in him beginning to boil.

"Captain, I don't know at all what you're talking about," said von Friedeburg hotly.

"You don't? Then you're the only one who doesn't, sir. I thought everyone must have enjoyed a conversation on that topic with our brothers in the SS. They always seemed to be quite forthcoming about it."

"Captain, the SS is not the navy. We don't concern ourselves with their activities, nor should we be expected to."

"Well, it doesn't sound like the British are buying that distinction, Herr Admiral. Not when millions of innocent men, women, and children get murdered."

"Captain Loerber, for the last six years we've been in a war, nothing more, nothing less. War is by its nature cruel, but that's the way it is."

"Herr Admiral, the death camps had nothing to do with the war."

"That's enough, Captain Loerber! I forbid you to say another word!"

"Yes, sir," barked Ziggy, bolting up from his cot. "I'll be outside if you need me."

He shoved back the tent flap and stepped into the rain, immediately coming face to face with a helmeted guard with a rifle. "Halt!" the guard shouted.

"Go ahead and shoot, you bastard!" Ziggy shouted back as he strode away down the narrow muddy pathway between the rows of tents.

"Captain of the guard!" the soldier yelled.

Ziggy kept walking, ignoring the man's shouts. Then a lumbering figure in a duffel coat stepped out from between a row of tents. It was Major Westerby again.

"Halt!" shouted the soldier.

"Oh, just leave him alone," said Westerby.

(24)

The next morning they were taken back to the empty mess tent, given breakfast, and then put aboard a twin-engine Dakota and flown to Rheims. The whole way, Ziggy sat in silence. Von Friedeburg had readopted his thousand-yard stare and the British delegation, which Ziggy noted did not include Westerby, kept their usual distance. When they landed several hours later, they were put into a green staff vehicle with a large white star on its side and driven directly to Supreme Headquarters.

Going to see Eisenhower! Ziggy felt a sudden elation. He supposed that every man in the German army had probably, at one time or another, fantasized about meeting Eisenhower. The great and famous General Ike; the American general with the German name; the man with the big friendly smile whom everyone in Germany alternately loved and hated. He was always grinning, an odd thing, since no German general would ever allow himself to be photographed that way. But good old General Ike smiled when he talked to Churchill or de Gaulle or any of the other bigwigs. He smiled when he was talking to ordinary soldiers. Ziggy remembered one time looking at a picture of him in a magazine, chatting with a Negro sergeant, as casually as two farmers talking about crop prices.

Supreme Headquarters turned out to be housed in a gray three-story school building. As they approached it, von Friedeburg emerged from his despondency and became animated. "Eisenhower will listen," he declared excitedly to Ziggy. "He'll understand what we're trying to do. I'm sure the reason Montgomery didn't was that he's only an army group commander. He didn't have any grasp of the political situation or its implications. But Eisenhower does. He'll understand."

As before, there was no honor guard or lined-up troops, only an unruly horde of uniformed journalists and press photographers, who were kept behind a velvet rope by a squad of white-helmeted military policemen brandishing polished nightsticks. Inside, a pair of grim-looking British and American colonels escorted them through the halls, past dozens of officers and enlisted men, all staring at them with murderous intent. Ziggy felt more in the presence of a lynch mob than a military high command. If this was what the office workers were like, then Ziggy figured they shouldn't expect anything much better from the big boss.

They were brought into a small room whose walls were filled with charts and battle maps. At a table before them sat two generals: a pleasant-looking Brit, and a sour-faced American. Neither looked at all like Ike. The British general pointed them to two chairs on the opposite side of the table. "I am General Strong," he told them. "And this is General Walter Bedell Smith, General Eisenhower's chief of staff." Von Friedeburg introduced himself, but the two only nodded perfunctorily.

Then von Friedeburg started to explain that he had been sent by the new head of the Reich, Grand Admiral Dönitz, to meet with General Eisenhower to arrange for a cessation of hostilities followed by the eventual complete surrender of German forces to the armies of the Western Allies. He told them how, with the breakdown in communication between units, the most effective thing would be a graduated progression of surrenders of intact units and the orderly handover of territory over several days. He added how they were not prepared to cease hostilities against Soviet forces because previous attempts to do so had invariably resulted in the wholesale massacre of surrendering soldiers along with the rape and murder of civilian women and children.

He went on to say how bad the refugee situation was, how desperately they needed food and medical supplies in order to avoid a humanitarian catastrophe. They also hoped the Western armies could move quickly into German territory before the Red armies occupied it.

Suddenly Bedell Smith put up his hand to stop him. "Before we go any further with these discussions, gentlemen, let me make one thing very clear to you," he said. "We are not going to discuss anything with you other than a complete unconditional surrender of all German forces on all fronts, including those facing Soviet forces. Now, are you prepared to sign an unconditional surrender or not?"

Von Friedeburg began to repeat his pleas for the refugees and the suffering civilian population, but Bedell Smith silenced him again. "Absolutely not," he snapped. "You must agree to an unconditional surrender on all fronts. No delays, no graduated surrenders, no ifs, ands, or buts."

So this is who the nice, smiling, where-you-from-soldier General Ike has doing his dirty work, thought Ziggy. It figured. He wondered how the old man could have sent anyone as basically mild-mannered as von Friedeburg up against an ogre like this. It was obvious Bedell Smith viewed von Friedeburg's presence as a public relations ploy to put a sympathetic human face on the Third Reich. Fact was, he detested von Friedeburg's niceness. Bedell Smith ate nice people for breakfast. All nice meant to him was weak.

"I thought we'd be discussing this with General Eisenhower," countered von Friedeburg.

Angrily Bedell Smith banged his fist on the table. "Admiral von Friedeburg," he said, "General Eisenhower is not interested in discussing anything with you or any other German, not until you've signed an unconditional surrender. And let me reiterate that it must be an unconditional simultaneous surrender to all the Allied armies. Anything short of that is unacceptable to us."

"But I'm not authorized to sign an unconditional surrender."

"So then why are we talking to you?"

"General," said von Friedeburg in a halting, trembling voice, "it appears you do not yet grasp the enormity of the threat that the West faces from the Soviets. At this moment the Red hordes are raping and murdering everything they can find."

Bedell Smith smiled pleasantly. "Well, I guess that is something your Führer should have considered before he made and then broke a pact with them."

"That may very well be true, General," said von Friedeburg. "But they are not going to stop just because the people they're facing are British and Americans. You must understand that they are not likely to wait very long before they turn their fury against the West. And if you wish to prevent the Red tide from continuing its sweep all over Europe, you'd be wise to attack them before they can regather their strength. General, Grand Admiral Dönitz is prepared to offer you more than a hundred German divisions to turn back that tide. Now, if I could just be allowed to speak to General Eisenhower and present our case—"

Bedell Smith sprang up from his chair. "I think I'll need to talk to General Eisenhower about this. Come with me, General Strong. If you'll excuse us, gentlemen." They got up and briskly walked out of the room, leaving Ziggy and von Friedeburg by themselves. "Maybe now we're getting somewhere," suggested von Friedeburg.

Ziggy got up and went over to examine the maps. "It's all lies anyway," von Friedeburg muttered. "You think they'd show us the real stuff? It's an old trick to make us think we're in a hopeless situation."

"We are in a hopeless situation," Ziggy pointed out.

"Perhaps," agreed von Friedeburg. "But not entirely hopeless. Now, if we can just get them to take us to Eisenhower."

"Do you think they will?"

Von Friedeburg didn't answer.

Then they heard excited voices coming down the corridor. As they got closer, Ziggy could make out one speaking quickly in thickly accented English. "General Bedell Smith, I must protest. This action is clearly intended to cut us out of the surrender negotiations and allow you to make a separate peace with the Germans at the expense of the Russian people!"

"General Susloparov," they heard Bedell Smith's voice answering, "if that is what you think, then I suggest you take your complaint directly to General Eisenhower. But we cannot let you participate in the surrender discussions."

"But why are you letting the British General Strong participate?"

"General Strong is my deputy. You, as a liaison officer, are not empowered to operate in anything but an advisory capacity. Now, if you'll excuse—"

"Then as an advisor I request that I be allowed to observe these discussions so that I can assure my government that no separate deals are being brokered behind the back of the Soviet Union."

"I'm sorry, General Susloparov, but that decision is General Eisenhower's."

"They tell me I cannot speak to him because he is asleep."

"General Eisenhower is under a lot of stress. I can assure you we're not cutting a deal with the Germans behind your back. Now, please, don't try gaining entry into this room. As soon as we know anything, I guarantee you I will explain it all to you personally."

"But General Bedell Smith—"

"Good day, General Susloparov."

A moment later the door opened and Bedell Smith and Strong reentered. "Gentlemen," said Bedell Smith, "your offer is out of the question. General Eisenhower has repeated that the only acceptable offer is of unconditional surrender on all fronts."

For several hours, Von Friedeburg tried again and again to engage the American general's sympathy. Each time, Bedell Smith let him say his piece and then promptly kicked the bricks out from under him. As it went on, Ziggy sat motionless, his hands folded on the table, an actor without lines, listening as the ideas went from German to English, English to German.

Finally Bedell Smith had had enough. He stood up and told von Friedeburg he was adjourning the negotiations for the day. They'd meet again at 0900 the next morning. But von Friedeburg remained seated. "May I say something to you, General Bedell Smith?" he asked.

"Go right ahead," answered the American flippantly.

"In all my years I have never treated a fellow officer with anything but courtesy and respect, regardless of whether or not he was my enemy. It has always been my understanding that in civilized society one should uphold certain standards of courteous behavior. The victor is supposed to treat the defeated not with rancor, but with magnanimity." Von Friedeburg stiffly got up from his chair, motioning for Ziggy to remain seated. He continued, "Now, I've come to you today representing a defeated nation whose armies have fought bravely and with honor and you treat me with no more consideration than a whipped dog. Why is that, General?"

Ziggy looked up at von Friedeburg, whose face was now shaking with indignation as angry tears welled in his eyes. Bedell Smith looked incredulously at von Friedeburg and let out a vicious laugh. "Why?" he asked, his face turning beet-red. "Why?" He held his hand up for von Friedeburg to return to his seat. Then he opened the door and shouted, "Burton, get me the latest issue of *Stars and Stripes*. And while you're at it, bring that file of photographs from Belsen. Move!"

A moment later someone came in with a newspaper and a thick photo file, which he gave to Bedell Smith. "Here, my fellow officer, take a look at these," Bedell Smith said to von Friedeburg, slamming them on the table.

NAZI MURDER CAMP LIBERATED, proclaimed the gigantic front-page headline. There was a photograph of people in striped clothing standing in front of some barbed wire next to a pile of something that Ziggy at first didn't recognize. Then, looking closer, he realized they were corpses. Von Friedeburg opened the photo file and they both began looking at the photographs. Seeing them, Ziggy blanched. After years of speculating about what went on there, he thought he'd at least be prepared. He was wrong. It was more horrible than anything he'd imagined.

One photograph showed a large pit, easily twenty meters long and ten wide, filled with bodies. They were so thin they hardly looked human. Arms strewn, legs spread, heads shaved, some still wearing striped blue and white prisoner's uniforms, but most naked and not looking like anything. There was a photograph, obviously taken quite some time before the Allied liberation, of an SS unteroffizer smiling proudly before a cart on which twenty bodies had been piled like cordwood. Another showed bearded prisoners kneeling before a corpse-filled ditch while an SS officer stood behind them, holding a pistol to the neck of one prisoner. Some showed limp bodies caught on barbed-wire fences; in others there were dead women, hundreds of dead children, charred bodies in crematoria. The dead ones at least looked dead. It was the images of those still alive that looked most horrifying. They were so emaciated they no longer seemed to have a discernible gender. Their eyes stared out uncomprehendingly. Having long since reconciled themselves to joining the others on the dead pile, they were no longer capable of expressing anything now that they'd been miraculously granted a reprieve. But from the look of them, it was easy to see they wouldn't long survive their liberation.

Ziggy couldn't take any more. He felt the welling and tightening in his stomach and he knew he couldn't hold it. He tried to get out from his chair, but before he could, the sick rushed up his throat and he began hurling his guts out onto the floor.

"Forgive me," he mumbled. He looked over at Bedell Smith and saw the thin, satisfied smile crossing his lips. But von Friedeburg didn't notice any of it. His eyes were riveted by the photographs. Slowly, gravely, he examined each one in turn, wincing at the sight of each new atrocity, but never averting his eyes. Like a blackmail victim examining incriminating photographs of himself, he stared transfixed, as if they were perversely already familiar to him.

Bedell Smith pointed at one. "And these are the gas chambers that they'd use to kill upwards of a hundred at a time. In order to get them in there they had them made to look like—"

But von Friedeburg finished the sentence for him. "Showers," he said weakly. "I know."

It went on like this for another twenty minutes, with Bedell Smith providing commentary where he felt necessary. Finally von Friedeburg was finished. Bedell Smith put the photographs back in the folder. "Anything you want to say, Herr Admiral?"

Von Friedeburg said nothing.

"Perhaps you'd like to tell us you had no idea, that you didn't know a thing."

Von Friedeburg looked away.

"Go ahead! It's what all you Nazi bastards are claiming! Say it!"

Von Friedeburg shook his head slowly and looked back up again at Bedell Smith. "What would be the point, General?" he asked.

"So you knew about it?"

"What do you want from me?" von Friedeburg asked.

"I want at least one of you Nazi rats to start admitting your responsibility."

"General, I only came here to surrender," said von Friedeburg. "Is this why General Eisenhower won't see us?"

"Yes."

Tears were streaming from von Friedeburg's eyes, but he forced his expression into stonelike impassivity. "I guess we'll be going now," he said.

"Go on, get out of my sight," hissed Bedell Smith. "I'll send for you when I want you."

Von Friedeburg got up from his chair. Bedell Smith reached for the folder, but von Friedeburg put his hand on it. "If you don't mind, I'd like to look at it some more," he said.

"Be my guest," answered Bedell Smith.

As they were leaving, they saw a Russian officer standing expectantly in the hall. He was a tall, thin, bald-headed man, not much older than Ziggy. As they passed, he glared at Ziggy as if greatly offended that Ziggy had not recognized him.

"Who is he?" Ziggy asked the escorting officer.

"That's General Susloparov, the Russian liaison officer. Does he know you?"

"I'm sure I've never seen him in my life," said Ziggy.

❨ 25 ❩

They were driven to a chateau for high-ranking visitors. Once inside the suite, Ziggy took von Friedeburg's hat and helped him out of his overcoat and jacket. "I guess I owe you an apology, Captain Loerber," said von Friedeburg. Then he went into the bathroom, closing the door behind him. Taking it as a dismissal, Ziggy went into the sitting room and saw that a table had been set up for them with two covered platters along with a water pitcher and glasses. He lifted one of the lids to find underneath a large steaming plate with roast beef, potatoes, carrots, and some leafy green vegetable he didn't recognize.

Von Friedeburg emerged a minute later and sat down across from Ziggy. They ate in silence, with a businesslike fixity of purpose. When they finished, Ziggy placed the dirty dishes and silverware on an empty cart left behind for that purpose and wheeled it out into the corridor. There, under the steely gaze of a helmeted soldier, waited another cart, this one with a white porcelain coffeepot, two mugs, and a bottle of cheap cognac on a tray. Ziggy picked up the tray and brought it inside. "We might as well be comfortable, Herr Admiral," he said. Von Friedeburg nodded without enthusiasm and they repaired to the coffee table. Ziggy set the tray down and poured coffee into the mugs. Then he uncorked the cognac and held it up to the admiral. Von Friedeburg nodded and Ziggy topped off both cups and placed one in front of him.

For several minutes Ziggy waited while von Friedeburg sat

motionless, staring at his cup. "Please don't wait for me, Captain," he said finally. Then he got up and went back into his room, returning a minute later with the folder. He sat back down and began studying the photographs a second time.

Seeing them, Ziggy immediately felt the queasiness return and, rather than go through another round, he stood up with his cup, gave the admiral a short, deferential bow, and said, "I'll be next door if you need me, Herr Admiral."

But von Friedeburg put up his hand. "Please don't go, Captain Loerber. I'd rather you stay here with me."

Ziggy returned to his chair and watched the admiral pore over the pictures. What's compelling him to do this? Just tell them you didn't know about it and keep repeating it until they drop the subject. It doesn't matter that they won't actually believe you. On the scale of all the guilty Germans out there, you barely rate.

But von Friedeburg wouldn't let it go. He kept staring at the mounds of corpses and the pits with the half-burned bodies, at the shaved heads, the dead eyes. Ziggy could see the anger and indignation building in him. His head began trembling and Ziggy knew another breakdown was on its way. Von Friedeburg probably knew it as well, but he had to look. Before he would act again as the grand admiral's plenipotentiary, he wanted to know all about the barbarity that he was now representing.

Ziggy knew he had to get him to stop or tomorrow was going to be a disaster. "Maybe you shouldn't do this, Herr Admiral," he said.

Von Friedeburg put down the folder. "So now we see what dwells behind duty and honor. I guess from now on, whenever anybody talks about Germany, this is what they will talk about first, before Goethe or Schiller or Beethoven," he said. "I can't say we won't deserve it."

He stared at Ziggy. "A couple years ago I went with a group of other military officers to an industrialists' conference on manpower and war production. There was a presentation about one factory director's experience using slave labor as a way of coping with the shortage of skilled workers. As I recall, they built rocket motors. Their initial problem was that the people they were getting weren't particularly skilled, even though many turned out to be quite educated. They'd start training them, but getting any of them up to speed took too long and by then most had died either of malnutrition or overwork, so they were never able to return the investment that had been put into their training. Since they weren't willing to consider feeding them better or not working them to death, the only apparent solution was to simplify the manufacturing processes to the point that they could be carried out by people as they were dying.

"They presented charts detailing the rate slave laborers' productivity would drop off as they weakened and died. You see, using the previous manufacturing processes, they were only able to work them from the fifty-five to the forty-seven percent range, after which they were too weak to do much useful work. But then they showed how, *aha!*, once they simplified certain key manufacturing steps, the slaves could keep it going until they were down to the twenty-three percent level. After that they would be removed and discarded and replaced by someone else. When they'd finished, everyone in the room applauded their wonderful breakthrough in industrial organization. So did we, because it was the proper thing to do.

"And I sat there listening to it and part of me started doing the math: how many people they were talking about training and replacing per month. Between the levels of output and the numbers of different factories involved, it was coming out to something like sixteen thousand workers being worked to death a month. And I thought about it for a second, but then I put it out of my mind.

"We all just sat there, not looking at each other, not raising our eyebrows or registering shock. We just pretended what they were talking about was nothing more sinister than the replacement of some worn-out pistons or machine tools, a purely technical matter possessing no moral dimension whatsoever."

Ziggy saw his opportunity to step in and put an end to von Friedeburg's confession while the admiral still had it together. "Admiral," he began, "what you did was what everyone else around you did. Okay, so you sat back and didn't speak up. You'd been in the navy for, what, thirty years, what were you supposed to do? Your job was to lead your men and obey orders. Navies aren't set up to allow you to pick which orders you'd like to obey. Sir, what you did really wasn't that bad."

Von Friedeburg looked hard at Ziggy. "Captain Loerber, just let me finish before you absolve me of my guilt. You see, after the conference was over, a group of us were all sitting together at a table over drinks, when one of the admirals from the shipyards' directorate did speak up. 'I don't know about you, but I don't want our U-boats to be built like that. It's dishonorable and if nothing else, it's unlucky.' The man was enraged. I remember how red his face got. 'How can they even talk like that?' he said to us. 'If they want them to work longer they should just feed them. What's so big a problem with that? It isn't as if the food isn't there. You see what those Nazi Party fat cats are keeping for themselves. It's disgusting,' he said.

"We all looked embarrassedly at each other, none of us knowing what to say. And you know what I did, Captain Loerber? I told the man to shut his mouth! That we were in a war for the survival of the German race and that tough, temporary measures must be taken to ensure victory and that once things started going again in our favor, surely we would alleviate those extreme measures and feed them better.

"'Admiral,' he said to me, 'that's a lie and you know it. The whole point is that they want to brutalize them and starve them to death. They'd rather be inefficient and cruel than efficient and humane.'

"And as soon as I got back, I reported him. I never found out what happened, whether he'd been arrested or not, but two days later he shot himself. And you know something, Captain? I put that out of my mind too. I didn't bother remembering any of it until now." He waved his hand to dismiss Ziggy. "Good night, Captain Loerber."

(26)

Ziggy went to one of the windows and pulled aside the curtains. As he reached to close the window, he noticed freshly marked graffiti on the side of the neighboring chateau: two parallel lines and a circle in the upper left corner. Why would anyone do that? he wondered.

Behind him, someone cleared his throat. Ziggy turned and there at the other end of the room, pointing a pistol at him, stood the Russian general. He was smiling at Ziggy as though they were the best of friends.

"So, Loerber, it would seem Reichsführer Himmler has allowed you to join the navy," he said.

"I beg your pardon," said Ziggy.

Susloparov shook his head gently as he stepped closer. "How many chances have we given you to come back to us? We've been more than generous, I'd say."

"I don't know what you're talking about," said Ziggy.

"Your first mistake was thinking you could give material to London without being caught. The second was not telling us about Source Moonpool."

Ziggy looked at the pistol pointing at him and at the smiling Russian general. He doubted that explaining to him that he wasn't Franzi would help much.

"You've put me in a difficult situation, Loerber," said the Russian. With his free hand he reached into his coat pocket and took out a large cigarette lighter and extended it toward Ziggy.

Suddenly Ziggy thought of something. Fixing his eyes onto the Russian's, he muttered, "There's some cigarettes over there," pointing toward the table with his chin. Just as he was beginning to squeeze the lighter, Susloparov glanced over at the table, causing his hand to dip slightly. Something tiny flew out of the lighter, missing Ziggy by a few inches and striking the wall behind him with a nearly inaudible plink.

The Russian cursed and raised his pistol so that it was pointing at Ziggy's head. "Don't move," he growled. As he fumbled with the lighter, trying to reset it, someone quietly stepped out from behind the curtains.

Susloparov's mouth dropped open as the pistol suddenly tumbled out of his hand and onto the floor. Then the general's eyes rolled back and he collapsed onto the carpet.

Ziggy stared at Susloparov lying peacefully on the floor, then looked up at the man who'd been hiding behind the curtain. He recognized him at once: it was Sebastian.

"Quick," he said to Ziggy. "We've got to get out of here!" He bent down over Susloparov and picked up the pistol and the lighter. "Check the corridor. See if anyone's out there."

Ziggy went over to the door and poked his head out. For once, the corridors were empty. He wondered how all the MPs could have disappeared just when the Russian had decided to come in and kill him. He closed the door. "It's clear," he said. Sebastian was still kneeling over the general, taking things from his pockets. "Is he dead?" asked Ziggy.

"No, but he's going to wish he was when he wakes up in an hour," Sebastian said with a chuckle. He held up a pair of very heavy-looking handcuffs. "Look what I found," he said.

Then a wicked grin came over Sebastian's face. "I've got an idea," he said. He pointed to the half-empty cognac bottle on the sideboard. "Bring that over here," he said.

Ziggy handed it to him and Sebastian poured some of it on the Russian's clothes, then opened his mouth and poured more in. "That's it," he said. "Everybody loves a drunken Russian."

They dragged him outside into the still-empty corridor. Sebastian snapped one cuff over Susloparov's right wrist and was about to clamp it around the other when Ziggy stopped him. "I've got a better idea," he whispered.

They dragged him over to the staircase, looped the Russian's manacled arm around the banister post, then pulled out his left leg and snapped the remaining cuff around his left ankle, leaving him hog-tied.

"There," declared Sebastian. "You're a genius."

He went back inside and returned with a trench coat, which he helped Ziggy put on and then handed him a slouchy-looking hat. As long as no one looked down and noticed his Kriegsmarine dress trousers and boots, they'd never think he was anything but a civilian.

They ran downstairs and then out the back of the building and over a wall in the back garden, jumping down into an alley. Sebastian led the way, keeping an eye on all the back windows of the houses they passed while Ziggy kept a few steps behind him, watching their back.

Once out on the street, they walked for several blocks looking for someplace where they could lay low for an hour, but all the cafés were full of British and American military. Finally they found one off on a side street, empty but for a handful of locals. They took a table and when the elderly waiter came, Sebastian ordered them coffee. As they waited, he took out Susloparov's cigarette lighter, placed it on the table, and pushed it over so Ziggy could examine it. "It's the sort of thing the Russians use on troublesome people," he explained. "It's got poison darts inside. They wanted to kill you without making a lot of noise."

"Kill me? You mean kill Franzi," said Ziggy.

"You're a Loerber Brother. It's the business we're in," Sebastian answered, with a sardonic lift of his eyebrows.

"So what were you doing behind that curtain?" asked Ziggy.

"I was waiting for you."

"What about him? You hadn't known he was coming?"

Sebastian shook his head. "Mere coincidence."

"Ah," answered Ziggy. The Loerber Brothers had a way of attracting coincidence.

"Lucky for me I got there five minutes before he did," said Sebastian. He flipped open a cigarette case and offered it to Ziggy before taking one himself. Then he pulled out a lighter, a Ronson, Ziggy noted, like General Kinzel's.

"What I don't get is why they'd send a big wheel like him after me," said Ziggy.

"You mean after Franzi."

"Right. But wouldn't you think he'd have been afraid that if something went wrong there'd be a big stir with Eisenhower?"

"There'll be a much bigger stir if Franzi starts telling what he knows."

"Is Franzi really that important?"

"Ziggy, right now he's wanted more than Himmler himself."

The waiter brought their coffee and left. Ziggy stared into his cup and the small white ceramic jars of sugar and milk. The war wasn't over yet and even a run-down French café like this one had coffee, and milk and sugar to go with it.

"I'm sure it's all been stolen from the Americans," said Sebastian. For a moment Ziggy wondered whether his brother had read his mind.

"I didn't have to read your mind for that. It's all pretty obvious," said Sebastian.

Ziggy glared at Sebastian. Sebastian looked back, exasperated. "Look, Ziggy, I'm on a job and I don't have the time or energy to turn it on or off just to be polite."

"On a job?"

"I'm with the Blood of Israel. We have to get Franzi out."

Sebastian leaned forward. "Let me ask you this, Ziggy. Have you thought about what's going to happen to us now that the war is over and the Nazis are beaten?"

"Us as in the Loerber Brothers?" asked Ziggy.

Sebastian gripped the table with both hands. "No, goddammit! Us as in the Jews!"

"Oh."

"Yes, we're the ones who've suffered the most in this war and now we're about to be conveniently forgotten. The West should be standing up for us, but let's face it, they'll be the first ones to act like the whole thing never happened. And where is that going to leave us? With nothing."

Ziggy nodded impassively. He particularly dreaded Sebastian's didactic discussions where the point was waiting, hidden somewhere among a minefield of polemics.

"Ziggy, the Jewish people need a homeland. The West owes it to us, for sitting on their thumbs while millions of us got butchered. But do you think they feel any obligation toward us? Hah! They're too busy cutting cozy deals with the SS to help fight their war against the Russians. It's not in their interest to acknowledge what we've been through."

Ziggy tried hard to imagine Bedell Smith cutting a deal with the SS, but he guessed the point would be lost on Sebastian. "What does this have to do with Franzi?" he asked.

"I'm coming to that, Ziggy. My point is that they're not going to give us our homeland out of niceness or guilt. The only way they'll do it is if we have a dagger at their throats. And with all the dirt Franzi has on everybody, they'll give us anything we ask for just to keep it from getting out."

Sebastian brought the coffee cup to his lips, but once it was there he put it back on its saucer without tasting it. "Listen to me, Ziggy. I can't do this alone. I'm going to need your help."

"Have you thought about using Manni for this? He seems like a better bet than me."

"No," said Sebastian, with surprising vehemence. "I can't work with Manni."

"Not even for Franzi?"

"No."

Neither said anything for a while. They drank their coffee and looked around the room. Outside, the sun was starting to set. Ziggy hoped von Friedeburg hadn't woken up yet.

Then Sebastian looked at Ziggy. "You think I like getting dragged back into all that Loerber crap? Believe me, I was a lot more eager to get away from it than you were. And magic? I only started doing the stuff with the dreams a couple months ago. I hate doing it, but you know something? This is war and in a war you use the weapons you have. Dreams sow terror in goyim hearts and that is priceless."

"I take it you don't care much for goyim," said Ziggy.

"I don't hate them per se, but I'm not going to pretend to be one just to save my lousy skin."

Ziggy felt the barb strike him. "I didn't do it to save my skin," he shot back.

Sebastian arched an eyebrow. "Oh? So then why did you go into the navy?"

Ziggy looked away. He thought about Lüth and Cremer. He thought about poor old von Friedeburg having his fitful sleep on that bed and what Dönitz had said to him on the bridge and all the men who'd kept his secret, all dead now, except for Cremer. I'd joined to prove I could be a good German, he thought, and no one could say I wasn't. And he thought about all the photographs and all the bodies. He looked back at Sebastian and thought, At least he'll never need to justify his sanctimoniousness.

"Sebastian, what do you want me to say? I made that choice twelve years ago. You can't change the past."

"But don't you see, that's where you're wrong," cried Sebastian. "You can join us. Put your past behind you and be what you always were: a Jew."

Be a Jew. Ziggy felt overwhelmed by the sheer simplicity of the idea. It felt right, the way it had echoed in his heart, sitting in temple when he was young, like waves on the ocean. It was also perfectly absurd. "Sebastian, I'm a U-boat captain." He pulled open the neck of his trench coat so his brother could see his Iron Cross. "Brilliants, swords, and oak leaves, Sebastian. There's no wiping that slate clean."

Sebastian shook his head. "Come on, Ziggy. You think you're the only one who did things they're ashamed of? Almost anyone who survived the camps did terrible things, Ziggy, things that make you look like a saint. You know what we tell them? We say, stop blaming yourself for what you had to do. Quit torturing yourself for the things that were outside your control. All that we demand is that you be a Jew among Jews."

"In Palestine?"

"Yes, of course, it's the only place we can ever be safe."

Sebastian sounded so convincing that even though Ziggy knew what he was saying had to be full of holes, he couldn't think of any arguments to the contrary. "So I take it you have a plan," he said.

"Well, yes, but it's not completely worked out."

"Explain what *is* worked out."

"Well," began Sebastian, "we know Himmler has set up his headquarters in a chateau a few miles outside Flensburg. The time to go in is now, while there are enough people that it'll still be easy to confuse them. By tomorrow they may have moved on to somewhere else. We've got a plane waiting, we could be there before midnight. We both put on SS uniforms, distract, confuse, act as decoys for each other. Get in close, grab him, get him out, like that!"

"It sounds harebrained," said Ziggy.

"We've pulled off more with less."

Ziggy nodded. It was true.

"It won't be without problems," said Sebastian. "Himmler's got a guy working for him named Macher. He's a particularly tough nut."

"I know, I've met him," said Ziggy.

Palestine. The idea had potential. Certainly there wouldn't be much point in staying in Germany. He didn't see why the Allies would be interested in rebuilding it. For all he knew, they'd let it revert to cow pasture. In Palestine, he'd be just another pioneer refugee, not a Magical Loerber Brother, not Hitler's Jewish U-boat ace. He could live with that.

Wipe the slate clean. Everything that had happened in the last ten years didn't happen at all or it happened to someone else, someone who lay dead on the bottom of the Atlantic in his iron coffin, or something very nearly like it.

They talked about it some more, the logistics, the weapons they had, the size of Himmler's force. Sebastian seemed to have a lot of backup manpower at his disposal. Some were already in the area disguised as Wehrmacht, others as British.

He watched Sebastian holding the coffee cup to his lips as he spoke. The sophistication he exuded was so natural, Ziggy could hardly reconcile it with the rough, fumbling affectations that had defined his memory of him. But then, we've all become some-thing else, made by the times and circumstances we've intersected with. Even the ships I sank, the ones I watched burn and break up, and making myself stand there on the bridge, listening to the cries for help I could not render, knowing myself at my most cruel and predatory, none of it will matter once it's put behind me. A memory is inherently false, frozen in time, yet endlessly buffeted by shifting context.

"If we're going to do it, we need to get going now," Sebastian said quietly.

"Right," said Ziggy. His throat felt constricted. He pushed the chair back and got to his feet, suddenly feeling like he was slip-ping off a trapeze. "I have to go back now."

Sebastian looked at him, but didn't say anything.

"Thanks for saving my life," Ziggy said and quickly went out the door.

(27)

The MPs were conspicuously back in place when Ziggy returned to the chateau. Though they regarded him with surprise and suspicion as he went up the stairs, none of them said anything. As he expected, there was no trace of General Susloparov anywhere. He settled back into one of the chairs and pulled off his boots. A little while later the inner door opened and von Friedeburg appeared at the threshold, looking worn and disoriented. "There was some noise an hour or so ago," he said. "Was something going on?"

"We had visitors. The Russian general came by," Ziggy answered.

"The Russian general? What did he want?"

"He thought he knew me, wanted to talk about old Berlin. I think he was drunk."

The explanation seemed to satisfy von Friedeburg. He turned and went back inside his room without bothering to shut the door. Ziggy walked over and looked in from the doorway. The folder was still open and the death camp photographs were spread all over the table, couch, and bed. "I know I shouldn't, but I couldn't stop looking at them," von Friedeburg said.

"You need to get some sleep, Admiral," said Ziggy, with more than a hint of authority. "You won't be any good to anyone if you're not fit tomorrow."

"I know," said von Friedeburg quietly.

Ziggy stepped in and began gathering up the photographs. "Now try to sleep," he said.

"I will," said von Friedeburg. "Just leave the folder."

"I'll tell you what, Admiral. You get some sleep and I'll look at the photographs." He could see von Friedeburg didn't like being countermanded. "Sir, I insist," he added.

Von Friedeburg stared hard at Ziggy.

"Grand Admiral Dönitz's orders, sir," said Ziggy.

Finally von Friedeburg acquiesced. "I suppose I should try to sleep."

"Good night, Admiral," said Ziggy firmly. "I'll see you in the morning."

Ziggy closed the door and stepped back into the sitting room. He stood by the window and had a cigarette. Looking out into the city, he tried to imagine what would have happened had he gone with Sebastian: a several-block walk to a safe house, guy inside who doesn't introduce himself, a phone call, a car shows up, two guys besides the driver. The only one who speaks calls himself Mordechai, or Schmuel, or Yitzhak. Small transport aircraft, probably one-engine, American markings. Somewhere in the process he's told to discard his uniform and given something nondescript to wear. After several hours of noisy, cramped flight during which nobody talks, they put down on an airstrip where everyone is in Wehrmacht feldgrau, though in unguarded moments they might here and there be heard whispering to each other in Yiddish. Behold: The Blood of Israel.

Stop, Ziggy told himself. He watched the subject slip from his mind, and knew he'd probably never think about it seriously again. He crushed his cigarette against the outside casement ledge and went to bed.

The next morning, just as Ziggy had feared, Admiral von Friedeburg was a mess. Throughout breakfast, he stared into the distance and mumbled things to himself while poking listlessly at his eggs and bacon with his fork. When they were brought back to Eisenhower's headquarters, Bedell Smith took one look at him and, slamming his files down on the table, snorted loudly, "This is ridiculous," and stormed out of the room. General Strong followed him out, turning to say, "Excuse us," as he did.

Von Friedeburg shut his eyes and began rubbing his eyelids with his thumb and middle finger. "I'm sorry," he said numbly. "I just . . ." Then his voice trailed off, but he made no further attempt at finishing the sentence.

The door swung open and General Strong came back in, looking embarrassed. He carried a small spiral notebook and a pencil. "I'm sorry," he said, "but General Eisenhower has decided that Admiral von Friedeburg is no longer acceptable to continue these surrender negotiations. We would like you to compose an *en clair* message to Grand Admiral Dönitz informing him of this and requesting he immediately send another representative, this one with the necessary power to sign a comprehensive surrender to all Allied forces in the theater." He handed the notebook to Ziggy. "I'll be back in five minutes," he said, giving Ziggy a significant glance.

Placing the notebook squarely between them to suggest collaboration, Ziggy wrote out in large individual letters a brief message, repeating Eisenhower's request, but giving little explanation as to its cause. Von Friedeburg looked on vaguely as Ziggy wrote, nodding his final approval. A minute later Strong came back, looked at the message, and, apparently satisfied, took it away.

An hour later, Strong brought back Dönitz's reply. He was sending General Jodl, head of the Armed Forces High Command's operations staff, to sign the surrender. An aircraft had already been dispatched from Montgomery's headquarters to fly him immediately to Rheims. Rereading the message, Ziggy was puzzled. Why Jodl? The man was a toad, an ass-licker, universally despised by the rank-and-file of the military. The only reason Ziggy could imagine Dönitz would turn to him was that, seeing that further negotiations were not possible, he'd decided to spare the navy the ignominy of surrender and had given the task back to Hitler's yes-men.

After they had been driven back to the chateau, von Friedeburg told Ziggy he wanted to lie down. Ziggy helped him out of his coat and boots and waited until he had closed his eyes before withdrawing to the sitting room, taking the admiral's boots with him. He drew a chair to the window and, with a piece of rag he found in a drawer, sat down and began cleaning the dirt and caked mud from the boots and polishing the black leather as well as he could.

As he worked the rag over the leather, Ziggy remembered his earliest days in the U-boat arm when he and Cremer were ensigns under Lüth, the first time they'd sunk a freighter, how they'd come to the surface and watched the ship slowly break apart as dozens of men struggled in the water. Having done what they'd come for, Ziggy naturally expected they'd revert to the ancient rules of the brotherhood of the sea and rescue the ship's crew, bandage their wounds, refloat their capsized lifeboats, give them food and water and a compass heading to the nearest land. He especially expected them to since Lüth had a reputation as the most humane and paternalistic U-boat captain.

But Lüth wouldn't let them. "We don't do that, Ensign Loerber," he had said. "They are the enemy. It's kill or be killed. Our water, our food, our medicine was given to us by the sweat of the German people's brow. It is not to be shared with the enemy. We have no room for them aboard our boat. If you find it too horrible to watch, Ensign, simply avert your eyes to their suffering. Let them die."

Ziggy remembered how shocked he was that Lüth could be so compartmentalized. The simple answer was that Lüth, a fervent Nazi, was callous and indifferent to the suffering of people who were not like himself. But true as this might be, the deeper reality was that, even if he'd wanted to, a U-boat's margin for survival was so narrow, any attempt at mercy was mostly an exercise in self-deception. The survivors' own ships were afraid of stopping to rescue them for fear of getting torpedoed in the process. More than once, U-boats attempting to rescue large numbers of enemy sailors by allowing them to crowd on their decks became targets for marauding enemy aircraft. To think that sailors in a lifeboat would live long enough to reach land hundreds of miles away was sheer fantasy. Eventually Ziggy got his own command, and though he swore he'd do things differently, it wasn't long before he was doing exactly the same. His heart may not have been as cold as Lüth's, but for the torpedoed sailors they didn't help, it didn't make any difference.

There was a knock on the door. Ziggy set the boots aside and stood up as two MPs wheeled in a metal cart with covered plates, which they placed on the table along with a water jug and some glasses before leaving and closing the door behind them. Ziggy considered waking up von Friedeburg, but decided against it. Instead he sat down at the table and helped himself to one of the plates. When he was finished, he returned to the window, smoking cigarettes as he stared out at the garden.

The spring was much further along here in Rheims than back in Germany. The leaves on the trees were already full and for the most part the blossoms were gone. Ziggy turned away from the window and saw the folder with the photographs on the table. He'd promised the admiral he'd look at them. He really should, he told himself. *I could have been any one of those people.* Except for his luck, except for old Gustav's endless glad-handing of Nazi leaders. *If you find it too horrible to watch, Ensign, simply avert your eyes to their suffering.* Ziggy decided to follow Lüth's advice. He may have been a Nazi, but he was the best captain Ziggy had ever served under. No commander ever cared more about his men than Wolfgang Lüth.

Ziggy wasn't sure exactly when it was that he'd spilled his guts about being a Jew. It had to have been at La Rochelle, during one of the drunken nights he'd spent with his friends going between bars and whorehouses. After four patrols, the terror of depth-charging had gotten to him and, once ashore, all he wanted to do was stay drunk and fuck his brains out. All sorts of things must have come out then. He had no idea which bar or brothel they had been in, or who was there when he'd unloaded his secret. All he knew was that two weeks into their next Atlantic patrol, while sharing a bridge watch with him, Cremer said, "You know, Loerber, next time you start praying aloud in a whorehouse, try not to do it in Hebrew."

Ziggy had blanched, but Cremer just laughed. "Oh, relax, Loerber, you think you're the only one? Well, you're not."

"Who?" asked Ziggy, in even bigger shock. Somehow he'd assumed he had to be the only Jew in the navy.

"Never mind who."

"Who else knows?"

"Who else? Jesus, everybody, Ziggy."

"Does Lüth?"

Cremer snickered. "The old man in a whorehouse? I don't think so."

He continued to eye the folder, wondering what Lüth would have done if he'd found out. Which set of his ideals would he have remained true to? *Simply avert your eyes.* No, to hell with that! Ziggy reached over and opened the folder and started paging through the photographs, the dead, the dying, the mutilated.

Who were these people? None of them looked like they'd ever been anything but victims, slaves. Had they been shopkeepers? Businessmen? Scholars, lawyers, tradesmen? Bankers, landlords, pimps, second-story artists with flashy suits and none-too-savory goy business associates? Why not? We were all across the spectrum. But for better or worse, they'd died as Jews, Poles, Gypsies, and queers.

And here I am wailing prayers to Jerusalem in whorehouses!

Eventually von Friedeburg emerged from his room, yawning and looking better than he had in days. Without saying anything to Ziggy he sat down, picked up his knife and fork, and began eating hungrily, pausing only to pour himself water from the jug. When he finished, he pushed away his plate and looked at Ziggy. "Well, I guess we're really in a mess now," he said in a flat voice. "I've failed the grand admiral. He was counting on me."

Ziggy fixed him with a droll smile. Compared to the state of everything else, Dönitz's disappointment had to rank fairly low. "Honestly, sir, I'm not sure the situation could have been improved or worsened. The grand admiral must understand this. Besides, the best you could have done was play for time. In that sense you succeeded."

"I don't know what I'm going to say to General Jodl," said von Friedeburg.

"Jodl? Screw him!"

Von Friedeburg gave a thin smile.

"But you're feeling better now, sir?" Ziggy asked.

"I'm relieved the job is off my shoulders," said von Friedeburg without embarrassment. "Have you any cigarettes?"

Ziggy lit two from the pack he'd taken from Westerby and handed one to von Friedeburg. For a long time neither said anything. Finally von Friedeburg took a long drag and said, "Well, at least we gave them a good run for their money."

"Yes, Herr Admiral, we certainly did."

"It's too bad we couldn't have gotten those Type XXIs out sooner, we might have made a real difference with them."

"Yes," said Ziggy. "We would have shown them a real good time."

"So what do you think will become of Germany?" von Friedeburg asked. "Will the victors divide it up among them? Will we ever be anything but a slave state?"

"I wish I knew, Herr Admiral."

"Can we ever regain our honor?"

"Probably not," said Ziggy. He looked at von Friedeburg, trying to gauge whether another collapse was looming. But von Friedeburg seemed calm enough.

There was a knock on the door. It opened and an MP stepped in. "General Smith wants you back at headquarters."

(28)

More like a bold conqueror than the emissary of a defeated nation, Colonel General Alfred Jodl strode into Supreme Allied Headquarters, determined that Eisenhower was going to see it his way. Unlike his more somberly dressed predecessor, Jodl, in his splendid gray and silver uniform, radiated confidence.

Accompanying him was a tall major with the narrow, pointed face of a greyhound. Jodl noted the admiring stares from all the American and British officers and men and he told himself that this would be a glorious moment.

The escorts led them to a small waiting room. Stepping inside, he saw the sunken-faced von Friedeburg sitting with his aide. Pathetic, he thought.

Ziggy nudged von Friedeburg, who hadn't reacted to their entry. Both got to their feet. "General Jodl," said von Friedeburg.

"Heil Hitler!" Jodl declared triumphantly. Neither man made any effort to salute, nor did they shake hands. Instead they regarded each other with palpable distaste. "This is my aide, Major Oxenius," Jodl said, and the major snapped into a *Heil Hitler* salute. "So what is the situation here, Admiral?" Jodl asked.

"The situation, Herr General," answered von Friedeburg, "is that they are not accepting any conditions whatsoever and all we've been able to do is delay."

"But haven't you explained to Eisenhower that we want to help them fight the Bolsheviks?" Jodl asked.

"General, we haven't even seen Eisenhower," answered von Friedeburg tiredly.

Jodl looked shocked. "That's utterly unacceptable," he said hotly. "You should have insisted you speak directly with him. I'm going to make that my first point."

Von Friedeburg gave a listless smile.

"What else?" Jodl asked.

"There isn't anything else," von Friedeburg answered. "All our appeals have fallen on deaf ears. Either we sign an unconditional surrender immediately or they say they will seal off the western frontier and start shooting refugees and anyone trying to surrender."

"But don't they want our help against the Bolsheviks? Didn't you offer them our divisions?"

"General, at present the Soviet Union is not their enemy, we are. If the West is planning a war against the Soviets, they have evidently not informed anyone in this building about it."

Jodl looked at him, astounded. "Are they crazy? Don't they understand what they face? Didn't you tell them what the Russians are doing?"

"General, I tried," said von Friedeburg in a hopeless voice. "Apparently they consider us a greater evil than the Bolsheviks."

There was a sharp knock on the door and then it opened. A British major stood in the doorway, flanked by two MPs. "General Jodl, if you'd come with us, please," he said.

"Best of luck, General," said von Friedeburg without enthusiasm. "I hope they'll listen to you."

Jodl shot him an ugly glance and strode out. Ziggy closed the door. Von Friedeburg settled himself onto the leather sofa, then pointed Ziggy and Oxenius to two tiny chairs. "Gentlemen," he said.

They sat down. Oxenius dug into his inner pocket and brought out his engraved cigarette case, which he offered first to von Friedeburg, then to Ziggy. Both refused. Oxenius lit one for himself and, seeing that neither of them was going to initiate a conversation, stopped trying to act sociable and turned to the door.

Hours passed. Nobody said anything. It was already late afternoon. Finally, Jodl returned, looking exhausted. "Who is this Walter Bedell Smith?" he asked disgustedly. "I don't believe I've ever heard of the man before. He wouldn't budge on anything regarding the conditions of surrender. I did manage, however, to get them to agree to some significant changes in the wording of the surrender document. They will acknowledge that the German armed forces have fought honorably. It's not much, but it's something. Damn it, we deserve at least that!"

Von Friedeburg seemed impressed. "You are a better negotiator than I am, General."

Jodl smiled bitterly.

"So then what's next?" asked von Friedeburg.

"Bedell Smith is having a meeting with Eisenhower," said Jodl. "When it's over, I suppose we'll meet again to agree on the final details."

There was another knock on the door. An American sergeant brought in a bottle of whiskey and several glasses. "General Strong sends his compliments," he said.

Oxenius took the whiskey and glasses from him and brought them inside. Jodl looked over at the bottle. "Pour some for everyone, would you, Major?" he said. "I'm not going to bother offering a toast."

"How about to the German army for fighting honorably?" suggested Oxenius helpfully as he poured whiskey into their glasses and handed them out.

"Yes, a splendid idea, Major," said Jodl, brightening a little. "Gentlemen," he said, raising his glass and waiting for the others to do the same. "To the German Wehrmacht for fighting honorably."

They emptied their glasses. Oxenius refilled them and they drank again. Then, as they were putting their glasses down, von

Friedeburg fixed Jodl with a friendly smile. "So, did General Bedell Smith show you any photographs?"

For a second Jodl froze. Then he glowered at von Friedeburg. "What of it?" he asked.

"So then you saw them?"

"Yes, I saw them."

Von Friedeburg's smile turned into a lunatic leer. "Pretty nasty stuff, wouldn't you say, Herr General?"

Jodl stared at him with visible displeasure. "War is nasty stuff, Admiral," he answered calmly, hoping von Friedeburg would let it rest.

But von Friedeburg was only getting started. "No, what we in the navy waged was war. What was going on in those camps was the mass murder of civilians carried out as national policy. Wouldn't you say?"

At this, Ziggy felt a cold sweat. He looked over at Oxenius and saw how nervous and wide open his eyes were.

"I wouldn't know, Admiral," answered Jodl evenly. "I am a soldier and do not involve myself in politics."

"But you knew of it?"

"Like I said, Admiral, I do not concern myself with political matters."

"So mass murder is simply a political matter?" asked von Friedeburg.

"What are you getting at, Admiral?" Jodl asked, his voice dead serious.

"I think they're going to hang us all, Herr General," von Friedeburg said, grinning maniacally, like he thought it was too funny.

Ziggy stepped forward. "Admiral, I think maybe you should sit down and rest," he said.

"Be quiet, Captain Loerber, and pour us some more whiskey," von Friedeburg said in a calm voice. "I'd like us all to raise a glass to Western civilization. To the intellectualism and humanism that makes us something better than barbarians."

"I've had quite enough of this," shot back Jodl. "I'm ordering you to shut up."

"Don't think you can pull rank on me, General. I'm head of the navy."

"You're a disgrace as a soldier, Admiral. For you to talk like this, you've obviously lost your sense of honor."

"That's right, Herr General. I have lost my sense of honor. I lost it the day I swore allegiance not to Germany, but to Adolf Hitler. We all lost it. And now look what we're all guilty of. And please don't insult all of us by pretending you didn't know."

Jodl was livid. "Half the German nation has made the supreme sacrifice in this war and instead of respecting their memory, you disgrace them all for a bunch of Jews!"

"Excuse me, sir," said Ziggy, stepping forward. "I'm a Jew."

The two men stared at him for a second and then turned back to each other. "When this thing is over," Jodl said, "I shall definitely report you to Grand Admiral Dönitz. This talk of yours is treacherous and . . . and . . ."

"Defeatist?" suggested von Friedeburg.

"You disgust me," snarled Jodl.

There was a knock on the door. Oxenius opened it. This time it was General Strong. "General Jodl, if I could have a word with you?"

"What is it, General Strong?" asked Jodl, trying to collect himself.

"Perhaps we should talk outside."

"That's all right, you can tell us all," said Jodl.

"General Bedell Smith informs me that General Eisenhower has ruled out any changes to the wording of the surrender."

"But we agreed. It is imperative that we acknowledge that the German armed forces have conducted themselves honorably."

"I'm sorry, but General Eisenhower considers that wording completely unacceptable." General Strong looked empathetic but uncompromising. He went on, "General Bedell Smith wants to know if you will accept the original terms for surrender."

Immediately Jodl countered, "In that case, we would like forty-eight hours' grace time before the articles of surrender fully take effect. Tell the general that."

General Strong shook his head. "No more delays, General," he said resolutely. "General Bedell Smith has ruled that out. Now, are you prepared to sign?"

Jodl stood silently for a long time. Then he nodded. "As I see it, I have no choice," he said angrily. "Yes, General Strong, I am prepared to sign."

General Strong nodded solemnly. "I shall inform the general immediately." He closed the door.

Jodl turned to the others. "Well, there you have it, gentlemen." Ziggy stared at the floor and hoped it would be all over soon. He and Oxenius exchanged a glance. *Your admiral is a loony and so are you*, Oxenius's eyes seemed to be saying.

Outside in the corridor, someone was approaching. The door opened and General Strong stepped in. "General, we're ready to begin," he said.

Jodl nodded. He reached into his jacket's inner pocket and took out something that he then fixed into his eye. A monocle! Jodl now looked like a Prussian played by Erich von Stroheim. What was he thinking? Did he somehow consider it vital that Germany be represented in her darkest hour by a walking carica-ture? Perhaps he was angling for a postwar career in Hollywood. From what Ziggy had heard, plenty of German and Austrian Jewish refugees had found lucrative careers playing Nazis in films. Jodl was the real thing. Why shouldn't he get some of it?

"Ready?" asked Jodl. Seeing everyone nod, he said to them, "Gentlemen, this is a black day for Germany, but I promise you, we will survive!"

"I wonder if Eisenhower will be there," von Friedeburg mumbled aloud to himself.

They walked down the corridor in single file, past the staring soldiers, General Jodl first, followed by Major Oxenius, then Admiral von Friedeburg, then Ziggy.

They were brought into a crowded, map-filled room, at the far end of which, under the glaring light from a bank of movie-studio floodlights, was a large rectangular table. Sitting there facing them were nearly a dozen British, American, and Russian generals with Bedell Smith at the center. Ziggy examined the faces of the other Allied generals, but none of them looked anything like Eisenhower. On the other hand, he noticed Susloparov glaring at him, though this time without the hint of a smile.

They took chairs on the near side of the table. Bedell Smith gestured to an aide, who brought Jodl a document. Scowling, Jodl examined it perfunctorily and then scribbled his signature on it before passing it to von Friedeburg, who did the same. The document then went to Bedell Smith, then to a British general, a French general, an American, and then Susloparov, all of whom added their signatures to it. Then another copy of the surrender made the rounds, followed by another and another and another.

When all the copies had been signed, Jodl raised his hand. "General, I would like to say a word," he said.

"Yes, of course," said Bedell Smith, sounding nicer than he had in any of their previous encounters.

Jodl stood up and began addressing everyone in the room. "General, with this signature the German people and the German armed forces are, for better or worse, delivered into the victor's hands. In this war, which has lasted more than five years, both have achieved and suffered perhaps more than any other people in the world. In this hour I can only express the hope that the victor will treat them with generosity."

Then they were marched out. The war was over.

❨ Part III ❩

(29)

That night there had been another shoot-out over in the west end. From his desk in the guard hut, Cremer listened to the details coming in over the phone and motioned for the senior petty officer to get a squad together. Ziggy, having nothing better to do, went along for the ride. Rifles were handed out, everyone grabbed their officially sanctioned three clips of ammunition, and they got into their open-roofed Kübelwagens and drove off.

It had rained earlier that evening, which seemed briefly to calm the city down. But the streets were still full of people, refugees, and soldiers; everyone was hungry, and if they weren't listless, they were angry and on the edge of revolt. The war had been over for a week but the velocity at which people died senselessly continued nearly unabated. The gods of war might have been sated, but the gods of disease, chaos, and stupidity still thirsted. Young men died in traffic accidents, drunken brawls, and shoot-outs with their comrades. And in response, Cremer and his guard battalion were assigned to clean it up. If there was even a chance one of these outbursts could be construed as a surrender violation, Cremer had orders to investigate and prepare a report for the grand admiral to give to the British.

They were in Flensburg, a small port city on the Danish border that served as Germany's new capital. There, at the old Marineschule, Dönitz had set up his government. Since returning from the surrender three days earlier, Ziggy had been assigned to the reception desk outside the grand admiral's offices. Most of his time was spent chasing away high-ranking Nazis who'd come seeking appointments and favors, a task that left him feeling wound up, angry, and restless. But once he was outside with Cremer and the others, roaming the streets, the night air and sustained jolts of adrenaline seemed to exhaust his nerves and he could finally manage a few hours of sleep before dawn.

When they got there they found a cluster of shore patrol and local police standing around, while a few feet away, in the blaze of automobile headlights, three Luftwaffe men lay dead in the street. A British officer crouched over one of the bodies, a pocket flashlight in his hand. It was unusual to see British out after dark when things became lawless. Then Ziggy recognized him. It was Westerby.

"Hey, I know this guy," he told Cremer.

"Well, he's been pestering me all week," said Cremer. "I can't tell what he wants."

They got out of their car, as did the others, and walked over. Westerby looked up from the bodies. "Good evening, Captain Cremer," he said. He stood up to shake Cremer's hand, a clear violation of the rules. Then he looked at Ziggy. "Ah, Captain Loerber," he said, feigning surprise. "I didn't know you were back with the guard battalion. Your name wasn't on the roster."

"Oh, Captain Loerber is just here helping out. That isn't a problem, is it?" said Cremer.

"Oh, no, no, no," answered Westerby, with a tug of his mustache. "It's good to see you again, Captain. How was your trip?"

"It was educational," answered Ziggy without enthusiasm. Westerby smiled, like he got the joke.

"So what have we got?" asked Cremer.

One of the civilian policemen stepped up. "It appears to be the result of a brawl that got out of hand."

"We agree," chimed in two of the shore patrol.

Cremer nodded. He'd already seen this sort of thing a dozen times.

"Curious thing, though," said Westerby.

"What do you mean, Major?" asked Cremer.

Westerby thrust his chin in the direction of the cops and shore patrol and raised his eyebrows.

"Would you excuse us for a minute, gentlemen?" Cremer said to them. He waited till they shuffled to the other side of the street. "You were saying, Major?"

"Look at their unit insignia, Captain Cremer. Does it ring a bell?"

Taking Westerby's flashlight, Cremer knelt down beside one of the dead men and shone the light on his chest. The eagle and rank markings were Luftwaffe. On the collar tab it said KG-200. Cremer looked up. "What about it?" he asked.

"KG-200," said Westerby. "They're the lads who flew up yesterday in those flying boats. The ones that got your grand admiral in such a huff."

Ziggy and Cremer exchanged sharp glances. No one was supposed to know about that, let alone Westerby. The flying boats had appeared in the harbor the morning before, without any explanation: four monstrous, six-engine aircraft, probably the biggest in the world. The crews wouldn't say why they were there or who their commander was. One look at them and Dönitz broke into a fury. "Why is this the first I've heard about them?" he shouted. He called over General Stumpf, who was currently in charge of what was left of the Luftwaffe, and demanded an explanation. Sheepishly, Stumpf confessed he didn't know anything about them except that they were a secret unit, run by the SS. For what? demanded Dönitz. "Besides secret missions, I think they were also used to supply the weather stations in Greenland," explained Stumpf. They stared out at the four lumbering behemoths, bobbing innocently in the blue water of Flensburg Fjord, and they all thought of the countless U-boat crews that might have been saved from their freezing graves in the Atlantic. But neither Göring nor Himmler liked sharing their toys and a U-boatman's fate was not their concern. "Weather stations," they heard Dönitz hiss in disgust before turning around and going back to his car.

Cremer spoke up now. "I'm sorry, Major Westerby, but we're not at liberty to discuss this matter without the grand admiral's permission. Perhaps you should bring it up with him."

Westerby ignored Cremer's suggestion. "One month ago, Reichsführer Himmler reorganized KG-200 into a Special Escape section, designed to get himself and his associates out of Germany and into safe havens abroad. Not just themselves, mind you, but also a large amount of gold and other treasures they have amassed. As for these men here," he said, gesturing toward the dead airmen, "we think they are being killed off to prevent such information from getting out.

"I'm asking for your help on this, gentlemen. There is much at stake here, and rather than bring in a lot of official attention, I think it would be better for the mission's integrity to keep knowledge of it limited."

"We haven't agreed to anything, Major," said Cremer. "As you know, we are bound by the articles of the surrender agreement and any unofficial activities are out of the question."

Westerby studied them for a long second. "Yes, yes, yes, of course," he said smoothly. "Perhaps I should have my colleague explain it to you." He turned around and shouted, "Corporal MacDonald, front and center!"

Looking down the darkened street, Ziggy noticed a jeep parked half a block away in the shadows. A Tommy driver stepped out and trotted toward them. It was Manni, Ziggy realized. He walked up to Westerby without giving a hint of recognition to either Ziggy or Cremer. "Sah!" he barked, giving an exaggerated salute. He had a long, thin, very British mustache and wire-frame glasses and on his shoulder was the mailed-fist insignia of a well-known Scottish regiment.

"At ease, Corporal," said Westerby, switching to English. "Explain to our friends here your plan for capturing the Reichsführer."

Manni turned and gave them both a wild-eyed grimace and then began addressing them in German. "We'd like you to have the flying boats towed to the northern cove where the harbor police have their outstation and repair yard. The aircrafts' crews should be removed, though a small skeleton maintenance staff may be allowed on shore in order to allay any suspicion on their behalf. You should convince the grand admiral to keep a naval guard of no more than twenty men on the site. We'll take care of the rest. The flying boats will serve as a way to lure Himmler out of hiding, and when he decides to fly away in one, we will have an ambush there to meet him. But since this is likely to result in a gun battle, it is imperative we first rescue one member from the Himmler party: his astrologer and masseur."

Westerby looked at Ziggy. "I meant what I said to you the other day at the aerodrome, Captain Loerber. Our highest priority is getting him out."

Cremer interrupted. "So you want me to take part in an ambush against the Reichsführer. You think I can order up a group of men on an unauthorized mission without everyone finding out about it?"

"We'll take care of the ambush, Captain Cremer," said Manni. "All we need from you is to get those flying boats moved up to the cove so that we can make things happen our way." He looked directly into Cremer's eyes before adding, "Can you do this for us, Captain Cremer?"

To Ziggy's surprise, Cremer nodded in agreement. "I don't see any problem getting the grand admiral to order that," he said. That was an awfully fast turnaround, Ziggy thought. But Manni had that special gift.

"Captain, something's coming!" one of the sailors shouted.

Farther up the road, a column of cars, trucks, and armored

vehicles was slowly making its way toward them. Ziggy heard somebody say, "SS!" Then he saw the flags with the swastikas and double lightning bolts and the helmeted, heavily armed men who didn't look remotely as if they'd been defeated.

It was the first time Ziggy had seen any SS since the standoff nearly two weeks earlier. They'd been keeping a low profile, staying away from the city, offering neither surrender to the Allies nor fealty to Dönitz; they remained a wild card and no one had any idea how much muscle they still commanded.

"There must be at least a hundred of them," Westerby said to Manni.

"What should we do? Should we stop them?" asked one of the petty officers.

"I don't think so," answered Cremer. "Everyone stand at ease. Hands off your weapons."

Everybody stood stock-still as the long parade of military might rumbled past them at an excruciatingly slow pace: half-tracks, Kübels, communications vans bristling with antennas like porcupines. Eight-wheeled Pumas with tank turrets and machine guns, trucks crammed with heavily armed Waffen-SS in helmets and camouflage smocks glaring down at them, ready to kill on the spot. And then they saw, in the middle of it, a six-wheeled Mercedes and Franzi's face looking out at them with a look of exasperation and helplessness. Next to him sat the Reichsführer, looking not all that worried.

"There's no one else we can turn to," said Manni, speaking in his old, familiar voice, which startled Ziggy. "British intelligence is completely infiltrated by the Reds."

Ziggy turned to look at him. Manni looked different, leaner, his face lined, and even behind the eyeglasses his eyes had a keen, determined look. "Manni—"

"No," jumped in Manni. "Not now. But I'll be in touch soon. We'll get him out, I promise." He gave a quick smile.

The SS column finally passed them. As the noise faded into the distance, everyone seemed to heave sighs of relief.

"That will be all, gentlemen," snapped Westerby. "Corporal MacDonald, we are returning to base at once." And they turned on their heels and marched off.

(30)

The subject that afternoon was fertilizer: nitrogen fertilizer. The nitrogen fertilizer needed to grow corn, corn to feed hungry people, but more importantly to feed the draft horses, which were in turn needed to plow farmland, on which to grow more corn to feed more hungry people and more draft horses.

And in order to do this, Grand Admiral Dönitz told the assembled cabinet members, they needed to reactivate, on a priority basis, Germany's nitrogen works. "Speer, how long would it take to bring them back on line?"

Speer stood up from his chair and started recounting the steps necessary to get gunpowder plants converted to fertilizer production. If they had the electrical generation on hand, and sufficient numbers of skilled repair crews, there was no reason something couldn't be operational within a week. But, more likely, they would have to bring the electrical power plants on line first. With luck and a lot of cannibalization, it could be accomplished in two weeks. Rail lines would also have to be brought back up so that coal could be transported to the power plants and, depending upon what bridges were still up, that might take an additional week.

"So what you're saying, Speer, is that it could take as long as a month to get the nitrogen production started?"

Dönitz was looking at Speer in complete shock, as though it hadn't occurred to him that everything they'd been discussing existed purely within the realm of fantasy. The reality was that all the nitrogen works and electrical power plants were in Allied hands and the Allies had so far shown not the slightest inclination to listen to any suggestions the Dönitz government might make about getting Germany's industries back in operation.

Dönitz sat at the head of the table, correct and steely-eyed as always. Schwerin von Krosigk, the chancellor and foreign minister, sat to his left, while Speer, in charge of the economic portfolio, sat at his right. The other ministers and advisors sat around the table, all of them looking very serious. Dönitz's government was now ten days old. At its inception, it had consisted of Dönitz, Speer, and von Krosigk, and a geographical realm that, besides northern Germany, included all of Denmark, Norway, Bohemia, and Crete, plus fragments of Russia, Latvia, Belgium, France, Greece, Italy, and even the British Channel Islands. Now there were more than a dozen ministries, several special departments, and more than sixty typists, clerks, and other staff members. The government's territorial jurisdiction, on the other hand, barely extended beyond the gates of the Marineschule.

They convened each day to have meetings, explore problems, issue orders, and attempt to establish some coherence amid the chaos. But what effect any of it had was hard to say. Whether their orders would be carried out, or, for that matter, even delivered, was largely beyond their control. The all-powerful Allied Control Commission was a bureaucratic hydra that stood in their way, without having any clear plan of its own. From time to time, its members would show up and nose around and issue orders and directives, whose meaning they usually seemed at a loss to explain.

The discussion on fertilizers went on for another twenty minutes and then they moved to the next topic on the agenda: churches. The question was whether a portfolio should be added for religious affairs. Dorpmüller, the transportation minister, suggested it might be a good idea, given everything the German people had just gone through, indeed it was necessary, that a Christian moral culture be reinstituted in the state.

People bristled at the idea. "Are you suggesting that just because National Socialists weren't Christian, they weren't moral?" one of the ministers countered.

"All I'm saying is we need to go back to old, traditional values. For more than a thousand years the Germans have been a Christian people. We need to emphasize that point both to ourselves and to the world. I think it would also be a good idea to embrace the contemporary Christian theology of human dignity."

"Do you have anyone in mind?" asked Dönitz.

"Yes, I do, Grand Admiral. I think Dietrich Bonhoeffer would be a perfect candidate. Last I heard he was still alive. We should see if we can locate him."

While an aide was dispatched to make some calls, the topic changed to banking issues. There wasn't enough money on hand to pay state employees or to fund purchases of emergency foodstuffs from Sweden and Portugal. The question boiled down to asking the Allies permission to print an emergency issue of reichsmarks. They were discussing it when the aide returned to inform them that Pastor Bonhoeffer had been executed by the Gestapo two weeks before.

The afternoon meeting wound down and Speer trudged back to his office to find a young Luftwaffe colonel waiting for him. It took Speer a second to realize it was Werner Baumbach, whom he'd often run into while kayaking on the Havel back before the war.

By the look of him, Baumbach was the happiest man in the world. He'd just arrived in Flensburg and only now had it occurred to him that he'd survived the war in one piece. And on top of it, it was May and everything was in blossom and he'd seen his first women in several months and they were even more beautiful than he'd remembered. He'd billeted himself at Schloss Glücksburg, a nearby castle owned by his friend the Duke of Mecklenburg-Holstein, and it was great!

"You Luftwaffe guys have all the luck," said Speer, trying to sound upbeat. "I just got kicked out of my quarters by the British." He told Baumbach how he and the rest of the government had been living aboard the *Patria*, an old Hamburg-Amerika liner docked in the harbor. But that morning they had been told to vacate it and were now crammed into the cadets' dormitories. He gave a sour look.

Baumbach laughed. "Well, that's great, then, Albert. You can stay with me! There's plenty of room, plenty of food, plenty to drink. Get your stuff together. Let's go!"

That evening, comfortably ensconced in the castle's best apartment, Speer and Baumbach sat in stuffed chairs before a crackling fire, busily putting a dent in a bottle of the duke's scotch. They'd swapped stories for an hour, Baumbach telling him about the art of dive-bombing bridges and Speer entertaining him with stories about Baumbach's much-unloved former boss, Reichsmarshal Hermann Göring. Then Baumbach asked Speer an odd question: "Albert, do you ever think about just flying away somewhere?"

Speer looked up from his glass, bewildered. "Fly away?" he asked.

Baumbach nodded earnestly. "Just get on an airplane and fly away from all this shit."

The idea was absurd. There were no aircraft leaving without Allied permission and nowhere that they could go without being arrested.

"Fly where, Werner?"

"Greenland, we could go to Greenland. What do you say?"

"Greenland?" said Speer.

"You could use a vacation, get some midnight sun, go fishing, hunt walrus. I've got some kayaks, plenty of food ready, camping equipment, tents, rifles. We could use grenades for fishing. And we can write our memoirs there. Albert, it'll be great!"

"But how are we going to get there?"

Baumbach grinned conspiratorially. "You know those gigantic flying boats in the harbor? They're mine."

Speer stared at him. "But those flying boats belong to a secret Luftwaffe unit controlled by the SS."

"I know, Albert. I'm commander of KG-200."

Speer was stunned. "I thought you said you'd been dive-bombing bridges."

"Oh, I was, up until about three weeks ago," said Baumbach. "Then I got pulled out and put in charge of the Special Escape Section that the SS was running to get its people out. I take my orders from the head of the SS. Except the problem is, officially speaking, Himmler is no longer head of the SS. The new head of the SS is Hanke, and Hanke is now dead, so that leaves me without anyone to take orders from!" He grinned as though he found the idea not the least bit troubling.

"Perhaps you should inform the grand admiral," suggested Speer.

Baumbach laughed. "Dönitz? Come on, Albert. You know we could do this. We could fly to Greenland and spend the summer there. We could fly there tonight."

Speer knocked back the last of his whiskey and gently set the glass down on the table in front of him. He shook his head in amused disbelief, which Baumbach took, if not as outright consent, then as a definite encouragement to go on.

"Look, I'm not saying go away and hide out forever, just until things settle down. Then we come back. I mean, why not? What's the point in staying here? You are not going to accomplish much here. Not now. Hell, Albert, imagine the inspiration we're going to get writing with icebergs and glaciers all around us. It'll be so clean and pure and uncomplicated. And when the world finds out we've written our memoirs while hunting walrus in Greenland, everybody will want to read about it!"

Speer smiled as he reached for the now-half-empty bottle. "I think it's a wonderful idea, Werner. Maybe we should."

Baumbach smiled, gratified, and settled back in his chair, cradling his glass happily. After that neither of them said much.

They just stared into the fire, each in their own thoughts. The whiskey felt good; so did the quiet.

Even after Baumbach staggered off to sleep, Speer continued to stare into the glowing embers. Up until then, whenever he slept, Speer had dreamt of being at party rallies, encircled by gigantic fluttering red banners, each with its huge black swastika, and following Hitler up a long, wide path of steps toward the podium, past seas of cheering people. And sometimes Hitler would turn around and smile only at him, as if to say, *We did this, Speer, you and I, our dream, we've made it happen!* And the flags flapping proudly, with the sky always a deepening azure and the clouds heavenly pink, and everyone cheering, cheering. Other times he'd dream of Germania with its monuments and avenues. Hitler would be there too. And each time he'd wake up from it feeling only a terrible void, wishing he were dead.

But that night at Schloss Glücksburg, Albert Speer dreamed of icebergs and glaciers. He dreamed of polar bears and seeing the sun rise over ice floes. For once, his debts to Adolf Hitler's memory were forgiven.

(31)

If the present is simply the intersecting point between past and future, then Flensburg was that unrepeatable circumstance where the two merely brushed against each other, like two party guests eyeing each other as they wait for an absent host to come and make the requisite introductions. And while the past stands solid and unalterable, and the future is but a swirling cloud of possibility, in Flensburg the opposite seemed to be the case. Here the future appeared fixed, bright and obvious, while the past was a murky shifting shadow, best not dwelled on, for its details seemed to change hourly.

And nowhere was optimism toward the future stronger than in the Dönitz government. The fact that it continued to grow was all the proof some people needed to believe that they had put themselves on the ground floor of a very prospective enterprise. They began seeking more and better furniture, larger offices with more windows and all the other appurtenances with which to demonstrate their recovered status.

Those stranded in the past, on the other hand, found themselves searching frantically for something, anything, that might help them ascend. Some lobbied for the creation of an "interministerial working group" to study undefined problems, while others sought diplomatic passports, medical certificates, or, failing that, a few sheets of office letterhead, as a protection against Allied arrest.

Ziggy witnessed all of this from his desk in the lobby outside

the grand admiral's offices. He was feeling ragged from not having slept all night, but, buoyed by a cup of synthetic coffee and a
cigarette, he once again assumed the character of a coldly efficient
staff officer and awaited the stream of supplicants.

The first were four gauleiters, all of them fat as hippos, who
waddled through the door in their brown-and-gold Nazi party
uniforms. They announced that they needed to see the grand
admiral on "a matter of national importance." Ziggy asked them
to explain. The four men traded nervous looks with each other:
*Should we? Shouldn't we? The plane leaves tonight. We have to get the
passports. But what about the money?*

Then, to his horror, Ziggy realized that what he was hearing
was their thoughts. Their telepathic roar hit him like vertigo.

*Tell him we need to go to Spain? Tell him about the conference?
Should we mention the meetings with Vargas and the Phalange?
Should we? Dare we?*

Ziggy hated mind reading. He hated the whole thing. Ten
years ago he'd managed to shut it out and keep it out.

*Spain . . . Swiss account number . . . Vargas . . . little contribution to
the Phalange . . . Tonight at Kastrup . . . Copenhagen . . . Should we?
Dare we?* Ultimately, they dared not and left.

The outer door opened and in walked a short, blond-haired
man Ziggy recognized from newsreels. "Alfred Rosenberg," he announced drunkenly. "Please alert the grand admiral at once. This
is a matter of extreme national importance!"

Rosenberg had been the Nazi Party's racial theoretician and
Reichsminister for the occupied eastern territories. But since the
party no longer existed and there were no eastern territories left
to occupy, Ziggy doubted Dönitz would want to talk with him.
He asked him to state the nature of his business. "I have come,"
Rosenberg proclaimed, "to offer the grand admiral my services
as theoretician! It is vitally important a conceptual framework be
reestablished to ensure continuity with our racial identity."

"I'm sorry, the grand admiral is very busy right now," Ziggy said. "He asks that you submit any request first to the Allied Control Commission, whose offices are on the second floor."

Rosenberg stared at him for a long time, then said, "Do you like fine paintings? Flemish masters? Brueghel? Wouldn't you just love to have one of your own?" He needed a diplomatic passport. He'd heard the British were looking to arrest him and he figured if he could drive into Denmark on diplomatic business, they'd have to leave him alone. "A bright young man like you, I can just tell you'd know who to talk to. No need to bother the grand admiral with this. Do this for me and the Brueghel is yours."

It went like this through the morning. When the time finally came for lunch, instead of eating, Ziggy decided to go outside and walk around to clear his head.

At the edge of the park was a hillside that overlooked the harbor. Ziggy lit a cigarette and stared out at the ships anchored there. Apart from the U-boats, there were destroyers, corvettes, minesweepers, patrol craft, and even a cruiser. And among all of them, probably not more than a few dozen crew still aboard. They were dead ships; the German Kriegsmarine was a dead navy. The victors would divide them among themselves. A few ships might live on for a few years as workhorses or testing vessels. The rest would be broken up for scrap, used for targets, or just sunk.

Suddenly he realized the flying boats were gone. Cremer must have already gotten them towed up to the cove. Manni definitely had a clever idea. Had the flying boats remained there in plain view, they'd quickly stop seeming special and simply fade into the mosaic of rusting, derelict warships. But now, having been revealed and then promptly hidden, their mystique would embed itself deeper into the imagination, making the prospect of flying away in one all the more tantalizing. And that was precisely how they wanted Himmler to react. He wondered when he'd hear again from Manni or Westerby.

Ziggy remembered Franzi's face in the car window. He looked a lot worse than he had that night in Plön. Since then, the SS had completely disappeared. There were reports of large numbers of them still hiding in nearby forests and the British were too wary of spreading themselves too thin to go on any extensive searches.

So where was he right now? Could he feel his way toward him? Once it had been easy to do, but he hadn't done any of it in so long that he no longer even knew where to start. Ziggy kept trying to imagine Franzi somewhere, in a forest or a house or inside a vehicle, but each time he did, the idea failed to grow into anything real. He knew he was going about it the wrong way.

Was it possible that, so many years after cutting Franzi off in his mind, Ziggy wouldn't be able to find his way back to him? And what was that ability anyway? What were the mechanics of perception? Perhaps if he just focused on one thing: Franzi, was he far or near? What were his eyes seeing? What was he thinking? What did his skin feel? Warmth or cold? Cold or warmth? Cold. Dry or damp? Dry. What was he smelling? Cooked cabbage and tinned beef, cold and greasy on a plate. Cigarette smoke, open window, and a night breeze, smell of pine. Pine trees outside the window, the wind blowing through them. They were in a farmhouse, inland, but still close enough to smell the sea. They were keeping within reach of Flensburg. There was a forest nearby, men hiding inside it. Lines of Kübelwagens hidden under camouflaged tarps. They were staying put, waiting for something to come. Inside, everyone was tense.

Ziggy opened his eyes. A bluebird was looking at him from a nearby branch. It chirped and flew away. Ziggy went back to the office.

Back at his desk, there were more supplicants awaiting him. One by one, he sent them away, not bothering to trouble the grand admiral about any of them. In the middle of the afternoon, the door opened and in walked Wolfgang Lüth. "Hello, Number One," he said.

Ziggy looked at him. The moment he had dreaded had arrived. "Hello, sir," he said.

Lüth looked surprised. "When did you get so formal? How've you been? I heard you went to see Eisenhower. Is he as nice as they say? Come on, Loerber, tell me what you've been up to. Seen any of the old gang?"

"Oh," said Ziggy, "besides Captain Cremer, I haven't seen much of anybody. I've been pretty busy."

Lüth gave a sour but good-natured look. "Busy? Sitting at a desk? What's going on with you, Loerber?"

Ziggy shrugged. But somehow he couldn't come up with anything resembling the usual banter.

Lüth looked at him and his expression grew serious. "I sent you congratulations when you got oak leaves on your Knight's Cross. I wrote you again when you got the diamonds. You never wrote back either time. I told myself you were busy, but now you've been here a couple of days now and you haven't even dropped by to see me once. What's going on?"

Ziggy shrugged noncommittally, but his heart was pounding.

Lüth continued, "When you didn't write back, I knew something was wrong. I wrote you again and you didn't write then either. What is it, Loerber? I've done something to offend you, haven't I?"

Ziggy said nothing.

"You should tell me what it is," said Lüth. "This is the time when we need to stick together. You know I've always considered you my brother, and if there is something wrong, then for the sake of our brotherhood, you should tell me what it is. This war has been bad enough. We shouldn't go into peacetime bearing grudges. It'll poison things."

Lüth was looking at him earnestly and Ziggy knew he expected an honest answer. He remembered again the times they'd stood together on a deck, witnessing the death groans of a ship they'd torpedoed as its insides ripped apart. "Yes, I do have something to say to you."

"Then say it."

"I'm a Jew."

Lüth stared at him a very long time. "I see," he said finally. "So I suppose there's nothing more to say, then."

Ziggy said nothing.

Lüth turned and walked away.

(32)

To just fly away.

What a thought! To separate oneself from all the details and involvements and get away to a place where life was down to its essentials. He could leave all this behind. Why not? They could take off in a flying boat in the middle of the night and by sunrise they'd be halfway to Greenland.

At least that was how it seemed to Speer while he sat through another morning cabinet meeting. Dönitz sat at the head of the table, correct and steely-eyed as always. Today's topic was housing. Some bright boy from the Transportation Ministry was explaining how to mass-produce worker housing. It would mean organizing construction into separate phases: one crew would put down piping followed by a concrete bed, the next crew would do the framing, another prefabricated side panels, another a roof and then a finishing crew would put in the electrical wiring and the interior. He argued that with a force of two hundred workers operating in teams, they could build thirty single-family cottages in a week. The idea was that they could quickly supply semipermanent family housing for areas where there were high-priority factories and industrial sites but a shortage of usable dwelling space. Speer watched Dönitz nod as he listened to the young man describe the processes and the breakdown of logistics, as though he agreed that under the right circumstances it might actually work. But as it was, they still had not gotten a single go-ahead from the Allied Control Commission on any of their proposals. They hadn't even gotten an acknowledgment that the proposals had gone anywhere besides the bottom of a desk drawer.

Eventually the subject switched to renewed Allied demands that the Dönitz government hand over Reichsführer SS Heinrich Himmler. "I've told them again and again that Himmler is beyond my control and that I haven't seen him since I turned down his request to be in my government," Dönitz told them. "Now they are claiming to have spotted him inside Flensburg the night before last. I intend to respond that I don't know anything about it. But please, if any of you hear anything, even just a rumor, bring it to my attention immediately. Anything positive we can tell them would probably help."

While he listened, Speer began doodling absentmindedly on the sheet of paper he had for making notes. He started with a small circle, then he began surrounding it with smaller circles, until it resembled a daisy. After that, he started putting down vertical lines, then horizontal ones, and almost without realizing it, he began sketching a house.

He started with the front door, making it wide and curved at the top. Then he drew the windows: a square one on the right and a long rectangular one on the left, both the same height, with shutters on the ends. After that, he drew in flower boxes. He then put in vertical lines, one on each end, to mark out the sides of the house. He followed these with horizontal lines—one to mark the top of the roof and the other the bottom. But no sooner had he drawn them than he realized it had been a mistake. The roof was too low. He wanted to put in a second story, one with a balcony and a long bank of windows and a door. He took out a small gum eraser and began carefully removing the top horizontal lines. Looking up, he saw Dönitz glowering at him. Speer put down more lines. Staring at it, he realized how much more he preferred small-scale to large-scale. Yes, small-scale suited him better. In school, his building designs were all for small-scale structures. That was where the original Speer was, but would anybody bother looking at his designs and trying to figure out where Hitler's gargantuan influence left off and Speer's more reasonable, intimate sensibility took over? Was there a chance that someday someone of rare talent and understanding might declare, *Here! You see! This element is pure Speer! See how the simple, elegant lines emerge!* A nice thought, but that might take centuries.

Abandoning straight lines for the moment, Speer's pencil began making squiggly lines and shapes on the paper to represent the irregular outlines of icebergs. Speer stared at the paper and imagined watching the sunrise from high above the shimmering North Atlantic. Flying west, he'd probably have to leave the cockpit and go aft to find a window he could observe it from. He thought of listening to the heavy drone of the aircraft's six engines with his hands on the cold metal bulkhead and his nose pressed against the glass and seeing the first rays of light spread across the dark surface of the water, then filling in to reveal the waves' white foam.

Back in his office, Speer stared out the window and suddenly noticed the giant flying boats were gone from the harbor. For a moment he felt a rush of panic as it occurred to him that Baumbach might have flown away without him.

He planned to leave early, but there was a meeting called at the last minute and he didn't get out until after dusk. Driving back to Glücksburg, he began feeling desperate at the thought of having no way out. As his Mercedes approached the castle forecourt, for a second he saw someone coming out of the entrance and then disappearing into the shadows. He never got a good look at him, but something told him it was Manni Loerber.

To his relief, he found Baumbach inside. He was in his usual good mood, having already worked his way through half a bottle of Black & White. He filled a glass for Speer and started telling him one funny story after another. At one point Speer brought up Greenland, but Baumbach acted as if he hadn't heard him and they never discussed it again after that.

❴ 33 ❵

The following morning, just as dawn was beginning to break over Flensburg Fjord, a flotilla of twelve midget submarines crept into the harbor. Seehunds, each of them seventeen tons fully loaded, with a crew of two and two torpedoes straddling their sides like saddlebags. They had escaped from Wilhelmshaven just as the British army was coming in. In that time they had painstakingly navigated all the way around the Danish peninsula and now that they were coming back into German-controlled territory, they were eager for fresh orders that would send them back out to exact some revenge on the enemy, and none more so than the flotilla's commander, Kapitänleutnant Hermann Rasch.

There was no question in his mind that the surrender was merely a sham, a crafty ploy by Dönitz designed to lull the enemy into letting their guard down. He knew what an unbending die-hard Dönitz was. All they would have to do was show up before him, salute, and say, *Ready for combat!*

Once his boats were all tied up along the quay, Rasch relit his last cigar and strode proudly up to the Marineschule. Filthy, bearded, dressed in an oil-stained leather jacket and trousers, his smudged white commander's cap tilted raffishly to one side, to the trio of young British subalterns who passed him on their morning stroll, he imparted the unmistakable air of a pirate.

But before he got to Dönitz's offices, his progress was blocked by a very stern-looking Kapitän zur See Wolfgang Lüth, who immediately pointed Rasch to his office and told him to wait inside. Then he picked up the phone and called Lüdde-Neurath. Lüdde-Neurath told Lüth he'd send someone down and then told Ziggy to go sit in on the discussion just in case anything got out of hand.

As he made his way downstairs, Ziggy tried to remember what he knew about Rasch. While he didn't know him personally, he'd heard plenty over the years. It wasn't that he was a bad officer or an unsuccessful commander; he had quite a respectable number of kills under his belt. It was that Rasch was a hothead and a troublemaker. He was prone to taking unnecessary risks. So they'd switched him over to midgets, an ideal place for cantankerous, highly motivated oddballs like himself. And there he thrived, creeping around the North Sea coastline wreaking havoc among Allied shipping.

When Ziggy got downstairs, he found Lüth standing in the corridor outside his office. At the sight of Ziggy, Lüth's eyes momentarily flared, but he quickly regained his officer's unflappable demeanor.

"Captain Lüth," said Ziggy.

"Captain Loerber," said Lüth and then began briefing him on the situation as if there were nothing at all amiss between the two of them.

"So it sounds like Rasch needs to be brought into the present," said Ziggy when Lüth finished.

Lüth nodded. "It would be better if you don't write anything down until it's over. Then we'll agree on what goes into the report. If we explain to the British that Rasch's radio was out and he hadn't received the surrender instructions, they'll probably accept it without too much of a problem." Ziggy agreed that was a good idea. Then Lüth told him he was going to try to get Rasch to accept it peacefully, since arresting him would also likely result in trouble with the British.

They went inside Lüth's office, where a ragged but exuberant Rasch sat waiting to present his attack plan. They let him go on for a minute, then began, gently at first, introducing him to the concept of unconditional surrender, explaining how under its terms absolutely no one, not even Rasch, was permitted to carry out any further military action against the enemy, no matter how richly the British deserved payback. The war was over. They had lost.

"You can't be serious!" Rasch shouted. "After all we've just been through getting here, past all those British assholes, you expect me to just sit back and let them take our boats away from us? That's just wrong! If you expect me to go along with this bullshit, you're crazy!"

That was all it took to set Lüth off. Ziggy watched him staring hard at Rasch, ready to explode. Ziggy couldn't imagine anyone had ever talked back to him, especially like that. When he spoke this time, his previous patient authority had turned to fire. "The war is over, Rasch. No matter what your opinion is, you will obey your orders or, so help me, I will have you hanged!"

Rasch's face was scarlet with rage. "Well, then, to hell with you, Lüth!" he said. Then, without being dismissed, he turned and stormed out, slamming the door behind him.

Lüth was ready to run out and have Rasch clapped in irons on the spot. Ziggy stopped him. "Just let him blow off some steam," he said. "He'll come around."

They composed the report together, boiling everything down into colorless, unemotional words and phrases, which drained all the tremor from the incident so that Rasch's near-revolt became nothing more than a purely administrative mishap, unlikely to spark any interest from their British overseers.

"Anything else?" Ziggy asked when they were done.

"No," said Lüth. Then he looked up at Ziggy. "Korvetten-kapitän Loerber?"

"Sir?"

"If I could say just one thing?"

"Please," said Ziggy.

"In case you're wondering, I never told any of what you said to me to the grand admiral."

Ziggy could tell Lüth was brokenhearted and part of him wanted to find something to say that would set things right between them, even a little bit.

He left again without saying anything.

⟮ 34 ⟯

This was the moment, Franzi told himself. If he wanted to get away, he had to act now. Macher was out on night patrol with two of the others, which meant they probably wouldn't be back for at least another hour. Himmler was also safely out of the picture, having retreated to the bedroom for another session with Fräulein Potthast. That meant the only people he'd have to contend with were Grothmann and Kiermaier, Himmler's personal bodyguards. The three of them were sitting in the front room, Franzi in the corner, while Grothmann and Kiermaier sat opposite each other at the table.

For the last three days they'd been holed up in a gamekeeper's cottage, deep in a forest somewhere near Flensburg. Before that they'd been continually on the move, never staying more than a night in any one place. When they had arrived, they found, to the surprise of everyone except Kiermaier, that Fräulein Potthast, Himmler's mistress, was already ensconced there. Macher didn't like it and neither did Grothmann, but as Franzi saw it, even though she got on everyone's nerves, at least she kept Himmler busy and out of their hair for hours at a time.

All he had to do now was put Kiermaier and Grothmann to sleep. Just get inside their minds, find the rhythms of their awareness, and then, like stepping into a chorus line, become part of it. Then, without them noticing it, induce a new rhythm. Make the flow of their thoughts change from a razor-sharp wave into a long, greasy, monotonous roll. Franzi and his brothers had grown up practicing it on their father. It had been easy, as Gustav Loerber was the rare individual whom self-doubt never visited.

Kiermaier, on the other hand, was alert and suspicious and entering his mind felt like walking barefoot across a beach of sharp rocks with the waves pounding casually beyond it. But gradually Franzi got him nodding. Grothmann, to his surprise, turned out to be relatively easy. The constant creaking and squealing coming from the bedroom had him so irritated that all Franzi had to do was set up a couple of counterrhythms to send him blessedly into oblivion.

Franzi rose from his chair and began making his way toward the door, carefully shifting his weight from one foot to the other so the floorboards wouldn't creak. But halfway across, he felt so overcome with fatigue that he had to stop and hold on to the wall. He tried to imagine running into the forest, up a trail, then cutting off to the side until he found some ferns or undergrowth he could disappear into. And after he got his strength back, he'd creep off like a badger. He figured they'd give up looking for him after a few hours, since they could no longer spare the men for a sustained search.

He made another couple steps toward the door. He reached for the handle, checking quickly behind him to make sure the two were still out. Suddenly a shrill scream tore through the stillness.

"Oh, Hanzeeeeeeee!" shrieked Fräulein Potthast from behind the bedroom door.

Franzi pulled his hand away from the door handle just as Kiermaier and Grothmann snapped awake.

"Oh, Hanzeeee, Hanzeee, Hanzeee!"

Oh, shit, thought Franzi.

Kiermaier's eyes were darting around the room. "What happened?" he asked, thoroughly confused.

"I don't know," answered Grothmann. He looked suspiciously at Franzi. "What were you doing? I didn't see you get up."

"I wasn't doing anything," said Franzi as he sank back into

his chair. He closed his eyes and tried to think. But his mind felt like it was full of cold, wet cement, his thoughts moving listlessly through it like dying animals.

By now Fräulein Potthast's screaming had subsided into little satisfied mewing noises. Grothmann gave a disgusted look and tried to focus his attention on the dirt under his nails while Kiermaier's face returned to its usual blank inscrutability.

Franzi had been trying to escape for a week now, and each time his attempts came apart at the last moment. Something always went wrong. Once he got Macher to run into a hall closet, believing it was a front door, but he barely bumped his head. Another time he'd gotten Grothmann and Kiermaier so angry at each other that they drew their pistols, but their training got the better of them and they soon calmed down again.

He remembered going through Flensburg that night and seeing his brothers there with Nigel Westerby. They had to be planning his rescue, which he absolutely had to prevent from happening. It didn't matter what resources Westerby had or what magic Manni could muster up for the occasion. They didn't stand a chance against Macher.

There was more creaking of bedsprings, louder, more jerking and arrhythmic. Grothmann's eyes narrowed. This weakness of character was something he had not heretofore suspected about the Reichsführer. But Himmler was insatiable. In the time they'd been here, he'd hardly done anything but have sex with Fräulein Potthast. Franzi wondered what it was about being the most hunted man on earth that could stoke one's ardency to this degree.

The creaking grew louder. "Jesus God, is that all he's good for?" muttered Grothmann. Kiermaier shot him a poisonous look. Grothmann glared back. It occurred to Franzi that if he'd had the strength, perhaps he might have been able to engineer another showdown between the two. But he didn't. Instead he closed his eyes and drifted off to sleep.

The next thing he knew he was being shaken awake by Grothmann. "Wake up, Loerber, wake up! The Reichsführer is having an attack."

Groggily, Franzi followed Grothmann into the bedroom. Kiermaier was already inside, holding down the writhing, naked Reichsführer, while Fräulein Potthast cowered in a corner, her dressing gown wrapped tight around her.

While Kiermaier held down his knees, Franzi began working on Himmler's stomach. Everything was knotted up, even worse than usual. Franzi let his fingers probe deep into the muscles and Himmler's screaming dropped to a whimper as he started to relax. Once Kiermaier felt certain Himmler was out of danger, he took Fräulein Potthast by the wrist and led her out of the room. Himmler's breathing began slowing down and he stopped whimpering. "Oh, Professor Loerber," he sighed. "You have saved me again."

"Thank you, Reichsführer," answered Franzi.

"You really are quite remarkable."

"Thank you."

For a few minutes neither said anything, but Franzi could tell Himmler had something on his mind.

Finally he spoke. "May I ask you a question, Herr Professor?"

"Certainly, Reichsführer."

"What do you think of General Schellenberg? Is he someone you would trust?"

"Sorry?"

"Let me put it this way, Loerber: Has he taken you into his confidence on occasion? You've done things for him, secret things?"

Franzi felt the tingling on the back of his neck.

"What were you doing for him most recently?"

"I was helping arrange the movement of some containers to remote locations. General Schellenberg wanted them dispersed into barns and cellars where they could be retrieved unnoticed."

"Containers, you said?"

"Yes, Reichsführer. Containers of intelligence files, relating to Source Moonpool."

"Did General Schellenberg tell you that?"

"No, Reichsführer, I just assumed it."

"Why?"

"Because Major Steiner was working on it with him."

"Major Steiner!" Himmler smiled. It was the answer he was looking for. "Major Steiner, yes," Himmler said. "But did he ever say anything about gold?"

Franzi acted startled. "Gold, Reichsführer? No, he never said anything about that."

"Did General Schellenberg ever name any of the locations where they were hiding the containers?"

"Not to me, Reichsführer." Franzi paused long enough to adopt a troubled expression. The fact was Schellenberg and Steiner had both, unbeknownst to each other, given him the lists of the locations of the gold. And each list was completely different.

Himmler went on. "Looking back on it now, with the virtue of hindsight, I think we can say fairly it was a mistake entrusting the location of the gold to the same individual running the special operations against the Soviets. General Schellenberg assured me the man was better than anyone at keeping secrets. But now they're both gone."

"Oh," said Franzi.

"This puts our negotiations with Eisenhower into a problematic area, since Schellenberg has not yet fully informed us of the details of the agreement he has reached with him. I can't very well go to Eisenhower myself, having no idea what the status is. That would be showing all my cards."

"Yes, it would be," agreed Franzi.

"So you wouldn't have any idea where he might have gone to?"

"None, Reichsführer."

"Can I ask you another question?"

"Of course."

"What do the stars say will become of me?"

Always the stars, thought Franzi. He hadn't seen a star in several days, since Macher wouldn't let him outside, other than for escorted visits to the latrine.

"Reichsführer," he began, "these are very difficult times. There is much uncertainty about. But know this," he said with all the stillness he could muster as he tried to think up something.

"Yes?" asked Himmler expectantly.

Franzi tried to mobilize his brain cells into a last-minute defense. "I see, I see . . ." And then he saw it. A vision, clear as crystal, and almost immediately the unplanned words came to him. "The change will come very soon, Reichsführer. It will come even before the moon wanes." He saw Himmler's face light up. Franzi went on, "In the east, two men wait. They stand surrounded by a bloody tide. They wait for their king, their new king."

Himmler gasped. "That must be Bulgakov and Rybchinski," he whispered. "Does one of them have glasses?"

"One of them sits on a horse with a golden mane, the other whirls through the air like a fish. They'll wait for you in the place where the sun shines at night and glows golden from the earth."

"You mean Greenland, don't you? This is amazing!" said Himmler. "Greenland is a place I've always dreamed of going to." But then he added worryingly, "Does it say how long I should stay there? When could I come back?"

Franzi shrugged. *Greenland?* he thought. Why on earth would anyone want to go there?

"The thing is," said Himmler, "I still have my career to think about. If I am gone too long, won't somebody else take the posts I am destined for? But go on, Professor Loerber," he whispered excitedly. "Please don't stop. Tell me more! What else do you see?"

"I see a maiden."

"A maiden? You see Fräulein Potthast?"

Franzi shook his head. "I see another maiden, with long golden hair, in a gown of feathery white. She stands beside an empty throne next to a stone altar where there is a golden helmet and a spear."

"That's the Spear of Destiny!" Himmler said breathlessly.

"With her right hand she points to the North Star, with the left to a castle, a castle with four towers."

"Four towers? That's Schloss Glücksburg!"

"There is a golden glow from the castle's west tower."

"Golden glow! You saw gold? That must be the treasure! We're supposed to bring it there. Does that mean it will come? Will the gold shipment arrive?"

Franzi nodded.

"So then I should tell Macher not to move again. Perhaps we should move closer to the Schloss? What do you think? Should we?"

Franzi nodded again.

"Does the maiden say anything?" asked Himmler.

"She says, 'Beware!'"

"Beware?"

"Beware!"

"Beware what?"

Franzi had no idea what. "Beware the Blood of Israel!" he intoned in a voice that frightened even himself.

"The Blood of Israel?" Himmler was shocked. "Not them? They're after my gold? Well, they're not going to get it," he snapped. "The gold is mine! I've worked hard for it. Does the maiden have any advice about what I should do?"

"The helmet will go to the true king, and with it the throne. But not before three bursts of lightning rain on the castle. The gold shall build a new kingdom in a land of kings where there is no king."

"That's Germany!" Himmler was beside himself with excitement. "She has to be talking about Germany. Germany is the land of great and true kings. Will I be the next king?"

"Beware the Blood of Israel. The Blood of Israel will seek its vengeance."

"It's a little late for that." Himmler cackled. "Hitler is already dead. I buried the hatchet with those people a month ago. We shook hands on it. It's Dönitz's problem. They don't have anything on me! In any event, I'll have Eisenhower deal with them once I am king."

After that, Himmler felt so much better he put on his best uniform and strode into the front room. Macher and the others were back now and everyone was sitting where they had been earlier.

Himmler smiled at Fräulein Potthast, who was now seated by herself, forlorn and frightened-looking, like she had the onus on her for the attack. "Come on, Hedwig, put on your nicest dress, let's light some candles and have some wine. We're having a party!"

Immediately she lit up and fluttered back into the bedroom, only to emerge a few minutes later in a shimmering lavender gown, elbow-length silk gloves, and wearing a long string of pearls around her neck. She was young, blond, and pretty, though in a horse-faced way. Now, reaffirmed in her position as the first lady of the SS, she greeted her guests with awkward formality, forgetting that they were all merely fugitives from an empire that had already evaporated.

Himmler wound up the gramophone and handed her a stack of disks and invited her to choose. She made a great show of picking one out, pulling it out from its brown paper sleeve. "Play this one," she said. Himmler put it on and lowered the needle. As the first notes surged out of the horn, he bowed and took her hand in his and they started to dance. The sad, happy rhythm and the swaying melody began filling the room.

It was "Harlem Rhapsody."

❨ 35 ❩

The day came when everyone wanted submarines.

There must have been a rumor that someone had been given one to escape to Argentina, or maybe it was the growing presence of British and American officers wandering around that unleashed fresh panic. Or perhaps it was just an idea whose time had come. Whichever the case, suddenly everybody who was anybody was back in front of Ziggy's desk, bombarding him with requests for the temporary loan of a submarine or two, along with an able-bodied crew.

" . . . But seriously young man, there have to be dozens of U-boats out there in the harbor. I'm sure nobody at all would mind if one were to disappear. The British couldn't possibly need them all!"

" . . . Now, I'm not asking for the biggest or the fastest one you've got. I'm not even insisting on my own stateroom. I'd be willing to work, pull my weight. Just let me have a hammock of my own. We can leave anytime, just the sooner the better. What do you say?"

" . . . Now, see here! I have secret orders requiring me to go to Rio de Janeiro at once. As you can see, they have been signed by Otto Ohlendorf himself . . . highest operational priority . . . It's not something the grand admiral has to actually know about. Please do not bother him. Just do as I ask."

" . . . You're a U-boat captain, aren't you? What do you say you help me out on this?"

Ziggy's answer to all these requests had been exactly the same. By order of the grand admiral, no submarines were available, no matter what the circumstances. Nothing was leaving, not now, not anytime.

Afterward, as he did every afternoon, he walked back to the hut where Cremer's guard battalion had its headquarters. It was a quiet, orderly place, rarely visited by higher-ups. Besides Cremer, there were usually no more than two or three people inside the dispatch office, answering phones and typing reports, while the rest were either out on patrol or in the other buildings. But this afternoon, as he approached it, Ziggy heard loud explosions of laughter from inside. Cremer's going to kill them, he thought. Off duty, he might be the biggest joker alive, but during working hours he was strictly business.

Ziggy wondered what he should do. Officially, he no longer had direct authority over the men, and didn't want to go around interfering in Cremer's shop. Still, he could just go in and drop a stern but friendly hint. No harm in doing that, he told himself. What should he say? He'd given speeches many times before and he knew that you had to appeal to their professionalism, their sense of history and tradition and shared purpose, their pride as German sailors, as U-boatmen. But as he stood outside, trying out the various arguments in his mind, he found the irony of their situation creeping up on him again, distorting any attempt at sincerity:

Now, guys, you know as well as I do how Captain Cremer doesn't want things degenerating just because we're on land and we've lost the war; we're still expected to act professionally . . .

. . . We're still the best of the best, and until the day comes that the British march up and disarm and strip us and rob us of our watches, rings, knives, binoculars, and belt buckles, we are going to keep up the appearance of the world's best-disciplined, most ferocious fighting force.

He continued to stare at the door and imagined their faces looking up at him respectfully and then he imagined Lüth standing there instead of him, dispensing his fatherly advice to the men who'd never failed to follow every tenet of his code.

This is the moment we're being judged by. Now we have to show those British what kind of men we really are. Even though we fought and lost for a criminal cause which our children and grandchildren and great-great-grandchildren will despise us for, we are still obliged to hold our heads high and not let those other things (like gas chambers and gas vans and ovens and barbed wire and Alsatian dogs) affect our character . . .

More shrieks of laughter. He wondered what could possibly be so funny. Oh, to hell with it, he thought. Maybe it was better for them to be laughing than to be getting drunk and morose and killing each other like all those idle soldiers out on the Flensburg streets. He pushed open the door.

There were at least twenty men standing along the walls and sitting on desks that had been pushed to one corner, while in the center of the room stood Manni—or was it Corporal MacDonald? This time he wasn't in British army uniform, though he still had the mustache and wire-rim glasses. And he was juggling.

Five balls in the air, three of them bouncing against walls, one being occasionally tossed to different members of the audience, who would obligingly throw it back. And all the while Manni was telling them a long, rambling, nonsensical story that had them all cracking up. Though it wasn't one Ziggy had heard before, it still sounded all too familiar. Behind the affability, there was cold-blooded calculation. Manni used stories like this to distract and lull people before playing one of his dirty tricks on them. He'd done it to him, he'd done it to Franzi and Sebastian and everyone else they'd ever known. Ziggy couldn't believe he'd be here, now, pulling it on his men. As he watched him closely, Manni appeared more predatory than ever.

One of the petty officers noticed Ziggy standing at the entrance and barked out to the others, "Officer on deck!" and everyone immediately snapped to attention.

Ziggy stepped into the guardroom. "What is going on here?" he asked sharply.

"But Herr Kapitän," protested the petty officer, "don't you see? It's your brother, Manni Loerber! You never told us you were one of the Flying Magical Loerber Brothers."

Looking around, Ziggy saw with growing dread how everyone's eyes were wide open with wonderment. *Korvettenkapitän Loerber is Ziggy of the Flying Magical Loerber Brothers, back from when we were kids!* If everyone in Germany possessed only one single happy memory, it was probably of the Flying Magical Loerber Brothers. How he hated having to smile and listen graciously to the same reminiscences and answer the same gushing questions about the four happy brothers and old Gustav and the idyllic days in old Berlin. And now twelve blissful years of anonymity had vanished in a heartbeat.

Ziggy fixed the men with his coldest stare and watched the excited smiles wither on their faces. Then he turned to Manni, who was standing in the middle of the room, five colored juggling balls resting in his hands and on his lips an expression of measured delight.

"You, outside," ordered Ziggy.

He marched him away from the guard hut, across the lawn to near one of the Marineschule's wooden storage buildings. They stopped. "Just what the hell do you think you're doing?" Ziggy demanded.

"Entertaining the troops, brother dear," answered Manni with a devilish grin.

"I'll not have you or anyone undermining discipline," barked Ziggy. "We've got a difficult job to do. Most of the time you British are being a bunch of pricks. And now you show up with your juggling balls and your stupid stories and that stupid fake mustache of yours and disrupt everything. We're trying to follow the rules you bastards have imposed on us and maintain some semblance of self-respect for these guys so that when they lose everything, they'll at least still have their dignity. If you want to entertain somebody, go cheer up the starving people on the street. But leave my men alone!"

"Are you through?" asked Manni.

"Yes."

"Good," said Manni. "Now I'm going to give you a piece of my mind. Seeing you here now, I have to say I'm completely disgusted with you."

"For what?"

"For pretending not to be what you are," said Manni.

"A Jew?"

Manni looked at him like he was nuts. "No! A Magical Loerber Brother! How is it even possible that not one of those men knew you were part of the greatest variety act in modern German history? How can you stand denying that?"

"Are you serious?" asked Ziggy.

"Of course I'm serious!"

"Then you're crazy," shouted Ziggy. "Goddammit, Manni, I'm a naval officer. I'm not here to entertain the men and be their pal. I'm trying to lead them and keep them all from getting killed."

"Ziggy?" said Manni.

"I don't want you talking to my men, Manni. Understand?"

"Ziggy," asked Manni, "can you guess why I'm here?"

Ziggy stared at him.

"I'm not wearing a uniform because I'm here under cover. I don't normally do this in broad daylight, so I had to come up with something that would throw people off and apparently it worked."

Suddenly Ziggy felt like a prize ass. "It's about Franzi, isn't it?" he asked.

"Yes. Cremer was supposed to meet me here, but since he doesn't seem to be around, I guess I'm going to need to brief you. May I proceed?"

"Please," said Ziggy.

"Major Westerby believes Himmler will make his move within

the next two to three days. From what he's hearing, there seems to be some holdup regarding deliveries of gold, but once that happens they'll want to leave quickly. Baumbach's boys would like to move sooner. They've already got a lot of passengers lined up, but apparently Himmler's group is where the real money is. They'd like to get it, but they know they can't wait forever. Are you getting all this?"

Ziggy nodded.

"All right, this is what we want you guys to do: First, increase the guards up at the cove and report any activity there that's even the slightest bit out of the ordinary. Second, keep your ears open for any Nazi fat cats in town suddenly checking out of their rooms. And let us know immediately if anyone starts asking questions about the flying boats. I can't tell you specifically where it might be coming from, but be very careful because these are some extremely nasty groups. Got it?"

"Anything else?"

"Tell Cremer we'll be in touch at the usual time," said Manni.

"Right. Anything else?"

Manni looked at him. "Yes, you and I need to talk sometime." And with that, he was off.

Watching him walk away in the direction of the south gate, Ziggy saw how, with a downward tilt of his head and an imperceptible slumping of his shoulders, Manni's flamboyant figure had transformed into a flat, reductivist version of itself that drew no curiosity and left no impression. So that's how he does it, Ziggy realized. No wonder he can get in and out of places without being noticed.

As he observed Manni fading from view while still in plain sight, Ziggy was wracked by a host of conflicting feelings. Manni drove him nuts, but still he was glad to see him. And as much as he hated being a Loerber Brother, those years of performing together had really been fun. How could he have forgotten that? He didn't want to get involved in one of Manni's gambits. Something was bound to go wrong and chances were Manni would come out of it untouched and anyone helping him would be left holding the bag. But still, the idea of pulling one over on Himmler thrilled him. And doing it with Manni, the Magical Loerber way . . . Suddenly he remembered Sebastian. He hadn't mentioned him at all to Manni. Next time, he told himself.

A few minutes later, Cremer drove up with a squad of guardsmen. He nodded conscientiously as Ziggy relayed the instructions Manni had given him.

"You know, we're not supposed to be doing this," Ziggy said after he'd finished. "This isn't something the grand admiral would approve of."

"Screw the grand admiral," said Cremer.

"Peter!" Ziggy was shocked. He'd never heard anyone speak of Dönitz that way.

"I mean it," said Cremer. "I'm sick of this stuff here, Ziggy. For two years now, they promised us those new U-boats would be ready, that we'd have them and get to wipe the British and Americans' asses with them all over the Atlantic. They promised us that we were fighting for civilization and for all the things that make Europeans better than everyone else. And everything they told us turned out to be a rotten lie. All these years I've given them; I want some of it back.

"Okay, so your two brothers are enemy spies. I can't blame them when I see what we've become. And don't let's pretend the Allies are ever going to let us forget it. Before they start feeding us and letting us rebuild, they're going to take their pound of flesh from us. They're going to humiliate us, make us feel like criminal worms. Westerby says your brother Franzi is a great hero. Let's save him. This is our last chance to do something we can be proud of. And if you're worried that we're going to get our men killed, let's be honest here, how many of these guys are even going to be alive in a few months? Life is cheap right now and it's about to get a whole lot cheaper."

Ziggy's eyes fell on the diamonds on Cremer's Knight's Cross. So this is how it all ends, he thought.

"You're in on it, aren't you?" asked Cremer.

"I guess I am," said Ziggy.

"That's great, old man!"

"So do you have any idea what Manni meant about those people we're supposed to watch out for?"

"Yeah, don't you know? It's those people you were talking about back in Hamburg."

"What people?"

"You know, the Blood of Israel!"

"Did you mention that thing about what I said in Hamburg to Manni?"

"Well, of course I did," said Cremer. "This is a military operation."

"And we're supposed to watch out for them? This Blood of Israel?"

Cremer nodded. "They're supposed to be real assholes."

Again Ziggy thought about Sebastian, but decided not to say anything to Cremer. Things were already getting complicated.

After that, Ziggy left the Marineschule grounds and headed into the city. For a while he walked along the quayside, trying to rid his mind of all the things that had been plaguing him that day: Lüth, Cremer, Manni, and those damn miracle boats.

Then he heard the words in his head: *The Blood of Israel will have its vengeance.* Ziggy stopped in his tracks.

"Don't turn," whispered someone behind him.

Ziggy recognized the voice. It was Sebastian.

"What's Manni up to?" he asked.

"He thinks something is about to happen," said Ziggy.

"Did he say what?"

"No."

"That's all he said? 'Something's about to happen'? I don't see why he'd take a trip over to the security hut just for that. You're not telling me everything."

Ziggy turned to see Sebastian standing a few feet away, pretending to be preoccupied with the contents of a shop window.

"Sebastian," said Ziggy, "I'm trying not to get involved in any of this. I don't understand what the problem is. Aren't you all supposed to be on the same side?"

"The situation is far more complicated than you think," said Sebastian. "Tell me this: Are they planning something?"

"Yes, they are, but I can't talk about it. It's a military operation and I promised to keep it secret. But I will tell you one thing he said: that we should watch out for the Blood of Israel. He said they're assholes."

"Did you tell him about me?"

"No, I didn't get a chance."

"Well, next time you tell Manni—"

"Tell him yourself," snapped Ziggy and walked away as quickly as he could.

(36)

Speer looked up from his desk to see a young American GI standing in the doorway. "Are you Albert Speer?" he asked in strangely accented German. He was wearing combat gear: helmet, a bandolier of ammunition, and a carbine slung on his shoulder. Speer had seen American officers at the Marineschule, but this was his first dogface. What was he even doing in Flensburg? Had he come to arrest him?

Speer decided to answer him in English. "Yes, I am Speer," he said. "Please, how may I help you?"

More than a little taken aback, the GI began to tell him about something called the United States Strategic Bombing Survey, which wanted to interview Speer on the effects of strategic bombing on the German wartime economy.

"Why, certainly," said Speer. "What precisely would you like to know?"

The GI looked confused. "Um, look, if you don't mind, could you just not go anywhere for a few minutes? Let me get Major Spivak up here."

The GI turned and left and Speer went back to the report he'd been reading. But he was too excited to concentrate. The Americans wanted to interview him about managing the armaments industry. He tried to repeat in his mind what the young soldier had rattled off, *United States Strategic Bombing Survey*. What could that possibly mean?

It only took Speer a second to guess. The American air war against Germany had been long, bloody, and, until its last six months, largely ineffective. Now their campaign against Japan was under way and they must have figured that whatever lessons there were to be learned from bombing Germany had better be learned quickly. Well, then, he thought, if that was the case, they'd come to the right man. Nobody knew more about the effects of strategic bombing than Albert Speer.

A half hour later, the GI returned with a bespectacled middle-aged man, short and heavyset, with a big nose, looking every bit the Jew from all the old anti-Semitic posters, only instead of wearing a black banker's suit and a bowler hat, he was in U.S. Army combat fatigues with a .45 strapped to his hip.

The GI said, "Major Spivak, I present to you Reichsminister Albert Speer."

Speechless, Major Spivak stared at Speer. Finally he muttered, "Holy cow!"

Speer stood up from his desk. "Good afternoon, Major," he said, as pleasantly as he could. He thought about extending his hand in greeting, but realized he shouldn't.

Major Spivak didn't return his greeting but continued to look at him with nervous distaste. He was thinking the same thing as everyone else: This man I'm talking to is *Hitler's best friend*!

Finally he recovered enough to say, "Sergeant Fassberg says you're willing to be interviewed."

"Yes, whatever you'd like to know," answered Speer. "It's about strategic bombing, you say?"

"Yes, the economic and other effects of daytime strategic bombing on the German wartime economy."

"Please, have a seat," said Speer. "I'm sorry I cannot offer you any coffee or other refreshment."

Brusquely Major Spivak shook his head, as if refreshment was neither expected nor desired. They sat down and both men began undoing the snaps of their shoulder bags and took out notebooks and manila file folders. "Sergeant, do you have the file on the abrasives industry?" asked Major Spivak.

"Right here," answered Sergeant Fassberg, handing him a sheaf of papers.

"All right, let's start," said Major Spivak.

He spent the next three hours asking Speer very detailed questions, first about abrasives and oil baths and then about specialty steels and problems with machine tools and manufacturing different kinds of screws and fasteners, nearly all of which Speer was able to answer easily off the top of his head.

Though it was obvious Major Spivak continued to regard Speer with extreme discomfort, he nevertheless conducted the interview with complete professional detachment. He'd ask questions, write down the answers, ask follow-ups, and write those answers down as well. In the end, as he sat looking over all his pages of notes, he turned to Speer and, shaking his head with amazement, declared, "Well, Sergeant Fassberg was right, Herr Speer. You're definitely the mother lode."

For one very long moment, Major Spivak stared blankly ahead, while inside of him the angels of light and darkness battled each other. Finally he looked at Speer and with the tiniest hint of cordiality asked if he'd be willing to undergo a more detailed debriefing by senior members of the survey team.

"Why, certainly," said Speer. "I'd be happy to cooperate in any way I can."

"Good," said Major Spivak. "I'll let the guys know. We'll be in touch."

They left without shaking hands or thanking him.

Speer went back to the castle feeling strangely let down. The Americans had come to him like heavenly messengers, only to vanish with the same abruptness with which they'd appeared. It had been the first time in months anyone had come seeking his expertise, and while Major Spivak had not been terribly courteous, he had at least acknowledged that Speer had something no one else had. He wondered what he'd meant when he said his colleagues would be "in touch."

Baumbach, on the other hand, saw it as a clear sign that his friend's bad fortune had reversed. "Well, congratulations, Albert. Now they'll have no choice but to bring you into their new administration. It's just like what they're doing with those rocket scientists from Peenemünde. You'll probably get flown out to Okinawa to join Curtis LeMay's intelligence staff."

"We'll see," said Speer.

"I'd say this calls for a drink, Albert." They settled into another night of drinking and storytelling and by the end of it the whole episode became just a half-remembered jumble in Speer's mind.

He awoke late in the morning with a terrible hangover. Staggering through the hall down to the kitchens, he debated whether to call in sick or just show up the way he was, since everyone else was in a similar state half the time.

As he was working his way through a cup of tea, he heard agitated footsteps running up the corridor toward him. The throbbing turned to a sense of dread. It was the captain of the honor guard that had been assigned to him for security.

"Herr Reichsminister, we have an emergency!"

"What is it?

"The American army is here, demanding to see you."

"What?"

"The Americans, Your Excellency! There must be twenty of them. They've come in jeeps."

"In jeeps? But what do they want? Are you sure they're not looking for Himmler?"

"No, Your Excellency. They say they want you. Reichsminister for War Production Albert Speer. Do you want my men to shoot at them?"

"No, absolutely not! Tell them to wait. I must get dressed first."

He went back to his room and found his best gray suit. Then he selected a French tie and put it on. He caught a glimpse in the mirror and thought that he looked pretty good.

The Americans were waiting for him in the courtyard. Twenty of them, just like the captain had said. They wore uniforms, but no helmets or guns.

Two very tall men stood together. One looked like a hawk, the other like an enormous owl. Next to them was a much shorter man who, by his sheer proximity to them, looked like a hedgehog.

"Good Morning, Herr Speer," said the owl. "I hope you don't mind us dropping in like this, but we were making everybody nervous at the Marineschule." They grinned good-naturedly at Speer.

"We've flown in from Frankfurt this morning to interview you," said the hawk. "Do you have some time to spare?"

"We should introduce ourselves," said the hedgehog. He began pointing out the various army officers and sergeants and reciting their names, though not their ranks. "This is George Sklarz, this is Burton Klein, Bob Gilchrist, Ernie Doyle, Walter Farley, Dan Watson." He went on and on with the names. Speer tried to take it all in, but the names and faces were more than he could process, so he just nodded and smiled like the good host.

Finally the man pointed to his tall colleagues. "This is George Ball, this is Ken Galbraith, and I'm Paul Nitze."

(37)

"For the last time, Reichsführer, Colonel Baumbach meant no disrespect," the Luftwaffe major was telling Himmler as they drove toward the cove. "As head of KG-200, he reports to whomever holds the title of Reichsführer SS, and since the Führer decided to . . ." He paused as he searched for the least offensive way to refer to Himmler's sacking two weeks earlier. "The Führer put him in that position when he gave the title to Gauleiter Hanke. All Colonel Baumbach did was follow orders. It wasn't personal at all."

Himmler made more disgruntled noises, but didn't argue the point. Baumbach, in a plainly mercenary turn, was now offering them passage to Argentina on one of his flying boats. He was demanding stiff payment, to be sure, in gold: one bar per person, payable before boarding. But then, gold was something they had plenty of, and at this point, getting out seemed to be the only thing they could do. In Argentina, they could use their wealth to buy all the safety and comfort they'd want.

Franzi stared out of the window, hoping to find some usable landmark. But it was all just dark woods and moonlit countryside. Fräulein Potthast sat at the other window, looking ahead, bored, while Himmler sat in the center. He had shaved off his mustache and instead of his uniform he had on a nondescript gray suit. Franzi knew that if he didn't find a way to escape in the next five minutes, he'd be going with them. Either that or Macher would put a bullet in the back of Franzi's head and use his gold bar for something fun.

The car was a Horch, driven by someone Franzi had never seen before, while directly in front of him sat Kiermaier, with the Luftwaffe major wedged between them. Behind them were two Mercedes, driven by Macher and Grothmann, carrying another half dozen men as security. The way Macher explained it, if anyone was going to try to ambush them, they'd assume Himmler was in one of the other cars.

"We're almost there," the Luftwaffe man said to the driver. "When I tell you to, blink your lights twice and wait for the countersignal."

"Say when," said the driver.

"Now."

The driver did as he was told and almost immediately there was a light blinking up ahead.

"Now slow down."

Two men came out onto the road with lanterns, waving for them to come forward. Immediately Macher's car pulled alongside the Horch and signaled the driver to stop. "I'll take over from here," he said. He brought his car into the lead. The two men pointed their lights to a side road and waved at them to follow it. "The boatyard is up ahead," one shouted.

They drove up the dirt road slowly. A few seconds later they went through a gate held open by a paratrooper with a machine gun. They entered a darkened boatyard and drove past rows of stacked pipe and shipboard machinery. Franzi could already hear Macher in his car thinking, I don't like this. Everywhere the lights were off: the harbor police buildings, the workshops, and the boat sheds. The moonlight seemed to illuminate only the rows of upturned whaleboat hulls, leaving everything else in shadow. Then he noticed all the abandoned cars lining the road.

"Keep driving, straight ahead," the Luftwaffe man urged them.

Then they saw it: a single streetlamp burning at the foot of a long jetty, its solitary beam thrusting like an accusatory finger into the black water. And in the circle of light beneath it, a large crowd of people dressed in heavy coats and hats with baggage stacked beside them.

Macher signaled them to stop and immediately jumped out of the Mercedes and walked over to them. "I don't like this," he said. "It smells like an ambush."

Himmler motioned to Fräulein Potthast to open the door. They stepped out. "Colonel Macher, you're being unreasonable," said Himmler. "It looks perfectly safe to me. The aircraft is right there." He turned to Franzi. "What do you think, Professor Loerber? It looks safe to you, doesn't it?"

At that, Macher gave a wild snort like he couldn't believe it had come to this. Even so, Franzi got out of the car and began surveying the darkness around them. Macher definitely had a point. There had to be dozens of places for shooters to hide. Personally, he hoped there was an ambush set up. If any shooting started, he could hide himself easily. He was tempted to tell the Reichsführer that the karma was in their favor, but seeing the way Macher looked at him, he said instead, "Reichsführer, I don't know."

Macher's sneer relaxed a bit. "That may be the smartest thing you've ever said," he grunted.

Himmler turned to the Luftwaffe man. "Tell Colonel Baumbach I would like to speak with him," he said.

"Certainly, Reichsführer, if you'll just come this way," the man answered a little too smoothly.

Kiermaier stepped forward to stop Himmler from going. "No, you tell Colonel Baumbach to come here," he shot back.

"I think Colonel Baumbach is extremely busy right now. He can't come up to talk to you."

"Tell him to come here, *now*," Himmler repeated, his voice suddenly cold and hard as ice.

The Luftwaffe man shrugged, then made his way down the hillside to the jetty.

"Everyone keep your motors running. Be ready for anything,"

ordered Macher. "Security, set up a perimeter." Three men jumped out of the car, machine guns in hand, and spread out in the darkness.

A minute later a different Luftwaffe man walked up. "Reichsführer, Colonel Baumbach regrets that he cannot come down and talk to you. He will be flying the aircraft himself and needs to oversee the rest of the preparations. He did ask me to remind you that he has offered you passage as a courtesy and if you're unwilling to accept the terms that have been stipulated, then you are free to seek passage elsewhere. And that includes handing in all weapons before boarding. If you like, we will return them to you once we have landed."

"You expect us to agree to that?" asked Macher.

"Whether you agree to it or not is your business, Colonel. But no one will be allowed on board with a weapon."

He started to leave, but Macher stopped him. "You're staying here," he said. Then he turned to Himmler. "I don't like any of this, Reichsführer. Maybe we should turn around now."

Himmler didn't answer, but it was obvious that he was hesitant. Out in the harbor, one of the enormous aircraft was coming to life. Lights blinked on along its fuselage, then the interior lights came on, revealing the silhouettes of two men in the cockpit settling into their seats.

"Maybe we should turn around and go," repeated Macher.

Himmler licked his lips as though about to say something, but didn't. He was staring at the flying boat.

Then Fräulein Potthast exploded. "What are you talking about? The plane is there! Look at everyone else. They're all going to go. You want it to leave without us? We can't stay. What are we going to do? Keep hiding in dirty farmhouses? Are you afraid of the dark, Colonel Macher?"

Calmly Macher turned to Himmler. "Reichsführer, either you shut her up or I will."

"Fräulein Potthast, be silent," said Himmler in a mild voice.

"No!" she shrieked. "The plane is going to leave without us. We're going to be stuck here. I'm sick of this. I want to go to Buenos Aires!"

"Be quiet, you stupid bitch," growled Macher.

But Fräulein Potthast wasn't listening. "Hiding in stupid, stinking farmhouses!"

Macher grabbed her by the lapel of her fur coat and slapped her hard three times, while Himmler stood by ineffectually. Fräulein Potthast looked around, outraged and embarrassed. Franzi gave her a polite half-smile, while Kiermaier never wavered from his blank expression.

Down in the harbor, the flying boat's six engines began to sputter loudly and the large, three-bladed propellers started turning, slowly at first, then faster and faster as the engines' metallic whine turned into a loud roar. At the same time, the passengers at the jetty started boarding barges that ferried them out to the aircraft. One of the Luftwaffe men shouted, "Make up your mind. We're leaving in five minutes."

"We're coming down," Macher shouted back. "Put out that light now!"

"We need it on! We're still loading!"

"That's your problem," barked Macher. "Kill it now!"

A moment later someone hit a switch and everything was back in darkness. "All right, then," said Macher. He ordered the remaining security men to walk ahead of the cars while the three men already on the perimeter were to take up the rear. Everyone else got back in their cars and with their headlights turned off, they began making their way slowly down the hill.

Then the shooting started. Machine gun fire erupted from all over the boatyard and flares shot up into the air, bathing everything below in cold white light. Macher's men returned fire, while out on the jetty the remaining passengers scattered and collided with each other in panic. People screamed. Grenades exploded. The three cars immediately slammed into reverse and, tires screeching, careened back up the hill, where they stopped long enough to pick up the rest of the men. Then there was a deafening roar as the flying boat exploded in a huge burst of flame that lit up the sky.

As they drove back toward the gates, Franzi looked out the shattered rear window and saw the monstrous aircraft breaking apart as it burned in the water, accompanied by a continuous cracking of smaller explosions as ammunition inside the aircraft cooked off. Himmler was nearly hysterical. This was all Speer's doing, he kept telling them. Speer was a usurper, Speer wanted his gold, Speer coveted his position as ruler of postwar Europe, Speer had always been plotting against him, Speer wanted to unseat him, from the beginning Speer had set out to unbalance everything! Well, he was going to show *him*.

Franzi looked around the inside of the car and realized all the windows were shot out. Everything was riddled with bullets, but aside from some minor wounds, no one seemed to be hurt. Fräulein Potthast held the collar of her fur coat tightly around the back of her head, shielding her ears, silent. Kiermaier looked unperturbed as usual. Franzi felt the cold wind blasting his face and wondered where they were going.

Then Macher called the cars to a halt.

Himmler leaned out the window. "What are you doing, Macher? We don't have time for this."

Macher got out of the car, pulling the Luftwaffe man out by the scruff of his neck and dragging him down in front of Himmler's door. "First we need to take care of this," he said.

It was a young man in the paratrooper sergeant's uniform, probably not even twenty, with dark hair, dark eyes, and olive skin, glaring back at them defiantly like a caged animal. He knows he's dead, thought Franzi.

Macher dragged him in front of the headlights and thrashed him with his fist. "Who are you?" he demanded. "Who are you with? Who sent you?" But the young man wouldn't answer.

Macher grabbed him at the throat and smashed his face with his fist. "Answer!"

"You tried to steal my gold!" Himmler shouted. "Well, you can tell Speer that gold is mine!"

At that, the young man's bloody mouth broke into a hideous grin. "No, it's not yours," he sneered back. "It's ours!"

"How dare you?" screamed Himmler.

The Luftwaffe man made a rasping laugh. "Who do you think you took it from?" he mocked, obviously pleased at how badly he was rattling the Reichsführer. "Now we're taking it back. And you, you're all dead!"

"You're a disgrace to your uniform!" screeched Himmler. "Look at you. A German paratrooper turned common thief."

The Luftwaffe man laughed again and held out his arm for them all to see. There were numbers rudely tattooed on the inside of his arm.

"The Blood of Israel will take its vengeance!" he announced with pride.

Himmler turned white. The young man looked satisfied. He was still grinning at them after Macher had killed him.

(38)

Cremer had chosen a roundabout route up to the schloss, so they wouldn't be noticed. Sixteen men in four open-roofed navy Kübels. Most had rifles, though one petty officer, in direct contravention of the articles of the surrender agreement, carried a machine gun. As for Cremer, in addition to his officer's sidearm, he cradled in his hands a massive pistol that only fired signal flares.

"So here's the plan, Ziggy," he said. "According to your brother, Himmler and his bunch will show up at the castle sometime shortly after ten-thirty. By now Manni should already be hiding inside and we're supposed to position ourselves at the southeast corner of the moat. There is an escape tunnel that comes out at the castle wall twenty meters up from the stone bridge. He's going to bring Franzi out there and they'll swim across the moat to where we're waiting."

Ziggy nodded and stared out at the gray and black mosaic of field and wood. He didn't like any of it.

Cremer went on, "Speer's own security is a joke. But of course there will be Himmler's boys and we already know what they're like. Manni thinks we should be able to pull it off without getting into a gunfight with them. I guess as long as we're on different sides of the moat it shouldn't get out of hand. But he said that if anything else starts up, we should stay out of it, except to provide covering fire."

"What do you think he meant by that?" asked Ziggy. "Who else could show up?"

Cremer shrugged. "He didn't say."

"Great," said Ziggy.

They drove through a forest where everything was dark, slowing down to make a succession of turns. A minute later they emerged again and there was the castle, Schloss Glücksburg, standing silently at one end of a lake. White walls and four towers glowing faintly under a sliver of moon. The lake was pitch-black, returning no reflection, with only the dark gray ribbon of the stone bridge running over the water, connecting the castle with a forecourt on the opposite shore. Everything was completely still; not a leaf rustled, not a tree branch groaned, no sound of a wild animal going through the brush.

They hid the Kübels and spread out along the bank, keeping low to the grass. Someone handed Ziggy a pair of night binoculars and, propping himself on his elbows, he began examining the outer walls and the bridge, looking for the spot where the secret tunnel let out.

He lowered the glasses and exchanged a glance with Cremer. "Two minutes," Cremer whispered.

Two minutes to what? wondered Ziggy. Manni was playing his games again, manipulating things and people like billiard balls. Two minutes until something causes Himmler to decide to come here, with Franzi in tow, right to the spot where Manni just happens to be waiting for them. Manni was an embodiment of the random and irreproducible. When they were kids, he could always figure out what Ziggy and the others were about to do, because, as he once explained to Ziggy, every seemingly spontaneous action was actually the confluence of established habits and patterns.

They heard explosions in the distance. Ten times louder than thunder; high explosive, a lot of it. There was a flash in the northeast, followed by the crackle of smaller ordnance going off. For a second the thought went through his mind that something had gone wrong and it was all over. But then he realized he was sensing Franzi at that moment, inside a car, cold air blasting at him through a shot-out windshield and Himmler babbling on and on about Speer's treachery.

"That was ten-thirty on the mark," said Cremer. "Everyone get ready."

A few minutes later they heard the roar of approaching automobiles, racing up the road as if the devil himself were chasing them. They came out of the woods, two Mercedes and a Horch, all three incredibly shot up. They careened up the road and into the castle's forecourt, and then reappeared as they went over the bridge. Looking at them through his glasses, Ziggy swore he could make out Franzi in the back of the Horch sitting next to Himmler. Then everything was silent again.

"Well, so much for that," said Cremer. "Now we wait for Act Two."

They settled back into their surveillance. The minutes ticked by, five, ten, fifteen. They heard more vehicles approaching. Not as loud, but a lot more of them.

C 39 D

Often it is the case that the further one sinks into despair, the more easily one is roused to brief fits of exhilaration. So it had been with Albert Speer when Baumbach had first suggested they escape to Greenland. For several days he had been barely able to contain his excitement at the thought of camping at the foot of a glacier and hunting walrus amid the ice floes. But once that prospect vanished, he was back in the company of the bitter chimera, which was all that was left of his brilliant dreams.

But today, following his latest session with the Strategic Bombing Survey, Speer was again walking on air. Suddenly the future was rising before him in Technicolor and it looked so tantalizing that even though he knew it might be an illusion, he had to drink deep of it.

Graecia capta ferum victorem cepit, captive Greece captured Rome. It was a phrase Speer had struggled with as a young student first learning Latin. How, he wondered, could a captive capture its conqueror? But now he understood. So charmed were his American interrogators by him that they had decided, by unanimous assent, to rededicate their inquisition "The University of Bombing," with Albert Speer their honored professor.

And maybe the Americans were as much in love with him as they acted. For all he knew they were already sending word back to their people in Washington that Albert Speer is one of *us*.

They'd spent the day discussing machine tools and the mixture of alloys for steelmaking. In Speer's experience, unless they were engineers or technocrats, any discussion about such things would inevitably put listeners to sleep. But these Americans weren't engineers. They were lawyers and economists and intellectuals and their passion for the ephemera of industry came from a different place. Like himself, they were driven to know the greater dynamics between machinery and human endeavor. These men understood that wars are not won merely by brave men with guns and force of will, but by production and logistics and unfettered supplies of oil, chromium, ball bearings, and tungsten carbide.

"John Kenneth Galbraith." Speer pronounced it slowly, savoring the sound of the words and then repeating them again, like an incantation, conjuring up a shimmering vision of policy-level meetings and advisory groups. "John Kenneth Galbraith.

"I tell you, Baumbach, this is a man who is going to matter in the postwar world. You wouldn't believe how bright the guy is. He tried to nail my hide to the wall when I explained how we dealt with the shortages of tungsten carbide. He never imagined we'd rather cut out production of heavier-caliber antitank ammunition in order to keep producing machine tool bits. He thought I was lying. But I showed him. I had the numbers right there in my head. And when he saw that he'd been wrong and I was right, he said, 'Well, then, I take off my hat to you, Professor Speer!'"

By now, of course, they were both quite drunk. Baumbach laughed and with a wide swoop of his arm snagged hold of the whiskey bottle from the table. Holding the bottle aloft, he proclaimed, "Let's drink to your John Kenneth Galbraith!" He refilled Speer's glass and then his own. Then, settling back onto the couch, he clinked his glass against Speer's. "Down the hatch!"

Speer drank the whiskey and leaned back in his chair. "I'm telling you, Baumbach, they ask such great questions."

Instead of answering, Baumbach pushed himself backward against the couch, snaking over the top until his head and shoulders pointed downward and his outstretched hands were touching the carpet. Apparently excited at seeing the world from upside down, he began waving his arms and addressing its inhabitants. "Well, hello!" he called out. "So nice of you to join us. I guess the fact that you're walking upside down must mean you're from Australia. I suppose this means you are also a marsupial. Be that as it may, sir, you are welcome just the same. Why don't you fix yourself a drink and come join us?"

At first Speer assumed Baumbach was speaking to imaginary guests. But when he looked over in the direction where Baumbach was waving, he saw they weren't alone. In the doorway stood a dumpy little man in a gray suit and ridiculous-looking square-frame glasses. Placing his feet on the table, Baumbach pushed himself even farther backward to get a full view of their visitor. The man stood there, looking so comically angry that it made Speer giggle.

Suddenly he realized the man was Himmler and in an instant the drunkenness dried up in him. He struggled to his feet. "Reichsführer, I'm sorry, I didn't recognize you!" he said.

Boiling with anger, Himmler stepped into the room, followed by several tall SS men with machine guns in hand. He smiled icily. "It was a nice try, Speer," he said. "But once again you were not successful."

"Whatever are you talking about, Reichsführer?" asked Speer. "I haven't done anything."

"You're not the Reichsführer," protested Baumbach. "The new Reichsführer is Gauleiter Hanke. I know. I personally flew him to Prague in a helicopter."

"Be quiet!" Speer hissed. "I'm sorry, Reichsführer, he means no disrespect. Please, is there something I can do for you?"

"What makes you think, even for a second, that you are entitled to my gold, Speer?" seethed Himmler. "I never took your things. Why are you trying to take mine?"

"But I haven't done anything," said Speer.

"Done anything?" Himmler cried. "You and your friends just tried to kill me, tried to take my gold! But it didn't work." Himmler gloated and raised his finger threateningly. He started accusing Speer of foiling his escape plan, taking over command of KG-200, blowing up his flying boat, and, oddest of all, selling him to the Jews. And now he was here to settle accounts.

"No, Reichsführer, you're completely wrong. I . . . we . . . haven't done anything. We've been just sitting here getting drunk all evening. There must be a misunderstanding. Isn't that right, Werner?" Speer turned to Baumbach, but he had fallen asleep on the couch.

For the first time since he'd come in, Himmler stared at Baumbach. "What's Baumbach doing here? He was supposed to be on the airplane, dead."

"What?" asked Speer, thoroughly confused. But then, seeing that Himmler's confusion was even greater than his own, he stepped forward and the next thing he knew, some other part of himself, shrewd, implacable, and unaffected by alcohol, had commandeered his mouth. There were ironclad reasons, he told Himmler, why neither he nor Baumbach could have had anything to do with the incident Himmler had escaped from. Speer assured Himmler that he had never, ever done anything disloyal to him— in fact, he had spoken up for him to Dönitz that very day.

He went on, making complex explanations and, to his surprise, saw Himmler nodding at different points he was making. Then Himmler waved him to silence. "In that case, Speer, yes, there is something you can do for me."

"Yes, just tell me what it is, Reichsführer, and it'll be done at once," Speer heard himself say.

"I need another airplane, Speer."

"Yes, of course, Reichsführer," said Speer. He suddenly felt the waves of drunkenness washing back over him. He wanted to sit down. He wanted to get rid of Himmler quickly so he could go lie down. He wanted to go to the bathroom, but he knew he couldn't ask Himmler to hold the thought for a second while he left the room.

"I need it now, Speer."

"Yes," agreed Speer. "Let me see what I can do." An airplane. He imagined snapping his fingers like a headwaiter. *An airplane at once for the Reichsführer!* "Airplane?" he repeated. "Yes, ummm, come to my office first thing in the morning and I'll have it taken care of at once," he said.

Himmler glared at him. "Not in the morning, Speer. Now!"

"Yes, Reichsführer."

Himmler was getting angry again. Speer tried to summon up the eloquent person inside himself to explain for him again, but that person seemed to have wandered off. "Ummm, unfortunately, under the current circumstances"—he paused to stare at the swimming ceiling—"my current brief as Grand Admiral Dönitz's chief of, ummm, economic and industrial"—his knees were beginning to buckle, Himmler's face now a grotesque caricature of something from some other time—"does not allow allotments of unauthorized"—he imagined having pliers to grab words with, the words like fish, fish like airplanes—"ummm, airplanes to, ummm, current or former members of the previous government, in accordance with Grand Admiral Dönitz's explicit, explicitly express, uhhh . . . agreement with the Allied Control Commission."

"Allies?" shouted Himmler. "It would seem to me, Speer, that you are considerably more concerned with insinuating yourself into their good graces than with preserving Germany's life spring! You always thought you were better than the rest of us, that you were exempt, just because you were the Führer's favorite. Now you think because there is a new order taking hold in Europe you can just disassociate yourself from us and become part of it. Well, it's not that simple. They have to have a reason to want you.

"Let me tell you something else, Speer. There are still numerous changes about to take place, changes you couldn't begin to grasp. Being able to design buildings isn't enough. Now they're going to want someone who knows what's going on in the streets, someone who understands the forces of destiny, of karma. You're nothing more than a grubby little technocrat, Speer. You will never be Eisenhower's architect!"

Speer felt the words cascading past him and wondered how long it would take for Himmler to tire and either shoot him or just go away. He was staring past Himmler and his aides to the doorway and to his shock saw Manni Loerber wedged between two men like a prisoner. Speer stared at him, but Manni looked away as though he didn't know him. What was going on? Was this one of the other Loerbers?

Somewhere in his drunkenness, Speer remembered that time in the Ruhr when Manni had told him, *If you ever want to trap Himmler, all you have to do is wait outside my office for him to show up in the middle of the night.*

" . . . for the karmic convergence requires very specific . . ."

Then Speer noticed a shadow moving behind the men in the doorway. From nowhere a hand clapped itself over one of the troopers' mouths. The other hand was clutching a knife, which plunged into the man's neck. Immediately the body went limp and was pulled noiselessly into the darkness. A moment later the same thing happened to the other trooper. The way they were taken, both seemed almost compliant in letting their throats be cut.

The assailant emerged, looking directly at Speer, finger on his lips. It was Manni, clearly Manni. He smiled at Speer for a second as he tapped the other Loerber Brother on the shoulder. A look of sudden understanding flashed through his brother's eyes, and then he too disappeared.

Almost immediately there was machine gun fire outside. Himmler's aides sprang into action, pushing Himmler behind them, running up to the doorway and firing shots into the corridor. There was a rapid exchange of fire farther down the hall.

"They've killed Bauer and Schmidt!" somebody shouted.

"How'd they get in here?"

"I don't know."

"We have to go now!" one of them shouted. "Reichsführer, stay behind us!"

Speer pitched forward, collapsing onto the thick carpet. He gazed up to watch Himmler and the others leave. Outside, there was the sound of a gun battle going on. But he couldn't tell what was real anymore and what wasn't.

(40)

"I see one of them coming out now!" whispered one of the sailors, pointing to a shadowy spot at the foot of the castle wall. Peering through his binoculars, Ziggy made out a dark figure coming out of the ground. It was Franzi, creeping along the bank, looking like he had no idea what to do next.

"Signalman, flash your light at him," ordered Cremer. "Let him know we're here." The signalman held out his flashlight and did as he was told. Franzi seemed to notice it, but still made no attempt to get into the water. "What is he waiting for?" hissed Cremer. "He needs to get moving before they start shooting at him."

By now the shooting had been going on for twenty minutes and was at its height. The British were pouring gunfire into the castle entrance, but to little effect. Though they had the forecourt, the SS still had both ends of the bridge and were shooting down from the castle's high windows.

None of it made any sense, thought Ziggy. If the Allies were so mad to capture Himmler, why had they decided to do it with such a paltry force? They could have easily sent in an entire armored division if they'd wanted to. Instead they'd elected to storm Schloss Glücksburg with a force of barely fifty men, whose shooting and assault skill was hardly equal to that of the much smaller but determined force inside. Luckily, neither side seemed to be aware of Cremer's group hiding in the tall grass along the bank of the moat.

"Signal him again," whispered Cremer.

Franzi looked in their direction and lowered himself down the bank, pushed away, and began swimming toward them. Almost immediately there was a burst of machine gun fire from one of the castle windows. Franzi dipped under the water and reappeared a few seconds later back at the bank.

"Covering fire!" shouted Cremer. Several of the sailors began firing their rifles at the men in the windows, who remained where they were, shooting bursts back at them, seemingly unconcerned about the prospect of getting hit.

"Captain," shouted one of the men. "Here come some Tommies."

Ziggy turned and saw a group of British soldiers crawling out from the forecourt and working their way along the side of the building toward the moat.

"Cease fire," shouted Cremer. "Everyone down."

Still unaware of their presence, the British soldiers came to the corner of the forecourt nearest the moat and started shooting at the castle entrance. The SS returned the fire, forcing the British back behind the edge of the building. Immediately four of the Tommies broke away from the wall and made for the tall grass where Cremer's group was hiding. Two were lugging a heavy machine gun, the others a tripod and belts of ammunition.

"Everyone stay down. Nobody shoot," hissed Cremer.

A few seconds later, the four Tommies found themselves surrounded by Germans with rifles. "Get down, and not a word from any of you," said Cremer in English. Startled, the four soldiers dropped to their knees and put their hands up.

"We're trying to get one of our men out," he told them. "Don't interfere with us and we won't interfere with you. Deal?"

"You are not SS?" asked one of them in oddly accented English.

"No, navy," Ziggy answered. Then something occurred to him. "You're not British, are you?"

None of them said anything.

"You're Blood of Israel."

They remained silent.

"Your enemy is across the moat, remember that," said Ziggy.

They nodded.

"All right, then," said Cremer. "We're going to be giving covering fire. We won't shoot at you. Take your position, and good luck."

As quickly as they could, the four ran to their new positions on the bank. A moment later they had the gun set up and were pouring fire into the castle entrance.

Cremer stood up and waved his arms. "Come on!" he shouted to Franzi. "Get moving!"

Franzi let go of the bank again and began swimming toward them with forceful strokes. The men in the windows opened up again with their machine guns, hitting the water only a few yards from Franzi, but he kept swimming.

"More covering fire," shouted Cremer.

By now the shooting was going on in all directions: from the castle, from inside the forecourt, from the bank next to it, from the windows and the bridge. But the hundred yards of water that separated the opponents prevented any of it from having much effect, other than trapping Franzi in the middle of it. He would dive under for stretches of twenty or thirty seconds, then come back up at nearly the same spot, and resume swimming erratically before being forced underwater again. It was obvious that at the rate he was going, he would never make it across.

Ziggy tried to think. They had to come up with something quick! Something to make the shooting stop. Something to entice Himmler and his group into breaking out. Something to—

Lightning over the castle.

The words jumped into Ziggy's head and kept repeating themselves like the lyrics to a music hall song: . . . *lightning over*

the castle . . . lightning over the castle . . . lightning over the castle . . .
He tried to push them out of his mind, but they kept coming
back. *Lightning over the castle.*

"Give me the signal pistol," he said to Cremer.

"What?"

"Give it to me!"

Cremer handed it over. "What are you going to do?"

Ziggy didn't answer, but raised the pistol high in the air and
fired it, sending a white-hot meteor blazing into the sky. It exploded in a blinding, molten burst before drifting slowly to the
ground.

Ziggy cracked open the pistol and removed the massive spent
shell. "Quick! Give me more rounds," he told Cremer.

"I've only got two," answered Cremer, handing them to him
from inside his coat pocket. Ziggy loaded a fresh round and fired
it, then the other one. As they watched them explode, a hush
came over the battlefield.

Now what? thought Ziggy. In another second everyone would
realize it was all a bluff and start shooting again.

But then they heard a screeching, excited voice echoing from
the castle's entrance. "It's the sign! It's the sign! The prophesy is
being fulfilled. Three lightning bolts over the castle. My time has
come. Macher, Grothmann, stop what you're doing. We must
leave this moment. Our karma, Macher! We're invincible!"

Moments later the two Mercedes and the Horch darted across
the bridge and into the forecourt. There was gunfire, but the cars
never slowed and a few seconds later they were back outside, roaring down the road and disappearing into the distance.

"I don't believe any of this," Ziggy heard one of the men saying.

In the water of the moat, he could see the splashes and ripples
as Franzi quickly swam toward the shore. He seemed to be doing
all right. In another few minutes he'd be there. The fake Tommies

on the bank had already removed the machine gun from its tripod and were carrying it away as quickly as they could, but the ones at the forecourt wall had turned to face Cremer's group, their rifles at the ready. One of them was running back to the forecourt entrance.

"I've got a feeling they are about to declare our little truce over," Cremer said to Ziggy.

A minute later, the Tommy reemerged with a man who looked like he might be their leader. He waved for one of them to come over.

"I'll go," said Ziggy and began walking toward them. The man came forward, walking quickly and keeping his hands out by his sides, palms open. They stopped a few feet from each other. Back by the forecourt, the soldiers had assembled in a line, looking like they were ready to start fighting again.

"Hello," said Ziggy in English.

"So what's this about?" the man asked in German.

"You tell me," said Ziggy.

"Who's this person in the water?"

"That's not your concern," said Ziggy.

"You're one of the Loerber Brothers, aren't you? Then you're also a Jew. You should be helping us instead of them," he said.

"I just did help you," answered Ziggy. "Now I want you to go and leave my men alone."

"That gold belongs to us."

"Well, go look somewhere else. We don't have it," said Ziggy. "Don't take it out on us just because you screwed up the whole thing."

"Don't think the matter is settled yet," the man said. "We'll talk again." And he waved to his men that they were leaving.

Ziggy walked back. Franzi was still in the water, but he was almost there. As he climbed up onto the bank, the sailors grabbed his arms and pulled him onto the grass. He was shivering from cold and exhaustion, his undershirt and shorts sticking to his skin.

Someone took his jacket off and put it on him. He looked around bewildered before finally fixing his eyes on Ziggy.

"Ziggy?" he asked. "Is that you?"

Ziggy was about to say, *Yes, Franzi, it's me,* but then he stopped. The face, the voice, was not Franzi's.

It was Sebastian.

(41)

"Korvettenkapitän Cremer," asked Dönitz, "did you not suggest to me several days ago that we move the flying boats out of Flensburg Harbor to the patrol station to the north?"

"Yes, Grand Admiral, that is correct," said Cremer. He stood rigidly at attention, the way they always did when reporting to the old man. Ziggy was next to him, waiting for the grand admiral's wrath to be directed at him, while in chairs a few feet away two Allied officers glared at them with undisguised malice.

"Didn't you also inform me that you were placing lookouts in the surrounding hills to keep an eye on them?"

"Yes, Grand Admiral."

"So then, logically speaking, you should have known anything that might have been going on up there."

"Yes, Grand Admiral."

"And yet you profess to know nothing of the incident which took place last night. How is that?" Dönitz regarded them both icily. He was furious. Twenty minutes earlier the British and American officers had stormed into his office, accusing him of secretly moving the flying boats out of sight in order to allow a large number of former Nazi officials to escape. To defend himself, he called in Cremer and Ziggy, the two men who were supposed to keep him on top of these things. But instead everything they were saying made him look like a liar, and worse, a fool.

"Well?" asked Dönitz.

"Grand Admiral," Cremer began, "at the time the incident at

the cove took place, my men and I were involved in an operation at Schloss Glücksburg, assisting a British unit in an attempt to capture Reichsführer Himmler, and therefore could not leave to investigate."

Dönitz sat still, like an iceberg that had just become infinitely cooler.

The British colonel raised his eyebrows incredulously. "Really?" he asked. "We are not aware of any effort by our forces to subdue the Reichsführer."

"Why wasn't I informed about this?" asked Dönitz.

"Because it was a secret operation," volunteered Ziggy and immediately regretted it.

"Secret? Secret from whom?" asked the American.

"Sir, we were asked not to tell anyone so as not to jeopardize the operation's success."

"Told by whom?"

"A British intelligence officer named Major Westerby."

The two Allied officers exchanged significant glances. For a second Ziggy thought he saw just the tiniest glint of relief in Dönitz's implacable mien, that perhaps this was all just a misunderstanding and that his trusted captains were merely doing what they'd been ordered.

"Were you?" asked the British officer. "And when did he call you to action?"

"Last night around eight-thirty," said Cremer.

"You're lying, Captain Cremer," said the American.

"Captain?" asked Dönitz. "I expect you to tell the truth."

"I am telling the truth," said Cremer.

"Captain Cremer," said the American, "Major Westerby has been dead for two days."

"Murdered," the British officer added.

Ziggy felt the coldness that always came over him whenever he learned a friend or former shipmate had died. Poor Westerby, he thought. He'd been right about the danger Franzi was facing.

"Actually, the request came from Major Westerby's adjutant," Ziggy said.

"Oh?" said the British officer. "And who might that be?"

"His name is Manni Loerber."

There was a very long silence. The British officer stared at Ziggy. Dönitz stared at Ziggy. The American looked like he had no idea what was going on.

"Manni Loerber?" asked the British officer in a shrill voice, like he knew he was being pointedly insulted. "Manni Loerber of the Flying Magical Loerber Brothers? Is this your idea of a joke?"

"My brother," said Ziggy.

"Grand Admiral." The British officer turned angrily to Dönitz. "What is going on?"

"Captain Cremer," said Dönitz, as coldly as before, "explain what your subordinate is talking about."

"Sir?" asked Ziggy.

"Not another word out of you, Loerber," said Dönitz. "Captain Cremer, report."

"Major Westerby approached us with his adjutant Corporal MacDonald, who in fact is Captain Loerber's brother Manni, who then called us last night to provide support for an operation against Himmler. He never said anything about flying boats or anything going on in the cove, only to expect Himmler's arrival sometime shortly after ten-thirty at Schloss Glücksburg. But since the flying boat blew up at precisely ten-thirty, I assume he must have had something to do with it."

"Corporal MacDonald?" countered the British officer. "I know for a fact that Major Westerby never had anyone working for him with that name."

The American jumped in. "I think we can stop this part of the discussion right here."

"But Colonel," protested the British officer, "if this Corporal MacDonald knows something, shouldn't we—"

The American cut him off. "This discussion is closed, Colonel."

Ziggy watched them stare at each other, the British officer red with indignation, the American angry at having had to reveal that he'd been holding back on some key information. The British officer looked away from the American and, facing the window, asked, "So then, Captain Cremer, was this joint operation you describe successful?"

"No, the Reichsführer and his men got away."

"Perhaps this phantom operation was actually just a way of helping Himmler to escape?"

Dönitz bristled. "Colonel, I can assure you none of my people have been helping Himmler in any way," he said. "We have been scrupulous in observing to the letter the terms of the surrender agreement, and any suggestion to the contrary is an affront to the navy's honor."

But the American was already in a hurry to wrap things up and get out. He stood up, forcing his British counterpart to do the same. "We've heard enough, Grand Admiral," he said. "We'll be making our recommendations to Supreme Headquarters. I can assure you that neither General Eisenhower nor the European Advisory Commission will take any of this lightly. Good day, gentlemen."

⁅ 42 ⁆

Ziggy returned to his post at the front desk dealing with the endless stream of supplicants. The day seemed to drag on forever. When his relief finally came in, Ziggy hurried into his coat and went to the park, hoping not to run into Cremer or anyone else he knew.

As usual the park was crowded equally with the victors and the defeated, all eying each other but otherwise doing nothing. Except for the British and German MPs clutching submachine guns as they walked side by side, no one looked particularly hostile. Instead of helmets, the British soldiers wore their blue, brown, or red berets, which together with the spring blossoms and flowers made things somehow appear festive.

Ziggy strolled the park's main circular path several times. By some mutual understanding there was no saluting either among friends or foes. Finally he spotted a freshly vacated bench and sat down on it. On the bench opposite him two Luftwaffe colonels basked in the sun, while on the bench adjoining his, three Scottish officers, all with identical walrus mustaches, chattered away over cigarettes.

Ziggy leaned back and stretched out his arms along the top of the bench. He let his eyes close just enough so that he could still see the sunlight filtering in. He was still boiling over the previous night's dustup at the castle. After spending an entire war doing everything he could to minimize his own casualties, he'd led his men blindly into something half-baked and amateur. And why had he done it? Because of his brothers! If any member of the public had been told that the Flying Magical Loerber Brothers had put together a military rescue operation, they'd have burst out laughing. Is this a joke? Is this a new routine? Correct on both counts! Nazi Germany had always needed its own version of the Keystone Kops! No wonder we'd lost. At least none of our guys got hurt, he told himself, feeling a little calmer as a result.

Suddenly the soft haze of sunlight in front of his eyes went dark. Someone was standing in front of him. Ziggy let his eyes open a crack and saw it was Sebastian.

"So you wouldn't help me, but you've been working with Manni," Sebastian spat out angrily.

Ziggy tightened down his eyelids. "Would you mind getting out of the way? You're blocking my sunlight," he said.

"I think you need to tell me what's going on," said Sebastian. "Why did you leave me in the dark?"

"I didn't leave you in the dark," answered Ziggy, trying to stay calm. "Manni and Cremer set the whole thing up. I just went along for the ride." He opened his eyes. Sebastian was standing before him like a petulant child. The Scottish officers were staring at him. Of all his brothers, Sebastian had always been the most prone to temper tantrums. Has he been throwing them all these years in front of strangers?

"No, I don't throw temper tantrums in front of strangers," hissed Sebastian. "It's just being around you guys . . ."

Ziggy patted the spot on the bench next to him. "Sit down, why don't you? You're making the enemy nervous."

Sebastian sat down and let out a long breath. "I'm sorry, Ziggy, but Manni really screwed things up for me with that cowboy act of his. Two of those guys he killed were my own people." He remained silent for a while before adding, "And Franzi is still Himmler's prisoner." He got up from the bench. "Come on, let's walk," he said.

They left the park, heading to the waterfront. Walking along the quayside, Ziggy observed that Sebastian looked much older than any of the others. His hair had thinned and there were creases and cobwebs of wrinkles radiating from under his eyes. Manni hardly looked any older than when they were still performing and from what he'd glimpsed of Franzi, he did too. I'm certainly older, Ziggy thought to himself. A thirty-year old U-boat captain is older than Methuselah.

"I'm putting together a new plan," said Sebastian. "I'm not sure how I'm going to do it, but we've got to offer Himmler another means of escape. Unfortunately, it can't involve KG-200. After last night, that thing is over. But I'm pretty sure I'm going to need Cremer and his guys. Do you think you can talk him into it? Talk to Manni too. Get him on board." Sebastian paused, looking directly at Ziggy. "It's for Franzi. Can I count on you?"

Ziggy had never had any difficulty saying no to someone. Being a navy officer made it extremely easy. But for some reason, he heard himself saying, "Yes, Sebastian, you can count on me. I'll talk to Cremer."

"Great," said Sebastian. "I'll be in touch." And with that he strode off like he hadn't a care in the world.

❨ 43 ❩

For the next two days Dönitz and the others continued to treat Ziggy with a version of the same icy correctness with which they were being treated by the British and Americans. No one spoke to him unless it was an order, and then with such disdain that Ziggy began to suspect he'd never return to Dönitz's good graces.

Then in the middle of the morning on the third day, Lüdde-Neurath came up to the front desk and began speaking to Ziggy in an altogether normal tone: "The old man wants you to go to the motor pool. Get a vehicle, drive up to Schloss Glücksburg, and fetch Speer. It sounds like he's playing the truant again. Bring him back, no excuses. The grand admiral doesn't care if he's dying of cancer. Do you think you can do it?"

"Jawohl," answered Ziggy, jumping to his feet. "I'll bring him back immediately."

"Well, try not to shoot the place up."

The motor pool assigned him a small Kübel with exactly one liter of fuel in the tank. Ten minutes later he was approaching Glücksburg. In the daylight, uncloaked from darkness and shadow, the Schloss hardly resembled the place where they'd fought a crazed gun battle only two nights before. Instead he saw a slightly garish tall white building, not at all fearsome, with narrow windows and uninteresting proportions.

Driving up to the front gate, he was met by a squad of armed but dispirited-looking Wehrmacht. Ziggy wondered where they'd been the night of the battle. Had they absented themselves by prior arrangement or simply fled upon seeing Himmler's men drive up?

The soldiers stepped aside and Ziggy motored slowly through the narrow forecourt passage. As he passed out of the rear portal and began driving over the bridge, something up on the battlements caught his eye. He looked up against the sunlight and saw the silhouettes of two men juggling. Stopping the car, he held his hand up against his forehead to shield his eyes from the glare. One of the men was unmistakably Manni. The other was not so tall, a little heavier and older, but also surprisingly nimble, like he'd been juggling for years. It was Speer.

Ziggy parked the Kübel inside the courtyard, next to some American jeeps. One of the sentries escorted him inside, past a small crowd of American officers sitting expectantly on some couches. Seeing Ziggy enter, they all looked surprised, as if worried that he might start shooting at them. Speer came down the steps, a secretary at his side, carrying a thick sheaf of papers. The Americans all got to their feet. Speer was smiling at them graciously. When he saw Ziggy his smile soured.

"What is it?" he grunted.

"The grand admiral wants you," answered Ziggy.

Speer rolled his eyes and nodded vaguely, as if reeling from the weight of all the undue demands Dönitz was putting on him. "Look, I need to take care of some things here, and I'll be right along. All right?"

Ziggy shook his head. "Tell them to wait. The grand admiral wants me to drive you back right away."

Speer let his annoyance show. "Very well," he said. "Would you give me a minute to talk to my guests?"

"I need to speak with my brother," said Ziggy. "Where is he?"

Speer looked bewildered.

"Manni Loerber."

"Your brother?" Speer gaped at Ziggy's face, searching helplessly in it for something familiar. Then it hit him. "Manni? Yes," he said. "Sorry. He's up on the roof. Second staircase on your left."

"Thank you," said Ziggy, running past him up the stairs.

Up on the battlements everything appeared deserted. Ziggy wandered around the walkways wondering if there was some other way down that Manni might have taken. The wind was blowing in from the Baltic and, looking out toward the harbor, Ziggy could see a lone freighter coming in. Was it Allied or one of theirs, a late straggler from the eastern territories that had managed to elude the Russians? A few were still creeping in, laden with refugees.

"Hey, Ziggy! Think fast!" snapped a familiar voice behind him.

Ziggy whirled around to see Manni hurling a red ball at him. He caught it and shot it back just as more balls came his way: a blue ball followed by a yellow one and then a green. Ziggy tossed each one back and in a second he was fully immersed in a juggling bout with his brother. How long had it been?

Manni laughed. "Well, it's good to see that your years in the navy haven't rendered you completely useless."

Ziggy grinned back. It was nice how some things stayed with you.

"I wish you'd told me about Sebastian," Manni said.

"You really didn't give me the chance," answered Ziggy. Catch it and toss it back.

"He really screwed things up being there."

"He seems to feel the same way about you."

Manni started tossing alternating balls to Ziggy in a high, arced trajectory.

"Jesus, what's he doing with the Blood of Israel in the first place?" asked Manni, a look of disgust on his face. "I mean, those guys are a disaster. You saw what happened at the cove."

"Oh? Is that what happened at the cove?"

Manni's smile broadened, but Ziggy knew he was worried.

"Westerby started hearing about it a year or so ago. Lots of SS all getting the same bad dreams. When he told me he thought it sounded like Sebastian's work, I told him he was nuts, that Sebastian was dead." Manni looked hard at Ziggy. "Turned out Westerby was right."

Ziggy interrupted. "I take it you know about Westerby."

Manni stopped arcing the balls. They were all coming at Ziggy straight now. "Yeah, I know about Westerby. Why do you think I'm hiding out here?"

"You're hiding out?" asked Ziggy. "This is your idea of low-key?"

"Absolutely," answered Manni. "Speer is my cover. Next to him I'm invisible. *The New York Times* was here the other day. They never noticed me."

"Who do you think killed him?" asked Ziggy.

"Westerby?" Manni stopped smiling. "It could have been anybody. Normally, I'd tell you the Russians. Westerby had been talking to Schellenberg's boy Steiner. Steiner was in charge of running a secret group they'd put into Soviet counterintelligence."

"Moonpool," said Ziggy.

"Yes, Moonpool."

Ziggy interrupted again. "Steiner was also in charge of hiding SS gold for Schellenberg. He's also Franzi's, um, boyfriend." Ziggy blanched with embarrassment.

Balls started falling onto the ground. Manni stared at Ziggy, his mouth gaping in amazement.

"How'd you know that?"

Ziggy didn't answer.

"Who told you that?"

"Franzi did."

"When?"

"Just now."

"Just now?"

Ziggy nodded.

"Franzi's . . . queer?"

"Is he?" Ziggy didn't know what to think. His brother was homosexual? As long as he didn't think about it, the whole question had seemed somehow like a foregone conclusion.

"Can you get him to tell us where he is right now?"

Ziggy thought about it a second. "He doesn't know where he is. He's hidden in a forest somewhere."

"Hey," said Manni, "just what is it with Sebastian anyway? Can you believe he'd snow his own family like that for twelve years?"

Ziggy told Manni about meeting Sebastian in the park. "He wants us all to help him rescue Franzi," he said. "He wants to know if you're interested."

Manni thought about it for a second. "Is the Blood of Israel going to be involved?"

"Presumably."

"They're losers."

"So what should I tell him? Are you in?"

"Sure, I'm in. What about Cremer?"

"I haven't asked him yet."

"Does Sebastian have any ideas?"

"I don't think so."

"Well, I do," said Manni, smiling suddenly. "As before, it's mainly a question of luring them out of hiding. Right now nobody seems to know where that might be. But we do know this: Himmler still has his networks of people with their eyes open. He's got couriers too. If a nice enough opportunity presented itself, he'd get word of it." Manni gave a foxy grin. "The best thing would be if they heard about an opportunity coming from someone known to be nursing a grudge against your Grand Admiral Dönitz. If that person had something to offer that was just a little out of the ordinary, well, they might just jump at it."

"Who are you talking about?"

"You really are an idiot, Zigmund," said Manni, rolling his eyes. "Don't you recall a high-profile incident only a week ago involving yourself, Captain Lüth, and a certain die-hard captain lieutenant named Rasch?"

Ziggy nodded, thinking it sounded like a bad idea already.

(44)

The new plan quickly began taking form. Following introductions by Manni and Cremer, Sebastian's associates in the SS had no trouble getting Rasch interested. Word soon made its way back to Himmler's web. Sure enough, the next evening Manni arrived at Cremer's hut with two of Himmler's representatives who wanted to meet Rasch and get a look at the midgets.

At first they didn't like what they saw at all. The craft were too small, they told Cremer. They could only carry two passengers besides the crew, and once they were under way communication between the boats was carried out via signal flags and semaphore lamps. Well, they got us here, didn't they? countered Rasch, visibly annoyed. Sorry, thanks, they told him, but we'll probably look for something a little more . . .

The next day they were back. Perhaps there might be a way to use them, they said to Cremer and Rasch. One of the men produced a written list of questions. Would it be possible for their destination not to be revealed until after getting under way? Could they, for instance, have all the midgets surface someplace where they could distribute maps to the different boats? They could, answered Rasch a bit irritably, but it would certainly guarantee an attack from enemy fighters. Wouldn't it be easier simply to have the passengers come aboard with sealed orders? The SS men didn't like it and left without saying anything, but then a couple of hours later they were back again saying they'd decided to go with it and offering terms that were by anyone's standards very generous indeed.

Rasch listened to their offer, then nodded and told them that there was still one little problem. Their tanks were dry. Following the flare-up, Lüth had judiciously ordered them pumped out. They would need to find fuel, not an altogether largish amount. With Himmler's resources it shouldn't be hard to get.

Did Rasch have any ideas? Actually, he did. A few docks away there was a flotilla of minesweepers that the British allowed to operate. They were still getting fuel, which they might be convinced to part with. The problem, of course, was their fuel levels were being closely monitored, but then that could probably be fiddled with, at least for the five or six hours it would take for Rasch's flotilla to get under way before alarms went off.

Listening to Rasch, Ziggy felt sick; the guy could be both so clever and so stupid. He still didn't understand anything about the treachery he was getting himself involved in. Rasch wasn't a bad sort. Under normal circumstances, Ziggy might simply have had a man-to-man talk with him to set him straight and bring him back to the fold. But instead, they were using his weakness to set him up.

After that Ziggy and Cremer got together with Sebastian and went over a seemingly endless list of contingencies. If they were to set up an ambush at such-and-such a place, where would the best place be to deploy Cremer's men? If Himmler's party were to meet Rasch's craft in the bay, could Cremer be waiting in boats hidden along the shallows? Could they drive them onto the shallows? If that was what they wanted to do, how would they stage it? If Himmler's party was traveling northward up the coast road, could they ambush them at the place where the road cuts sharply right?

Things seemed to be coming together until two days later when the minesweeper flotilla got moved north and everything suddenly came to a halt.

(45)

"Experts and planners simply did not appreciate that the social and economic life of a large city will survive even when its physical structure is severely damaged. Life has a way of going on. Housing proved to be a highly elastic resource: bombed-out families doubled up with relatives and friends or were reaccommodated in factory dormitories or barracks or even schools. Transportation is much less elastic, but even there much can be done: nonessential travel can be restricted, sightseeing buses diverted into the regular transit system, empty cabs filled, and people can turn to bicycles.

"I was surprised myself how quickly everything was back up and running after bombings. Factories were relocated, machinery got shifted to intact buildings. Workers were put on second shifts where previously there had only been one. Everyone kept working and morale stayed high."

Ken Galbraith held up his left hand as he continued scribbling furiously with his right. "Professor Speer, when you talk about housing being unexpectedly elastic, I'm wondering, can you tell us the degree to which the apartments and homes of people sent to concentration camps enabled this shifting?"

"That's an interesting question," allowed Speer. "I am sure it must have had some positive effect, but I do not have any information on this issue. Perhaps you should pose this question to Transport Minister Dorpmüller."

But Galbraith wasn't satisfied. "But weren't you in charge of the forced deportation of the Berlin Jews?"

Speer frowned. "I think what you are referring to is that just before the war, as general architectural inspector for the city of Berlin, I did give orders for the forced evacuation of several Berlin neighborhoods, or approximately twenty thousand apartments, which would be demolished to make way for the planned Grand Avenue and the urban structures which would be built along it. It is true that these did involve numerous Jewish-owned flats, but they also included even more flats that were occupied by non-Jews. And while I did give the orders for the demolition of these neighborhoods, the evacuations themselves were carried out by the Goebbels ministry."

"Aren't we getting a little off-topic here, Ken?" said Paul Nitze.

After that they broke for lunch.

(46)

Ziggy was asleep in his quarters when there was a frantic knocking on the door. "Captain Loerber, wake up. It's an emergency!"

He sprang from bed and went to see who it was. One of Cremer's petty officers was standing in the hall. "There's been a shooting out on the Black Path. We need you to come and take charge."

"Where's Captain Cremer?"

"He's away."

Ziggy put on his clothes and followed the sailor outside. Heavy rain was coming down and the wind was howling. It was the kind of night anything could happen. There'd already been a number of shootings and grenades going off in the nearby woods and, as a result, Lüth had ordered sentries posted all over the Marineschule grounds with orders to shoot after only one challenge.

Walking toward the main buildings, Ziggy could make out a small group of people clustered together up ahead, pointing a flashlight at something on the ground. At the sailors' approach, they shone it toward them. "Who goes there?" one of them shouted.

"I've brought Captain Loerber," answered the petty officer.

As they got closer Ziggy realized with a sinking feeling that the man lying there had on the long black leather coat with the braided epaulettes of a navy officer. He forced himself to keep an even stride even though his heart was already racing. When he got there, even before they shone the light on the dead man's face,

Ziggy knew it was Lüth. He lay there with wide-open eyes and half his forehead blown away.

"He didn't answer the sentry's challenge," explained someone in a shaky voice. "He was challenged, but he didn't answer."

They brought up a stretcher and carried the body to the Sporthalle, where a doctor was already waiting along with the same British colonel who had interrogated Ziggy and Cremer in Dönitz's office a few days before.

"Is it Captain Lüth?" he asked.

"Yes, Colonel," said Ziggy.

The British officer ran his hand over his mouth, extremely worried. A few minutes later Lüdde-Neurath and Dönitz came in. "What happened?" Dönitz asked quietly. He listened as the chief sentry recounted the facts.

Then the British officer stepped forward. "Grand Admiral, if I may?"

"Yes, Colonel."

"This matter needs to be taken care of at once. There are already rumors flying about, everything from suicide to a plot by the SS. If this gets out of hand it is unlikely either of us can hold order in the city. Can we count on your cooperation?"

Dönitz nodded tiredly. "We'll have the Board of Inquiry convened first thing in the morning. You may expect our report at noon."

The colonel nodded and left.

Ziggy stared at Lüth, still open-eyed as though sleepwalking. He'd spotted him several times in the days before, walking around the city with groups of displaced women and children who'd been evicted from their flats by the British. Once Ziggy had actually walked up to help carry some suitcases. But while Lüth thanked him, it was obvious he was so fatigued he didn't recognize him.

Dönitz walked over and reached out his hand to close the dead man's eyes. For a while he just stood there. *You shouldn't have died like this,* his face seemed to be saying. *Surviving against all those odds, all those battles, only to die during the coda.* Then he turned back to Ziggy and Lüdde-Neurath. "We need to go tell his wife," he said. "You were his friend, Loerber. You will come with me. Lüdde-Neurath, stay here and take care of the rest of it."

In the morning the inquiry was convened, with several British and American officers in attendance. Testimonies were presented and it was quickly concluded that the whole thing had been a tragic accident, nothing more. But out in the city, things were anything but calm. People were angry and rumors continued to spread and intensify. The local newspaper presented many as facts, including a front-page headline that read, *Hero Shot from Behind.* As the story continued to spin out of control, the British retaliated with a bold gambit. There would be a state funeral with all the honors and privileges that have a way of transforming a mob's anger into a mood of somber reflection.

The next day, swastikas flew again over Flensburg. All the banners and flags with gold cord and bunting, all the splendor and dash of dress uniforms, all the glittering Nazi regalia that had been put away were brought back out one last time.

And in the center of it, flanked by six senior U-boat captains, each with a sword and wearing the Knight's Cross, was Lüth's flag-draped casket, mounted on an artillery caisson drawn by eight horses. Behind it walked Dönitz, followed by Frau Lüth and her four children and then senior navy, army, and Luftwaffe officers. There were generals and field marshals, colonels and majors, along with a blue sea of sailors, looking smart and undefeated.

In front of the cortege marched a single Korvettenkapitän holding out a velvet cushion that bore Lüth's many medals and decorations: the Spanish Cross, the Italian War Cross, the Knight's Cross with swords, oak leaves, and diamonds. He had been Lüth's shipmate and former executive officer whom he'd known even before the war. It was the widow's express wish that the honor go to Ziggy Loerber, and he performed his task with a gravitas that belied the conflicting emotions that raged inside him.

As they marched down Mürwicker Strasse, past the formations of troops and flags and banners, Ziggy felt an inseparable mixture of horror and pride. It was all perfect. Lüth would have loved it. The navy that was his pride and joy had all come together to remember their best. And they did it in the way he believed in: as Nazis. Their navy, bloodied but unbowed in defeat, marching with their heads held high.

A thousand soldiers and civilians lined the mile-long stretch of road leading down to the churchyard. Some cried for what they'd lost and would never get back, others looked dry-eyed and sullen, *Haven't we already suffered enough?* Farther down, groups of British looked on, keeping silent. There were Americans too, though in much smaller numbers, who seemed confused and uneasy about what they were witnessing.

Ziggy stared past them, keeping pace with the clopping hooves behind him.

When this war is over, Loerber, you and I ought to get appointments as district magistrates in the new eastern territories. You can bet they'll be giving them away to any officer with an Iron Cross. It'll be great, Loerber, we'll be country squires without a care in the world, raising kids in the country. You really need to get married, Loerber.

How many times had he told Ziggy he should get married? Lüth loved his wife and children and felt everyone else should taste the same happiness. Ziggy's protestations that he preferred to wait until after the war made no sense to someone who remained convinced of victory.

Ziggy wanted to shout out, *This man passing before you was a warrior, sailor, father, husband, inspired leader, and an ardent Nazi.* He never pretended otherwise, so why bother whitewashing him? He was a Nazi. He was my friend, my brother, my father, my superior officer. He was the very best, and he carried the worst alongside it as a virtue.

How could I have done that to him? How could I have been so unkind? Because he was a Nazi, and I am a Jew. Because I have to be at least as proud of being a Jew as he was of being a Nazi.

He would have given his life for me as he would for any of his men. And he demanded the same of each of us and got it. For those he commanded he would give everything, for those he met in battle he had not an iota of compassion. He wasn't a cruel man, just indifferent to his enemy's suffering.

How many times had I listened to him talk about the Jews, the dirty Jews, the human bacillus, the mongrel race that hated us for our purity, they take our money and defile our women, for the sake of humanity the world must be rid of them? So why do I feel remorse, damn it? So what if for me he would have made an exception? I'm not an exception, I'm just a Jew.

And perhaps I wouldn't have told him if I knew he would die a few days later.

Mürwicker Strasse turned into Bismarckstrasse and then the road turned, leading into the churchyard at Adelby. It was a small church from an earlier century when this was still Denmark. It was built low, with a high-peaked roof and a square steeple.

They stopped outside the churchyard walls and broke ranks to file inside through the narrow wrought-iron gate. The yard was full of trees and flowers, all in full bloom. The leaden sky had let up and sunlight was beginning to break through.

The casket was brought in. A naval hymn was sung, a squad of riflemen stood outside and fired three volleys into the air. The casket was lowered into the ground, and one by one the mourners filed past, shoveling dirt into the grave. And then it was over. The banners and flags were folded up and put away, never to be seen again.

People were milling around the churchyard, chatting with each other as they prepared for the walk back. Ziggy looked at the trees and flowers and the lichens covering the older graves and thought,

If you wanted to spend out your days as a country squire, I guess this is close enough, Lüth.

Then someone touched his shoulder. "Hello, Captain Loerber, it's good to see you." It was von Friedeburg.

"Admiral," said Ziggy. "How have you been?"

Von Friedeburg looked composed. "Come walk with me a little, Captain," he said, taking his arm.

They walked up the road toward the Marineschule. "A beautiful day, in spite of everything," von Friedeburg remarked.

"Yes, Admiral," said Ziggy.

"It's funny that we haven't spoken since the surrender, Captain. I know it's only been two weeks, but it seems like an eternity."

"Yes, a strange sort of eternity," said Ziggy.

"How have you been?"

"Honestly, sir, it seems like everything is flying apart."

"I know," said von Friedeburg. After a while he added, almost cheerfully, "I have become a pariah, Captain. People don't like you once you've come back from the other side of the looking glass."

They walked the rest of the way in silence.

(PART IV)

(47)

After Lüth's funeral, things were quiet for a couple days. Anyone who had actually managed to carry their optimism that far ditched it then. If the future promised anything, it wasn't for them. Ziggy spent his evenings patrolling with Cremer, breaking up brawls, tallying the dead from the accidents, the shoot-outs, and the suicides. Both wondered if anything was going to come of Sebastian's plan.

Then one afternoon, to their great excitement, they received word from Sebastian to meet him at an address in the old town. The operation was back on.

That evening Ziggy and Cremer walked the two miles from the Marineschule to the house. When they got there, Ziggy rang the bell and an old lady opened the door and led them through a darkening corridor into a back parlor, where they found Sebastian sitting with Manni at a small table by the window, drinking tea.

"Come have a seat." Sebastian waved them in heartily. "Great seeing you guys."

They sat down and Sebastian filled their teacups.

"I'm glad you guys made it," said Manni. "Sebastian here was worried that—"

"No, I wasn't," snapped Sebastian.

"Yes, he was," sneered back Manni. "He was afraid you might have had a change of heart after parading in that funeral the other day."

"No, if anything, it makes me want to break free from all this damn moroseness," said Cremer.

"And what about you, Ziggy?" asked Manni. "Are you raring for action?"

"Eager," said Ziggy. "What have you got?"

Manni looked over at Sebastian. Sebastian grinned back like they had already discussed it and it was all settled between them. "All right," Sebastian began. "Let me say first that a lot of things have changed with this operation. Without going into any of them, I'll just say that it's been decided to bring you two a lot deeper into the picture."

"I thought we already were in the picture," said Cremer, with the slightest hint of flippancy.

Sebastian flashed his most velvety smile. "Actually, no," he said. "My superiors previously ruled out anything but very limited involvement from your group. They had doubts as to where your loyalties lay." He cleared his throat. "They thought you might still be connected to the, ahh, old order."

Ziggy cringed. Was Sebastian afraid of offending Cremer? What would he say next: *I'm sure there were some good Nazis?*

"The navy is what the navy has always been," Ziggy said.

"That's exactly what I told them," said Sebastian hastily. "They're willing to accept that now."

"Good," said Cremer. "Because I want to personally nail Himmler for you."

"Well, tomorrow you're going to get your chance." Sebastian smiled. "Now, here's the plan: Tonight we're moving the midget subs to another location, where we can wait for Himmler's party to arrive more or less at their leisure. We want your men divided into two teams: one on land to help in the ambush, and the other in patrol boats that would be used to drive the subs into shallow water to keep them from escaping. How well do you know Gelting Bay?"

"Well enough," said Cremer. "We trained there in sailboats, didn't we?"

"Sure," said Ziggy, remembering with a flitter of nostalgia a carefree summer ten years earlier. He knew Gelting Bay like the back of his hand.

"Good," said Sebastian. "How hard would it be to drive those subs onto the shallows?"

"At low tide? Very easy," answered Cremer. "At high tide it would be harder, but there are still some shoals there that you can get stuck on if you don't know what you're doing."

Sebastian began explaining how the subs would be moved down the coast to Gelting Bay, where they would wait half submerged until Himmler's party arrived, probably sometime after nightfall. After exchanging signals, Rasch would bring his subs closer to shore and then send a rubber dingy for Himmler's party. Then the final payment would be taken and they'd begin rowing back to the waiting subs.

"And that's when we hit them with the lights and start shooting," said Manni. "If any of them manage to get aboard the subs, it's going to be up to you to keep them from getting out of the bay." He paused for a second before adding, "My job is to get Franzi."

"What do we know about Franzi?" asked Ziggy. "Does he have any idea what we're up to?"

"No, because Sebastian has been having concentration problems."

"I have not!" Sebastian shot back.

"Well, he hasn't been able to send out any dreams since last week," explained Manni. "But I'm sure we'll manage anyway."

"Of course," smirked Sebastian. "Manni will do his song and dance for Macher, who will just look away while Franzi sneaks off."

"Well, at least my magic still works," said Manni.

"That's because nothing that annoying qualifies as magic," countered Sebastian without missing a beat. "Magic requires an accompanying sense of wonderment." They both grinned.

Listening to their bickering, Ziggy felt an odd elation. For a moment, it was exactly how it used to be, the endless, quick dressing-room repartee. A glance at Cremer told him he was enjoying it too. But then, their friends had always aspired to attach themselves to the Loerbers as a group. Cremer was just the first one in ten years to be given the opportunity.

A few minutes after that, Manni stood up and said he had to go. Then he asked Cremer to come along with him so they could check out the staging area. Once they were gone, Sebastian set aside the teapot and brought out a bottle of scotch. Ziggy wondered what was going on with him. Had he really lost his ability to project dreams or had he simply decided he didn't want to do it anymore? Whichever it was, the easy smile on his face wasn't giving away anything.

Sebastian poured each of them a drink and shoved one over to Ziggy. "L'chaim, you Nazi son of a bitch," he said with a chuckle.

"L'chaim, piss off, and down the hatch," answered Ziggy. They emptied their glasses. Ziggy put his down. "So is everything all right on your end?" he asked.

Sebastian leaned back in his chair and let out a long sigh. "Yeah, finally it looks like it's all happening. But I tell you, this last stretch has been really difficult," he said. "That guy Macher keeps outsmarting us and every time that happens I got good people losing enthusiasm and they get replaced by fortune hunters, all of whom have their own ideas how things should operate. They'll nod and agree to anything and then turn around and do something entirely different.

"A couple of weeks ago you could still count on a level of cooperation from the British and Americans. It was all under the table, of course, but it was pretty good most of the time. Now? About all anybody wants to do is get laid and stay drunk. The war's over, that's all they care about. They couldn't care less that there are a million SS wandering around. And the gold? They're all hot and horny to get their hands on it, until somebody starts shooting, and then they change their minds."

Sebastian brought the bottle over and refilled Ziggy's glass and then his own. "But the important thing is we'll get Franzi back and then we'll get out of Europe for good," he said.

"Palestine?" asked Ziggy.

Sebastian nodded. "The one place where no one will look, no one will want to remember. They say people there never talk about old Berlin. I think Jews need to forget about Europe any-way. I think that as a people we bought a little too much into the whole thing about Western civilization."

"Oh?" asked Ziggy.

"I mean, look where it got us."

Ziggy wondered if Sebastian was going to try to persuade him again to join them. Had he made a similar pitch to Manni? Had Manni accepted? They certainly had been acting pretty chummy.

"You know, I still can't believe you're alive," said Ziggy.

Sebastian gave a sad smile. For a while he didn't say anything. He drummed his fingers against his glass. Then he looked at Ziggy. "So how did Father take my disappearance?" he asked.

"How do you think?" answered Ziggy. "We all thought you were dead. Or worse, that you were stuck in some scratch-built prison. You know what it was like then. Father looked everywhere. He went to his friends in the Gestapo and in the Criminal Police, but nothing ever turned up. I mean, a celebrity like you disappears and nobody knows anything? For a while everybody thought you might be in one of those amateur prisons Göring had set up, but they were afraid to ask for fear of getting Göring riled up against them."

Sebastian looked taken aback, as if the answer he'd spent years hiding from had finally landed in front of him. "Come on," said Ziggy. "Didn't you discuss any of this with Manni?"

Sebastian shook his head. "No, he wouldn't talk about it. He's still mad at me. Look, I'm sorry I had to do it that way, but I had to take advantage of the chaos. You said it yourself; everything was fragmentary, twenty different police forces, overlapping jurisdiction, every question that arose was bound to cause problems. Nobody wanted to start a turf war, so nobody looked very hard. It was perfect."

"Well, you could have written."

"No, I could not have written."

Ziggy decided not to argue it. "So who is Blood of Israel?" he asked.

Sebastian gave an ironic smile as he refilled their glasses. "Better you should ask, who isn't Blood of Israel?" Ziggy waited for him to elaborate, but instead Sebastian said, "We're buying land in Palestine, at least my group is. Putting in kibbutzes, nice places, everybody gets along, everybody shares. We've started raising vegetables, oranges, grapefruit, lemons, olives. Have you ever seen an olive tree, Ziggy? They're incredible."

Sebastian's face darkened. "But, of course, that's just our group. There are others; antisocialists, ultrasocialists, revisionists; the Jabotinskys, Lehi. More than you can keep track of. Most of the time we work together okay, but now it's getting funny."

"Is that what happened at the cove that night?"

"Honestly, I don't know what happened. All I know is the day before there were all these Jabotinsky-types dressed as Luftwaffe. The next day they were gone. Even I get told only so much."

"So how do we know this isn't going to happen again?"

"Relax, there aren't that many people involved. And we only came up with our current plan yesterday when we got the fuel. Plus, the flying boats attracted too much attention. Everybody suddenly wanted to get into the act. No one will bother to think about midget submarines at all."

"So how did you get the fuel?"

Sebastian shook his head and laughed. "I don't mind telling you it was truly epic. The kinds of things that happen. We arrange to pump some from the minesweepers and right before we can do it, what happens? They get ordered north by the British. We divert a tanker truck full of diesel from the British, what happens? It gets hijacked by some Scottish infantry who for all I know probably have a deal going with the Danish gangsters who're taking over all the trucking in this part of Germany.

"And then I realized the solution was right here under our nose. The German navy might not have a drop to spare, but the Marineschule keeps a nice little store of its own for training cadets in handling large harbor craft. The British didn't even know about it. It was just a question of finding a way of getting it released to us.

"I'm telling you, it was a lot easier when the war was still on. Things were a lot more cut-and-dried. See a guy in an SS uniform, your first thought isn't how can I get him to do things for me, it's how do I slit his fucking throat to maximum effect and still get away."

"And that's what you did the whole war?" asked Ziggy.

"Well, not the whole war. The real killing campaign only started this year, when it became easy to send people in. Before that, we'd infiltrate people into SS units and get information from them, occasionally blow something up, but mostly just basic intelligence stuff. Not that different from what Manni was doing." Sebastian paused a moment, then added, "In fact, Manni's been doing plenty of assassinating himself. He won't tell you that, but our people spotted him in the Ruhr. Once he even got one of our people out of a Gestapo jail, without even knowing who he was. Just went in and did it. It's not what the British hired him to do, but you know Manni, he likes to do things on his own."

Ziggy shrugged. "War turns us all into killers."

The parlor had striped wallpaper, peeling and weathered at the edges, with groupings of tiny framed paintings. There were so many, it was difficult to focus on any one. Ziggy looked at Sebastian, who had fallen silent, a troubled look on his face. His eyes avoided Ziggy as he stared at the wallpaper. Finally, he spoke. "Manni doesn't think we should go to Palestine," he said quietly. "He thinks that once we get Franzi out we should take the gold and fly to Spain. We can keep the fuel money. Nobody knows about that."

He paused again, rubbing his fist against his lips. Then he stared back at Ziggy. The light had gone out from Sebastian. Now all he looked was tired and desperate.

"I want to get away from this shit, Ziggy." Sebastian dug his thumb and forefinger into his eyes. He let out a breath. "I don't want to keep doing this Blood of Israel. I'm tired of it. I'm tired of the killing."

Ziggy stared at Sebastian. "But what about Palestine, Sebastian? I thought your dream was going to a kibbutz and raising olives."

"Fuck olives," mumbled Sebastian. "I'm tired of all this."

"Tired of being a Jew?"

"No! Yes! No, of course not! I'm tired of the cause. I just don't want to be part of it anymore. I don't want people pointing at me and saying, 'Do you know what he did?'" Sebastian gave a sheepish grin. "Besides, how long would I last on a farm? A half hour? Fuck Palestine. Let's just go to Spain."

Ziggy had to laugh. "If we go to Spain, we'll spend the rest of our lives with everyone thinking we're Nazis."

"I don't care," sniffed Sebastian.

"How many times can you put the past behind you, Sebastian? I'm sick of new beginnings."

Sebastian suddenly brightened. "But don't you see? It won't be a new beginning at all. We'll be going back together, to what we were."

"And how are we going to get to Spain?"

"With the gold the SS gave us for the fuel."

"What are you talking about?"

"When the SS agreed to give us gold to pay for the fuel, we

still knew Manni would have one of his own people taking over the fuel dock and we'd get the fuel for free."

"Take over from whom?"

"Lüth."

"Lüth was in charge of the fuel?"

"He was rector of the Marineschule, wasn't he?"

"Well, yes, so you would have had to pay off Lüth to get the fuel?"

"Yes, that was where everything stalled."

Ziggy looked at Sebastian and suddenly felt everything crumbling around him. "You killed Lüth?"

"Hey, we made him a nice offer and he wouldn't take it. He acted like a complete prick. He even asked if we were Jews. Can you imagine that? After all we've been through, to have some goddamn Nazi prick ask, 'Are you Jews?' I mean, the nerve of some people!"

"You killed . . . Lüth?"

"What do you care? It's one less Nazi in the world. And he was a real Nazi, wasn't he?"

"Yes," said Ziggy, staring back at Sebastian. "He was also my captain."

"I know who he was."

They stared at each other in leaden silence. "Why did you have to kill him?"

"I beg your pardon, Zigmund, but do you think I need an excuse to kill a Nazi? You really have been in the navy too long." Sebastian shook his head incredulously. "If you have a problem with it, try remembering that we're doing this for Franzi and to bring those SS bastards to justice."

"And you killed him over fuel oil?"

"I did it for Franzi!" Sebastian's irritation was now in the fore. "I mean, this is stupid, Zigmund. You need to get over this. We've got a big task ahead of us and there's not any point talking about some fucking dead Nazi."

"It's not about Lüth," said Ziggy, calmly staring at his brother as if from opposing cliffs. "It's about Cremer and the men. If they knew any of this, they wouldn't want to help you. And I'm not going to drag them into it. This is not how the navy does things."

Sebastian was furious. "Who the hell do you think you are? You're suddenly too good for us? Have you already forgotten what you were a part of?"

Ziggy shook his head. "I'm through with this. I don't want to talk to you again. Keep away from me and Cremer."

"You're going to let Franzi die, just so you and your men can keep your white gloves immaculate? I'm not going to let this operation go down because of your willful, high-handed selfishness." Sebastian stared hard at Ziggy. "Don't for a moment think we're going to let you back out."

(48)

Storming out onto the street, Ziggy flagged down a jeep and ordered the British sergeant driving it to take him to the Marineschule. The guard hut was empty but for two sailors manning the desks. "Grab some rifles and follow me," he told them.

They commandeered a Kübel and drove out to the inlet. This whole idiot operation has to be stopped, he told himself as they motored past the outskirts. To hell with freeing Franzi and catching Himmler. Cremer might allow himself to be swayed by Manni, but that didn't mean Ziggy had to. Franzi was going to have to find his own way home. Someone else would have to bring Himmler to justice. His responsibility was bringing his men into peacetime alive, not settling scores.

A mile from the inlet, the road narrowed to a single muddy lane and they were forced to pull over to the side while a couple of British trucks passed them in the opposite direction. One, he noticed, was a fuel truck with a civilian driver, whose blond hair and cloth cap looked distinctly Danish.

"Step on it," Ziggy told the driver. "We don't have a minute to lose."

They arrived at the inlet as the sun was beginning to set. The midget U-boats were clustered in rows along the side of a long pier, at the top of which sat a slightly larger harbor tug, like a shepherd overlooking its flock. On the dock, a crowd of sailors in denims and leather jackets was busy loading supplies. Even in the dimming light he could make out Rasch in his white commander's cap, giving orders to his men and helping pass containers onto the boats.

Ziggy told his driver to park the Kübel behind a row of upturned boats. "Sling your rifles," he ordered. "I want this to look purely social."

Rasch saw them approach and waved them to come forward. Walking toward the pier, Ziggy did a hasty count of the boats. Nine, ten, eleven, twelve, they were all still there. All over the dock there were stacks of baggage and personal kit along with packages of food, canisters of water, and fat round tins of motor oil. By the look of it, they had enough supplies to last each boat several days, certainly enough time to get them past Denmark, maybe even up to Sweden.

Rasch threw Ziggy a jaunty salute. "So you've come to see us off?" he asked.

"That's right," said Ziggy. "You've got your fuel?"

"Finally," said Rasch.

"So, what's next? Gelting Bay?" asked Ziggy.

Rasch nodded. "We should be there by morning. Then it's just a question of waiting for our passengers to arrive. We've told them that if they're not there tomorrow at six, we're heading out without them."

"Did they say where they're going?"

Rasch shook his head. "I told them our one condition is a little stopover in Copenhagen. Intel reports there's a nice fat British cruiser in the harbor, along with escorts and auxiliaries, all just asking to get sunk." Rasch gave a wicked smile. "You know, I've got room if you want to come along. I hear you're good luck. What do you say, Herr Korvettenkapitän?"

Ziggy noticed some men stepping off the tugboat onto the dock and realized they were in SS battle dress. "What are they doing here?" he asked. "I thought you weren't picking them up till tomorrow."

Rasch turned to look at them, then raised his hand and gave them a wave. "Oh, them?" he said. "They're just the advance team. They'll do the run with us and do the signals with the men on the beach. They're all right."

Ziggy stared at Rasch. The man was an innocent. He hadn't a clue about what he'd gotten himself and his men into. U-boatmen didn't know the first thing about conspiracy or double-dealing. To Rasch, pirate or not, a man was as good as his word. Ziggy looked back at the SS men staring hard at him and knew he had to act.

"Kapitänleutnant Rasch," he said coldly, "I must inform you that you are under arrest."

Rasch looked confused. "You're joking," he said.

Ziggy fixed him with his eyes. "I'm not. You're under arrest for insurrection."

Rasch's face turned scarlet. "Insurrection? I don't believe this! This is all bullshit," he snarled. "You set me up."

The SS men could see that something was going on. One was reaching into his pocket. Behind Ziggy, his men swung their rifles in their direction. The SS men froze.

"Shut up, Rasch!" barked Ziggy, taking out his pistol. "All right, everyone, pay attention!" he shouted. "You're all under arrest for violation of the surrender agreement. Everyone put down your weapons on the deck and form ranks. Now!" Ziggy half turned to his men standing behind him. "Petty Officer, put the cuffs on him. Rasch, put your hands out."

"You're crazy," said Rasch. "We've got you twenty to one."

"I said put your hands out, Rasch," barked Ziggy. He looked at Rasch's men. "I gave an order. Put down your weapons and form ranks!" He turned to his men, who stood wide-eyed behind him. "Get the cuffs on him, now!" he told the petty officer. Then he motioned to the other. "Any of these SS birds move the wrong way, shoot to kill."

Nervously, the petty officer stepped forward, holding the handcuffs while the other kept his rifle on the two SS men. "Take your hands out of your pockets and drop your weapons," he shouted. But the SS men didn't move. Neither did Rasch.

"Listen to me, Rasch, it's over," said Ziggy. "Even if they don't hang you, do you really want to spend the rest of your life as an outlaw?"

Rasch glared back at Ziggy. But his expression turned from defiance to angry resignation. He held out his hands and looked away as the petty officer snapped the handcuffs around his wrists.

"What the hell is going on?" shouted one of the SS men. "I can't believe you're going to let this prick tell you what to do. We've already paid you."

"Raise your hands or I'll shoot," said the sailor with the rifle.

Slowly they put up their hands. "I don't believe this," one said.

"Petty Officer, remove their weapons," said Ziggy. He waited as the two sailors disarmed the SS men. Then he turned to Rasch's men. "Prepare the boats for scuttling."

Everybody looked at him in surprise. Rasch was livid. "What are you talking about, Loerber? This is a dirty trick."

"You heard me," said Ziggy.

"But you know scuttling has been forbidden."

"Do you think I'm going to let you sail out of here to rescue Himmler and attack the British fleet?"

"Whose side are you on, anyway?" Rasch said, frowning.

"Rasch, the war is over."

"These are not the orders the Führer gave us," said Rasch.

"Rasch, the Führer is dead. The grand admiral is in charge now and he says it's over."

"Oh, come on, Loerber, you don't really think the old man wants us to do that, do you?" Rasch shook his chains with exasperation. "Goddammit, man! Half the British fleet is up there. You're going to make us pass up an opportunity like that?"

"Rasch, for heaven's sake," said Ziggy under his breath, "I'm doing this to keep you guys from getting murdered."

Rasch looked back at Ziggy and for the first time looked as though something was sinking into his thick skull.

"Captain Rasch, what do you want us to do?" one of the men called out.

"Do as he says," Rasch told them sullenly. "Kirschbaum, Meyer, Stahlmann, get to it."

"What about scuttling charges?"

"No charges," said Ziggy. "Remove all lines, open sea cocks, leave the hatches open. How deep is the water?"

"Twenty feet, sir."

"Fine. Then the British can recover them if they want them that much."

The sailors set to work, untying the subs from each other and climbing inside each boat's conning tower hatch to turn open the sea cocks. As soon as they were finished with one, they hopped off its deck, while others used long poles to push the boats away from the dock. For the longest time, nothing happened. Ziggy watched nervously as the sailors moved from one sub to the next, and it occurred to him that they might only be pretending to be following his orders. Why wouldn't they? They were being paid in gold. How could obedience to orders stand up against that?

And then suddenly the first boat pitched forward and plunged into the dark water. Moments later another leaned over and sank.

Ziggy heard frantic shouting behind them. He looked down the pier and saw Sebastian and Cremer running toward them. "Stop it! Stop it! What are you doing?" they shouted.

Sebastian grabbed Ziggy by the arm. "Make them stop!"

"Sorry," said Ziggy.

"But Zigmund, this is madness." Then Sebastian turned to

Rasch's men. "Everybody stop what you're doing. Don't let any more of those submarines sink. Save them! There's gold in it for you!"

"Loerber, what do you think you're doing?" shouted Cremer.

"Peter, I'm not going to risk our men in this operation." He looked over at Sebastian. "He killed Lüth. His guys will kill us just as easily."

Sebastian looked shocked. "I can't believe you'd say that!"

"Is this true?"

"Zigmund, how could you do this to me?"

"Sebastian!"

"Will someone tell me what the hell is going on?" asked Rasch.

"You men!" shouted Sebastian. "Stop what you're doing! Save the boats! I've got gold for you!" He pulled a small, shiny yellow ingot out of his pocket. "See?"

Rasch's men stopped what they were doing and looked at each other.

"Don't listen to him!" shouted Ziggy. "You have your orders. Carry them out!"

"Close the sea cocks, switch on the pumps!" shouted Sebastian.

"No! Don't listen to him!"

The confused men stared at Sebastian and then at Ziggy. Suddenly their faces lit up with recognition. "Who *is* that guy?" one asked.

"He looks *exactly* like Captain Loerber! Is it his brother?"

"He just called him Sebastian . . . Sebastian Loerber?"

The men looked at each other in amazement. "Does that mean Captain Loerber is . . . ?"

"The Flying Magical Loerber Brothers!"

"Oh, my God! Does that mean . . . ?"

"Sebastian Loerber is alive!"

"Sebastian Loerber is alive!"

"This is unbelievable!"

"What the hell is going on, Loerber?" asked Rasch. "Who is this guy? Is he your brother?"

"He's the one running this operation," said Ziggy. "Blood of Israel, pretending to be SS, pretending to be Blood of Israel, pretending to be SS, I'm sure he doesn't even know."

"Ziggy, you're talking crazy," shouted Sebastian. "Of course we're not SS."

Another sub dipped its bow and disappeared into the water.

"Ziggy, make them stop!" pleaded Sebastian. "I'll explain it to you, I promise."

"It's too late, Sebastian," said Ziggy. "I'm not risking our men on any more of your harebrained—"

"Zigmund, we have to take the risk," shouted Sebastian. "It's for our people!"

"What's he talking about?" asked one of the SS men.

"I have no idea," said Rasch. "Loerber, what is going on?"

"It's the family, isn't it, Zigmund?" said Sebastian. "That's the real reason you're doing this!"

"Loerber, what are you doing?" shouted Cremer. "Stop the scuttling immediately!"

"It's the grand admiral's orders," said one of Rasch's men.

"Belay that. Loerber, did the old man tell you this?"

"Peter, I can't explain this right now, you have to trust me."

For a moment Cremer stood staring at Ziggy in confusion. But then Sebastian stepped in, swift and seamless as a breeze, sidling up next to Cremer, jamming a pistol hard against his neck.

"Zigmund, in the name of justice, you have to stop thinking like the rules still matter. Look around you! Don't you see it's all gone out the window?"

Ziggy pointed his pistol at his brother. "I'm not going to let you do this, Sebastian. Put the weapon down. Let Cremer go."

One of the SS men stepped forward. "Would somebody please stop the boats from sinking?"

"Drop the weapon, Sebastian, and let him go," Ziggy said.

"Zigmund, don't be an idiot," said Sebastian. "We have to save Franzi. The rest of you get moving and save the boats! There's gold in it for you."

"Yes, gold!" echoed one of the SS men.

"Put the gun down, Sebastian. Let him go."

Sebastian drew Cremer closer to him.

Ziggy felt his finger tightening against the trigger. He saw his brother smile the way he used to when they'd catch each other in the air. Then Sebastian's forehead exploded in a cloud of red.

(49)

There was a British checkpoint in the middle of a bridge half a kilometer up, reported Grothmann. Nothing to it, just two very bored Tommies with Enfields and a field telephone. Even so, they all traded looks with each other. It was, after all, their first enemy checkpoint.

They'd go through one at a time, Macher told Franzi and Himmler. "It'll be easy," he said. "Keep twenty yards apart. When you get there, go right past the sentry. Don't look him in the eye, but if you're challenged, don't avoid them." He gave Himmler and Franzi each a tap on the shoulder. "Don't worry, gentlemen, you'll be fine. I'll be right behind you."

Then he took Franzi aside. "All right, Loerber. This is where it starts. Once we cross that bridge, we'll be in enemy territory. I assume you know how to act. We don't start anything, but we'll finish it when it comes to that. You understand?"

He waited for Franzi to nod that, yes, he understood. Macher went on. "Now listen, there's no reason we can't walk through every British checkpoint we come across. There's too many people out there. As long as you don't call attention to yourself, they'll never see you.

"We can walk to Munich in two weeks," said Macher. "Once we get there, the networks will take over and everything will be easy. Once we get to South America and have the chief settled into some hacienda somewhere, I'll cut you loose with a nice fat share for you to disappear with. Sounds good, doesn't it, Loerber?"

Again Macher paused and waited for Franzi to nod, then he went in for the kill.

"Now, I have to know I can count on you. I have to know that if I go off somewhere to check something out for ten minutes you're not going to be sneaking off somewhere. Because if you do that, you know what I am going to do?"

Franzi nodded that, yes, he knew the answer to that. Macher nodded for him to say it aloud.

"You're going to hunt me down and kill me," he said.

"That's exactly right," said Macher. "Now, can I count on you as a brother-in-arms?"

Franzi nodded effusively. "Yes, Colonel, yes! You can count on me!" Franzi said it with complete earnestness and sincerity. Franzi Loerber was ready to follow Macher to the ends of the earth, which was roughly what Macher had in mind.

Macher was incredible. Never in his life had Franzi seen any-one who came close to him. No one had his awareness or his in-stincts. Nobody moved like him, like a shadow or a panther. And the casual way he killed put even Manni to shame. No one, except perhaps Grothmann.

"You can count on me, Colonel," Franzi said again and then added, "I swear, sir."

Macher nodded solemnly. "All right," he said, giving Franzi's shoulder a punch. "Now go get the Reichsführer ready."

Franzi walked back to the other end of the clearing, where Himmler was sitting on a tree stump. Macher made it sound so easy. To get to Munich all they had to do was keep walking and not attract any attention to themselves. But of course there was a problem: Himmler. For twenty years the spotlight had been on him. He was someone the whole world had looked at and pointed out and now he was completely incapable of blending in, of becoming just one in the mass of humanity. He stood out like a sore thumb and now it was Franzi's job to teach him otherwise.

Himmler was sourly examining his new set of identity documents.

"What is it, Reichsführer?" Franzi asked wearily.

"I don't see how this is going to work," he said, his voice tinged with hysteria. "Here, look at it." He thrust the papers into Franzi's hands. Franzi looked. The name on them didn't say *Himmler*, but *Hitzinger, Heinrich,* a sergeant in the Special Field Police, demobilized a week earlier. The face in the photograph wasn't Himmler's either, but the resemblance was good enough to get through any cursory inspection.

"Honestly, Reichsführer," said Franzi. "It's just fine."

"But look at this," said Himmler, tapping his finger on the demobilization certificate. "It looks like it was run off on a mimeograph machine."

"I'm sure it *was* run off on a mimeograph machine, Reichsführer," he said, trying not to sound exasperated. "But that's how it's being done these days."

Himmler shuddered. "But it's all so cheap, so unconvincing."

Jesus, thought Franzi, what does he want? An engraved, watermarked parchment? Even now, when Himmler's empire was down to five people walking on foot, the man's expectations flourished on a grand scale.

"Reichsführer," said Franzi. "Forget about the documents. They don't matter. What matters is you."

He stopped and waited for Himmler to say something or to look him in the eye. Finally he did.

"You have to learn to make yourself invisible."

"Invisible?" asked Himmler, cringing at the idea.

"You have to carry yourself like you're nobody. The way you're walking now tells the world you're a king in disguise. And that will get you caught. Tell yourself I'm nobody, I'm nobody, I'm the same as everyone else here. I'm tired, I'm hungry, I'm scared, I'm nobody. Nobody."

Himmler grimaced unhappily.

"Reichsführer, think of King Alfred and the cakes."

"He was English."

"He was Saxon, just like Henry the Fowler."

"Well, Henry the Fowler never had to," grumbled Himmler.

"He didn't have to because it wasn't his destiny," said Franzi. "But it is your destiny, Reichsführer. It is what the stars demand."

Himmler let out a bitter laugh. "The stars? Sometimes I think my stars have abandoned me. Why else would things have gone so badly?"

"Reichsführer," said Franzi, "things are not going that badly at all. We'll be in Argentina soon. And never think that your stars have abandoned you. The stars always know who they belong to."

At this, Himmler seemed to brighten. "Really?" he asked.

"Absolutely," answered Franzi.

"Well, then they have an odd way of showing it," sniffed Himmler. "Look, Loerber, I just don't know how to act like I'm nobody. I wouldn't know where to begin."

Franzi had an idea. "Reichsführer, you know the song 'Harlem Rhapsody,' don't you?"

Himmler sniffed. "Well, of course I do," he muttered. "What does that have to do with anything?"

"Well, you know the words, don't you?"

Himmler looked confused. "I didn't know it had words," he said. "I thought it was just a tune."

"You don't know the words to 'Harlem Rhapsody'?" Franzi rolled his eyes like it was hilarious. "Not even how it begins? Honestly, Reichsführer!" Franzi wiggled his finger and made sure he had Himmler's attention. "Reichsführer, it starts like this." He began singing the opening bars, the ones everyone would always whistle or hum: "Doo dah dah doo—doo doo, sing it with me. Doo dah dah doo—doo doo!" And Himmler sang it with him in his whimpering voice. "Doo dah dah doo, do do! Doo dah dah doo, do do!"

And then Franzi added the words. "Nobody knows—my

330

name." And Himmler sang it with him. "Nobody knows my name. Nobody knows my name."

And then it dawned on Himmler. "Nobody knows my name," he sang. "Nobody knows my name. Nobody knows my name."

"You've got it?"

Himmler nodded.

"Good."

"Is he ready, Loerber?" asked Macher.

"He's ready."

"Let's go!"

They joined up with Kiermaier and Grothmann, who were waiting for them at the edge of the woods, looking down on the crowded roadway. They moved in a group down the embankment to the road and stepped into the mass of people making their way toward the checkpoint.

Argentina would be nice, Franzi told himself. Once he got there, maybe he'd even change his name to Ramon! Of course, in order to get there, he'd have to hold Himmler's hand all the way to Munich and then across the Apennines to Italy or Spain. He'd prefer not having to do it, but he didn't want Macher to kill him either. Franzi wanted Macher to like him and he could tell Macher almost did.

Franzi looked over at Himmler trudging up the road, flanked by women and two old people wheeling bicycles. He paid them little notice, he just kept singing to himself as he walked along. *Nobody knows my name. Nobody knows my name.* And sure enough, Himmler's fledgling waddle had already started to even out. He wasn't quite the sore thumb he'd been earlier. Perhaps they just might make it to Munich.

They came around the bend and saw the bridge and the two Tommies with their Enfields. Just as Grothmann had said, they weren't showing any interest in any of the hundreds of people who were passing by. They seemed to be there purely as signposts, to indicate that this was now British territory.

A hundred meters from the bridge, Macher had them stop and then started sending them across one at a time. Grothmann went first. He situated himself alongside a woman with her family, carrying one of the children. After that Kiermaier went, also without any problem. Once he saw them both on the other side of the bridge, Macher clapped his hand on Himmler's shoulder.

"See you on the other side. We're right behind you."

Himmler put up his hand. "Just one thing before I go," he said, turning to Franzi. "I would like to ask you something, Loerber."

Franzi stared at him. "Reichsführer?" he asked.

"You are a homosexual, aren't you?"

Franzi felt his mouth drop open.

"Reichsführer," said Macher, "I don't think this is the time—"

Himmler put up his hand. "Answer my question, Loerber, and don't lie!"

"Reichsführer," said Franzi, trying to contain his rage, "I don't know what to say."

"Well, you do know it's wrong, don't you?"

"Lots of things are wrong," muttered Franzi.

"Don't change the subject, Loerber," said Himmler. "It's one thing to have to do bad things because of operational necessity. But it's another thing to do it because of weakness of character."

"I've always tried to do the right thing, Reichsführer, but it's difficult," said Franzi, pretending he wasn't boiling on the inside.

"I know that, Loerber," Himmler answered, sounding suddenly paternal. "I just want you to promise me that when we get to the Argentine, you'll stop and find a nice Aryan girl and settle down. It's easier than you think."

"I promise I will, Reichsführer."

"All right. That's all I have to say," said Himmler. He reached out to shake their hands. "Colonel Macher, Professor Loerber. I'll see you men on the other side."

Himmler walked up the road, humming quietly as he did.

They watched him approach the bridge. He walked easily, like he'd been walking for weeks and had the hang of the road.

"It's working," said Macher. "Good work, Loerber!"

"Thank you, sir," said Franzi.

"Cut out the 'sir,'" grunted Macher.

Franzi thought about Buenos Aires for a moment, then changed his mind.

He had to get the sentry to notice Himmler. He had to make the sentry wake up and see that the meek little demobilized field police sergeant was the one they were supposed to be keeping an eye out for. And at the same time he had to make Himmler start calling attention to himself again. And he only had about twenty seconds left to pull it off!

He focused on one of the Tommies. The soldier's gaze was leaden. He'd been there since morning and his brain was barely functioning. Franzi started hitting him with little mind-bursts on the right and left hemispheres, which got his eyes opening and shutting in mild spasms. The sentry shook his head and started examining the people going past him. But it only lasted a few seconds before his awareness began to deaden again. Franzi hit him with a stronger burst. *Wake up!* The sentry shook his head again. He was awake. Good. Now Franzi focused on Himmler, ambling comfortably toward the sentry. *Nobody knows my name. Nobody knows my name,* he hummed, moving with the notes. Franzi decided it needed an extra beat.

"Come on, Reichsführer. Just thirty more feet," whispered Macher. "Just twenty more feet, just ten more feet. That's it."

Nobody knows my name, hummed Himmler, to which Franzi added, *Cha-cha-cha!*

"Nobody knows my name, cha-cha-cha!" sang Himmler, twitching to the left. "Nobody knows my name, cha-cha-cha," and a twitch to the right.

"What the hell is he doing?" gasped Macher.

"Nobody knows my name, cha-cha-cha! Nobody knows my name!"

Franzi jumped back inside the sentry. *Look over there! Look at him! That's the one! Him! That's the guy! Look! See!*

And seeing through the man's eyes, Franzi saw him fixing on the half-dancing figure coming up to him. But even though the man's movements were starting to register, the sentry's brain slipped back to half sleep.

Himmler walked right past him, quietly humming as he did. Himmler was clear! Macher nudged Franzi.

But then Himmler did something strange. He stopped and turned and then walked back to the Tommy, and once he had the man's attention, he showed him his papers. They could hear him saying, "Are these good?"

The Tommy, now thoroughly awake, put his hand up to stop the line and began politely thumbing through Himmler's documents.

"What the hell?" whispered Macher.

They could hear the British soldier saying to Himmler, "It says here you're discharged from the Geheime Feldpolizei. That's SS! I'm afraid I'm going to have to take you in for questioning." He put his hand firmly on Himmler's shoulder and said something in English to the other soldier. Himmler looked back at Macher helplessly.

"Wait here," Macher said to Franzi and began pushing his way through the crowd to the checkpoint. As he approached them, the two Tommies brought up their rifles and pointed them at Macher. Macher reluctantly put up his hands. One of the soldiers began searching him and pulled out his pistol and knife. Next thing he knew, both he and Himmler had handcuffs on.

Franzi stood there for a little while, frozen with disbelief. Then it suddenly occurred to him that he was free and he turned around and began walking back to Flensburg.

It was nearly nightfall when a Red Cross truck pulled up and the driver leaned out and asked if he wanted a lift into town. "There's something very big going on there," he said.

"Really, what?" asked Franzi.

"Haven't you heard? They're having a funeral for Sebastian Loerber."

(50)

It was, Dönitz realized, probably the closest he would ever come to official recognition. There were two of them: a uniformed general and a man in civilian clothes. The general's name was Rooks. He was from Eisenhower's staff, and the other man introduced himself as Robert Murphy of the EAC by way of the U.S. State Department.

By now it had become abundantly clear that the Flensburg government's days were numbered. But for some reason, today the two of them had insisted on coming over to his office to talk. They didn't offer to shake hands when they came in, but Dönitz no longer expected it. He let Lüdde-Neurath point them to the chairs in front of his desk and, once they were seated, asked how he could help them.

The first thing they wanted to know was what proof he might have of the legitimacy of his accession to power. So Dönitz called Lüdde-Neurath back in and had him bring in the folder with the two telegrams from the bunker.

The Americans examined the telegrams, rubbing their fingers on them as if to further verify their authenticity. "It says here he committed suicide," said Murphy, tapping the sheet. "I'd be curious to know why you chose not to reveal it to the German people in your radio broadcasts."

"It is not something one customarily does," Dönitz replied coldly.

The two Americans handed back the telegrams without any further comment.

"So you've been in office three weeks now," said Murphy. "What are you hoping to accomplish?"

Dönitz looked at them and wondered if they'd only come here to insult him. "Gentlemen," he began, "as long as you ask, I would hope to convince you that your alliance with the Russians is about to fall apart and when it does, you will need Germany as a partner to fight them. Whether you are willing to recognize it or not, the battle line between East and West is right here and irrespective of your opinion of this government, you will need Germany on your side. As I tried to tell General Eisenhower, we can offer you more than a hundred divisions and millions of people willing to stand with you against the Soviets. So what I would hope to accomplish, gentlemen, is to get you to look beyond the optimism of the moment and see things the way they really are."

Murphy stared at Dönitz with disgust. "It sounds like you're expecting us to just forget about the millions of innocents that you people have cold-bloodedly murdered and turn you into our allies, in order to kill people who are already our allies," he said.

"I don't expect you to forget anything," answered Dönitz. "I am simply asking you to recognize that the only thing that will keep the rest of Europe from being overrun by the hordes of Red barbarians is you joining forces with us. If General Eisenhower thinks any differently, then he is a fool and so are your superiors at the EAC, whatever that is. You came here and asked me what I hoped to accomplish. I've just told you. Now, is there anything else?"

Murphy was still sneering. "Grand Admiral, after all the barbarity the Germans have inflicted on the world, I don't believe you're in any position to suggest what course Europe should take."

Now it was General Rooks who spoke. "Grand Admiral, we

came here today because there has been concern among the Allied leaders that you are attempting to drive a wedge between the West and the Soviet Union. Having spoken to you firsthand, I can see that those concerns were justified. We will now report our findings to General Eisenhower." And with that they left.

Later that afternoon Rooks sent another message telling Dönitz, Jodl, and von Friedeburg to report to the *Patria* at precisely nine o'clock in the morning. Dönitz called in his ministers and passed it around for them to read.

"Pack your bags," he told them.

Dönitz spent the rest of the afternoon alone in his office reading reports and writing down recommendations for whoever would be taking over. At six his dinner was brought in, and afterward he returned to his desk and worked a little longer. Then he went back to his quarters to pack his bags, one to take with him, the rest to be sent to his wife. Then he put a disk on the gramophone and over a cigarette listened to Bruckner.

He stared at the mantelpiece where he kept photographs of his two dead sons, both killed in the war. There was also his brother, who'd died in a bombing two years earlier. After that he found his favorite Beethoven record, but it was too rousing for his mood and he turned it off. He thought about having a drink, no reason not to, but then decided he didn't actually feel like it. So he sat alone in the dark for a while, trying not to think of anything, with only the wall clock ticking for company. I'll be damned if I show them anything, he told himself grimly. Then he went to bed.

(51)

Manni had just gotten up from his chair and gone into the next room for either a smoke or something to eat when one of the men in the back got up and sat down next to Ziggy. He'd been there all evening, sitting in one of the chairs near the door, farthest from where Sebastian's body had been laid out.

People had been coming and going all evening. Though most exchanged words with Manni, so far none of them had introduced themselves to Ziggy, he presumed because of his uniform. They were mostly men in their forties and fifties, all of them thin, worn out, and quietly angry.

Most would come in, sit, and stare silently at the body for five or ten minutes, and then leave without saying anything to anyone. A few stayed longer, breaking up their vigil with forays to the next room, where Ziggy could hear men murmuring back and forth between cigarettes and pipes and glasses of something, which they'd clink together to toast Sebastian. Though Ziggy had been there for some time, he stayed where he was, sensing he was not welcome there. He assumed they had to be Blood of Israel, though for all he knew, some of them could have been local Jews who'd miraculously found their way back from the camps.

The body had been dressed in a shroud hastily made from a bedsheet and laid out on a long table covered with a white table-cloth. Bordering it were several vases of flowers and two large flickering candles at his head and feet. It created a sense of enclo-sure that almost made up for the absence of a casket.

The man next to Ziggy turned and gave a polite nod. Ziggy nodded back.

"I am a colleague of your brother's," the man said. "We were friends. Allow me to express my sorrow at our common loss. I knew your brother quite well. We worked together many times. He was a very brave fighter, very selfless. I had hoped he would be one of us who grew old in the peace. But sadly, this was not to be. Did you get to talk to him at all, besides business?"

"We only had our first real conversation yesterday evening. The last time we talked was in 1933."

"Twelve years," said the man. "I spoke with him many times during those years. If I may say this, Herr Loerber, in many respects all the years of struggle made him a bitter man. He took many risks, put his life on the line many times, but because he was Jewish underground, he never got any respect from anyone. The rare time he wasn't nothing was when people recognized him from the cabarets. Then they'd want to talk about old Gustav, Grock the Clown, the Magical Loerber Brothers, and the good old days in old Berlin. He didn't enjoy reminiscing.

"The underground never got any respect, no matter what we did. Once he compared us with the prostitute that the banker visits every Thursday afternoon." A thin smile came to the man's face. Ziggy remembered that was something Gustav had liked to say.

"You know, of all his brothers, he liked you the most. Once he said to me that he hoped you hadn't lost your sincerity. Another time he said he envied you getting to go to your father's funeral. The others weren't there?"

"No. Franzi was away. I don't know where Manni was. No one would say."

"But everyone else was there. The Führer, Göring, von Ribbentrop. But not his own people."

"The Nazis *were* his own people," said Ziggy. "They loved his magic and never asked touchy questions."

"Sebastian never forgot what he was. He was proud to be a Jew. Most of the time he acted with righteousness, but as time wore on and his bitterness grew, he let the wrong things influence his decisions and overstepped the boundaries. In most respects, it didn't matter, vengeance being what it is, but at the same time, it changes a man and sometimes there's no going back. I think what he tried to do last night with your buddy was an example of that. You must not blame yourself. You acted properly to protect your shipmate. We respect that."

Surprised, Ziggy looked at him. "Are you saying that the Blood of Israel will not have its vengeance?"

"Well, I can't speak for the Blood of Israel in its entirety. That's a lot of territory. But I will say this: our section considers you a righteous gentile."

"But I'm a Jew," whispered Ziggy.

The old man chuckled and pointed his finger. "Not in that uniform, son. But go forth and be righteous." He stood up. "Good night, Herr Loerber," he said, leaving the room, the others following like shadows behind him until everyone else was gone.

Ziggy stared down at the body. Looking at his brother, he still didn't know what to feel. Regret? Loss? Inconsolable sadness? None of them were there. Perhaps they'd come later.

Manni came over and sat down across from the table.

Ziggy looked at him. "He told me you were an assassin," he said.

"And you're a U-boat captain with the Knight's Cross," Manni answered. "How many ships did you sink?"

"Including my time with Lüth, fourteen."

"That's a lot of ships," said Manni.

"Manni, do you feel the British gave you enough respect?"

Manni blew a burst of air through his nose, letting Ziggy know that what he'd said was funny, though not amusing.

"Where were you when Father died?" asked Ziggy.

"In Canada," he answered. "Did you hear where Franzi was?"

Ziggy shook his head.

Manni offered a wry smile. "Tibet."

"Tibet?"

"Ahnenerbe field trip."

"Did he find anything?"

"Aside from a bad case of the clap? I don't think so."

The door opened and the old lady who owned the house gestured to Manni from the threshold. He got up. "Look," he said, "we're going to have to decide what to do about Franzi. We'll talk about it when I get back." He followed the old lady out into the hall, closing the door behind him.

Ziggy stared down at the threadbare carpet and the stray strands splitting off from the worn spots and suddenly knew the path that lay ahead for Franzi. Himmler's group wouldn't stay together much longer. It wasn't possible. Things were so unstable now that even the slightest obstacle would cause them to fray and spin out in different directions, and once that happened, Franzi would be free. He saw it with diamond-sharp clarity.

Suddenly the sadness was tearing him apart. If only Sebastian had known this. How long had he been dead? He looked at the reddening sky outside the window. Twenty-four hours, the same as eternity.

He stood up and brushed his hand against Sebastian's hair. He found himself remembering the old days when they were performing. Had he ever known how brilliant he was? Had he ever looked beyond the top hats and tails, the five-six-seven-eight razzmatazz, and seen what the rest of the world all took for granted? That the seedy glamour and corniness were nothing more than a picture frame in which genius ran free? Ziggy had hated the reminiscing too. But they really had been something. Better than cartoons, as good as jazz.

The door opened. Ziggy looked up and saw Manni reentering the room, followed by a man in a dark suit. It was Speer.

"Ziggy, you've met Herr Reichsminister Speer, haven't you?" said Manni.

Speer put his hand out and Ziggy shook it. "Please, allow me to extend my condolences over the death of your brother," said Speer.

"Thank you," said Ziggy.

Speer looked down at Sebastian's body and tears welled in his eyes. He turned to Manni. "Honestly, Herr Manni, after all we've been through, I didn't imagine anyone's death would bother me this much, but it does. I don't understand why.

"It's funny how you hope for things. I thought that with the war ending we'd all get to see you perform again." A tear ran down his cheek. He gave a polite bow and left.

Ziggy and Manni returned to their chairs. They sat for a while, then Manni said, "Sebastian is dead. That can't be changed. Now what are we going to do about Franzi?"

Ziggy shrugged. "Franzi doesn't need our help."

"What are you saying?"

"He's on his way," said Ziggy.

The hostess returned again. "We'll talk about this later," said Manni. "Let me see what she wants."

He came back in a few minutes, a bemused smile on his face. "So can your premonition tell you anything about what's going on outside?"

Ziggy thought a second. "A crowd!"

"Let's go," said Manni.

Two men were waiting on the front steps. One held a notebook prominently in his hands, while the other stood over what seemed to be an extremely large metal suitcase. Behind them, jamming the street and the sidewalks, were hundreds of people.

"Mallmann, *Flensburg Nachrichten*," said the first man.

"Brentwesser, Radio Flensburg," said the one with the enormous suitcase. "We apologize for bothering you in this moment of grief, but don't you think it would be better for all concerned if you allowed us to record something for all the grieving fans out there?"

Ziggy looked down at the suitcase. "What's that?" he asked.

"Portable recording equipment," answered Brentwesser. What they would like, he told them, was for the two brothers to talk with them about Sebastian's life and their celebrated career in prewar Germany.

It seemed that people were struck by how Sebastian, twelve years after disappearing, returned just long enough to die in a senseless accident. That he reappeared only to melt away like a snowflake. They wanted to know something, anything about the time he was back. They wanted to know about the Loerber reunion.

For ten minutes Ziggy and Manni stood together on the porch recalling stories of mishaps and emergency improvisations, and the backstage pranks that Sebastian specialized in. Of their recent time together they said little, beyond that it had been brief, it had been an extremely happy time, as if they'd never been apart.

While they were talking, the people in the street began swaying and humming bits of song: "Call of the Enchanted Isles," "From Monday On," "My Little Green Cactus." The crowd was like an ocean, observed Ziggy, with its own energy and mood and common rhythm and the waves of grief sharing the space with those of happy memory.

"So you're going to be playing it on Radio Flensburg?" asked Ziggy when they'd finished and the radio reporter was wrapping up his microphone cables.

"Well, yes, but it's also already been sold to Radio Atlantik," he said. "We're just putting the segment together. We've got a Brit in the studio to record the English-language text."

Suddenly there was a rumbling among the crowd. He looked at the brothers. People were excitedly shouting something to each other. Franzi! Franzi! It's Franzi! Franzi! Franzi!

"What is it?"

"It's Franzi!" someone said. "Franzi Loerber is here!"

Ziggy and Manni looked out into the crowd and they could see it parting so someone could make his way through. It was Franzi, making his way toward them; even from the far end of the street, they could see he was laughing and crying at the same time. They saw a man climb up onto the hood of a parked truck. He put a bugle to his lips and the crowd fell quiet as the notes poured out like silver into the evening air. Ziggy couldn't imagine how anyone could play "Harlem Rhapsody" on a bugle, but he played the song, sweet and sad, exactly like everyone remembered it.

> *Nobody knows my name.*
> *No one can feel my sorrow.*

The recording machine's green light flickered and the reporter was holding out his microphone to capture the song. He smiled at Manni. "This is going to be so good," he whispered.

(52)

When it was all over and the Americans began to leave, Speer didn't bother getting up from the couch. Those who tried to say thank you or good night found him sullen and cold. But then, the magic spell had been broken and he was no longer Albert Speer, colleague, but Albert Speer, war criminal.

It wasn't supposed to have ended like this, Speer told himself bitterly as he poured the last of the whiskey into his glass. This should have been the day the Americans offered him the job of overseeing Germany's reconstruction.

And it had all started out so promisingly. The daily government meeting had ended and Speer had driven back to the Schloss. There, to his enormous relief, he found Galbraith and the others still waiting in the courtyard, guarded by the dozen-odd troops of Speer's security detachment.

"I'm very sorry to have kept you gentlemen waiting," he told them. "But the grand admiral insisted." But rather than acting annoyed by the delay, the Americans clamored to hear details of what a real Nazi cabinet meeting was like. "Oh, it's all like second-rate Warner Brothers," joked Speer. They all laughed.

They'd brought two large bottles of Haig & Haig whiskey, an even more flagrant violation of the anti-fraternization rules than anything they'd done previously. "I hope you're in the mood to answer a lot of questions today," said Ken Galbraith.

"I'm sure I cannot think of a more pleasant way to spend a May afternoon." Speer smiled graciously and led them back upstairs to one of his favorite salons. He opened a glass cabinet and broke out some glasses and passed them around. The University of Bombing was back in session.

"All right, who wants the first question?" asked George Ball after everyone had settled in with their drinks.

For the first hour or so, it went on its usual way, with questions about ball bearings and hydrogenation works and alloy steels. But the questioning lacked real direction and only fueled Speer's suspicion that today, perhaps, they might have something quite different in mind that they wanted to discuss. He got the feeling that they were just looking for the right moment to pop the big question to him: *Professor Speer, we've been communicating with some people we know back in Washington and they share our enthusiasm for what you've managed to accomplish and they think, as we think, that you're the best person to oversee the postwar reconstruction of German industry, no, Germany!, no, all of Western Europe!*

Finally, just as he expected, they dropped the technical questions altogether. "Please," one of them said, obviously speaking for everyone, "tell us what it was like in the bunker." Hearing it, Speer had to smile. It hadn't even been a month, and already the bunker had reached mythic stature.

He obliged them with his best, most revealing stories. He told them about Hitler directing nonexistent divisions against the Red army, and the situation conferences where real-life facts never graced the agenda. He described the endless cocktail party with its bourgeois niceties, and how even at the final hour Hitler's primary concern had been playing his few remaining followers against each other.

He told them about Göring: his flamboyant dress and rouged cheeks and the lions wandering about his palace. He told them about Rosenberg, with his unfathomable theories of race; Ley, the perpetually drunk Labor Front chief, who had once come to Speer with blueprints for a "death ray," which, it turned out, required parts that hadn't been produced in sixty years; how von Ribbentrop, the foreign minister, had laid down on Hitler's threshold until the Führer finally agreed to see him. Then of course, there were Hitler's two military chiefs, Keitel and Jodl, who refused to visit the Russian front, until finally the front came to visit them.

He talked and they listened with such rapt attention that he was almost puzzled by the appetite they had for gossip and stories of bizarre personalities. But then, he thought, so much the better when the time comes for me to state my case, and high time I did.

So he began telling them about his break with Hitler that previous fall. How they went head to head over different matters: offensive or defensive war, fighter planes over bombers, production of miracle weapons, whether to cut out whole classes of medium-caliber ammunition, until ultimately what they were arguing about was whether victory was even possible. He told them about the long slide downward, the looming inevitability of defeat, and, finally, the Nero Decree. He told them about how his relations with the Führer got worse and worse, to the point where Hitler stopped acknowledging his presence at the daily situation conferences.

After that, Speer described his own quest for redemption: traveling about the Ruhr with his stalwart band of fellow conspirators, countermanding Hitler's orders, pleading with and coercing the gauleiters and army commanders, sabotaging deliveries of explosives, diverting nitrogen away from ammunition plants to fertilizer production, and doing whatever it took to preserve Germany's industrial heartland for the future.

Next thing he knew, he was telling them about the strange young man he'd met then, a onetime vaudeville performer with the uncanny ability to talk anyone into anything, and the extraordinary adventures they'd had.

The Americans were dumbfounded. "A former child star? And he taught you to . . . juggle?"

Speer grinned.

Ken Galbraith cleared his throat. "Could you . . . juggle for us, please?"

Speer looked mischievously at his audience. Dare he?

He went over to the glass cabinet and pulled out four small cut-crystal glasses. One by one he threw them in the air, and soon he had all four going, around and around. For nearly a minute he juggled them and didn't drop a single one and when he was finished he gathered them all inside the crook of his right arm and took a very theatrical bow. His audience went wild.

Thank you, thank you, gentlemen, Speer wanted to say, *and for my next trick, I'm going to put all the war-ravaged economies of Western Europe back on their feet. But I'm going to need a few assistants . . . from the audience . . .*

He put the glasses on the table and sat back down on the couch. He looked expectantly at Galbraith. Galbraith only smiled. Paul Nitze raised his hand and asked him if he'd been afraid that Hitler might hang him if he found out what he'd been doing in the Ruhr.

"Certainly I was afraid," said Speer. "But we were all facing death anyway. It had all gone too far. But don't let me paint myself as too heroic, gentlemen. What you have to understand about Hitler is that when it came to the people closest to him, he was infinitely forgiving. For him to acknowledge that people had turned against him meant acknowledging he'd made a mistake choosing them in the first place. That was why he preferred the Luftwaffe be destroyed to sacking Göring."

"But how did you put up with it?"

"My secret was to focus all my energy on my work. As long as a task was challenging enough, I could completely lose myself in it." He gave a sad smile. "It is ironic, gentlemen, that work was what got me in this mess with Hitler in the first place. I was never interested in politics or power. All I ever wanted was work and he kept giving it to me."

He paused, seeing them nod in sympathetic agreement. Well,

of course they would, Speer told himself. They know all about hard work. Now, what do I have to tell them to make them bite?

"I can't tell you how glad I am that this whole ugly episode is finally over. And that the new day we have all waited for is finally here. I just hope we can put the horror behind us and work together toward a peaceful, prosperous world. I can only hope I will be allowed to participate in this rebuilding."

For a long pregnant moment no one said anything. Then a shrill, reedy voice shattered the meditative silence.

"I don't get you, Speer." A bookish, bespectacled little captain stood up. Speer could tell he was drunk.

"You talk all this wonderful stuff, like you're so rational and decent and just like us, and that's what's most horrifying about it. Here we are drinking with you, relieved that you're not the monster we imagined. But what good is any of it if all you do is sell out to someone like Hitler just so you can design some fucking building?"

"Easy, Burton," said Galbraith.

"No! Fuck this whole thing! Don't you see? As long as you get to maintain your irony and circumspection and don't have to march around like a thug in jackboots, you'll happily serve the biggest murderer in history. And you don't simply serve the regime, you become Hitler's friend, his only friend. God Almighty! And don't tell us you didn't know about the millions of people he murdered, just because he didn't bring it up during his little tea parties."

"Burton, that's enough!"

"The hell it is! You're pathetic, Speer, and I hope they hang you. Now I'm finished. You can continue with your line of questions. Good night!"

He stormed out of the room and they heard him stomping down the hall, cursing loudly as he did.

It didn't last long after that. There were a few halfhearted questions about ball bearing works and then someone suddenly recalled a late-night meeting they had to attend aboard the *Patria*.

Alone now, everything silent around him, his glass finally empty, Speer surveyed the dark room. The only flicker of light came from the fire, nearly down to its embers. He stared dully at it, imagining it was the light of a thousand torches and he was back at one of the great nighttime party rallies before the war.

Speer walked over to the fireplace and, poking the embers, watched the sparks fly up. He felt a careening vertigo, brought on by all the whiskey, and staggered back to the couch, laying his head back and closing his eyes.

And there it was, Germania, the Great Dome, bigger than sunrise and colder than an ice mountain. Speer wiped his hands over his eyes, but it wouldn't go away. Then he saw all the others: the vast plazas and boulevards, the gigantic ministries and monuments, Soldiers Hall, the Armory, the Party Academy, the Triumphal Arch, and the tall, narrow columns topped with eagles lining Unter den Linden, which seemed to go all the way to the horizon.

We did it, Speer, you and I.

Coda

The way it looked from Dönitz's office, it could have been any other May morning in Flensburg. The sun was already up, making the water glisten in the bright light. Near the boat dock, a host of seagulls floated complacently, while farther out in the harbor the vast disarray of unmanned destroyers, minesweepers, gunboats, and small craft bobbed discordantly from their tethers.

Then a line of turreted, four-wheeled armored scout cars came rumbling down the waterfront, causing the seagulls to irritably flap their wings. About what he'd expected, Dönitz told himself bemusedly. He looked at his watch and saw there were fifteen minutes left. Having the watch on was a mistake, he realized. It should have been packed and sent with the rest of his belongings to his wife. Perhaps he could still give it to one of his men as a gift, rather than let some souvenir-hungry Tommy steal it. But, he thought, to hell with it. Let the bastards have their fun.

There was a knock on his door. Lüdde-Neurath opened it and announced, "General Jodl and Admiral von Friedeburg are here."

Dönitz nodded. "I'll be right out."

Stepping into the foyer, Dönitz saw that Jodl looked nervous, his nose a little redder than usual, while von Friedeburg appeared nearly lifeless. Nobody said anything during their drive over to the *Patria*. When they arrived, it was obvious what was happening. Gathered outside the Marineschule gates were dozens of British jeeps, armored cars, and trucks, and hundreds of soldiers in full battle dress. When they reached the dock, there was a small crowd gathered at the foot of the gangway, all of them with the excited look of movie fans at a premier. They were witnesses to history. Stern-looking MPs stood on each side of the gangplank in case anything got out of hand.

Dönitz turned to von Friedeburg and Jodl. "Well, gentlemen, shall we?" They walked in a line up the gangway and stepped onto the promenade deck, where a horde of reporters and press photographers barraged them with questions and snapped their pictures.

They were led down narrow passageways to the ship's wood-paneled bar. There, at a long table, General Rooks sat flanked by his British and Russian deputies. He motioned for Dönitz and the others to sit. Then he stood up. "Gentlemen," he began, "I am in receipt of instructions from the supreme commander, General Eisenhower, to tell you that he has decided, in concert with the Soviet High Command, that the acting German government and the German High Command shall be taken into custody as prisoners of war. Thereby the acting German government is dissolved." Rooks paused, and then added, "If the grand admiral has any comment to make, he may do so now."

Dönitz stood up. "Any comment would be superfluous," he said and returned to his seat.

After that Rooks began reading from another sheet of paper, informing them that they would now be taken back to their quarters, allowed to pack their bags, given lunch, and then taken to the airfield and flown to an undisclosed destination.

With Dönitz called away to the *Patria*, it had fallen on the chancellor, Schwerin von Krosigk, to preside over the morning's government meeting. No sooner had he called it to order than the doors were kicked open and in stormed twenty British troopers, brandishing rifles with fixed bayonets, shouting, "Hands up!" The ministers, their deputies, and the staff stood up, raising their hands as they did. They were lined up against the wall and searched, stripped, and relieved of watches, rings, or anything else that appeared of value or interest.

Ziggy had been sitting calmly, hands folded, at the reception desk when the British came in. "Hands up!"

Slowly Ziggy raised his hands.

"Souvenir!" shouted one, pointing at Ziggy's watch.

"Souvenir!" shouted another, pointing at his Knight's Cross and U-boat badge.

"Souvenir!" shouted a third one, pointing at his belt, pistol, and holster.

Ziggy felt the medal being yanked from his neck at the same time the watch was pulled off his wrist. The pistol took longer, since he had to take his jacket off for it.

They did the same to Lüdde-Neurath, then went in to ransack Dönitz's office, looking for anything they could put in their pockets, while Ziggy was left at his desk, his hands still up in the air. Then the Germans were led downstairs, past corridors full of pillaging soldiers, and together with other officers and staff were marched out to the parade ground, where another group of soldiers began going through their pockets. When they realized that all the good booty had already been taken, they grew angry and violent. "Get 'em off! Get 'em off!" one shouted. As Ziggy began removing his leather coat, the man went berserk, grabbing it and knocking Ziggy to the ground. "Get 'em off! Get 'em off! Get 'em off!" he screamed. He pulled Ziggy back halfway to his feet and punched him in the side of the head, knocking him down again. Somewhere in the process, Ziggy was stripped and left lying naked in the morning sunlight, his mouth swollen and sides aching, waiting for someone to tell him he could put his clothes back on.

A few feet away a general was being stomped and kicked by a group of Tommies. They ripped off his jacket, then his shirt, and then started pulling off his trousers. But because of his tight cavalry boots, the trousers wouldn't come off. They left them in a tight jumble below his knees and began kicking him again. The general cried out hysterically, which only enraged them further.

"Get ahold of yourself!" shouted another general who was on the ground nearby. "Be brave!"

The man stopped screaming and gritted his teeth as the Tommies continued to kick and stomp him and punch him in the face.

Then it was all over. The Tommies lost interest and moved on to someone else. The general lay in the dirt for a minute, then rolled over and sat up, his trousers still bunched below his knees, while the other general sat nearby, examining his own ripped trousers.

"Are you all right?" asked Ziggy.

The general nodded. Then a Tommy came by and, offering his hand, pulled him up to his feet before moving on.

As he put his clothes back on, Ziggy looked over to the main building and noticed that even now, Cremer and his men were still standing guard at the different entrances in helmets and rifles. Getting to his feet, Ziggy waved over to Cremer, who waved back.

After that they were told to stand in a line for processing. Then they were fed lunch and led off to a prisoner-of-war stockade, which, when they got there, hadn't yet been fully set up, owing to a shortage of barbed wire.

It was him, all right, thought the intelligence officer when they brought the little man into the room. Heinrich Himmler, head of the SS, biggest mass murderer in history. Problem was, he didn't look like anything. Meek little man, that's what he looked like, not a military leader, not the head of a grand police state, not the architect of genocide.

He'd come in wearing dirty, shabby clothes and a makeshift eye patch; his papers had identified him as a sergeant in the Geheime Feldpolizei, but he'd admitted who he was.

They made him undress and took his clothes away. Searching them, they found two brass capsules. One still held a glass phial that looked like poison. The other one was empty, but he wouldn't say why. They offered him some British army trousers and a shirt to put on, but he refused them, saying he was afraid they'd let photographers in to take his photo. So they gave him an army blanket to wrap around himself.

And for the next few hours it was just Himmler and the intelligence officer, sitting in a room waiting for the interrogators from headquarters to arrive. "Don't try interrogating him yourself," they'd told him. "Leave him alone until we get there. Just keep an eye on him, that's all."

Except that Himmler wanted to talk. So they talked. They talked about the weather, and how the intelligence file photo they had of him was out of date, since it showed him in his black SS uniform and he hadn't worn that since the beginning of the war. He clucked with visible self-satisfaction at that. Then the intelligence officer asked him about his hobbies. Did he garden, have children, keep pets? Dogs?

"No, I don't like dogs," snapped Himmler, as though everyone were supposed to know that.

They talked about other things: automobiles, airplanes, travel, dancing. Himmler told him how he'd been walking since that morning, that things had not gone well, and that the people wandering about were miserable and disorderly and that he hoped they would all be put to something useful in exchange for food.

"I'll bet you must be hungry," the intelligence officer said.

Himmler brightened. "Yes, I am," he said. "I haven't had anything all day."

"I'll get something for you to eat."

"Yes, that would be nice," he agreed eagerly.

"Stay in the chair," ordered the intelligence officer. Then he opened the door and shouted, "Bring up some food."

"Bring up some food," repeated Himmler, recognizing that it might be a useful phrase to know in the future.

The intelligence officer smiled at Himmler. "We'll have

something for you in just a minute. But first I'd like you to look at some photos I took."

"Oh?"

"Bergen-Belsen," said the intelligence officer, handing Himmler the photographs. "I was just there. Take a look."

Politely Himmler examined them, one after another, each for a couple of seconds, then he'd move on to the next. Stacks of dead bodies, ditches filled with skeletal figures, children. He looked at the last one and then handed them back. His expression wasn't any different. Bland, accommodating, uninvolved.

"So, do you have anything to say?" the intelligence officer asked.

Himmler looked almost surprised by the question. "Am I to blame for the excesses of my subordinates?"

"Are you?"

Himmler seemed affronted. "Should I be?"

"Yes."

"Well, that's just your opinion," said Himmler.

The intelligence officer was about to suggest something else, but Himmler asked, "Do you know when the food will be here?"

There was a knock on the door and a corporal brought in a tray with bread and thick slices of cheese. The intelligence officer set the tray down on the table and gestured for Himmler to eat. With a nod, Himmler began chewing on the bread and cheese.

"Good?" asked the intelligence officer.

Himmler smiled and nodded that, yes, it was good.

After that they talked some more. Himmler told him how he'd get terrible stomach cramps, but that he'd had an excellent masseur who also did his horoscope and was a wonderfully sympathetic person who'd previously been a famous entertainer.

"Really?" asked the intelligence officer, wondering if headquarters might know anything about it.

Then the door opened and three men came in. One was Colonel Murray, commander of the unit. He'd been made colonel only two weeks earlier and was, by the intelligence officer's own estimation, something of a massive prick. Along with him was Command Sergeant Major Austin, who wasn't much better, and an older man in the uniform of a captain in the Medical Corps named Wells, whom he had never seen before.

"How is everything?" asked Murray.

"Everything is just fine, sir," the intelligence officer answered.

"Any problems?"

"None at all, sir. He's just had his lunch and before that he was telling me about how much he loves dancing."

"Does he speak English?" asked Murray.

"No, sir, I don't believe he does."

Himmler coughed, covering his mouth with his hand momentarily.

"What else did he talk to you about?"

"He has two children and doesn't like dogs or gardening."

"Ah," said Murray, like it might mean something.

"I showed him the photographs."

"You did?" Murray's face colored. "You weren't supposed to do that on your own. I was supposed to be there to record the reaction."

"Well, there wasn't much reaction, sir."

"What do you mean, no reaction? Did he deny it?"

"He doesn't seem to think it has anything to do with him, sir."

"He doesn't?" asked Murray angrily. "You've ruined the whole thing. This was supposed to have been done in an expert way so we could maximize the effect and properly document the proceedings."

The intelligence officer shrugged apologetically. "I'm sorry, sir, but the prisoner wanted to talk. So we talked. I merely obeyed the first rule of intelligence, 'Strike while the iron is hot!'"

Murray didn't like that. For the next two minutes he rained abuse down on his head, much to the amusement of Himmler, who grinned at him from his chair. He opened his mouth a crack and in that moment the intelligence officer thought he saw something lodged in his upper back teeth.

"Sir," he said to Murray, sotto voce, "I think I just saw something in the prisoner's mouth. Don't turn, don't say anything."

"I thought you said he'd already been searched and poison was removed."

"Yes, sir, but—"

"You just fed him lunch. How is he going to eat a sandwich with a poison phial between his teeth?"

"Sir?"

Murray was livid. "You've completely fouled this investigation," he shouted at the intelligence officer. Then he turned to Wells and barked, "You're the doctor, examine the prisoner for poison."

"Sir," snapped Wells, "I am a doctor, not a detective. Let the sergeant conduct the search."

At that, the young colonel exploded. "You will do as you're told!" he shouted.

With much unpleasantness, Wells approached Himmler and began looking into his half-opened mouth. "Yes, I think I do see something in there in between his back teeth," he said.

"Colonel," said the sergeant, standing behind Himmler, "if you'd like, I can sandbag the prisoner."

"No, don't," said Murray. "Look closer," he shouted to Wells. "What do you see?"

Wells moved closer to Himmler, who had now shut his mouth. "Open your mouth," he ordered.

But as Wells grabbed him, Himmler jerked his head back and bit down on what he had in his mouth. There was the tiny crunch of thin glass and the harsh smell of cyanide filled the air. Himmler fell to the floor, twitched a few times, and then went still.

As Dönitz had expected, by the time he'd been brought back to his quarters, they had already ransacked the place. His orderly handed him his bags, they exchanged salutes and said goodbye.

He was then driven to Flensburg Police Headquarters, where he was promptly stripped naked and his bags were rifled through. He stood impassive and calm while the British officers helped themselves to his watch and ring. After he put his clothes back on, they pulled his arms behind him and snapped on a pair of handcuffs. He was led into a room where Jodl was sitting, also shackled.

"Hello, General. You're looking nicely ransacked," Dönitz said, giving him a droll smirk.

Jodl grimaced. "I wonder what comes next," he said.

"Oh, I think we're about to explore the delights of British cuisine," said Dönitz. "That must be why we're in handcuffs. They're looking forward to force-feeding us."

The door opened and in came Speer, dressed in a gray suit and a light-colored trench coat.

"Grand Admiral, General," said Speer somberly.

"So nice to see you, Speer," said Dönitz. "So you've decided not to wear your party uniform for the occasion. I'm disappointed in you."

Speer gave a sour look.

Dönitz went on. "I must say I'm heartened that you chose not to accept their offer to run their reconstruction effort. You chose to set aside your pathological opportunism to take the high moral ground with the rest of us. I'm sure someday you'll thank yourself."

"Someday," answered Speer.

Then a British major led them outside to a courtyard, where a group of press photographers and reporters pelted them with questions.

"General, is this the end of the Third Reich?"

"Admiral, what are your plans now?"

"What do you have to say about the murder of the Jews?"

"Are you looking forward to meeting General Eisenhower?"

"Admiral, what are your feelings about being Hitler's successor?"

"What do you think history will say about the Flensburg Reich?"

Hearing the barrage of questions, Dönitz almost had to laugh. So this is what it must have felt like for poor von Friedeburg during the surrender. This multiplied by three. No, much worse than that! How will history judge the Flensburg Reich? It won't remember it! The world has already moved on. This won't even make it to the front page. It'll show up somewhere next to where they put the talking dog stories. If von Friedeburg were here, I bet I could make him see the sublime ridiculousness of this moment. I could even make him laugh. Where is he anyway? He turned to the others. "Has anyone seen Admiral von Friedeburg? Speer? Jodl? Have you seen him?"

They hadn't.

He went over to the major, who was standing smugly between them and the photographers, no doubt to ensure his picture made it into the papers.

"Major, where is Admiral von Friedeburg?" he asked. "Isn't he supposed to be here?"

The British major grinned. "Von Friedeburg kaput," he said.

"Sorry?"

"You heard me. Your friend's killed himself."

Dönitz turned away as he felt the ache hit him. All the tears that he'd not allowed himself for all the endless loss he'd felt during the past six years suddenly welled in his eyes. He looked at the major. "Please get me out of here, just for a minute."

The major grabbed him by the arm and brought him back inside into a small interrogation cubicle. "Five minutes," he barked as he shut the door.

Dönitz began to weep. "Oh, Hans," he cried. "Did you have to do it to yourself?"

Historical Postscript

When I first started researching the Flensburg Reich, most of the major figures were still alive. Now they have all passed on; some died violently, some mysteriously, most in their own beds, but at least one in someone else's.

Albert Speer was sentenced to twenty years at Spandau Prison, where he wrote his bestselling memoir *Inside the Third Reich*, which, in addition to detailing his relationship with Hitler, describes his campaign in the Ruhr and time in Flensburg, including his and Baumbach's dream of escaping to Greenland to hunt walrus and write their memoirs together. During the 1970s he published his prison diaries, and a book on the infiltration of German industry by the SS. He died in London in 1981—shortly after appearing on *Good Morning America*—under what some regard as suspicious circumstances.

After his release from Allied custody, **Werner Baumbach** moved to Argentina, where he became a senior officer in the Argentine air force. He died mysteriously in 1953 when the British Lancaster bomber he was test-flying blew up in midair. His memoir continues to sell, and while an interesting read, it makes no mention of Speer, KG-200, or any dream of escaping to Greenland.

Grand Admiral **Karl Dönitz** served ten years in Spandau Prison. Following his release in 1956, Dönitz retired to a suburb of

Hamburg and wrote his memoir *Ten Years and Twenty Days,* which has remained sporadically in print for nearly fifty years. He spent the remaining twenty-five years of his life as a sort of living historical artifact, answering all letters and giving frequent interviews to historians and documentary filmmakers, in what is generally regarded as a successful effort to rehabilitate the navy's image from the taint of association with the Nazi regime. He died in December 1980, two weeks after John Lennon.

Captain **Walter Lüdde-Neurath** remained close to Dönitz after the war. In 1950 he wrote *Regierung Dönitz,* the official history of the Dönitz regime. The last time anyone checked he was still alive.

Fregattenkapitän **Peter Cremer**'s name was inexplicably omitted from the British arrest lists and he was promptly released to the civilian world. He went into the import/export business before becoming general manager for Sperry Electronic Systems in Hamburg. He wrote his memoir *U-Boat Commander* during the 1980s. He died in 1994.

The mystery behind **Wolfgang Lüth**'s death has never been solved, though it was officially attributed to a jittery sentry. His writings on leadership of U-boat crews continue to be widely read among naval professionals and submarine officers around the world.

Though Captain Lieutenant **Hermann Rasch** was suspected of involvement in Lüth's death, nothing was ever proven. He became a journalist in Hamburg and died in 1974.

SS General **Walter Schellenberg**'s rise to the top of German intelligence was early and swift, but his fall was equally meteoric. Released after a surprisingly short imprisonment, he provided testimony at the Nuremberg War Crimes trial, after which he moved to Switzerland, where he wrote his memoir *The Labyrinth,* which remains in print. Somewhere after his release, he developed a mysterious ailment, suspected to be the result of an exotic, slow-acting poison. When he died at age forty-five in 1955 he was, by all appearances, a very old man.

Felix Kersten was decorated by the Dutch government for his role in preventing the deportation of the Dutch people to the East. He became a Swedish citizen in 1953 and died in Stockholm in 1960.

SS Colonel **Werner Grothmann** became a businessman. Over the years he allowed himself to be interviewed by only a small number of historians. He died in 2003.

SS Colonel **Heinz Macher** also gave only a few, very selective interviews to historians. He died in 2001.

The fate of the **German Surrender Delegation** to Montgomery does bear telling. By the time Admiral **Hans-Georg von Friedeburg** committed suicide, two members of the party were already dead. Major **Friedel** was killed in a road accident a few hours after the surrender while carrying Montgomery's instructions north to Field Marshal Ernst Busch. Major General **Eberhard Kinzel** remained behind at Montgomery's headquarters as a liaison, transmitting British orders to the various German commands. After two weeks in that capacity, he asked for and received permission to hire a personal assistant. When it was discovered that his assistant was a very young, attractive blonde, he was told to get rid of her. Kinzel's reaction was to promptly shoot her and then himself.

By the time Admiral **Gerhard Wagner** was released from Allied imprisonment in 1947, he was already assisting in efforts to gather information for different military history projects. He was a member of the Naval Historical Team until 1952, after which he rejoined the navy and ultimately served as director of the NATO Planning Staff and commander of the Allied Naval Forces Baltic Sea Inlet. He died in 1987.

Major **Wilhelm Oxenius** served as a defense attaché at the West German Embassy in London. When he tried to enroll his son in the exclusive St. Paul's School, he found the path had already been paved through the intercession of one of the school's alumni, General Sir Bernard Law Montgomery, the man to whom von Friedeburg had first surrendered.

Colonel General **Alfred Jodl** was found guilty of war crimes at Nuremberg and hanged.

Supreme Allied Commander General **Dwight D. Eisenhower** left the army and served as president of Columbia University before becoming President of the United States for two terms in 1953–61. He died in 1968.

General **Walter Bedell Smith** later served as U.S. ambassador to Moscow and director of the Central Intelligence Agency. He died in 1961.

After the war, General **Kenneth Strong** was given both the CBE and OBE and served as director general of intelligence at the British Ministry of Defense. He then moved to Australia, where he died in 1980, after having written his memoirs.

General **Ivan Susloparov** disappeared from history immediately after the Rheims surrender. As a member of the SHAEF delegation, he flew to Berlin for the third round of surrenders. But upon arrival, he was immediately snatched from the limousine by

Russian secret police and is believed to have been executed shortly afterward. Whatever the case, the Russians have never offered any explanation as to his fate.

Sixty years after the **United States Strategic Bombing Survey** released its hundred-plus-volume report, its findings remain highly controversial. To those who read no further than the executive summary, it appeared to merely affirm their strongly held beliefs in the effectiveness of strategic bombing. But anyone who read further found heresy. It not only raised serious doubts about the efficacy of the whole doctrine of daytime precision bombing, it also damned with faint praise the usefulness of the heavy bombers such as the B-17, which performed the bulk of strategic bombing missions against Germany. Some concluded that if it was so difficult to knock out the armaments industries of highly centralized industrial nations like Germany, trying to do the same to less developed nations such as Russia or North Vietnam would be nearly impossible.

The Survey's three directors—John Kenneth Galbraith, George Ball, and Paul Nitze—all went on to distinguished postwar careers.

George Ball became a staunch Europeanist, free-trade advocate, and assistant to Jean Monnet, the founder of the European Community. He served as an undersecretary of state in the Kennedy and Johnson administrations. In this capacity, he came to prominence as an early critic of American involvement in Vietnam. While he remained a favorite colleague of Lyndon Johnson and Dean Rusk, his disagreement over the war caused him to resign from the Johnson administration. He later served as ambassador to the UN. In subsequent years he became known as a high-profile critic of American foreign policy in the Middle East. He died in 1994.

Though perhaps not as well known to the public as the others, **Paul Nitze** was probably the single most important shaper of American defense policy during the Cold War. He served in the administration of nearly every President from Roosevelt to George H. W. Bush. He was director of policy planning for the State Department under Truman, secretary of the navy under Johnson, and deputy secretary of defense under Reagan. He also served as ambassador at large and special advisor to the President and secretary of state for arms control. He died in 2004.

John Kenneth Galbraith became one of America's best-known liberal economists and public intellectuals. From his tower in Harvard, he frequently courted public disfavor with his criticisms of conservative economic policy. He served as an advisor to many presidents, and was appointed by President Kennedy as ambassador to India. His writings included dozens of books on economics and politics, several of which became best sellers, as well as memoirs and a novel, *The Liberal Hour.* He died in 2006.

Captain **Burton H. Klein** became a prominent economist at the RAND Corporation and later at the California Institute of Technology.

As for the two unnamed German generals who were being roughed up and de-pantsed on the Marineschule grounds, one later became head of NATO intelligence, while the other became head of NATO.

ACKNOWLEDGMENTS

First of all, I would like to thank my agent, Larry Weissman, for his patience, tenacity, and vision. Second, Colin Fox and David Rosenthal at Simon & Schuster, for reading my story and liking it enough to buy it. Special thanks to my editor, Sarah Hochman, genius and taskmaster, for grasping what the story was about and then explaining it back to me and helping me to write it that way.

I would also like to thank Paul Nitze and John Kenneth Galbraith for talking to me at length about their experiences at Flensburg interviewing Albert Speer.

A lot has been written during the last sixty years about the end of the Third Reich, and within this vast universe the story of Grand Admiral Dönitz's three-week Flensburg Reich rattles around in aimless obscurity. While Flensburg has been mentioned in countless memoirs, where its surrealistic oddness is sometimes described at length, inevitably it gets overshadowed by the horrific events preceding it.

For anyone wanting to learn more about Flensburg, Albert Speer's memoir, *Inside the Third Reich*, is invaluable. Galbraith gleefully recalls it in his memoir, *A Life in Our Times*, as does George W. Ball in his *The Past Has Another Pattern* and Paul Nitze in *From Hiroshima to Glasnost*.

I am particularly indebted to Jordan Vause, the best of the new generation of U-boat historians, whose book *U-Boat Ace* tells the full, unvarnished story about Wolfgang Lüth. He does it with such balance and objectivity that the Lüth who emerges from it is even more compelling than the whitewashed man of legend. I dread thinking of the Lüth I would have written about had it not been for Jordan Vause's indirect guidance.

I would also like to thank my family and friends who put up with me during my endless thrashings about, but there are too many to mention here, and besides, you all know who you are. But I would like to thank my mother, who prayed for my success every day for much too long. If there is one friend to single out for thanks it would be Pete Capelotti, arctic explorer, archaeologist, author, and fellow flying boat fanatic with whom I served unsupervised apprenticeships in researching obscure and overlooked history. If not for Pete's own estimation of the possible, I might have gotten a job and never bothered trying to write this.

Finally, thanks to all the gang at the Starbucks on Lower Greenville in Dallas, without whom the years of writing would not have been nearly as much fun.

ABOUT THE AUTHOR

Before turning to fiction, Brendan McNally worked as a defense journalist, first at the Pentagon and later in Prague, where he investigated the Eastern European arms trade. His investigative work included uncovering the Czech government's role in helping supply nuclear technology to Iran for *The Prague Post* and Iraqi use of chemical weapons for *The New York Times*. He lives in Dallas, Texas, with his wife and daughter. *Germania* is his first novel.